"You Have the World. . . ."

he said so softly she had to strain to hear him. "What can I give you?"

She answered the only way she could, by bringing her lips to his, by pressing her aching body against him. "Show me, Mark darling. Show me what you can give me," she pleaded, certain he would understand that she meant more than sex, more than the immediate need she felt for him.

His kiss was impassioned and contained an element of torment, as if he felt that he was bringing her the same gift that had been rejected before. Yet his arms held her tightly, savoring her, slipping down over her slender back. . . .

"Mark!" She swayed slightly as he released his urgent grasp on her. Then his lips met hers for another kiss, and this one carried a different message, a question that she remembered from so long ago. Smiling, she answered this one with ease, with assurance, with a heart filled with happiness. "Oh, yes, Mark, darling. I do want you. I want you so much. I've waited so long."

Dear Reader:

We trust you will enjoy this Richard Gallen romance. We plan to bring you more of the best in both contemporary and historical romantic fiction with four exciting new titles each month.

We'd like your help.

We value your suggestions and opinions. They will help us to publish the kind of romances you want to read. Please send us your comments, or just let us know which Richard Gallen romances you have especially enjoyed. Write to the address below. We're looking forward to hearing from you!

Happy reading!

Judy Sullivan
Richard Gallen Books
8-10 West 36th St.
New York, N.Y. 10018

All Mine To Give

MARSHA ALEXANDER

PUBLISHED BY RICHARD GALLEN BOOKS
Distributed by POCKET BOOKS

This novel is a work of fiction. Names, characters, places and incidents are either the product of the author's imagination or are used fictitiously, and any resemblance to actual persons, living or dead, events or locales is entirely coincidental.

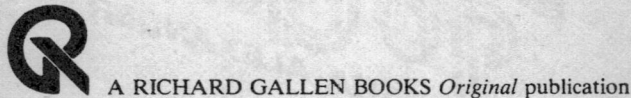

A RICHARD GALLEN BOOKS *Original* publication

Distributed by
POCKET BOOKS, a Simon & Schuster division of
GULF & WESTERN CORPORATION
1230 Avenue of the Americas, New York, N.Y. 10020

Copyright © 1981 by Marsha Alexander

All rights reserved, including the right to reproduce
this book or portions thereof in any form whatsoever.
For information address Pocket Books, 1230 Avenue
of the Americas, New York, N.Y. 10020

ISBN: 0-671-43539-6

First Pocket Books printing September, 1981

10 9 8 7 6 5 4 3 2 1

RICHARD GALLEN and colophon are trademarks
of Simon & Schuster and Richard Gallen & Co., Inc.

Printed in the U.S.A.

ACKNOWLEDGMENTS

With special thanks to Jan Myers and Joan Passanante of the Redken Laboratories, Inc., for their generous help; to Terry Williams and Norman Lowenstein; to Linda Innes, Jane Wirth, Yvonne MacManus, Jo Anne Prather and Joyce Madison for their time, love and selfless dedication.

To a special swan
Leah Durchin
mother and critic *ne plus ultra*

BOOK ONE

*All his . . . own geese are swans,
as the swans of others are geese.*

—Horace Walpole,
Fourth Earl of Orford

CHAPTER 1

The wind, characteristically savage in mid-January, tore around the corners, over the rows of parked cars and between the lanes of heavy afternoon traffic. Its fury unabated, it swept on past wildly flapping awnings to chill the pedestrians hurrying along the streets in the heart of San Francisco's most fashionable shopping district. The cold had a way of heightening The City's cosmopolitan atmosphere and stepping up its brisk pace.

As soon as the light turned green, a delegation of shivering Chinese people in traditional garb abandoned the outer edges of Chinatown to dart across the street, hoping to escape the wind in the shadow of the modern white building with the bronze-tinted windows. The silver imprint on its wide gold awning identified it as the headquarters of MagnifiScent, the newest and most successful cosmetics firm in the world.

But a bunch of artsy-craftsy types from North Beach and a couple arguing in volatile French were already gathered under the awning, and the Chinese group moved on. A smartly dressed woman just made the light in spite of her unhurried step, a refusal to compromise with elements beyond her control. As the group crowding the doorway dispersed, her face became animated with pleasure and she walked through the tinted glass doors into MagnifiScent's exquisitely appointed beauty salon where she would be luxuriously pampered by MagnifiScent's staff of expert cosmeticians.

The light changed again, and two stylishly anorexic teenagers stopped short at the curb, cursing quite distinctly, unconscious of the dark-skinned man wearing a turban whom they jostled with their unexpected stop. Disconcerted, he stared at them with an expression of malice and subliminal lust.

Only Olivia DeSante, gazing out of Thea Wallace's office window, caught the look on the turbaned man's face. It brought a faint smile to her lips, a gentle corruption of a mouth so flawlessly shaped it could have belonged to a Botticelli water nymph. Everything about Olivia suggested a finely executed work of art. She was not tall, but her slender, long-legged body with its graceful neck and elegant face gave the illusion of regal height. Olivia was wearing a superbly tailored smoke-white Lanvin dress, just short enough to reveal flawless legs. The dress was complemented by finely hammered white gold earrings that emphasized her swanlike neck. Her natural platinum hair and exceedingly fair skin made people think of the Snow Queen. But most pale blondes would never indulge in Olivia's studied avoidance of color for fear of fading away. There were few women who possessed Olivia's impeccable sense of style, her poise, or, for that matter, her outstandingly elegant features. One famous San Francisco columnist, at a loss to describe her stunning golden beauty, had compared her to a young but infinitely more chic Grace Kelly.

Olivia had smiled at the comparison—she had worked very hard to develop her extraordinary style, her uniqueness. Because she had grown up in Hollywood, where beautiful women were commonplace, she understood that beauty in itself wasn't enough. Beauty was only a raw ingredient and would require great skill from its owner to develop its full potential. As the dynamic ruler of a cosmetics empire, it had been imperative for Olivia to establish an image that was as elegant as her products. She had succeeded.

Thea Wallace, frantically shuffling through the papers on her desk, glanced up and saw Olivia's amused smile. "What in hell are you smiling at? I was half-expecting buckets of tears, love." Thea's long brown hair was caught back in a pony tail, held by an unpretentious tortoise-shell clip that immediately identified Thea as a member of the select Mill Valley horsey set. Thea was unmistakably another of the privileged daughters of Beverly Hills who gave herself away with every gesture. She looked as though she held the magic keys to any kingdom, as though all the world were her private Disneyland.

Olivia turned away from the window, the smile fading. "I'd say I have a thing or two to smile about, Thea," she answered with a trace of defensiveness. "This isn't exactly ashes, you know." Her fingers fluttered vaguely, encompassing much more than the office or even the conglomerate called MagnifiScent.

Thea's grin flashed quickly. "You're right, you know, darling. Righter than you think. It's actually a bit ludicrous, the suggestion of pity I was working up for you. How can anyone pity the wonder of two worlds? A million women with humdrum lives are probably sitting around right now thinking about you and turning an absolutely ghastly shade of—"

"What am I going to do?" It was such an astonishing thing for her to ask that Olivia looked as surprised as the friend whose help she was soliciting.

Thea pushed the heap of papers away and closed her eyes for a moment. "I know it looks bad, Olivia. But you can't seriously *believe* that Marlissa would sell you out? I can't believe it. You don't truly think it's a possibility, do you?"

Olivia rested a hip against a corner of the desk, trying to avoid looking at the cluttered papers on it. Clutter was as natural to Thea as organization was essential to Olivia. She had no idea how Thea managed to get any work done in such chaos, but the fact was that the woman's specialized department ran as smoothly as any other executive office at MagnifiScent.

In many ways Thea's role in the organization was particularly complex. At first Thea had been drawn into Olivia's emerging business as the company's only sales representative in the United States. Olivia had asked her girlhood friend to sell the Deloffres' creations to a group of select women, those with an abundance of money and a desire to own cosmetics unavailable to the world at large. From saleswoman to symbol was her next step in helping Olivia realize her dream—Thea was solidly planted in society, and her affiliation with MagnifiScent gave the growing company a certain luster that Olivia wouldn't have been able to create at that time—not in the United States, at least, and in Europe she would have had to lean heavily on the DeSante name and reputation for recognition, which she was determined not to do.

Once MagnifiScent was fully evolved, Thea's position was at first hazy. Her presence continued to reassure that portion of their clientele who needed to believe that although MagnifiScent had gone public, its products still maintained its former standard of excellence. With intuitive shrewdness Olivia came to understand that Thea could contribute heavily to the company in other areas as well. She had flawless taste and a fine understanding of every woman's desire to feel pampered and glamorous. Eventually a new department was developed, a liaison division between product creation and product presentation, headed by Thea. It served two important functions. The first was to assess the market for possible innovative products. Her department suggested cosmetics that would either assimilate two existing products into one, such as the fine all-in-one lip balm and lipstick Marlissa had created at Thea's suggestion, or, conversely, motivate sales of an already existing product by realizing the need for a second cosmetic to make the first more appealing. One example of her inventiveness in this area was China Doll, a neutral eye product to be applied to the upper lid before shadow. It smoothed the lid and helped conceal the folds caused by aging. China Doll was not only immediately successful but also opened up the market to exotic blendings of shadow not appealing to older customers before, those conscious that shadow often gathered unattractively on the lids only a short while after application.

The second important function of Thea's department was to operate as the watchdog of the marketing branch. As in every other cosmetics company, MagnifiScent's marketing department sometimes got carried away with an ad campaign. Thea had an impeccable feeling for cosmetics advertising, sensing instantly which layout would best convince women that MagnifiScent alone could help them realize their dreams. Because her importance to the company was growing while her dilettante nature prevented Thea from throwing herself into work as conscientiously as either Marlissa or Olivia, Thea had wisely staffed her department with carefully selected personnel. For this she had shamelessly lured away employees from Revlon and Estée Lauder, from top ad agencies in New York, and even from a highly esteemed Paris perfumer's retail department. And she had had the intuitive wisdom to take as her personal assistant Justine Brandon, the immeasurably helpful, experienced former executive at a rival cosmetics company. Justine had begun her career at *Elan,* a short-lived but ultrasophisticated fashion magazine.

Thanks to her competent staff and especially to Justine, Thea was currently free to spend as much or as little time at MagnifiScent as she wished. She would be away visiting her family all the next week.

"When are you catching your plane?" Olivia's voice held a note of tension.

"Olivia . . ."

"Let it go. For now, anyway. I have to think about it a little more, and I can't, not today. Not this weekend." She passed a hand wearily over her eyes, something she dared not do while using any line of makeup other than her own. It was more of the genius of Marlissa Deloffre . . . the smudgeless shadow in a wide range of delicious colors, the wonderful liners that customers could easily apply and know that their finished effect would rival that of a salon. Marlissa . . . no, she couldn't think of it now. Thea was right; it was impossible to suspect the woman. Marlissa more than anyone, perhaps even more than Olivia herself, was responsible for making MagnifiScent what it was today . . . Marlissa, who had helped Olivia turn a dying little shop in Meiringen, Switzerland, into a cosmetics empire.

Yet there could be no doubt that someone was leaking their most cherished secrets to Riviera Cosmetics. Olivia thought about Riviera's stunning new line with a flash of panic. How else could they have suddenly whipped up a collection so close to her own? Riviera, a steadily dwindling firm that up until last month was still catering to women who expected cosmetics to cake and run, whose plastic-packaged wares littered every cut-rate drugstore and supermarket . . . No, not Marlissa! "When are you leaving?" she asked Thea, to take her mind off the painful subject.

Thea grimaced. "The plane leaves at midnight."

Olivia felt an intense longing for a cigarette, the first such craving since she'd stopped smoking almost three months ago. "Thea, surely they've given up? Your family is incredible. Do you really think they're going to trot poor Everett out for you again?" As she spoke, she thought of Mark Lyman, whom she would be meeting in less than five hours, and felt her craving go in an entirely different direction.

Thea's laugh was vaguely theatrical. "What amazes me is that Everett hasn't given up yet! Do you realize it's been almost a year since I've seen him, and I'm absolutely certain nothing's changed. He's as patient today as he was that mad evening you and I took off for Europe and left him standing there in his tennis drag. Remember?"

For the first time that day, her smile felt completely genuine. Olivia let it widen into a grin. "How could I forget?" They had both been twenty-two and burdened—Thea with money and family obligations, Olivia with bitterness and poverty. It had been an escape for each of them, but they didn't know it at the time. At thirty-two and looking backward they shared a keener vision. But then they had simply been two young and beautiful girls with very little to lose, careening through Europe looking for that mysterious something that would give their lives meaning. And after she met and married Jean-Pierre DeSante, Olivia believed she had found it as the wife of Switzerland's architectural genius, land baron, and favorite young millionaire, the handsome, tremendously charming Jean-Pierre. How little she had known.

The thought of her late husband effectively erased the smile from her mouth. It evoked other memories, other scenes—mountains of brilliantly white snow; cherry-cheeked children on skis; the melting warmth of spring; delicate flowers amid green, green grasses; dozens of feathery waterfalls mistily trickling into cold crystal springs—all part of the magnificent Alps.

But most of all it conjured up day upon day of meaningless existence, when she served no purpose, had no place in the cyclical scheme of nature. She had not even had the satisfaction of believing that she was in some way vital to Jean-Pierre. She had been an ornament primarily, and an ornament, however beautiful, however precious, once it is broken or lost, can always be replaced. Every time she thought about her life in Meiringen—the ultimate outcome of any reminiscing about that trip to Europe—she was beset by a flood of mixed emotions. She could not bear to remember how Mark Lyman had begged her to stay with him, first in Los Angeles and then in New York. She didn't want to hear the echo of her own voice denying them what they both had wanted. The first time it had been because in accepting Mark, she would also have had to embrace his poverty, to live with him in his artist's garret. The second time she had called her reluctance honor and loyalty to Jean-Pierre, when she had known it was really a terrifying blend of guilt and fear.

Olivia sighed, willing the images to disappear. Twice she had left Mark, the only man she'd ever deeply loved. And tonight, in less than five hours, she would meet him again. Tonight, the past could be rectified. Tonight.

"*You* remember!" Thea got up and impulsively hugged Olivia. "I hope you also remember that you let me go home alone. And there was Everett, still waiting! Fortunately not in the same tennis things, of course, but nevertheless. . . ."

Olivia shook her head and started for the door. "I have a million things to do before meeting Mark tonight. Give your parents my best. Everett, too. Why not? I thought he had marvelous knees."

With a shrug of the pony tail, Thea looked up. "Tonight, is it? God, I'd forgotten! Jesus, how long has it been?" She eyed her friend closely as she reached the door. "How do you feel?"

Olivia clung to the brass doorknob. "Tonight," she said softly. "Three years. How do you think I feel? No, don't answer that. Eager."

"Frightened?" For once Thea's face lost most of the slightly enchanted but largely disbelieving expression that had become her trademark over the years. "Are you?"

"Have a good week. Give me a call Monday." She closed the door firmly behind her. "Scared stiff," she whispered.

CHAPTER 2

For a change the hallway was empty. Gratefully Olivia walked to the elevator, her face composed but preoccupied, moving rapidly enough to avoid a chorus of greetings from the various secretaries sitting just beyond the open doorways. For once she wanted to escape the demands of business and social pressure. Too much had hit her at once. Riviera's new line; Marlissa; most of all the phone call from Mark, the fact that he was this minute in San Francisco, either settling into his hotel room or, more likely, making the rounds of the art dealers he had come to see. In Mark's mind, she was not the obvious reason for this trip. But Olivia knew better. Or rather, it was essential to believe that she knew better. She had waited so long for this chance.

A young secretary with an armload of papers scurried out of an office, almost colliding with Olivia. The girl's eyes widened, and her skin reddened with her embarrassment. "Oh, Mrs. DeSante! I'm terribly sorry. I didn't see. . . ."

Olivia smiled briefly and pressed the elevator call button a second time. Usually she made a point of being friendly and gracious to her employees. She had felt the need to break through the distance imposed by her wealth and fame. Ever since she'd returned to America as Jean-Pierre's beautiful young widow, to set the cosmetics industry on its ear, she had gotten a lion's share of publicity. Pictorial coverage of her salons, her office building, her home in Pacific Heights, even her fabled jewels, had created the image of a perfect human being. Only a few knew the real Olivia DeSante, a woman with inner conflicts, a woman who questioned her decisions. The attention she had received because of her brilliance in business, however, gave her savage pleasure. And yet in the end all her success had accomplished was to keep her as far apart from people as her poverty had. Her wealth in this country and in Switzerland ran into the hundreds of millions, but no amount of money could make her complete. Above all she felt a loneliness that couldn't be explained by the cliché about being alone at the top; she had been alone at the bottom. She had been alone when Hollywood offered to make her a star; perhaps she had been most alone as Jean-Pierre's envied wife. Only with Mark had she not been alone. She had told Thea that it had been three years since she'd last seen Mark. But it was closer to ten years since they'd really been together.

The elevator was silent and swift, a polished cage with ivory walls. On days when the demands on her were too pressing, Olivia often longed to stop in mid-floor and hide out in the silent, womblike chamber. But now it couldn't transport her to her office fast enough. She understood what she was doing. Because of her unwillingness to dwell on thoughts about either Marlissa or Mark, she was filled with a compulsion to move physically from one place to another. She had left home more than an hour early, not touching the breakfast her cook had served along with a spray of freshly cut orchids, hurrying to the office, only to leave it almost at once to wander through the building in total distraction. The salon didn't open that early, but it was always a beehive of activity, a white, gold, and silver palace dedicated to the care of discerning, pampered women who demanded and gladly paid for only the best. All her salons were identical, ultramodern workhouses for the purpose of transforming patrons into living works of art.

Olivia made a point of touring each salon every three months, using the company jet and taking either Thea or

Marlissa with her on the five-day trip. Sometimes Miles Holbrook, MagnifiScent's salon director, came along to terrorize the individual branch managers. They saw enough of Miles as it was, since his job consisted of rotating among the various salons to make sure every detail of the operation was perfect. The salons were an important but not essentially prosperous part of MagnifiScent. They were the icing on the cake; they were luxurious palaces representing the image every woman was seeking when she purchased the uniquely packaged products they sold.

Olivia had rejected all thoughts of conventional merchandising when she first started the MagnifiScent collection. A drop of luxury: she had seen it so clearly in her mind, the alluring little bottles and jars, each topped with a bit of jeweled glass, as magical and promising as the fountain of youth. She knew she would make good on that promise, too, because she had the Deloffre family—humble little wizards who were then creating miracles in a hopelessly inadequate factory tucked into the side of a mountain—to make it all possible. Oils and creams, lotions and cakes, each so superior to anything Olivia had seen anywhere that she knew from the first she could not fail.

The shop with its back-room factory had been going broke when Olivia found it. The meeting was opportune for the Deloffres and herself. Desperately bored, she had been delighted to find treasure in one of the many unbelievably quaint shops in the Bernese Oberland. She had been married to Jean-Pierre almost six years at the time. The pressure on her to produce children and ensure the family name was growing more intense by the day. Against her better judgment the idea was gaining in appeal. A baby would fill the long days, give her something to do, take the place of the books she devoured night after lonely night when Jean-Pierre was away on business trips . . . and other trips that had nothing at all to do with business.

It seemed dishonest to have a child to compensate for the emptiness in her own life. It would compromise her personal set of ethics. But there was the other side, of course, the desire to have a baby, to feel the pull of chubby arms around her neck, a greedy little mouth at her breast. In Switzerland Olivia lived more intensely with nature than ever before. She felt the rhythmic swell of the seasons, the purposeful sweep of time. Like all the creatures who danced to its infallible beat, she felt a longing to be useful, too, to be fruitful, to multiply.

If she hadn't found that little shop, she might be in Meiringen yet, surrounded by children but perhaps still toying with the idea of striking out on her own. In a way Marlissa had saved her life . . . Marlissa, the plain, dark-haired girl who had sold Olivia her first bottle of perfumed oil with the delectable scent that had triggered MagnifiScent, an empire, and turned Olivia into its empress.

Even in the elevator and in spite of an excellent filtering system, the faint fragrance of perfume prevailed. Olivia breathed it in with bittersweet pleasure, forcing her mind to shy away from the mounting evidence that hinted at betrayal by a cherished ally who might this minute be quietly selling her out.

Olivia remembered a lesson in trust she had been given many years ago. "Trust is a badly misunderstood concept. You think that if my intentions are good, I can be trusted. Nonsense! Skill is the other part of trust, and every bit as important. No matter how good my intentions toward you, you'd be a fool to trust me to . . . tune your piano, for example. I might have every intention of helping you out, but since I lack the skill to do it properly, you shouldn't trust me with the damn thing at all. On the other hand, if I happen to be an excellent piano tuner but I also happen to hate your guts, you'd be equally wise to deny me your trust. . . ."

Mark. It had been one of his rudimentary lessons on living, served up with cheap white wine in a water tumbler.

It had taken less than a minute to move from the depths of reluctant paranoia to the heights of dizzy anticipation, from Marlissa to Mark. She seemed to have no control over her thoughts.

The elevator stopped on the top floor. Olivia crossed the silver carpet to her office, silently willing the hours that separated her from Mark Lyman to pass quickly so that she would know once and for all if he still wanted her. The question hung in her mind, refusing to go away since he'd called almost a week before. His voice had brought it all back—his touch, the way he smelled always of turpentine and oils, those dreadful Greek cigarettes he liked so much . . . the way his mouth parted with that tender little smile before he kissed her.

She stopped before the desk of her personal secretary, Myoko Harper. "Any urgent calls? No, don't tell me." She breathed in a reviving whiff of white tulips from a silver vase on the corner of the desk. "Lie to me."

The dark-haired woman who turned every cliché about Japanese females upside down studied her boss with a coolly appraising eye. "Nothing earthshaking, for a change. I put the pad on your desk. *Newsweek* called to remind you about Monday. Ten sharp. You don't look overly thrilled."

Olivia made a face. "When they start talking covers, I'll be thrilled." She walked past the older woman as calmly as she could. If Mark had changed his mind, a note canceling their date would be on the pad. Myoko had too much tact to mention it directly. Her gracefully aging face masked a mind as swift as a computer, as subtle as an abacus. It had been Myoko who took the first call from Mark, had seen the color drain from Olivia's face. Myoko would grant her the dignity of complete privacy in which to vent any feelings generated by this caller. It was one of the many reasons the woman drove a Seville while other secretaries scrambled for a trolley or cable car at five.

Olivia closed the door behind her and stared with none of her usual pleasure at what had been called the most tasteful yet outrageously elegant office in the industry. It was becoming a cause célèbre in its own right, this room she had so painstakingly decorated. She had set out to make it a larger expression of her personal style, a swan's nest of purity and perfection. Color was kept to a minimum, an understatement of vitality and passion. The rich but subtle Golden Lotus carpet, for which she had paid a king's ransom, covered the floor. Matching pointe d'Hongroise curtains were deliberately narrow to keep from obstructing the breathtaking view of the Golden Gate Bridge and the water below, with its traffic of ships and barges. The bronze window glass merely tinted the view from the inside, blunting the sun, shading the frequent fogs, so that whatever the weather, Olivia's office always seemed to be vaguely underwater, the jeweled submarine of a Croesus. She had contrived a congruity of style that borrowed from every culture, every century; it should not have worked but did, bringing together a harmony of golden spaciousness.

"*Ne plus ultra,*" Thea had breathed upon seeing it for the first time. Olivia had been delighted by the tribute—Thea was a dear friend, but she could also be and frequently was a nasty little snob. "We who are born to the purple salute you. Definitely a *ne plus ultra.*"

No more beyond . . . it had symbolic significance more meaningful to her than her cherished office itself. Olivia was at the top now; she had arrived. Nothing could put her down ever again. She had wanted this too long to let it go, no matter what happened. If Marlissa were suffering from some secret jealousy or seeking revenge because it was Olivia and not she who had piloted the Deloffres' miraculous skill to this lofty eagle's nest of power, Olivia would deal with it somehow. That, more than the accolades, more than the publicity, was what this office of treasures did for her—it filled her with strength, with respect for her own capabilities.

CHAPTER 3

Olivia stared blindly at the sterling-silver cartouche with its engraved MagnifiScent logo on the wall behind her desk. Many thought that her company was erected on the indestructible tower of Jean-Pierre's wealth. Nothing could be further from the truth. MagnifiScent had been launched without a dime of DeSante money. Only the buildings themselves were in any way connected to the fortune she had inherited from her late husband's estate, and that was a strict business investment, with the mortgaging carefully structured between her personal corporation and Jean-Pierre's vast holdings. Thea and her lawyers had not understood why she had insisted on setting it up that way.

"It's all your own money, darling," Thea had protested. "It's like borrowing from your right hand to fortify your left!" But it was more of her uncompromisingly rigid ethics again—and she saw to it that MagnifiScent's debts were paid promptly. She would never be indebted to any other source but herself for what had been accomplished. She, with the help of the Deloffres and Thea, had been responsible for it all.

Olivia twisted her bracelet, her fingertips moving over the band of small but flawless blue-white diamonds. It would be difficult to cope with her feelings about Marlissa if the information she'd been given was accurate. But cope she would. Olivia glanced around the office again, then slid her ice-blue eyes over the blanc d'argent velvet couch with its fierce lion's-head woodwork to stare at the graceful span of the bridge being enveloped by a rolling fog. She would also have to cope with her feelings if Mark no longer wanted her.

The thought of his possible rejection brought a tightness to her throat. She knew that her fear was reasonable. Years separated them. There had been that bitter scene. He wouldn't have forgotten—how could she assume he'd forgiven her?

He'd understood the first time, when she had left him for the untested wonders of Europe. He'd been hurt, certainly, but he had his work, his great dreams to sustain him. They bolstered him against every reality of life—irate landlords, unpaid utility bills, even her tearful departure. Mark had understood that her escape wasn't so much from him as from his poverty, from his dedication, which had no room for a wife.

But the second time—how could he have understood that?

Olivia had not thought about Mark when she planned that trip back to the States. He was the unresolved but buried past, the man she had silently pledged to forget when she agreed to marry Jean-Pierre. Her total concentration had been on business, on the sudden inspiration that had come to her in something akin to a vision.

Under Olivia's control the little Swiss cosmetics business was by then selling to Thea's wealthy friends in America. It had been Thea's idea, motivated by a sudden need to make some money, because her family, infuriated at her repeated refusal to settle down and accept the man they had chosen for her, had played their trump card. They had cut off her allowance. Although her trust fund would have been adequate for an average family of five, it was barely enough to cover Thea's rent at the Sunset West. She proved to be an adroit saleswoman, genuinely enthusiastic about the sensuous, exotic Deloffre perfumes. She was supplying Olivia with so many eager and rich American customers that they'd begun to hire help at the factory. Money was pouring in, but Olivia had seen a much larger potential.

She knew that the good things in life were ardently desired by all women. Better than most she understood the comfort of using the very best products, of feeling that nothing had been spared to bring out the best in her. Having lived on both sides of the economic fence, Olivia knew that the chief difference between the groups was that one group wanted and the other had. The rich took the best for granted. Certainly they had to have it—quality, once experienced, jades the palate. But it was the less-coddled women who needed touches of luxury the most. Olivia believed that women in every economic bracket were discriminating creatures, by and large. Finances kept many from indulging themselves, not indifference. Given the opportunity, they would gladly use the oils and the superior cosmetics the Deloffres were developing. But she also knew that her potential buyers were nursed by the same Madison Avenue hype she was—the best had to cost more. And on the practical side, Olivia's products could not be made cheaply. Any compromise in quality would destroy their perfection. How, then, to make the best available to the most?

The slogan was already in her mind. *A drop of luxury.* By packaging her products elegantly but in tiny fractions of an ounce, Olivia could market her cosmetic line to the world and still keep her product the most expensive of its kind. She was positive she could do it.

Under her mask of composure Olivia had been nervous about telling Jean-Pierre of the business trip she intended to take. She had barely mentioned the little perfumery she'd bought into with a pittance, then bought out with the first flush of her profits. During five years of marriage she'd heard the words *"A man of my background and position"* too many times to have any doubt about his reaction to her venture. She was not surprised to hear it again.

Jean-Pierre had been coldly furious.

He'd paced the large master bedroom with the lithe grace of a restless predator. "A man of my background and position does not have a wife in business." He put special emphasis on the last word, his beautiful mouth tightening over it, spitting it out. Olivia visualized a hunched old woman with one hand clutching a tattered babushka, the other clawed and quivering, extended to catch a few pieces of silver. The image made her smile, a reaction she instantly regretted. "I'm sorry, Jean-Pierre—but you make it sound so sordid."

He turned to her, towering over her. He was not tremendously tall, but he was a man of vast and tyrannical energy. He had been born to authority; it was second nature to him, and he used it magnificently. He was also impressively handsome, which meant less and less to her all the time. When he wanted to, he could also be the most charming man she'd ever known. It was not the tack he would use on her with this issue, however. Olivia had met his intense blue stare firmly, knowing that she would never give in on this. It meant too much to her.

"I would very much like you to understand what it is I want to do," she had said softly, picking her words with care. Long before he'd arrived home, she'd worked it out in her own mind, had tasted her own desperation. "Your life is so full, Jean-Pierre. Important. You wouldn't have it any other way. Yet you want me to stay home and do nothing beyond functioning as your wife. I could spend my days tucked into a closet, and you could pull me out when you needed me! Can't you understand that I need something real to do? I need to feel that my life serves some purpose. . . ."

"My mother lives a life such as yours and deludes herself by thinking it rewarding."

She let the sarcasm pass, sorely tempted to drop a few scathing remarks about his mother. "Jean-Pierre, this is my opportunity to create something significant. I need to build something of my own!" She had anticipated the pitfall, of course, but she had hoped that this one time he would rise above his own desires.

"A child would distract your mind from this foolishness."

In the end she had left for the States anyway, his rage still unabated, the growing coldness between them finally surfaced. She promised herself that she would make it up to him when she returned. She had to go. Thea was at heart a dilettante—Olivia's concept of mass producing the most luxurious cosmetics in the world could not be entrusted to anyone but herself. She had always come second to Jean-Pierre's other interests, and this once he would have to come second to hers.

She hadn't looked for Mark. She'd had no idea he was even in New York. When he called at her hotel, she had been pleased to hear his voice, but her mind was swimming with the success of her first business conferences. If she had responded to his call with more than simple pleasure, she would never have agreed to go to his studio to see his work. It had been so long since they were lovers that perhaps now they could be friends.

At thirty-two Mark was more handsome than she'd remembered. His dark hair was shorter and his body more muscular, less boyish. His work was going well. He had begun to sculpt as well as paint, and his progress gave him an edge of excitement, a source of pleasure that had nothing to do with his restrained happiness at seeing her again. He was not bitter over her marriage, but he wouldn't believe that the inclusion of Jean-Pierre had in any way altered the current between them.

He was right.

As soon as he took her hand, looked into her eyes, Olivia knew she had made a mistake by seeing him again. But she was not the same emotional girl she had been. Jean-Pierre had taught her composure. Masterfully she hid the effect Mark still had on her. She marveled over his work, particularly impressed by his fiery oils and the staggeringly sensitive compositions of marble and terra-cotta. She felt a stab of anguish when it was time to leave, but not even her eyes betrayed her. If he hadn't touched her, she could have escaped without giving herself away. He might have stayed where he belonged, locked in the past, a ghost who had ceased to haunt her when Jean-Pierre reached out for her in the dark warmth of their bed.

But Mark had touched her. First her face, moving his fingers with infinite gentleness. Then, without a word, he'd swept her into his arms.

"Don't leave, Olivia. Don't do this to us again. Stay. You can't love him. You belong here with me." He had been much more confident than before. His art was just beginning to sell. Things were going well. She was back, and he wanted her more than ever.

She had trembled in his embrace, averting her face in terror that he might kiss her, knowing what his kiss would do to her.

His strong artist's hands were gliding over her back, burning through the businesslike Chanel suit she had deliberately worn, urging her closer. His touch was magic, erasing the years. It stimulated memories of them together in bed, his mouth insatiable for her kisses, his lovemaking one endless statement of impassioned adoration. Nobody had ever touched her in quite the same way before or since. No one else had known her feelings so exactly, had understood her needs or confronted her as skillfully, gently but firmly peeling away the layers of doubt and confusion to put her in direct contact with her inner self. Mark didn't have the faintest idea of what a single-minded charade sex with any other man could be. He put into lovemaking what he put into his art: his uncompromising best, his total attention. His kisses probed her deepest yearnings. *Am I touching you?* the first kisses asked, never growing more intense or demanding until hers responded with eagerness for the next level. His sensitivity to her was unparalleled. As a lover he was the most politic friend, solicitous of her needs, challenging Olivia to drop all pretensions. His love was a gentle insistence on mutual fulfillment. Within its golden spell she found a joy for life, a glowing peace within herself that transformed love for him into love for both of them. Each time she left his bed, she had been reborn into something better, something stronger, a woman who, with feet on the firm ground of reality, had been given the power to touch the fingertips of the gods.

His embrace had brought it all back. She'd clung to him because she was falling backward in time. She'd dissolved into parts—eyes that held his precious image, lips that parted in feverish desire for his, a body that ached for his touch. "No," she had whispered. Another vision had crowded her senses: Jean-Pierre's face, the weight of his ring on her finger. "No!"

The protest had sprung from her mind, not from her heart. But Mark had taken it for what it represented. He was not a man who could accept anything less than total, uncompromising commitment—not from his art, and not from her.

"Someday," he had said, without masking his fury. "When you are ready."

The famous San Francisco fog had taken great bites out of the bridge, but Olivia hadn't noticed, her gaze looking through years instead of bronzed glass. Only one tower stood untouched by the murky mist.

She crossed the office with its museumlike furnishings and put an unsteady hand on the embossed knob of her desk chair. The familiar feel of the wood was comforting. The chair was old and very important to Olivia. One society editor had dubbed her office the throne room of the cosmetics empire, an inspiration prompted by this splendid chair. It was ironic that the chair had inadvertently established the tone of the room—it was the only item in the office that hadn't been shamelessly extravagant. It had, in fact, been unearthed at a secondhand shop in Santa Monica eleven years before, not long after Olivia had first fallen in love with Mark.

Mark had found it under a pile of fraying carpets. It had been a sorry sight, with a moth-eaten velvet seat, a dangerously loose back leg, its beautiful wood completely hidden behind scratched green paint.

Olivia saw its potential immediately. With great patience she had sanded it down to its original grain. It, too, had come a long way. From some initial service in the company of its elegant peers, the chair had fallen to near annihilation in a junk store. Olivia had given it salvation in the garret under Mark's spellbinding paintings and afterward sent it to Switzerland and Jean-Pierre's award-winning house. From there it had traveled to the finest furniture restorers in the Bay Area. Finally it had come to crown Olivia's office. Perhaps someday it would end up enshrined, like FDR's wheelchair or Archie Bunker's overstuffed horror on display at the Smithsonian.

Olivia sat down in it and immediately reached for a filtered Balkan Sobranie. Her fingers were shaking as she brought the blue flame of her desk lighter to the cigarette and inhaled deeply.

There were five messages on the pad, none of them from Mark.

She looked at the cigarette. It was stale, tasted like yesterday's fire, and filled her with childish pangs of guilt. She crushed it out rather ruthlessly in the crystal ashtray. "No point in going to hell just yet," she said cheerfully to the fog, which had now reached her window.

She picked up her silver phone and got to work.

CHAPTER 4

"How did it go?"

Justine elbowed shut the front door and put down her briefcase, then turned to lock the door she had just entered. Shrugging her thin shoulders, she crossed the large living room and collapsed into a large, overstuffed armchair. Without looking, she extended a hand to receive the martini her mother always prepared for her homecoming.

"That bad?" Flora Davies asked anxiously. "Trouble?"

"No, no," Justine reassured her mother quickly, annoyed at the necessity of having to do so. "Nothing's wrong. I'm just tired. Why do you always assume something's gone wrong?" It grated on her nerves that no matter how high she clawed her way up the ladder, her mother anticipated disaster on every rung. Certainly losing her job—which was the disaster her mother feared most—would be a hardship. They were living beyond their means even at her salary, but by now she would have expected her mother to realize that Justine was more than capable of supporting them by finding a new position.

"I didn't assume, dear. I was merely concerned, that's all." Flora carefully cradled her own martini until she gingerly lowered herself into the chair opposite her daughter.

Justine watched her mother's stiff movements and felt a flash of remorse. It was difficult to believe, but the woman was past seventy now—not that she looked it—and fears about security came easily to older people. But the wave of compassion dissolved with her first sip of the martini. Her mother had always lacked faith in her success. Aging had just made the faithlessness show more. *The older you get, the more so.* . . . Where had she heard that? It didn't matter; it was true. Part of the reason her mother pushed at her so was because she had always lacked confidence in Justine's ability to triumph.

"You're only concerned about yourself!" she retorted hotly, narrowing her eyes while she sipped at the reviving drink. "You don't give a damn about me!"

"Now, Justine, you know that's not true," Flora said, sniffing and lifting her own glass.

Justine shrugged again, momentarily too exhausted to continue the battle. It was an old pattern, the accusations and bickering, completely understood and needed by both. For Justine it was comforting, being with her mother. She could unwind and say whatever she chose without having to mask her feelings behind pretty smiles and carefully chosen words. For her mother it was the same. To her friends Flora revealed only sweetness and charity, but with her daughter she could vent her intolerance for their stupidity.

"What happened?" Flora asked, putting down her glass and leaning forward expectantly, all trace of injured feelings quickly forgotten in her desire to keep abreast of Justine's daily battle to gain her deserved recognition at MagnifiScent.

"Well," she began, savoring her meager news as if it would grow in importance if she nursed it herself, "Olivia is starting to understand that Marlissa might be selling her formulas to Riviera. Even Thea is beginning to have a doubt or two." Quickly she repeated a few comments she had heard pass between the two women, filling in the blanks with her own speculation.

Her mother sat back, her lips primly closed. A small woman with a figure better than her daughter's, Flora had an excellent ability to broadcast disapproval without saying a word. "I thought the situation looked . . . hopeful," Justine said carefully, again glaring at her mother.

"Well, since you force my opinion, I'll give it." She first took another sip of her martini. "Justine, you'll rot in that nothing job of yours till the day they cart you away if you wait for Olivia and Thea to act on any suspicions they might have."

Trying to suppress the anger she felt at the demeaning way her mother chose to describe her well-paying job, Justine was nevertheless compelled to agree with the brief analysis. "I don't know what else I can do at this point."

Flora smiled grimly. "You can keep your eyes and ears open, that's what you can do! And if nothing happens you can make something happen! No one ever got anywhere in business by being the nice guy, you know. Olivia DeSante is obviously too close to the Deloffre woman and Thea Wallace to give you the position you deserve. Get rid of *them,* one way or the other, and you'll get somewhere. You've done it before, in other companies, and you can do it here. It's a dog-eat-dog world out there. God knows, I've tried to make you see that time and time again."

Cowering, Justine silently studied the Sultanabad carpet she had recently bought. Then her temper flared again. "What would you suggest I do? Plant incriminating evidence in Marlissa's lab coat?"

"If it takes that, yes!" With the help of her hands grasping the chair's arms, Flora got up. "Whatever it takes! Until they go, you stay where you are! Someone is selling the secrets or formulas, whatever you call them, and that someone has to be Marlissa Deloffre or one of her staff, from what you've told me before. If you can't point the finger of fact, point the one of suspicion so hard that Mrs. DeSante forgets about friendship and concentrates on business, as she should. It's your duty to your company. And also to yourself." She picked up her glass and smiled lovingly at her daughter. "Would you like another martini, darling? Dinner won't be for a little while yet."

Justine nodded and returned her mother's smile. "Thank you, yes, I think I would. It will help me think."

"Now that you know what to think about, it won't be difficult at all. You'll see. Trust Mother."

Justine nodded, grateful that there was at least one thing she could trust. Perhaps her mother pushed at her and lacked complete confidence in her abilities, but she never doubted in the slightest that her mother was solidly on her side, in her corner, rooting for her success. A sudden inspiration came to her. "What if," she began, stopping her mother from leaving the room, "Marlissa wasn't betraying the company directly, but if she was accidently revealing her secrets to some outsider who was then selling the information?"

"Then you don't believe Marlissa would sell the formulas herself?" Flora asked with a trace of disappointment.

Justine reviewed what she knew of the chemist. "No," she answered shortly, not bothering to elaborate, knowing her mother would accept her judgment because Justine was too good a judge of character to be wrong about anything this important. "But suppose she shares her work with someone close to her, just as I tell you what I'm doing every day. That's reasonable, isn't it?"

Her mother thoughtfully nodded. "Even as a child, you were a good little detective, always finding out this and that about people. And when you were married to that dreadful truck driver—"

"Please, Mother," she interrupted, not wanting to remember.

"You almost drove him crazy by letting him know you were wise to his infidelities," she continued smoothly. "Well, now you have your work cut out for you—your direction, at least—and if anyone can find out who this Deloffre woman is close to, I'll put my money on you, Justine." She sighed contentedly. "Now let me get you that drink, darling."

Forcing back the pained memory of secretly prying into Peter's affairs, Justine wondered whom Marlissa might be seeing away from work. She was young and not unattractive, for all her failure to make the most out of herself. *This might even,* she thought to herself, *be fun.*

CHAPTER 5

Justine Brandon felt her lips tighten. With great effort she softened her expression and bent over her note pad, scratching a few words on the bright yellow paper. It was a twofold gesture—it gave her a chance to compose her features before they betrayed her impatience, and her note taking added to her already established image of industriousness.

But inside she was seething with irritation. It never ceased to disturb her, these undisciplined executive meetings in Olivia's fabulous office. Justine pretended to listen attentively to the discussion of MagnifiScent's newest line, but a part of her mind was aloof from the proceedings, replaying a favorite tape of critical analysis about the flaws of the company for which she worked.

For one thing, Justine believed that Olivia DeSante, whom she grudgingly admired, was undermined by sentimentality. She treated both Thea and Marlissa like friends rather than employees, and certainly both women enjoyed far too much power, especially Marlissa, who, after all, was merely a chemist. If Justine held the reins of MagnifiScent, Marlissa would remain where she belonged: in her laboratory, receiving orders. She would never be in this office, daring to take part in the direction of future lines. And Thea, Justine's boss, routinely got away with murder, teasing and chiding Olivia in front of Miles Holbrook and the rest of the executive force.

Before coming to MagnifiScent, Justine had worked always with top professionals who ran their affairs efficiently and with no quarter given for personal relationships. She ached to be given a free hand, to winnow out the hangers-on, to restructure the top-heavy management from Olivia on down. Her own department was a good example. Once she had been hired, Thea's own position in the firm had become unnecessary. She could not only do everything that Thea did, but she had the background and experience to do it better. Never would she have hired an assistant who could outperform herself, as Thea had done. Justine's initial function had been to free Thea to follow her playgirl whims, and yet she was sticking closer to MagnifiScent than ever, denying Justine the title and salary she deserved.

Not that she wasn't being amply compensated for her work, Justine acknowledged to herself. More than once she had used the amount she made to silence her ambitious mother. As assistant to Thea, she was making more money than she had as an executive with her own department before.

Even so, money wasn't the only consideration. Being Thea's assistant negated a goodly portion of the satisfaction her salary warranted. At forty-six Justine knew that she was rapidly entering her peak years, that she had to get to the top and quickly, or never get there at all. And it was not enough to be at the top of a lesser organization. She had set her sights on MagnifiScent ever since the then-small Swiss company had exploded into the American market. She had courted MagnifiScent like an ardent lover, never once showing her intense desire to affiliate herself with the growing concern. She was too smart for that—she had let them come crawling to her by holding out the right bait—her own brilliance.

Olivia and Thea didn't know it, but Justine had deliberately jockeyed her way into her executive position at the rival firm to get their attention. It was a long, carefully plotted campaign, and she had done her homework well, knowing all the important details that were to bring her to MagnifiScent. She had gone to the other firm because she knew—through manipulated informants—that the company was in trouble, and she was therefore able to convince them that she could be instrumental in solving their particular problems. She had worked long and hard to get a solid reputation, then saw to it that the rapidly mushrooming MagnifiScent heard about her.

Initially her plan was to come to MagnifiScent in some secondary position, using it as a springboard to climb higher. Thea's offer was perfect. Justine would relieve Thea of her workload, then ease her completely out of the company. Olivia would remain as the figurehead, but she, Justine, would be the power behind the throne. Olivia could enjoy her queenly media image, but the real world of business would know who the controlling force was.

The one flaw in her otherwise-perfect plan was the discovery that MagnifiScent's leader had some quaint, romantic image of herself as some latter-day Musketeer, with Thea and Marlissa her loyal right and left hands. There could be no opportunity to snatch the prized position away from Thea, to establish herself as a significant power, with Olivia's two watchdogs guarding the pyramid as they were. In Justine's mind she could clearly see the great benefit to not only the company but to Olivia DeSante herself if she and Justine, unhampered, spearheaded the organization. And Justine was more than willing to do the work for both of them. She could run both marketing and product development with an iron hand, bulldozing MagnifiScent into monopolizing the cosmetics industry. She was suffused with ideas and new directions for the company.

She had already introduced many of her ideas, either directly to Olivia or through Thea. Some had been accepted and were currently in operation, while others had been shelved or completely discarded. She still fumed internally over the rejection of her suggestion to move heavily into the area of hair products. Olivia herself had demurred, claiming that existing companies like Redken were putting out the products in this market that already met MagnifiScent's exacting demands. Justine had argued sweetly, reminding Olivia that Redken, whose line was undeniably excellent, still refused to retail, selling their wares only through salons, leaving wide open grand-scale merchandising to companies like MagnifiScent. But backed by Marlissa and her tiresome research, Olivia came back at Justine armed with data proving that in this select area, the standard of MagnifiScent products could not be maintained in mass-market retailing. Hair products were too individual, so that a perfectly good shampoo for one person would be all wrong for another. This, even though other conglomerates were swelling their purses on mass-marketed shampoos every day!

And that was a perfect example of the weakness in MagnifiScent. While Justine acknowledged that it was extremely important to put out quality merchandise, she also understood, apparently better than anyone else present, that far more important than the actual quality of the product was the illusion of its quality—women bought dreams, not cosmetics. Hadn't Charles Revson taken the same basic nail polish that Cutex sold and founded his empire by simply doubling Cutex's price and convincing the public that he was selling something more glamorous? And who really believed that garbage about Helena Rubinstein having a darkly guarded secret formula for her face cream? The impression of being allowed in on a secret formula was what sold the cream, not the value of the cream itself. MagnifiScent was now too big to continue to play around with idealistic precepts. Billions rather than millions were ready to be garnered, and nitpickers like Marlissa Deloffre were keeping them back.

"I have an idea that might be appealing," Marlissa was saying.

Justine looked up, an encouraging smile glued to her face, revealing none of the disdain she felt. She was too seasoned a player ever to tip her hand. But she promised herself that she would sooner or later get Marlissa, if only to pay her back for Olivia's ultimate rejection of Justine's hair-products suggestion.

While Marlissa explained her idea—something that she could very nicely have kept to herself and worked out in the lab without taking up Olivia's valuable time, not to mention Justine's own—Justine thought of her situation with more than usual dissatisfaction.

Time was running out. Not only was she a decade older than these women to whom she had to humble herself, she had never been good-looking. She lacked the basic ingredients of beauty and had never been appealing to men. She had married once, briefly. Fortunately, Peter Brandon had abandoned the responsibilities of marriage shortly after their first anniversary. At least in hindsight it was fortunate, because his leaving had prompted Justine to pursue a career, although at the time his leaving, his rejection of her, had devastated her. Afterward, she had gone back to live with her widowed mother, herself a frustrated career woman who had given up her small business to be a wife and mother long ago. At her mother's urging Justine had completed her schooling, securing a degree in business administration. With her mother behind her, constantly pushing her to reach higher, demand more, she had risen steadily, and last year she had been able to afford their wonderful house in St. Francis Wood, not so very far from Marlissa's own home. She had inadvertently put herself in a position where she could watch over Marlissa not only at work but at home. She was ready to pounce on her slightest weakness.

It had already been established that Riviera had access to Marlissa's formulas. Justine had planted seeds of suspicion about Marlissa through Miles Holbrook, who had Olivia's ear. Chance remarks here and there—never directly from her—were working their way up to Olivia, each from a separate office. It was absurdly easy to direct speculation toward Marlissa. Meticulous in every other way, the chemist was sloppy about security. Justine had made it her business to discover this flaw. Even if she could not find some way to pinpoint the leak directly to Marlissa, she could guide thoughts to the realization that Marlissa was responsible for the leakage.

"Excellent, Marlissa," Olivia said at the conclusion of the chemist's report. But there was a slight tension in Olivia's smile that Justine, looking for a sign, immediately noticed. "Any other new thoughts?"

Justine straightened in her chair. She pointedly smiled at Thea, going so far as to clear her throat to get her boss's attention. Thea, who had been tapping at the ash of her gold-tipped cigarette, looked up blankly.

"The new layout?" Justine prompted good-naturedly, as if she, too, shared these amateur businesswomen's casualness and wasn't overly concerned that her week-long research would be overlooked through Thea's absentmindedness.

"Oh, yes!" She scanned her notes and sighed. "Justine, darling, why don't you explain? It's really your project, anyway, and I'm simply a million miles away today."

First a glance of sympathetic concern for Thea, and then a bright-eyed eagerness for Olivia's benefit. Then, consciously grandstanding her authentically excellent findings, Justine began to speak.

CHAPTER 6

"Quality!"

Rita Vanalden flinched as the pale hand struck the massive, glass-topped, mahogany desk with unexpected force. Since Marlissa's hazel eyes seemed to have singled her out from the others, Rita kept her face solemn. Under the younger woman's gaze, Rita felt foolishly guilty, barely managing to resist the urge to squirm like a schoolgirl taken before the principal.

"MagnifiScent was, is, and *shall always be* synonymous with quality!" Marlissa Deloffre paused dramatically. "I shouldn't have to explain what I mean by quality to this select little group standing in front of my desk, should I? And not only you senior chemists, but *every* chemist, laboratory technician, and *janitor* in each and every laboratory we own must keep this word fully in mind. My family slaved to create the finest, purest perfumes and cosmetics the world has ever known! Remember that! Our products are miracles of chemistry, technology, and art, miracles that are revolutionizing cosmetics. Not since Madame Helena Rubinstein showed the world that beauty is an acquired art has one organization so strived to take this art to the pinnacle of perfection. MagnifiScent's products must exemplify the ultimate in this esoteric art. Our salons, our packaging and publicity departments convey this image to the outside world—but the final burden of perfection falls upon our *usually* competent shoulders. Each of MagnifiScent's products must be tested and retested at every stage of development. If at any point there is uncertainty, the entire process must begin again! Our end result must represent the highest quality of any like product on the market. MagnifiScent *is* quality! Remember that," she said forcefully in her softly accented voice. "Olivia DeSante has built an empire based on quality."

Marlissa looked down at the sheaf of papers in front of her on the desk. They were neatly stapled into an impressively thick packet. "This," she said quietly, the muscles in her face working as if constricted with sudden pain, "is not quality."

Rita watched Marlissa disdainfully push the offending report to the edge of her desk, accusingly closer to where Rita and the nine other biochemists summoned to this office stood mutely. The dark-haired director of laboratory research had propelled the papers with only the tips of her fingers, as if loath to contaminate herself by prolonged contact with the defective analysis. Again Rita felt singularly reproached, as if the report were her exclusive work rather than the combined effort of the complex as a whole. It was, in fact and thank God, one that had fortunately required only a routine test from Rita's department. *A competently executed and completely satisfactory analysis,* she reminded herself, still fighting down the infantile discomfort Marlissa's displeasure generated in her.

Wishing this session would come to an end, Rita moved her eyes from her boss's face and scanned the familiar office. She had made this same quick visual scan every time she had visited Marlissa's wing of the building, partially out of curiosity but more often to ease the nervousness she always felt in the immediate presence of this somehow intimidating young woman from Switzerland.

And, as always, the superbly decorated room vaguely bothered her, gave Rita a sense of discomfort, as if something was not quite complete. Yet it was an elegant, tasteful office with its own bar and lounge area for small gatherings. Marlissa never used that area during a session in which she was forced to tell her staff she was displeased with the work presented to her. In vain Rita tried to identify the source of her vague discomfort, an unidentifiable something that disturbed her at odd moments. At home with Stephen, while watching television or preparing a meal, Rita would find herself thinking of Marlissa's inner sanctum and almost grasp the delicate flaw, only to lose the knowledge once again.

After a short, highly technical discussion among Marlissa and the chemists from toxicology and the lab-evaluation departments, Rita and the others were curtly dismissed with the weary admonition to rework the unsatisfactory report on the new facial mask. She was the last one to file out of the office and into Marlissa's secretary's cubicle. Relieved now that the meeting was over and she had emerged unscathed, Rita lingered a moment in front of the large oval mirror on Barbara Cantor's wall. Rita's approach to any reflection of her physical self was cagy—a quick, acutely self-conscious glance at her image, achieved by the briefest roll of her eyes, followed by a hasty retreat. Her mind recorded her rather bulky, less-than-feminine shape, slightly minimized by the white lab smock, the unremarkable features of her round face, the functional cut of her neither blond nor really brown hair. In shifting her eyes from the unkind reality, Rita noticed a small bowling trophy on Barbara's desk.

Marlissa's secretary stopped typing and also looked at the trophy. "Isn't it silly? I won it almost three years ago, and then only because half the other girls were out with the flu. But I can't seem to make myself toss it out."

"I think it's nice right where it is," Rita answered absently, redirecting her gaze to a photograph of Barbara's family. It was flanked on one side by a white porcelain coffee cup with the initial *B* in bright red and on the other by a tiny model of an expensive car Rita knew Barbara hoped one day to own. These represented the trivia of a life separate from a job, personal touches, a dab of individuality that subtly altered the contrived impersonality of Barbara's office.

Rita thought of the wall behind her own desk. It was emblazoned with the threads of her existence—the framed degrees in chemistry, the eight-by-ten of Stephen and herself taken on their honeymoon the year before, a stiffly handsome portrait of her parents, and a sketch of a lop-eared dog done by a favorite niece. Next to it was a snapshot of Stephen taken less than a month ago. It showed his handsome face crinkled by a broad grin, his dark hair attractively tousled by the rampant San Francisco wind.

Rita hurried back to her laboratory, noting with relief that Marlissa's rare but not unprecedented meeting had lasted until the end of the working day. As she hung up her jacket, washed her hands, and took a swift look around to make sure that she had left nothing urgent undone, Rita turned her attention to more comfortable, mundane matters, particularly the mental survey of the contents of her refrigerator at home. There was more than enough of the stew she had made the day before, but Stephen didn't really like leftovers.

Carlos Ruiz, one of her lab technicians, flashed her a sunny smile. "I hear the facial compound got snuffed, huh?" He smoothed his glossy black hair into place. "Did our ice maiden give you a hard time?"

She had heard this unflattering description of Marlissa before and wondered why it always put her on the defensive. "Of course not, Carlos. And she was right, you know. It was a sloppy report."

He shrugged. "Not our fault." He glanced at his watch. "Time to go! I've got a hot date." His thickly lashed eyes closed in anticipation of a good night ahead.

Rita watched his lithe body slip around the desk and out the door, his exit as graceful as a dancer taking a curtain call. From long habit she observed him furtively through the plate-glass window of the various laboratories. The whole complex was like a glassed-in maze, making it easy to watch her assistant as he made his way toward the exit. He always took the time to say a word or two of farewell to everyone he passed, his handsome, dark face open and cheerful, in spite of his professed rush to meet his date. Carlos was a particular favorite with women of all ages, radiating a slightly exotic sensuality with the practiced charm of a gigolo.

Rita's relief that she had never revealed her own attraction to him during the first two months he had worked for her bordered on hysteria. Never would he guess the nights she had tossed in her bed thinking of his muscular body, his golden skin, his strong hands that worked so steadily in her laboratory.

She had recognized it immediately as an absurd attraction. Carlos was twelve years her junior and obviously partial to melon-breasted beauties half her age. Acute loneliness was responsible for her ludicrous feelings; the same bitter loneliness that, more than once, had made her consider giving up this job she loved to escape back into the protected boredom of the town she had left in Washington, where scores of sisters and brothers and nieces and nephews would keep time from hanging so heavily on her hands. But, she reminded herself, she had held out; she had not disgraced herself by saying anything foolish to her sexy Chicano assistant. Then, miraculously, Stephen Vanalden had come into her life and saved her from returning home or making a fool of herself with Carlos.

She closed her eyes and swayed slightly, still intoxicated with the wonder of having married such a man. She remembered the exact moment she'd seen Stephen for the first time.

He'd come alone to the Bannermans' party, arriving late and wearing clothing that marked him as different. It was perhaps that very quality that had caught her immediate attention, had impressed her more than the fact that he was so terribly handsome. He had looked disdainfully removed from the other carefully suited men, dramatically above them, a prince among pretentious peasants. The snug jeans and dark blue shirt with the bold dragon design in gold seemed to emphasize his inner confidence. Rita, stiffly insecure in spite of the great effort she'd made to look her best, admired him and longed to share the secret of social success people like Stephen Vanalden seemed to possess.

Rita rarely went to parties. But the Bannermans' invitation had come at a moment when another empty weekend had seemed unendurable. They were a nice middle-aged couple who lived across the hall in the expensive high-rise apartment building into which she'd recently moved, and this was the third invitation they'd extended. She'd lived in San Francisco almost two years and had yet to establish a close friendship or even to master her small-town terror of walking into a roomful of strangers. Yet the fear of spending the remainder of her life alone was a greater horror.

Rita had done very well for herself professionally. In her hometown of Chimacum, Washington, her dedication to work had won her the position of chief chemist at a small cosmetics factory. At first she had scoffed at her brother Raymond's suggestion that she apply for the job with MagnifiScent during a vacation in San Francisco. She liked her job, and the money was more than ample for her needs. Ray's wife, Edie, had found the ad in the newspaper, but it was Ray who had urged her to investigate further.

"Look, sweetie, you know there's nothing for you in Chimacum. San Francisco's exciting! It would be a whole new life for you!"

"I like my job," she'd protested, panicked in spite of her infatuation with what she had seen of The City.

She watched him search for a tactful way to express his concern. "A job can only do so much, kiddo. It's not a life. You're a warm, loving woman. A woman, Rita. I watch you with my kids, and I . . ."

His pained expression cut into her soul. "Then there's the family," she'd protested softly. "I couldn't imagine living so far away from you all." Guiltily she'd wondered if Raymond subconsciously resented her for horning in on his family's vacation. He and Edie had encouraged her to come, and she'd tried to repay their kindness by baby-sitting with the three kids so that they could enjoy a few nights out on the town. Was it possible that at thirty-nine she was already an embarrassment to her family? The old maid that everyone pitied and tried to find a place for? His next words had seemed to suggest as much.

"It's not the same as your very own family, Rita." He had taken her hand and squeezed it gently. "You need your own family. Don't live your life through us. You deserve more than that."

The interview with Marlissa Deloffre had gone smoothly. Rita's college background was exactly what MagnifiScent was looking for in their biochemistry division, and her knowledge and experience in the cosmetics industry was an added advantage. She was awed by Marlissa, who was becoming a legend in the field, but she admired the way Marlissa handpicked her extensive staff. Rita had taken the job, and every time she got a promotion along with a generous raise, Rita had moved, first from a staid woman's hotel, then to a quaint Victorian, and finally to the ultramodern high-rise less than a mile from the MagnifiScent building. Only Rita's personal life was a vast wasteland. She was trying to get by on hope salvaged from the tattered remnants of her girlhood dreams. Out of desperation she had agreed to go to the Bannermans' party.

Her acceptance activated a flurry of ambitious resolutions. She would walk to work daily. She would pay more attention to what she wore. She would join a health club. She had starved herself for the entire week before the party in a last-ditch attempt to bring some trace of symmetry to her stocky body. Her sacrifices were rewarded by the rare experience of finding a really flattering dress, a bottle green watered silk, at a small specialty shop just off Maiden Lane. Learning of the party, Bonnie Tyler of the radioisotope lab, whom Rita barely knew, had insisted on getting one of the makeup girls from MagnifiScent's downstairs salon to give her a bold new face. Bonnie had also talked Rita into a smart haircut by her own beautician.

As a result, Rita had gone to the Bannermans' feeling like an elegant fake. Bonnie had raved about the transformation. But at the party, surrounded by animated, sophisticated strangers, Rita knew that all her efforts and Bonnie's kindness had been in vain—underneath she was still the same shy, drab, unexciting Rita Moore who sat on the edge of couches and prayed she would remain unnoticed.

Stephen arrived at the moment Rita, having stayed long enough to make an unobtrusive exit, was plotting her escape. He was tall and casually dressed, but the jeans had an expensive label and the shirt an expensive look. He was so gorgeous she thought he might be an actor, but she overheard someone mention that he sold real estate across the bay. Rita had stayed at the party not with the hope of meeting him but simply because she wanted to look at him a little longer. Stephen hadn't noticed her immediately, but after chatting with the Bannermans, he had sought her out.

"The lady chemist, I presume?" he'd said, standing by her, his face creasing into a wonderful, boyish smile. She saw that he was younger than she, but not by much, and that close up he was even more handsome than she'd thought. He had a square jaw, a thick neck, and sensuous lips. She could feel the exciting warmth of his body as he sat down next to her. His deep-set eyes held her gaze, and she felt imprisoned in their vaguely restless depths.

He had done most of the talking, skillfully drawing her out by asking endless questions. He had seemed genuinely fascinated by her job. His interest made her forget that she wasn't beautiful, that even her barely adequate appearance at the moment had been achieved through unusual dedication and great expense. She gave him her phone number with trembling fingers.

Even when they were seeing each other regularly, Rita didn't allow herself to dream that Stephen might be serious about her. She'd seen the way other women, beautiful women, looked at him when they went out. Few of them made the effort to mask their interest in him in front of her, probably dismissing her as a maiden sister or business date. They didn't take her seriously—how could he?

When he asked her to marry him, she went through the motions of considering his proposal rationally. There were, after all, several good reasons to hesitate. He was not a success at his work. He disliked selling and at thirty-seven had yet to find himself. She earned far more money. Being married to Stephen would mean a lifetime of unasked questions on the faces of strangers, naked surprise even from family and acquaintances—how could a woman like Rita get such a man? His beauty dwarfed her. She could not believe he could want her.

Miraculously he had understood her dark thoughts as she deliberated. Both knew she would accept, of course. She had already accepted, for all her mute hesitation, her eyes brimming with happiness and gratitude. They were alone in her lovely apartment, sitting together on the tan suede sofa he had helped her select. She was already dependent on him, on his sense of style, his ability to make instantaneous decisions. He had touched her hair with gentle understanding. "I know you, Rita Moore. I know what's going on in that little mind of yours. In spite of your success at work and all you've done for yourself, you're a funny bundle of self-doubt."

She pretended a confusion she didn't feel. He slipped his arm around her. The contact made her hands turn to ice. Even breathing was difficult when he was close to her. She wondered if he sensed how much she wanted him.

"Hey, listen to me, baby. I want you to hear what I'm saying." He kissed her ear. "I know you don't think of yourself as beautiful, desirable. So you don't understand that I do. Because *you* don't, you see? Did you ever think about what a selfish sequence of thoughts that really is? *You* don't find yourself attractive, so I'm supposed to share your opinion, right? You, you, you!" He'd laughed softly, hugging her as if she were a child confused by a bad dream. Then he'd kissed her, lingeringly, deeply. He'd kissed her before, but not like this, not so slowly and lovingly, never with such boundless tenderness. His voice, when he finally spoke, was husky and hypnotic. "Let me show you how desirable I find you, Rita. My body can speak better. Give me a chance. Give us both a chance, okay? Let me show you, baby. . . ."

It was not the first time she had made love. There had been a very few others in her past. Not men who mattered. With deep shame she had remembered the handful of times when loneliness had made her accept an hour of passion from a near-stranger, hurried, embarrassed moments that had seemed vital to her at the time. But no one had ever opened the world of slow sensuality to her the way Stephen did that night.

She had married him before a breathless assembly of family members who had gladly made the trip to San Francisco to share her limitless joy, never openly questioning her choice or his.

Even so, after more than a year she still felt as if she were seeped in a wondrous dream. Her only prayer was that she might never awaken.

Flushed from her unbidden thoughts, Rita grabbed her purse, fumbled for her car keys, and remembered the thick porterhouse in the freezer. Stephen loved a thick steak, preferably blood rare. It gave her such pleasure to feed him well.

CHAPTER 7

The high-pitched screech of a departing 747 drowned Daniel's last words.

"What? I can't hear you," Thea yelled over the noise. Daniel had driven her to the San Francisco airport, and now she began to wish her plane would be announced.

"I said you wouldn't be this tense if you jogged." He lowered his voice as the plane outside disappeared into the dark sky. "A little exercise. . . ."

Her answering laugh was a little shrill. "Between exercising a horse and sailing, I get more than my share of workouts, Daniel. You don't have to run through the streets at some ungodly hour. . . ." She let it go, aware that he had only been trying to give her well-intentioned advice. Again. Daniel was beginning to bore her. Thea noticed that each new man seemed to last a shorter and shorter time in her life lately. She'd been seeing Daniel less than a month, and between his lengthy dissertations about the trials and tribulations of manufacturing auto parts and his passion for jogging, it had seemed like years.

A muffled voice over the public-address system advised that boarding for her plane would begin in five minutes. Thea put a hand to her hair, which she wore loose and brushed back. "You were a darling to take me to the airport, Daniel. I shouldn't have let you do it. I'll be landing in L.A. before you even get home. Don't wait until I get on." She lifted her face for a kiss.

"Do you have everything? Would you like me to dash to

the newsstand for a magazine?" He kissed her quickly. "I get damn restless flying if there's nothing to read. It'll only take a minute."

She shook her head and let him kiss her a second time. It was a habit with him; first a brotherly peck and then, as if remembering who she was, a sensuous second kiss with his hands touching her briefly but powerfully. Routine or not, he did it very nicely, reminding Thea that he was far less boring in bed than out of it.

"I'll call you Tuesday, darling. Monday's impossible and I have that business thing at night. You're sure I can't get you something to read? Even short flights can seem interminable."

Thea smiled and patted his arm. "You wouldn't be so restless if you didn't jog all the time." She smiled to let him see she was teasing. He had almost no sense of humor and would frequently be offended by her teasing if she didn't give him some immediate indication that she was less than serious. "Talk to you Tuesday."

She walked toward the gate, hoping he wouldn't get lost while attempting to find his big brown Mercedes. His lack of a sense of direction was even more ludicrous than his lack of humor. She hadn't been joking about arriving in Los Angeles before he got home. If he found his car without several false starts, he'd very likely go in circles on the trip back to The City, even though he made the trip with regularity.

Immediately she turned the annoyance she felt to herself. Why was she always so quick to find the flaws in a man, and why did they bother her so much? Daniel Phelps was a perfectly acceptable man. He was tall, handsome, intelligent, unquestionably successful, and very attentive as a date and a lover. He was even halfway in love with her. What did she want? So he didn't tell jokes or know north from south. So he wasn't perfect. Was she?

Thea followed a young couple onto the plane. Each was holding a sleeping baby, their identical faces bobbing against their parents' shoulders. The flight attendant was still smiling at the open-mouthed, closed-eyed twins as she took Thea's boarding pass. She waited until the couple had maneuvered past the first-class section, then took one of the comfortable seats herself. She wondered idly if the couple had bought seats for the babies or would have to endure the whole flight with the infants numbing their shoulders. She couldn't imagine traveling with a baby, not without a capable nurse, anyway. Thinking about babies made her think about Daniel. No. Impossible. Never.

She watched the steady string of passengers moving by her seat. She had always been curious about people, although she sensed a certain lack of understanding about those whose life-styles differed too greatly from her own. Olivia had accused her of being a snob more than once, and Thea supposed the label was justified—a good example was that she couldn't help wondering at these hurrying people who refused to part with a few dollars for first-class seating, preferring the cramped quarters allotted to flying at bargain prices. She could almost hear Olivia's indignation.

Did it ever occur to you that some of these people couldn't afford what you call a few dollars?

The chief flight attendant, neat as a pin in her red uniform, droned out the standard announcement prior to takeoff. Absently Thea fastened her seatbelt. She flew so often that she felt less apprehension or excitement in a plane than she felt in a car, particularly when she drove with Daniel, who was not a good driver, or with Henry, her parents' chauffeur, who was rapidly approaching senility.

She settled into the cushioned back of her seat while the plane accelerated, smiling as she thought of Henry, who had been old even when she was a child. His stiff formality amused her. He would, of course, be meeting her in spite of the late hour. His job wasn't particularly taxing, as her father drove his own car to the office and her mother had needed his services only infrequently since her gall-bladder operation last May.

Henry would look impeccable in his severe black uniform with the peaked cap over his close-cut gray hair. He was so reassuringly predictable. He would inquire about her health, the comfort of her trip, the weather in San Francisco, then ask for her baggage check. Then he would escort her to the black Mercedes, hold the door for her, put her baggage in the trunk, and be as silent as a tomb as he drove her to her parents' home in Beverly Hills with the unintentional recklessness of the old and unaware. Flying, in contrast, was a snap.

Thea accepted coffee from the flight attendant, regretfully passing on an offered cocktail. She had killed a bottle of wine with Daniel before coming to the airport, and she needed a clear head for the inevitable meeting with her mother. She had no doubt that her mother would be waiting up for her. It was an old ritual between them, but this predictable meeting was never wonderful or reassuring like her dialogue with Henry.

Her mother would be seated in the living room, peering through the pince-nez glasses she didn't need at a magazine or a book. She would remove the glasses and take a quick, all-encompassing glance at her only daughter to reassure herself that Thea hadn't deteriorated physically, that she was still marriage material. Their conversation would be as calculated as a mathematical formula, and while her mother no longer had the intestinal fortitude to inquire too obviously about Thea's love life, every word would be directed toward discovering if there was a worthwhile man somewhere in the periphery of her daughter's alien world. If she was up to it she would probably mention Everett's name somehow, now that Everett was a widower and therefore eligible again.

Thea couldn't remember how the whole thing with Everett Hamlinton had begun. Although their parents were friends, she didn't remember seeing much of him when they were children. He was away at school, or she was busy with lessons and parties. When she began dating, Everett began to be a common, everyday household word. She hadn't ever been especially impressed by him, nor had she been repelled. He was just another local boy wearing expensive clothing, driving a good car, experimenting with cigarettes and alcohol. There was no logical reason not to date him when the boys she went out with were so much the same, but her mother had made the typical mistake of pushing too hard at a time when Thea was just tasting her first breath of independence. Without any conscious intent and through no fault of his own, Everett became a battlefield for her mother and her and, eventually, his name alone became a symbol of all she didn't want.

Her coffee was cold. She gestured for a refill, and while the flight attendant was bringing her a fresh cup, Thea let her eyes drift over the half-dozen others in her section. There was a middle-aged couple reading in the seats before hers, a teenage boy dressed in ragged jeans with an old blue backpack on the seat next to him, his studied poverty laughable in view of his gold Corum watch, Ralph Lauren polo shirt, and new though scuffed sixty-dollar tennis shoes. A well-dressed older man in the first row of seats was contentedly absorbed by the papers in his overstuffed briefcase. He reminded Thea of her father, who always approached business with an expectant eagerness, as if he were returning to an especially exciting game of Monopoly in which he held all the assets.

Thinking of her father took some of the mild anxiety away from this trip home. Her father was the easy one. He would be glad to see her, would ask a few questions about her horse Legacy, talk business a little, probably encourage her to play golf with him, and otherwise leave her alone. His interest in her marital status had waned long ago. Now that her brother David was solidly entrenched in Wallace Enterprises and had fathered a son, he was free to enjoy his daughter without imposing expectations on her. Carrying the Everett torch had become her mother's exclusive burden.

Thea realized she wasn't being quite fair. She stared out the sealed window at the blackness and wondered if this battle between her mother and herself was completely one-sided. Once poor Everett had given up the quest and married Anita Horton, Thea had actually found herself liking him. She had never given herself a chance to like him before. Everett had ceased to be a person when she was seventeen—he had become instead an issue.

The drone of the plane was hypnotic. Thea felt drowsy. She also felt a tremendous wave of loneliness settle over her. For a moment she could think of her mother's life with a trace of desire. To have a husband, children, a comfortable place in a comfortable world . . . why had that always repulsed her so deeply? Because it was boring. Since childhood Thea had craved excitement. But what had she found?

Closing her eyes, Thea reflected on her own life. A predictable childhood, girlhood crushes, her first experimentation with booze and sex and drugs. Standard fare. Two summers in Europe with her parents, a semester in England at school. A return to begin the battle about Everett. Her decision to pass on college and her mother's renewed energy about her getting married, preferably to Everett. Or someone in the same mold.

Only now it was so difficult to remember what she had wanted to do with her life instead. Recalling the restlessness in her blood was easy. She felt it still. Then life had been an unopened present, with all the charm and potential of the exquisitely wrapped packages she used to get from F.A.O. Schwarz when she was a child. She couldn't imagine settling down with one man.

She had been a pretty girl, her face promising a beauty that had never really come to fruition. Not that anyone knew that. She knew all the tricks, had access to the best. The world saw a sophisticated, beautiful woman who rivaled the best. Only Thea, looking in her mirror when she awakened, saw something else. It was beginning to frighten her, the woman she saw then. Tiny lines were the least of it, easily camouflaged. Her brown eyes, still flecked with gold, were the worst. What had happened to the light in them? Eyes were said to be the mirrors of the soul. Her soul, then, she knew, was sick.

It was in many ways her deepest, darkest secret, this sickness of her soul. She guarded the knowledge with varying intensity. Her mother must never suspect. Marlissa, for all her frightening intelligence, could never guess because she saw Thea as the epitome of all she herself strove to be. Even Olivia, her dearest friend, was not permitted to catch more than the slightest hint of the sickness of her soul. Once, only once, she had exposed herself to someone, and then a stranger.

Thea's opinion of psychiatrists had been formed when she was little more than a girl. It was the thing to do in Beverly Hills, a sort of fad at one time. All her mother's friends had psychiatrists, and their animation when discussing these professionals had amused Thea greatly. She could remember telling Olivia on their European escapade that these psychiatrists were little more than gigolos. *Don't you see, Olivia? These women have found safe lovers for themselves. They pay money to have this other man in their lives. With them they can have a big, meaningful affair, even if it's all on an emotional level and nobody mucks around in bed. It's all so clean! And such bullshit. My mother comes home from her sessions looking like she just got laid. Mind whores, that's what they are. No thanks. If I ever get decrepit to the point where I have to pay for my kicks, I'll start thinking about suicide . . .*

She remembered her smugness at the time, that amazing confidence of youth. Olivia had argued at the time that there were valid reasons for psychiatry, and later Thea had eaten her words. Shortly after her thirtieth birthday, Thea found herself in Dr. Leon Julius's office. Reaching thirty had hit her hard. For more than a year Thea hadn't been able to sleep without pills, get through a day without a drink, and her craving for sex had made her seek out faceless strangers. She was barely surviving the days to come alive at night in smoke-filled discos. She draped her body in confetti-sequined tulle dresses or skintight jeans with skimpy tops; she was always laughing, always dancing, the objects of her flirtations ranging from popular European royalty to self-consciously overdressed young men who saved all week to afford one glorious night out. There was always someone to take home to her apartment at the Sunset West, someone to dazzle her senses until the pill took effect and she could escape into sleep. Those were the days when she was starting to make money of her own by selling perfume for Olivia, when she should have felt good about herself, because at last, at least financially, she was gaining freedom from her parents.

Under all her frenetic energy Thea felt herself dying, slipping away, becoming entombed in the debris of her own wasted life. Other women she knew married, had babies, and were learning to run their households with a semblance of grace. She knew she didn't want that, but what did she want?

"Do you think—possibly, just possibly—you are suffering from a conflict in your own moral standards?" Dr. Julius had asked after three visits. "You cannot accept the sort of life your mother wants for you, yes? But on the other hand, perhaps you feel that you now live too casually. There is a conflict for many women in your age bracket. They have been raised with certain standards, yes? A certain morality, a face they are expected to show to the world. Affairs are carried on with discretion. Sex is considered the outcropping of affection, never the sole purpose of a relationship.

"Yet the generation just behind yours has defied all that. Now a woman is expected to seek her own gratification in much the same way men have always been permitted to indulge themselves. Now, women initiate sexual advances. You are caught between two worlds, yes? You pursue the pleasure of one world and suffer the guilt of the other, perhaps."

Thea was furious. The man had implied that her discontent stemmed from being raised as a lady and conducting her life like a whore. He saw her as a guilt-ridden puppet, one more of the mass of empty-faced girl-women who couldn't seem to find themselves. If that was who she was, she didn't want to know about it. She had come to a psychiatrist out of desperation, only to be told a glib string of generational nonsense.

Even so, Thea had changed at least externally since that third and final visit with Dr. Julius. First there was Jean-Pierre's death and her flight to Meiringen to help Olivia through the first shock. Then her time became filled with

MagnifiScent, and for the first time in her life, she knew what it was to be absorbed in something other than herself, what it was to work, and work hard. It was merciful, because she didn't have time for the alcohol, and she would tumble into bed too exhausted to need her pill. Moving to San Francisco had been good, too. Olivia had given her a piece of the new company, and money was streaming in. Thea had also come into an inheritance, and after three months of looking had found an ideal house on the Marina.

Her social life had also changed, and Thea had never known for sure if it was as a result of her new schedule and position or if Dr. Julius's words had touched something in her. She had what could be called real relationships with men and let sex be a part of those relationships rather than the purpose of them.

But for the last year she had felt her grip slipping again. She had gone home for a weekend and had seen Everett, who was recently widowed. He had once more suggested marriage. She refused, but on her return to San Francisco she was edgy and unhappy. She was forced to go back to Los Angeles when her mother was in the hospital, but refused to so much as answer Everett's phone calls. Never one for consistent work, she tried to spend more time at her office downtown and less alone, had bought her horse and taken up sailing. She dated men like Daniel and saw every show, every opera, every ballet.

And, keeping it a complete secret, she returned to the sleeping pills, the booze, and, finally, the quick, humiliatingly gratifying sex with faceless strangers. She foraged for men with the restless abandon of a jungle predator, keeping a secret and unpretentious apartment in The City for this purpose rather than bringing these men to her house on the Marina. She was conscious of her position at MagnifiScent and took pains to keep a separate identity at the dives she frequented for these casual meetings. Alone, she would return to her house, to her pills, to her troubled sleep when it finally came.

It was a terrifying double existence. What she had once accepted as a life of erotic daring was rapidly disintegrating into a shoddy and shameful compulsion. She told herself that she simply craved excitement and that taking risks with strangers was fun and unique. But she had read *Looking for Mr. Goodbar* with a sense of panic, and her fear of death became more immediate and chilling. She feared other things as well—an unexpected meeting that would give her away, a seemingly accidental overdose of sleeping pills on one of those nights when self-disgust overcame her, the embarrassment of perhaps contracting a venereal disease and passing it on to Daniel or whoever was her current man.

What had started as a simple desire to find her own place and avoid a life chosen for her by her mother had exploded into degeneracy. Olivia seemed to be handling her life competently enough. She put the greater part of her energy into building her empire, a creative, positive use of the same restlessness. Marlissa, who had left the man she loved behind in Switzerland, seemed to be able to get through the evenings without a dependency on drugs or constant sex. Only she was unable to cope. Thea understood that in some ways her easy life was now working against her—these other women had resources she didn't have, had far-reaching goals, had responsibilities. Thea had only herself.

By her own choice. She remembered how she had looked at the sleeping twins who had come on the plane before her. Daniel would be happy to give her babies. There had been other men, even more acceptable to her, with whom she could be building a more stable, less frightening life. And, of course, there was always Everett, whom she liked when it was safe to like him.

The pilot announced their impending arrival at Los Angeles, the No Smoking sign came on, and Thea roused herself with relief. It wasn't often that she allowed herself this kind of painful introspection.

She looked out through the window and saw the twinkling lights of Los Angeles spread out under her. It was an unusually clear night, and the city looked alive and glittering. Perhaps somewhere out there was an answer.

Thea waited in her seat until most of the other passengers had filed out of the plane. She was in no hurry. Henry wouldn't mind waiting a few minutes longer. He was used to waiting. With any luck her mother would mind waiting so much she might even give up the hour or so she would be planning to spend with her daughter for bed. If Thea was lucky, that is.

Feeling much older and more than a little tense, her nerves calling for a stiff drink, she made her way off the plane. She peered wearily through the mob of deplaning passengers and greeters for the familiar peaked cap over the cluster of close-cut gray curls.

Instead, she found herself staring into the excitement-flushed face of Everett Hamlinton.

CHAPTER 8

Mark's smile looked slightly unreal, as if a gifted sculptor had fashioned it but had momentarily forgotten there was no smile in the eyes. "So it's been . . . how long?"

Olivia parted her lips to form some sort of answer to his meaningless question. She knew the exact date of their last meeting, of course, but when it came to Mark, time itself moved at a surrealistic pace. When they were together, whole months had seemed little more than minutes, and when they were apart . . . she couldn't finish the thought. How could they have ever been apart?

"Forgive me, Olivia." He brushed aside her feeble attempt at an answer with a wave of his astonishingly graceful hand.

She stared at the hand mutely, the lean, strong, sensitive fingers with the fine network of bluish veins, the eloquence of the artist evident in every gesture, no matter how casual. "Forgive you?" It had been her first words to him.

He sighed. "Of course I know how long it's been since I last saw you. Down to the minute." His smile made his face tragic. "More than three years. Three years! Olivia, damn it, when you walked out of my studio that day, I . . ." He waved his fingers in mute dismissal, gazing at her with those dark brown eyes that absorbed all light and yet were strangely unfathomable. "Hell with it. It's good to see you."

Olivia thought of all the casual, noncommittal welcomes she had worked and reworked to perfection during the long hours since she had left her office. And now none of them fit, because in her wonder at actually finding him at her house, she had not even had the simple presence of mind to usher him inside. He was still framed in the doorway, the soft light from within and from the gate lamps outside the door illuminating him oddly, intensifying the spectral image of Mark to which she'd clung so long. Until he'd spoken, Olivia hadn't accepted him as a reality. She laughed finally, but it was a hollow and disembodied laughter that she hoped would cloak the rush of overwhelming emotion she wanted desperately to conceal.

"Why are you just . . . *standing* there, Mark? Come in! Aren't you freezing?" She turned her smooth cheek for a kiss as she might to any guest and knew, by her own gesture, the depths of her own terror of this long-anticipated meeting.

He stepped into the dim foyer, but instead of grazing her offered cheek, he touched her hand. "Olivia?"

She looked up at him, and before she had time to comprehend his intention, his lips touched hers very, very gently. "That's better." He smiled, a real smile.

Like a dedicated historian cataloging every scrap of trivia, Olivia's mind recorded the trace of a smile on his lips just before he had kissed her. She remembered a thousand such smiles followed by as many kisses. Some had been gentle greeting kisses like this one and others had burned with passion. "Let's sit down, have a drink. Talk."

"Why not?" A quick grin.

The familiar grin made Olivia realize that nothing had changed between them. The intimate knowledge they had always had of each other was solid and unignorable, and it made her hours of frantic preparation a mindless exercise in imbecilic nervousness.

She had forgotten the sense of continuing intimacy they shared, and had to see him again to remember that he was the one man who required no artifice of her, who had always accepted her in any guise. He had loved her at her best, but just as deeply, with just as much fire, when she awakened from sleep, her hair mussed, her face naked. How could she have forgotten? But still she had had to go through those frantic hours, for thinking of the practical details of what to wear had calmed her. Only through familiar ritual could she survive until that moment when she would see him again.

Dressing for a date with Mark inevitably posed a problem. She hadn't the faintest idea of what to expect. Feeling helpless, she tried to decide if Mark would appear in his usual studied inelegance or in something more appropriate to a San Francisco evening. It had always been difficult to second-guess him in such matters. But this was a hundred times worse than ever. So much time had passed.

The very young Mark Lyman she had first known took pleasure in flouting convention. The Mark she had seen briefly three years ago had emitted a subtle serenity, and with it a confidence that implied a deeper degree of maturation. After selecting and then rejecting a dozen or more outfits, she had finally settled for a versatile Oscar de la Renta braided suit in soft dove gray. It went perfectly with her tiny shell earrings and her favorite gold watch.

Mark hadn't specifically mentioned going out to dinner when he'd called. She'd been far too drenched by shock, happiness, and excitement to question him. The hour he'd suggested implied dinner, but with Mark that could mean anything from a snack at some greasy hole frequented by artists to an elegant dinner at some special spot he'd found. It could also mean staying at home and raiding the refrigerator.

Afraid to take a chance, she had asked her cook to prepare a simple but sumptuous dinner for them, topped off with her specialty, a rich mousse au chocolat encased in thin shells of fluted chocolate. Then she worked out a signal with Maureen, her favorite maid. In the event Mark had not intended dinner out, the meal could be served as if the invitation had been implicit during her stilted end of their conversation.

For dinner at home the suit simply wouldn't do, but it suggested another de la Renta costume she adored, a beaded and embroidered gold rayon-and-velvet evening jacket with matching zouave pants that went perfectly with a pale gold shirt of soft panné velvet. It could be worn at home or out. She exchanged the shell earrings and the watch for a matching bracelet-and-necklace set worked in Black Hills gold, set with small squares of emeralds and imperial jade.

Once that torment of indecision had been resolved, Olivia immediately began debating about what scent to wear for him. After rummaging through her personal storehouse of MagnifiScent products in her brilliantly lit, mirrored dressing room, Olivia had finally selected Premier Enfant—First Child—their first and still her favorite commercially packaged oil perfume. Two other exquisite blends had since been formulated by Marlissa with Olivia in mind and even named for her—Oli and Eau DeSante. Olivia was delighted to stand next to Revson with his Charlie and Coco with her Chanel Number 5, but Premier Enfant remained her personal choice, especially for new beginnings.

Olivia had felt the rapid beating of her heart as she dabbed herself with the intoxicating fragrance. It made her think of their last ad layout in *Vogue*. An artfully blurred couple were surrounded by feathery ferns and bathed in yellow moonlight; the woman was as fair as Olivia, her coiled blond hair woven with seed pearls, her chantilly gown flared as she spun toward her darkly handsome lover. Above, in thinly embossed gold script, were three simple words. *That special night*. And below, the now-familiar logo: MagnifiScent. A tiny jeweled flask of Premier Enfant lay on its side in the upper left-hand corner, spilling out the dreamlike vision like wine from a decanter. The ad breathed promises of that one memorable moment in time: the perfect night, the perfect dress, the perfect man.

Olivia had wanted to subdue her own surge of expectation as she anointed herself before Mark's arrival. For the moment logic came to her aid and whispered in her ear. Mark had called because he was in town. After all, she surely qualified as an old friend. Certainly he would want to see her. If only to reject her, as she had twice rejected him.

"You were saying something about a drink?"

Aware that she had been staring at him, she laughed softly. "Forgive me. I think I'm being bombarded by fallout from the past. Mark, you look . . . wonderful."

"No. I'm the same. It's you who look wonderful, Olivia. Is it possible that you're even more beautiful than I remembered?" He glanced around as he followed her into the living room beyond the plush foyer. "Certainly the setting is. It suits you better than my studio. You were right about that," he added with irony, although he kept the smile on his lips.

She took his hand and urged him to sit on the sofa next to her but said nothing as his eyes studied the rare eighteenth-century Piranesi etchings, the Picasso prints, and the Velásquez portrait on the opposite wall. It was so like Mark to pay almost no attention to the artistry of the room as a whole while devouring its iconoclastic collection of paintings, sketches, prints, and etchings that included works ranging from the twelfth century to the present time. There was even Mark's formal and scrupulously lifelike portrait of her next to the Jean Arp sculpture on its polished stainless-steel pedestal.

Olivia was as proud of her home in Pacific Heights as she was of her office at MagnifiScent, so proud that she frequently overcame her mania for privacy and allowed the house to be photographed for magazines. Hers was not the largest house in the exclusive area, but it stood alone in uncluttered elegance. Its rather formal brick exterior was neat and majestic, and the view of the Palace of Fine Arts and the bay beyond was breathtaking. Black wrought-iron gates and brick posts kept the house from the street, helped by a string of trees crusted with gnarled ivy and a thick bank of passionflowers. It was far too large for herself and her three live-in servants, but she needed ample room for all the treasures she had brought back from Switzerland and the furnishings and works of art she had bought since.

The interior had been her own creation and, in a way, was a tribute to Mark, or rather to all she had learned from him. He had taught her long ago to love art, to ignore the formulas of interior decoration. Here her carefully cultivated signature style was offset by brilliant splashes of color. Her living room was an eloquent tribute to simple elegance. Frosted pearl walls were mere backdrops for an extravaganza of pictures, magnificently framed.

In contrast, the furnishings Olivia had chosen reflected the simplicity and flawless taste for which she was known. The fabrics and woods of the various pieces either picked up the faintly luminous quality of the pearly walls or played against them in compatible shades of white. But the striking colors of the pictures were carried further into the room by Olivia's vast collection of Tiffany and Venetian glass, and again by the generous clusters of vivid flowers, changed each day by Maureen.

The total effect of the room in which she sat with Mark was that of a gallery of carefully amassed, stained-glass splendor cradled in a lovely white-satin frame. On first entering her house, all Olivia's guests tended to be overwhelmed by the beauty she had achieved and were then pleasantly surprised to find the place as comfortable as it was beautiful.

Mark finished surveying the room and nodded in silent approval as he accepted the glass of Manzanilla sherry she offered. "You always had remarkable taste, Olivia. I really like the Piranesis. Always have."

"I picked them up in Geneva a few years ago."

He tasted the sherry and smiled. "You remembered."

She smiled back at him. "How could I forget?" When Mark's mood was good, he drank Manzanilla sherry. When his work wasn't going well, he drank gin. Bottles of it. She shrugged off the thought.

"So tell me, Mark, and quickly—I can't stand it—what's

blasted you out of New York? That cryptic phone call about being in San Francisco . . . are you going to be here for a while?" She couldn't remember ever seeing him in a suit before, and while the formality of the one he wore was softened by a chocolate brown turtleneck shirt, it was still a new image to her. She settled back against the white satin pillows, hopelessly drunk although she had barely tasted her wine.

Mark tried but failed to hide his excitement from her. "DeBeers from the Dakota Gallery wants to talk to me tomorrow. He thinks . . . well, he might be interested in a one-man show."

"Mark! That's wonderful!" She placed the gallery quickly. While it couldn't be considered a top gallery, it was nevertheless established and recognized.

He shrugged, looked at her appraisingly as if realizing that he wouldn't be likely to earn enough from the entire exhibit at the Dakota to equal the price of the clothes she was wearing. "It could be a real step up for me, but suddenly it feels like small potatoes. You've done all right for yourself, Olivia. Better than all right." His laugh was tinged with strain.

Olivia felt her old defenses rising like a corpse from a grave. "Yes, I suppose I have, Mark." It was the same argument between them, tattered bits of a conflict unchanged by time or circumstance. "Can't you be . . . just a little proud of me?" She was surprised by the depth of the need she felt for his approval.

He was instantly contrite. "Hey, of course I am, Olivia. You've made it, just like you said you would. But don't expect me to pretend surprise. I knew you would. When you told me about your little cosmetics operation the last time we saw each other, I knew you were onto something big." He shook his head in reluctant admiration. "I had no idea how big. I figured marrying DeSante would have been making it enough, but this. . . ."

She took a sip of sherry, hoping it would dissolve the lump in her throat. He could always evoke her anger quickly, as quickly as joy, excitement, desire. "I did this myself, Mark. This is mine. Thea helped, and the family who started the business, the Deloffres. But I built it into what it is now without any help from Jean-Pierre—without a cent of his money."

He touched the short cap of her nearly white hair, his eyes holding hers. He spoke without apology but with warmth and sincerity. "Calm down, Olivia. I guessed that. I also knew you wouldn't have married DeSante unless you loved him. That's what hurt the most. If I could have believed it was just for the money. . . ." He finished his sherry and refilled their glasses.

"Listen," he continued in a lighter vein, "do you have any idea how hard it is to pick up a magazine without running into you or your MagnifiScent? Catchy name, by the way. Yours?" He smiled at her brief nod. "Thought so. Even so, the magnitude of your success only hit me last week. It was a shock, let me tell you. Staggering." He raised an eyebrow significantly. "I was doing this crossword puzzle, see, and there you were, 16 across: a six-letter word for the first name of the first lady of beauty. Knocked me out!"

She laughed, not entirely sure that he was teasing her. He had always had a mania for crossword puzzles. "I guess I've arrived." She caught Maureen's eye from the next room and indicated that the maid should bring them some hors d'oeuvres. "Tell me about your work, Mark. The sculpture you were doing when I saw you last." His work was safer ground than hers.

As always, Mark couldn't resist a chance to talk about any portion of his work that especially pleased him. His features became animated. "I've just completed a series of mythical animals, Olivia. For a while now I've been absolutely captivated by the challenge of combining fantasy with motion. Unicorns, winged horses . . . all of them. The thing is, they live only in the mind, so capturing them in a solid form is tricky. They have to move. They have to move so well that you get the sense of elusiveness, as if you couldn't just reach out and grab them, like they could slip away from you if you tried." Rather sheepishly, because he had always disdained the ostentatious use of precious metals and gems in contempory art, he admitted that he had finally managed to get the fluid quality he wanted by plating the pieces in fourteen-karat yellow gold. "The eye slips over the curves, giving the figures life, whimsy, activity."

Olivia watched him closely as he spoke. There were changes, certainly, but her mind got in the way of her vision, memories clouding what her eyes perceived.

On a purely physical plane the years had treated him well. His body had ripened. The skinny, boyish look had given way to muscular manhood. He drank his wine with moderation, sipping it appreciatively rather than gulping it for the sake of its effect.

Olivia remembered the nights she had worried about his drinking. That was during periods when his work was going poorly, when gin was his escape from frustration. She also remembered that sherry had once seemed to work on him like an aphrodisiac, and he would pull her away from a party or bar in a frenzy to be alone with her in the studio where they lived.

And then—only then—the huge room with its peeling ceiling, paint-spattered furniture, ghost-white canvases stacked against the cracked walls, and the stench of too many cheap meals, turpentine, and oils would cease to matter to her. When Mark held her, when his lean body rose naked and strong over hers, then, for a little while, she was precisely where she wanted to be.

It came back to her with a shocking wave of undiluted sweetness, the memory of his body against hers. Only the discreet entrance of Maureen with a tray of hors d'oeuvres kept her from reaching out for him.

"Thank you," she said weakly, turning blindly toward the girl. She trembled, feeling trapped in this structured charade of casual reunion. She no longer wanted to hear about his work. There was time enough later to talk, to dine. Now she wanted—needed—a more powerful feast. Him. His body. His lips. His stroking, soothing hands on her naked, burning flesh.

"Mark! I'm so glad you're here." It was the best she could do. Time and distance did matter. She was no longer free to reach out for him as she had in the past. He could be lost to her forever. There could be another woman, one perhaps who was content to live a simple life if he was by her side.

She picked up a cheese puff as the maid walked out of the room. Her heart was thudding in her chest, and Olivia knew she would be sick if she tried to eat the canapé. "And you . . . Mark—my God," she managed a little laugh, "are you married?"

His eyes smiled. "Of course not. Don't you think I'd tell you if I were married? Are you?"

Her laugh was more natural, brought relief to her tensed throat muscles. "Don't you think I'd tell you if I were?"

"Oh, hell, Olivia, put that damned thing down." When she didn't move, he took the hors d'oeuvre from her and put it carefully back on the tray. "Come here, you," he coaxed, reaching out for her.

She sank into his arms gratefully. Then she lifted her face for the kiss her lips demanded. First there was only the warmth of his mouth, then, after a moment, the searching sweetness of his tongue. He broke the kiss in the end. She hadn't the strength or the will to end it herself.

"Dinner's probably ready," she said dreamily, looking up into his dark eyes.

"Can it keep?" he asked huskily, his arms still around her, the heat from his body penetrating the layers of clothing that kept them apart.

She nodded. "You're not hungry?"

He laughed and kissed her again. "Very. Olivia . . ." It was a question and an urgent appeal. "Where?"

She got up, her hands ice in his, her entire body conscious of his nearness. "The best," she whispered, remembering the way they used to quote poetry to each other, "is yet to come."

CHAPTER 9

Never had the house seemed so huge. Olivia felt as if she were moving through a dream as she led Mark through room after room, then up the wide staircase to the second floor. This time he ignored the paintings and the oriental tapestries hanging on the walls.

The deciding factor in buying this particular house had been the view from the largest bedroom, but it was the furthest thing from Olivia's mind as she opened the door and stepped back to let Mark enter. He stopped in the middle of the room and stared through the gigantic, almost wall-to-wall window at the breathtaking sight of the distant Palace of Fine Arts and the bay, still further away, festooned with lighted ships.

Olivia waited, allowing Mark a long moment to gaze through her bedroom window, to share at last the splendid vista she had shared with precious few men before, and none so precious as he. She could afford to wait now; her fears and doubts were rapidly fading. He was hers again, and this time, she vowed, she would not make the mistake of letting him go. She didn't waste time or energy regretting the past. Before they had been lovers meeting at the wrong time. She had not been ready for a commitment until now. She had had her own dragons to slay. But now, at last, she was ready. More than ready. She ached for him, yearned in every corner of her soul for a completion of self only this man could bring to her.

She walked up to him and touched his arm gently.

His ruggedly handsome head was in profile, outlined against the backdrop of night and twinkling lights. She saw that it was a noble head, as cleanly drawn as a Michelangelo sculpture. Her hand reached out to trace its outline.

He turned back to her, his eyes bright as if they had absorbed the distant lights. "You have the world," he said so softly she had to strain to hear him. "What can I give you?"

She saw that he hadn't really meant it as a question. His words were instead a statement of bitter fact, expecting no denial, tolerating no soothing lie. Olivia would have liked to give the reply that came impulsively to her lips, to assure him that without him, she had nothing. Much as her heart believed those unspoken words, she knew them to be childish untruths. Even without him, she had a lot. Far more than most. Without him, she would still have this view, still live in this fabulous house, still own MagnifiScent. Without him, she would continue to have her successes to enjoy, her failures to swallow. A part of her mourned the simple beauty of a love only children knew, an all-encompassing love that led Juliets to their deaths and Romeos to follow to their own.

She answered the only way she could, by bringing her lips to his, by pressing her aching body against him. "Show me, Mark darling. Show me what you can give me," she pleaded, certain he would understand that she meant more than sex, more than the immediate need she felt for him.

His kiss was impassioned and contained an element of torment, as if he felt that he was bringing her the same gift that had been rejected before. Yet his arms held her tightly, savoring her, slipping down over her slender back so that his marvelous hands could imprison the backs of her thighs through the velvet cloth, could then slide up over the firm roundness of her buttocks, press into the small of her back, reach out and surround her, caressing her shoulders so that there was no room between them.

"Mark!" She swayed slightly as he released his urgent grasp on her. Then his lips met hers for another kiss, and this one carried a different message, a question that she remembered from so long ago. Smiling, she answered this one with ease, with assurance, with a heart filled with happiness. "Oh, yes, Mark, darling. I do want you. I want you so much. I've waited so long."

The glow from a full moon helped by the distant pinpoints of light threw more than enough light into the room. Olivia had furnished it with a shrewd understanding that the window with its stupendous view was decoration enough. The large canopied bed, the roomy Régence bombe commodes with their marble tops, even the lovely Louis XV Marquetry Bureau à Pente mounted in bronze doré were placed so as not to distract from the view. Both the thick, furlike, hand-tufted Viennese rug and the satin de Bruges bedspread were a stark white, as were the Burano lace draperies that had never been drawn. Olivia's bedroom was an ice palace, the throne of a Snow Queen who chose to look out upon a less sterile world.

She walked to the corner fireplace and found the matches, then knelt to ignite the fire. When she stood, her face was flushed from the quickly spreading fire, and she was bathed in its orange light.

Mark was a beautiful statue, frozen in place while his eyes followed her every gesture. He made no move to throw off his own clothing, betrayed no boyish eagerness to get on to the next stage without first fully savoring this one.

Olivia had undressed for other men, of course: Jean-Pierre, and a very few other men who had been welcomed, however fleetingly, into this bedroom. Yet undressing for Mark was a completely different experience, an act complete in itself. His rapt expression paid homage to her loveliness without evoking the slightest trace of coy vulgarity. His appreciation seemed to be as much for the gracefulness of her movements as the unveiling of her body. She basked in his gaze, able to tolerate the flaming desire she felt because he was there, waiting for her. There was also a fierce pride in being able to present something beautiful to this man who was, above all, an artist, although she sensed that she would always be beautiful to him, even after time had ravaged her body, had cut lines into her face.

"Your face is a wonderfully mobile thing, Olivia," Mark said, breaking out of his trance. "I see so much in that face. Tell me what you're feeling right now," he said softly.

She rested against him briefly, dwarfed by his compassion more than his larger frame. "I feel . . . heavy with years, Mark." She glanced at him quickly, afraid he would misunderstand. "I don't mean what happened to us. Well, yes, that, too."

He held her away so that he could study her light eyes. "Ghosts and goblins, and it's not even Halloween." His laugh was gentle. "We don't walk alone anymore. Not the way you do when you're twenty and in love and in lust, huh? Don't mind that you remember other nights, even other men. Remember when I told you a long time ago that it's a buy-and-sell world? When you bought innocence and youth, you paid with immaturity and discontent. Now you've bought that back and more, and the price is lightness of spirit, newness perhaps. Is it such a big price for you?"

"Isn't it?" She took off her blouse and tossed it uncaringly on the chair next to the window, on top of the evening jacket. She faced him in her sleek pants and satin-and-lace beige bra, aware on so many levels, unable to speak of any of them.

"Not for me." His hands cupped her breasts. His face was radiant from the flickering fire that played on her back. He closed his eyes as he fondled her, like a blind man who remembered by touch. "I consider myself a tough merchant. I always get my money's worth. At a glance I'd imagine you to be an even better one. You paid your dues, Olivia. Enjoy the ride. Everthing that happened made you who you are. If it wasn't worth it, you wouldn't have done it."

She wasn't entirely sure she understood what he was telling her, but as quickly as the sadness had come, it went away. Mark was with her again. The ghosts were gone, and goblins turned into pumpkins with the dawn. His hands had opened the bra, pulling it free, and closed over her again.

In the orange glow of the fire, they peeled away the clothing that separated them. The bed accepted their bodies without a sound of protest. His mouth was hot on hers, finished with questions now, intent only on raising her desire to new heights. He led and she followed, passive only because she was numbed by the vastness of her need. His warm flesh was a thousand grasping hands, covering her, exciting and tormenting her until at last, at the end, it was Olivia who led, Olivia who demanded, Olivia who roused him so greatly that

Mark trembled in her arms, his final moan a sob of gratitude and adoration.

She would have liked to have fallen asleep in his arms, but just as she remembered, he was starving afterward. While Mark dressed, Olivia slipped into a dressing gown, ran a comb through her hair, and went to the kitchen to send June, her cook, and Maureen to bed. Over their protests, she fixed a tray for Mark and herself.

Fully dressed, he was almost a stranger again. "I was going to bring this upstairs," she explained, meeting him at the bottom of the curving marble staircase.

"Can't wait." He took the tray from her and brought it to the inlaid table by the couch. He barely waited for her to sit down before he began to eat.

Her own appetite fully sated, Olivia nibbled at her food and watched him devour the contents of his plate. "Hungry, I see." She felt marvelous. It had been a long time since she had felt this good, this happy.

"What is this stuff?" He took another bite. "Never mind, it doesn't matter. It's terrific."

She smiled and poured steaming coffee into their cups.

He pushed back his plate and reached for his mousse. "Wow! I like the way you rich guys live."

She laughed. "Really? I thought you hated this decadent life-style. I see you have changed, after all."

He grinned. "Not really. This beats the hell out of my loft in New York, I will admit. I think I could force myself to live like this."

Olivia felt a not unpleasant tightness in her chest. "I'd say that's a good idea, Mark. An excellent idea." She wanted to be casual, to throw the words out as if they didn't mean so terribly much to her, as if her entire future weren't hanging on his answer. "God knows there's plenty of room here. You always were my favorite . . . roommate." She swallowed quickly, staring down into her ornate Persian coffee cup. She felt his eyes on her but couldn't look up yet. It was miraculous to her, the way he affected her after all these years. She would have been frightened if it hadn't been for those moments in her bed. Remembering them, she was able, at last, to look up at him.

"Olivia . . ."

She saw the sadness in his face, heard the refusal in his voice. "You haven't seen the house," she said quickly, unable to accept what she knew he would say. "There's a sort of greenhouse out back that would make a perfect studio. The light is exactly right. And you would have complete privacy. I'm gone so much . . ." The desperate appeal in her voice embarrassed her. Yet she had to go on, had already gone too far to turn back. "San Francisco has everything for an artist. Everything."

His face reflected pain, but his mouth revealed determination and a touch of anger. "I can't live here, Olivia. Don't you know that?"

"Why?" she asked, knowing the answer and hating it.

He got up and paced the floor in front of her for a moment. "Damn it," he spat out, stopping across the room from where she sat stiffly on the couch. "Do you really think I could ever live off you? In your shadow? Do you think I could work under those conditions?"

She struggled with an answer, quietly stunned that she had let her own desires overwhelm her reason, her knowledge of him, her memory of his damned pride. "No. The Mark I used to know probably couldn't. The boy I used to know." She let the words drip like acid from her lips. "So you've gotten even with me at last, Mark. Is that it?" She looked at him with scorn, her anger comforting her more than sorrow. "I rejected you for your poverty. Now you reject me for my success."

He kneeled in front of her. "No, damn it." He was silent a moment. "Yes, I suppose it's something like that. But not for the sake of revenge, Olivia. Don't you know that? Don't you know that I love you? Do you think you alone carry ghosts? Don't you think I wish it were possible to marry you today? What do you know of my loneliness, of the nights I've prowled the streets looking for you, settling instead for someone who would make me forget you, just for a few hours? As bad as it was when you went to Europe . . . how the hell do you think I felt when you married DeSante? I couldn't work, I didn't sleep, I thought my life was over." He grabbed her, pulled her up and into his arms. His mouth was savage on hers, as if recalling a time of bitter hunger. He released her, turned his back to her.

She stared at him, at his familiar body so unfamiliar in its dark brown suit, at his thick, wavy hair. His hair was still mussed from her hands. She reached out, smoothed it with her trembling fingers. "Then why, Mark?" she asked softly. "Why not stay? Why not grab the moment? I have never loved anyone the way I love you. What does it matter—this house, my money? How can it possibly matter now?"

He stiffened under her stroking hand, then turned back to her, catching the fingers, bringing them to his lips. He spoke into them. "It matters, Olivia. To both of us. Don't you understand? I want to come to you as an equal. They call you the swan, Olivia. I read that in some magazine." He smiled sadly. "The swan. This thing at the Dakota—who knows? Maybe it's a start. Maybe it'll get me out of the marshes and into the pond. My work is good. It's everything I've got. If I make it, then we'll try it again, okay?" He kissed her fingers and walked slowly toward the door.

She watched him go through a film of tears, knowing there was nothing she could say to change his mind, to keep him with her now.

He stopped and turned toward her. He was masked by shadows from the darkened foyer. "Olivia?"

She stared at him.

"You asked how it could possibly matter now. Let me ask you something. Would you give up all this and come away with me right now? This minute? Would you give up everything?" He waved his hand in a broad sweep.

She couldn't see his eyes. What was he asking? She thought of this house, and MagnifiScent, the empire she had created from her own ingenuity and labor. And because she could never lie to him, she slowly shook her head.

"You see?" he said very gently. "It matters."

Quietly he walked out of her house.

Out of her life.

CHAPTER 10

Up until the age of twelve, Olivia's life had been predictable but interesting, comfortable, luxurious, and busy. She had attended The Lindly School with her best friend, Thea Wallace, and was an apt and eager student. After classes there were tennis lessons, a racket-ball class, a weekly drama class, and riding lessons at the Equestrian Club in Thousand Oaks. When the weather permitted, she swam with Thea and other friends in the olympic-size pool at home or practiced her tennis on her own clay court with Thea, who even as a child was an unbeatable opponent. Olivia had already reached the age at which she had achieved a certain indifference toward her parents in an effort to struggle out of childhood into the tantalizingly provocative world of adulthood. She had never been especially close to her parents, anyway—true to Beverly Hills form, her parents were engrossed in business and recreation that kept them away much of the time.

Her father, James Franklin Nash, a successful stockbroker, was almost forty-five at the time of her birth, a childless widower until his marriage just over a year earlier to Olivia's mother, Marta Sarreid.

There had been the usual talk at the time of the wedding, but middle-aged men of means who marry beautiful young women without money or family are common fare in Beverly Hills society. And Marta had been lovely, with platinum hair, large blue eyes, and a flawless figure. She was well educated and genuinely appreciated art and music. These facets of her personality saved her from being called a gold digger.

Olivia had often wondered why her parents had married. Even as a young child she had seen them as an unlikely couple in every way. Her father was home rarely. As chairman of the board of Nash, Adams and Blake, which had been founded by his father, he traveled frequently, especially to New York, the home office. When he was at home, he spent long hours in his office on the second floor of the large colonial home, laboring over paperwork or talking to business partners on his private line.

Her mother, on the other hand, was in and out of the house all day long, her most pointed absences occurring in the evening when her husband was technically at home. Olivia often thought it was a miracle that she had been born at all. Even as an adult she found it impossible to imagine her parents in any situation that brought them close enough to produce a child.

Nash had lost his first wife to a rare lung disease two years earlier. After her death, he distracted himself with constant work, and this got him through the first year and a half of his grief, but he continued the habit of hard work after his second marriage. During the second year of his widowhood, he began to long for the comforts of a wife, and he began to renew his earlier desire for children. Julia, his first wife, had been a sickly woman, and after nearly dying from the complications of a therapeutically aborted pregnancy, was warned against trying again. She and James had begun to think of adoption at the time the lung disease was first suspected.

Undoubtedly when he had first seen Marta at a party in New York thrown by a business associate, the girl he saw must have represented life itself after his year of mourning. She had been at her most animated at the party, because earlier that day she had been given a speaking part in an off-Broadway play, the culmination of over a year's hard work of pounding New York's dirty streets looking for something that would give her a chance to make it as an actress. She had left her immigrant Norwegian parents and brothers in Pennsylvania to pursue the career of her dreams, only to find herself one of countless beautiful and talented young women. Through that year she had made many compromises, had worked at many disillusioning jobs, had walked across a number of stages without getting a chance to say a word. Nash had known none of this at the time. All he saw was a lovely young woman with sparkling blue eyes and the smile of a happy child. It was the first time he had noticed a woman since the death of his wife, and the only impulsive act of his entire life was to ask Marta to dinner the next night.

Olivia knew her mother had accepted that date because Marta had confused James with Edgar Nash, a well-known critic and syndicated columnist, who she had heard was at the same party. She might have canceled at the last minute once she discovered her error if she hadn't returned to the apartment she shared with two other aspiring actresses to find out that the play for which she had been cast that morning had lost its financing.

Harriet, the roommate with whom she had gone to the party, after straightening Marta out about her dinner partner for the next evening, counseled her against breaking the date so quickly. James Franklin Nash was a wealthy and lonely man. Marta, though she was only twenty-four, was already competing with girls younger than herself, many of whom had more experience and resources. Losing what would have been her first speaking role in a play hit her hard. Her money was almost gone, which meant another three or more months of working in some sleazy nightclub to accumulate enough cash to make the theatrical rounds again. Marta knew she wasn't the first girl to contemplate a frightening future and consider instead the life she might have as the wife of a wealthy older man. She kept that date.

They saw each other twice more before it was time for Nash to return to California. Once he was home again in the house he had shared with Julia, he felt the loneliness settle over him, and his mind returned to Marta frequently during the next week. His second impulsive act was to call her in New York and suggest she come to California for a visit. He vaguely thought he might rent her an apartment where he might pass some of the hours that hung so heavily when he wasn't at the office.

Marta was at first tempted by the offer. She doubted that there was much more work in Hollywood than in New York, but a change would be welcome, and Los Angeles sounded like a magical world where she might forget there were things like snow and sleet. But she was wise enough not to want to trade in her insecure life as a would-be actress for the life of a kept woman, who might as easily be replaced by another woman as a role could be taken from her by a bad review or lost financing. She encouraged Nash's interest but rejected his invitation, quickly agreeing to go to dinner and a show with him when he returned to New York in less than a month.

Almost as if to prove to herself that she would be foolish to ignore the opportunity of marrying the wealthy stockbroker, she took a particularly demeaning job as a hatcheck girl in a Broadway nightclub and watched parts she might have suited go to other actresses. With far more determination she charmed James Nash into loving her. It was an embarrassingly simple chore. Nash had been married for almost fifteen years and he was not sophisticated about women. Marta knew this was a precarious time in his bachelorhood, and a smart young woman would make the most of James Nash's infatuation without a moment's hesitation.

Yet she had hesitated once Nash had proposed during their third weekend together. After almost two months of manipulation and plotting among her older and wiser roommates and herself, Marta very nearly rejected the proposal she had schemed to evoke.

She had always been a girl with a dream: She wanted to be an actress. It hadn't proved to be as easy as she'd imagined back in Tamaqua, Pennsylvania, as a girl on their dairy farm outside of town. She'd had other girlish dreams, too, of the handsome young man, likely a decorated war hero, who would fall madly in love with her and reveal himself as an aspiring actor as well, with whom she would rise to glory like Fairbanks and Pickford, Lunt and Fontanne, or any of the other romantic couples. But the war was over by the time Nash proposed, and the heroes were working nine-to-five jobs, and the handsome young man had already paraded through her life, more than one of them, leaving nothing in his wake but soiled sheets and an ultimate frustration.

If she married Nash it would be her way of conceding that it had all been childish dreams, that the life she had envisioned for herself was over. Still, marriage to a rich man would give her a certain leverage. She could possibly develop contacts in Los Angeles that might further her theatrical career. Beverly Hills was a nest of producers and directors, and more than one actress hit Broadway after making it in the movies, instead of the other way around. She would be able to pamper herself, dress well, take on polish. If she continued as she was, whatever freshness she had would be lost in the struggle for existence. She would age and harden, her light dimmed by disappointment and eventual bitterness.

She looked hard at the man who waited for her answer. He was beginning to gray and had already thickened at the waist. He did not excite her sexually. She found him about as stimulating as her own father, in spite of his business acumen. But he was generous and undemanding, and Marta knew life would not easily yield another man so eager to be her husband who could make her nearly as comfortable as this one. Hoping James mistook the tears in her eyes for happiness, Marta agreed to become the second Mrs. James Franklin Nash.

A year after Marta's marriage to James, she gave birth to her beautiful little daughter. But the role of doting mother lasted less than a year before boredom set in. James had hired an able nursemaid for little Olivia, and Marta was free to look for other diversions. After attempting to interest more serious playhouses in her talent, she finally settled for working in a West Hollywood theater. At first she played smaller roles in the season's offerings; but the director, unimpressed with her looks and talent, suggested she could be more useful as an Angel. Marta chafed at the suggestion. The Angels were the ladies who sold tickets, helped behind the scenes and, presumably, added a little class to the company through their well-heeled contacts. Marta left the playhouse and spent the next few years trying to get roles at still smaller theaters, arriving by process of elimination at the Hollywood Argyle Workshop, a tiny theater just off Hollywood Boulevard where the fare was standard and the audiences light. The headliners were predominantly stars who had faded long ago but had names that were remembered by a public who knew nothing of the alcoholic excesses that had negated whatever talent had brought them to an earlier stardom.

For Marta it was an ideal showcase, because she quickly found out that the purchase of solid rows of the cheap seats would ensure better roles at the Hollywood Argyle Workshop. And understudying the female lead whenever possible meant something here—the star was almost sure to miss a performance or two a month.

At first James dutifully attended her performances, sitting alone in acute discomfort in the nearly empty little theater. Although he eventually begged off coming to the theater at all, he paid Marta's mounting bills without a word, and his abdication marked the end of any pretense that the mismatched couple shared more than their marital bed.

From the time she was eight or nine, Olivia knew Nick Thatcher as one of her mother's friends. She dimly remembered Nick's wife, a nervous, red-haired girl who worked in a Hollywood bank, undoubtedly supporting Nick as he tried to break into show business. Later she found out that the redhead had eventually discovered his affair with her mother and divorced him.

Like most children, however, Olivia grew up in her own world, and her parents formed only the shell of her existence. Her father was unfailingly kind toward her, and her mother was more like an older sister, warm and generous at times, sullen and unapproachable at others.

Thea lived only two blocks away from Olivia, and they had been fast friends since their first meeting in the third grade at The Lindly School. Even in the third grade Thea was a smaller version of herself as an adult: pretty, polished, calculatingly flamboyant, masking a certain inbred snobbery behind a rebellious nonconformity. Olivia knew that Thea's mother didn't approve of her own mother and therefore was not happy about her close friendship with Thea, although Thea took pains to conceal this fact from Olivia's discerning eyes. More than anything it was Thea's fierce loyalty that touched Olivia, her firm insistence that Olivia be treated well on her frequent trips to the Wallace mansion on Beverly Drive.

Olivia understood Mrs. Wallace's discomfort, knowing even then the nuances of Beverly Hills society; that which was "done" and that which was "not done." Her father and his first wife had been perfectly acceptable, even to the eastern-born Vera Taywell Wallace. She had no doubt approved of the sedate life-style of her father and his first wife. And his background and money were also old and well enough documented—one of Olivia's paternal ancestors had arrived in the New World in the wave of ships following the *Mayflower*—to make James Nash well respected.

Even the faux pas of later marrying a would-be showgirl would have been overlooked if Olivia's mother had had the good taste to abandon such interests and wait quietly to be accepted into the Beverly Hills society over which Vera Wallace reigned. Or if she had become an accomplished actress of the legitimate theater, her profession would not have been held against her or her daughter. But Olivia knew that Thea's mother and others of her ilk regarded Marta as little better than a social climber who lacked the good taste to appreciate what she had acquired through her marriage to James Nash. Instead, Marta had chosen to flaunt her interests without the slightest discretion.

Marta would have been delighted to find herself a subject of scorn by this group. Beverly Hills society bored her. She had no interest in managing a household staff and hired a personal secretary to do it for her. At first she spent months buying anything that appealed to her. When that pastime paled, Marta began to give parties. Since the only friends she had made were actors from the playhouses in Hollywood, she had stopped at nothing to make these events theatrically exciting and this had the effect of permanently excluding her from Vera Wallace's set. Her friends of the moment, however, were thrilled with the avalanche of catered food, excellent booze, and special effects she ordered for the night's entertainment. Yet the handful of would-be stars who attended were painfully few in the backyard tents she had erected for her parties, and even the bottomless stomachs of starving playwrights and actors couldn't hope to put a dent in the mountain of food and drink. Although James said little about the waste of his money, he once again excused himself from so much as a token appearance.

The party phase passed quickly, and Olivia saw few of her mother's friends and almost as little of her mother. Olivia did not find her situation unusual. Many of her friends saw their parents infrequently and were more strongly attached to the servants and governesses who had a more direct hand in raising them. The books Olivia read and the television shows she watched told her about a different kind of family, with close ties between parents and child. But these were like modern-day fairy tales, and if there were moments when she illogically longed for a happy, noisy family around her, she and Thea would assuage them as they shopped on Rodeo Drive or swam in her pool or worked themselves to a frenzy on the tennis court.

In one of her moments of generosity and goodwill, Marta threw a fabulous party for Olivia's twelfth birthday. Almost all the pupils in the upper classes at The Lindly School came, and there was a cloaked magician, a rock 'n' roll band, and a folk singer to entertain them. Olivia could easily have passed for sixteen at the time, and her glorious, nearly white hair hung long and loose down her back. It had been a wonderful party, and her mother was very much in attendance for once, looking especially pretty in a long white dress, her own blond hair caught up in a mass of curls. Olivia had felt close to her mother that afternoon and evening. In her happiness she was blind to Marta's unusual nervousness, harboring not the slightest suspicion about her mother's obvious desire to please her. Her birthday presents, always elaborate, were exceptional. Boxes and boxes of clothing and games from the best shops bore her mother's signature, and her father arrived home in time to watch her cut the three-tiered birthday cake and give her his own present, a delicate gold necklace with a tiny, perfect diamond in a seed-pearl heart.

Seven days later, dazed, her eyes burning with unshed tears, Olivia was moved into a two-bedroom apartment with her mother and Nick Thatcher.

It had been an otherwise uneventful day. She had gone to school, had lunched with Thea on the pretty terrace behind the auditorium, and had worked out the plans for Thea's birthday the following week. That afternoon Thea had to stay after school, and Olivia returned home alone, but for once not to an empty house. Both her parents were there, though the servants were curiously out of sight.

They had been fighting. Olivia knew that at once by the tense lines on her mother's face and the deep creases in her father's high forehead. Neal, the butler, had come to the doorway of the room where her parents stood on either side of her, coughing softly to catch their attention.

"I've put the last suitcase in the car, Mrs. Nash," he had said, glancing at Olivia and then quickly away.

"Thank you, Neal. That will be all." her mother replied in a flat voice, dismissing him.

Without a word and without glancing at Olivia, her father turned and followed the butler out of the room. She could see him slowly climbing the stairs on his way to his office, but this time moving slowly, without his usual purposeful step, as if he was simply retreating rather than going to work.

"Olivia, dear, I have something to tell you," her mother had begun as soon as the office door had closed behind her husband. "You'd better sit down."

It was a discussion Olivia never remembered with any clarity. The words her mother was saying made no sense. The two of them were leaving right away. They were going to live in Hollywood, in an apartment. Her parents were getting a divorce, and her mother was going to marry Nick Thatcher. The sentences were short and to the point, but all Olivia understood was that a woman whom she barely knew was leaving a man she barely knew to be with a man Olivia didn't know at all, and because of this preposterous nonsense her entire life was going to change.

The questions came later, when she could think again, just as it took time for Olivia to understand just how drastic a change the trip of a scant few miles would make in her life. She found out that her questions were pointless by the time she was left alone in the square cubicle that was to be her new room. She had suddenly ceased being a person. She was merely an appendage of her mother, required to move when Marta moved. Marta and Nick were in love and had been for a long time. The charade of living with her father was over. Nick's divorce had become final, and they would be married as soon as her own came through. They would pursue acting careers in earnest together. Things would be less comfortable for a while, until they were established. She would not be expecting any alimony or child support, either. The break had been clean and final, with no strings attached on either side. This fact seemed very important to Marta, as if it established that Nick loved her for herself rather than the money a more devious separation might have supplied.

Looking back in time, Olivia came to think of her mother

and Nick's position as suicidally childish. It reeked of bad theater, with the lovers spurning luxury for the gratification of each other's arms. Neither had proved a creditable ability for self-support in the past, and it was unlikely that either would in the future. Perhaps they had actually believed that by the time Marta's jewels had been sold, her furs hocked, whatever money she had salted away spent, their careers would be assured and money wouldn't be a problem.

Even at twelve Olivia had known what the next years would bring. If Marta had doubted her ability to compete with the masses of aspiring young actresses at twenty-four, it was ludicrous to believe she could do it now, at thirty-seven. And Nick at thirty-one hadn't earned enough in his entire acting career to support the family for more than a few months.

CHAPTER 11

Two days after the move a stunned Thea telephoned Olivia. Thea had found the number by asking James Nash's butler for it. Olivia, without asking, knew Thea was calling her against her mother's wishes, and at first the conversation was stilted. Neither of them knew what to say. Olivia was in the position of a powerless child, being moved around like a pawn on a board. But Thea knew that something precious would be gone from her life if their friendship were not kept up. She reminded Olivia of her birthday party five days hence, and Olivia, choking at the thought of facing her former friends, braced herself and agreed to go. It would be the last time she would see those friends. Only Thea had the grace and steadfastness to remain a part of her life.

After Olivia talked to Thea, she wondered again about her father. Why hadn't he called? He certainly couldn't want her to leave, to live in a cramped apartment with a screeching mother and three constantly running children over her head, on a street without a single tree and a noisy drive-in restaurant on the corner. Why hadn't her father stopped them? Why had he stood there so defeated, letting her go without so much as a word? A sense of innate pride kept her from calling him, and for months Olivia waited for the phone to ring, waited for her father to rescue her, to take her home where she belonged.

The following Monday she started school at LeCompte Junior High in Hollywood, taking her place in a classroom overflowing with children who seemed both younger and yet wiser than those in her considerably smaller class at The Lindly School. It was a frightening experience for her. She had never been to a public school in her life, or any but the one she had started in with all of her neighborhood friends. The classes were absurdly easy in comparison, but she got no pleasure out of the excellence of her work.

Coming home was even worse. Now her mother was there almost constantly, and Nick was there, too. Sometimes the apartment would be filled with their friends, drinking beer and talking glorious fantasy futures, all seeing themselves as stars living in the style Marta claimed to be glad to have abandoned. In fairness Olivia knew that her mother was trying to make it up to her to some degree by encouraging her to bring home friends and even by being there when Olivia returned.

But Olivia didn't want to see her mother. She especially didn't want to see Nick. The streets were the only way to avoid these people who had wrested her from the only life she had known, without so much as telling her first, giving her time to prepare herself. Her feelings toward her mother were curiously mixed—she was beginning to think of Marta as a child with a cheap, shiny new toy. But for Nick she felt nothing but cold hatred. He had fed her mother the broth of his dreams, depriving her of the protection of her husband, who alone could keep from her the harsh realities of the career she had never had.

Nick was a perfect target. He didn't care. He saw women as a blend of assets and liabilities, and Olivia was a liability he accepted as one for the prices for having Marta. If Olivia had raged her hatred at him directly, he would have shrugged it off as one might stoically ignore the annoyance of a fly. Instead she chose to treat Nick as if he weren't there, and this made things less complicated still for him. Olivia was free to hate him, but nothing touched him at all.

Surprisingly, Marta got a very small part on a television

soap opera through a connection at the Hollywood Argyle Workshop. It kept her busy for almost five months. During that period Olivia, alone at last every afternoon except for the once a week she spent with Thea, had the time she needed to get a grip on herself and comprehend all aspects of what had happened.

She found that she enjoyed her hatred of Nick. It gave her a safe way to discharge her anger. He was the only one she cared so little about that hating him was a gratifying outlet. She couldn't afford to hate her mother. At least her mother had cared enough to want to take her along, much as Olivia might have wished she had not. She couldn't hate her father, not while there was the slightest chance that he might someday come for her.

But her father had given her her biggest lesson about love. By his silence he taught Olivia that it was possible to love someone and then push her from your life as if that person had never been born.

She had not known such a thing was possible before coming to Hollywood. She had never thought very deeply about the question of love. She had supposed her parents loved her, in their fashion. Her father had never been demonstrative. There was an enormous gap of years between them. He was almost old enough to be her grandfather, and business seemed to occupy most of his time. Yet Olivia had never doubted his love for her, his only child. He had never denied her a thing she asked for, nor had he ever failed to remember birthdays or even lesser occasions. When she was very small he would sometimes take her to the Los Angeles Zoo. When she was five and bored with being house-bound by a series of rainstorms and resulting sniffles and sore throats, he had transformed the room next to the nursery into a small movie theater for her own use, stocking shelves with cartoons and full-length Disney movies. There were a dozen red velvet seats and a matching curtain over the screen, with a popcorn machine and a soft-drink dispenser in the tiny lobby as well. It had become Olivia's favorite entertainment for years after, with the movies changing with her tastes. Through such kindnesses Olivia had felt her father's love.

She didn't stop hoping her father would come for her until the night of her thirteenth birthday. It had been a full year since she had last seen him. The divorce had become final long before, and her mother and Nick had gotten married. Still she waited by the phone all that evening. Her mother had offered to take her to a movie to celebrate her birthday, but she had refused. In the end Marta and Nick had gone to a party where they might be seen by someone important, and she had no witnesses to her long vigil by the phone. At midnight she had gone to bed, and never again did she search the streets for her father's long black Cadillac or jump at the ringing of the telephone.

Love, she had painfully discovered, was for the moment. Not for eternity. *Forever* was another word in fairy tales, a fiction believed by children and dreamers.

Growing up in Hollywood was an enlightening experience for a young girl previously swaddled in the protective folds of comfortable Beverly Hills. It was like adjusting to a foreign country, where squalor lived side by side with decadent grandeur. She walked to school along Hollywood Boulevard over golden stars commemorating movie idols, while filthy drunks staggered by, dodging the morning sun like vampires scurrying for cover. Chauffeured limousines and Bentleys roared by while sick-faced perverts muttered lewd suggestions in her ears. After twelve years of living in a quiet, large, clean home run by silent, efficient servants, Olivia now found herself in a cluttered, dirty apartment overflowing with strangers, from which the only escape was the comparative solitude of her bedroom, which she kept immaculate and off limits even to her mother.

For the first year she made no attempt at all to find new friends among her classmates or the children who lived on her block of apartment buildings. She spent her time reading instead and sustaining herself with the promise that someday she would have everything she wanted and have it on her own terms. She would never be dependent on anyone ever again. She looked forward to the times she saw Thea, but their conversation centered around Thea and her dreams of her future. Olivia had always been a proud girl, and she did not want even Thea to know how much her father's rejection had hurt or how much she hated the muck her mother allowed to surround her.

She began to understand the power of money, not only for what it bought in goods but for what it delivered in the sense of the quality of life itself. As a child in Beverly Hills, she had been treated with consideration and respect. Servants deferred to her wishes, shopkeepers treated her with courtesy, even teachers exercised a certain decorum toward her and her friends. She was accustomed to being treated in this manner and was initially confused and then infuriated to find that in her new world things were different. There were no servants; store clerks in her neighborhood ignored her in favor of adults, and public-school teachers had little reverence toward their charges.

At home it was even more humiliating. For her mother this changed status was merely a reversion to life as Marta had known it before James and obviously something of a relief. She disdained housework and embraced what she thought of as a colorful, bohemian manner. Nick, eternally playing Brando, walked around the apartment in a yellowed undershirt and ragged jeans. Their friends, all dubiously connected with the theater, sprawled over the furniture, and their dialogue with Olivia was in the third person—"Marta, get the kid to get the beer," or "Kingman is casting kids for a movie. Why don't you take her down? She's damn pretty. Can she act?"

The last was a line she was to hear often in the next decade. "Can she act?" But she wanted no part at all of her mother and Nick's world, and Marta and her friends were all she knew of theater people.

Eventually she made enough of an adjustment so that the days ceased to drag and she stopped fantasizing about a speedy return to her father's lovely home. But the pride that kept her sane also kept her captive in the drab apartment in Hollywood. If her father wouldn't reach out to her, she'd never come crawling to him or anyone else.

The only time she thought of contacting him was when she was going to Hollywood High School and heard about a school in Switzerland a girl she had met was planning to attend the following year. It was just outside Zurich and sounded wonderful. The girl gave Olivia the brochure for the school, and Olivia kept it for a week, fighting with herself over the possibility of asking her father to give her the money for her tuition. It was the first time she had thought of him for a long time. She would not have dreamed of approaching him for anything since he had so obviously chosen to forget her, but she wanted to go to this school badly. It would take her far from her mother and Nick and their fighting, which had begun less than a year after her parents' divorce. Both had begun to realize that dreams didn't pay the rent and put food on the table and beer in the refrigerator, and they had taken part-time restaurant jobs between their infrequent acting parts. A slow, sure hostility had entered into their marriage, and while Olivia felt a small, childish satisfaction over this, it increased her own discomfort to witness their battles. Susan, her friend who was going to the Swiss school and in whom she had confided, had urged her to see her father.

"He owes you something, Olivia," Susan insisted. "The divorce wasn't your fault. When my parents separated, my father went on paying for me. That's the way it's done. Your mother was really dumb to let him off the hook. The least he could do was see that you went to a decent school. Call him. For all you know, he'd be delighted to send you away. At least then he wouldn't feel guilty about dropping you."

Susan's realistic appraisal had hurt, but it had also activated an edge of anger toward her father. He did owe her something. It wouldn't be crawling to stand up and demand no more than was due her. Yet she put off making the call for a full week. She was sitting at the kitchen table looking at the brochure when her mother returned home. Marta was working at a restaurant on Hollywood Boulevard. She sat down heavily in a frayed kitchen chair, her face creased under the heavy makeup she wore.

"What's all that?" she'd asked, looking at the color picture of the little school tucked against the Alps.

She told her mother about the school then, watching Marta's face for a reaction.

"Must be expensive. We don't have that kind of money, Olivia. Not anymore."

"My father does," she'd answered boldly, surprisingly relieved at the opportunity to try out her plan on her mother. She watched her mother's eyes change, grow soft and then flinty. Olivia realized that Marta had aged and changed in the last few years. She looked older and harder, and the girl wondered if the thick makeup was an attempt to make herself look younger. Olivia hadn't noticed it before, but she saw that her mother looked every bit of her six years older than Nick. For the first time in her life, she found herself pitying her mother, but Marta's next words destroyed the sudden wave of compassion.

"You can't ask him, Olivia." Her eyes pleaded for understanding. "He doesn't think he is your father. When I told him I was leaving, I also told him that Nick and I had been lovers for thirteen years." She paused to let her words sink in.

When she saw that Olivia was looking at her blankly, not comprehending, her voiced dropped to a raspy whisper. "I told him that you . . . were Nick's daughter."

Later that night Olivia burned the brochure. She did it very carefully and slowly, performing a sort of ritual over the procedure, swearing to herself that she would get to Europe someday, somehow. After her mother's words had penetrated, her first reaction was fierce anger at her mother. But that phase had passed quickly. She had been angry at her mother for so long already, had long ago classified her as a child incapable of separating reality from fantasy. Her second and lasting reaction was a final dull sense of disappointment in her father. Knowing Marta, how could he have accepted her lie so easily? How could he have not probed further, considered her motives in saying what she had? To Olivia it was obvious—how better to convince James that he shouldn't try to detain his wife and daughter if he was told that he in fact had no wife or daughter? If she could see through the thin strategy, how could her father be fooled?

It was a bitter disappointment, but like everything, it taught her a valuable lesson. Anything she would get in life she would have to get for herself. And only by getting it for herself could she hope to keep whatever she had. Love was nothing on which to depend, and hate was ineffectual, draining the energy she would need to conserve in order to get where she wanted to go. She didn't know how, but sooner or later she would have her chance, and when it came, she would be ready.

CHAPTER 12

A year later the chance came. It would enable her to be independent from Marta and Nick, but she knew she couldn't take it. Olivia's arrival at Hollywood High in the early fall of 1964 was highly visible. Her beauty made her outstandingly attractive to boys, and she was sought after by all the sororities. Even the exalted league of cheerleaders wanted Olivia to decorate their team. But most of all, the would-be thespians converged on her, urging her to join their ranks, where they were certain she belonged.

With a surprising lack of vanity, Olivia understood exactly why she was getting all this attention and considered the value of her beauty for the first time in her life.

Now that she was older, her fine features were beginning to clarify and show the beauty of her bone structure. Her eyes were a startling azure, her cheekbones were delicately hollowed, and her skin was glorious. Her figure complemented the glory of her face and luminous platinum hair; long tapering legs, a small waist, and perfectly shaped breasts made her a magnificent woman.

That early in life Olivia had had the sense to understand that beauty could be enhanced, and she saved her lunch money to buy cosmetics. She bought the best and applied them sparingly, enriching her natural beauty rather than masking it under a sheath of artificiality. Maintaining an elegant style was a direct way of stating her uncompromising position in life.

Her seemingly impenetrable air of confidence, combined with her mature beauty, brought her an avalanche of attention at Hollywood High. She began to date, and because she was popular without being "easy," the girls wanted to align themselves with her as well. She continued to do well in her studies—the work in public school was absurdly easy after the firm foundation she had received at private school, but she also had a social life with which to fill her hours. She passed on the cheerleading and the sororities, but the theater-arts crowd persisted in their efforts to catch her up in the popular dream of eternal stardom.

Because of Marta and Nick, Olivia was one of very few Hollywood beauties who didn't entertain the fantasy of climbing the bandwagon of fame and fortune through a show-business career, who didn't daydream about catching the eye of a talent scout while playing Juliet in the school play. But the interest created in motion pictures by her father's present of the well-stocked home-movie theater and the movies she saw frequently as she grew up made her regard acting as an art and look upon serious actors as artists. One did not have to be beautiful to be an actress, but she couldn't deny that beauty would in no way be a liability, either. Somewhat ambivalently she agreed to try out for a minor role in the next school play. She found that she liked acting because it gave her a safe way to elude a reality that wasn't altogether pleasant. When the part of a lovely young girl going through the pangs of first love in an original play by one of the more talented young school playwrights came along, Olivia was begged to accept the starring role. It was not a particularly challenging or complex part, and she felt she handled it with passable aptitude and professionalism. Her mother and Nick sat through both performances and were vocal in their praise, but more astounding was the fact that a fairly important producer from one of the major studios attended the final showing, and he liked Olivia.

It was the stuff of dreams, and when he sent his card backstage and requested that Olivia come to his office the following week, her fellow actors were ecstatic.

She slept poorly the night before her meeting with the great man. For all of Nick's and her mother's praise and the enthusiasm of her friends at school, she knew that her performance did not qualify her for stardom. Her teacher, while he was kind and encouraging, had not overwhelmed her with accolades. He could not answer that question she had heard so many times—"Can she act?"

The producer arranged a screen test quickly.

In a daze Olivia found herself in a small studio in Hollywood, dressed in a hastily fitted evening gown, clutching a short script of a scene she vaguely remembered from a play she had once read. Lights were playing over her, and people whose functions she didn't know were moving in every direction in front of her.

The director, who had introduced himself as Dick Swanson, returned with a tall, good-looking blond man. "Olivia, I want you to meet Vince West. He will play the scene with you."

She greeted the actor, noticing little about him other than the whiteness of his teeth.

"Okay, Olivia," Dick Swanson began, taking the barstool next to hers on the set while Vince West moved aside to endure the ministrations of the makeup girl, "I want you to relax and try to enjoy youself. This will be fun, I promise. I'm going to talk to you first—look into the camera, that's it. Okay. Listen, you're a pretty girl, you know that? Come on, give me a smile. That's good. I hear you were the lead in your school play. Tell me about it."

Aware of the camera on her, Olivia tried to speak naturally and appear relaxed, but she felt wooden and shallow, inept and graceless. Her throat felt constricted as if by a hand tight around her neck. He asked her questions, which she somehow answered. They were simple questions, designed to put her at ease.

"And who's your favorite movie star?"

"That's hard to say . . . I don't go to the movies all that often." Immediately she reddened at her tactlessness.

He laughed. "Well, who's your favorite director?" He lifted a dark eyebrow archly.

She wasn't about to miss the bait. "You, of course," she answered, smiling naturally for the first time.

"Ah, I bet you don't even remember my name."

She had to laugh. "I don't," she admitted mischievously. "But you're the only director I know, so you have to be my favorite."

In some ways stumbling through her lines with Vince West was easier, if only because she was distracted out of her acute self-consciousness by having to concentrate on her lines.

Three days later she was back in the producer's office, breathing in the rich scent of good leather and highly waxed furniture.

"You come across, Olivia. I thought you would, but you'd be amazed at how often we're wrong. The camera sees things the human eye misses and misses what we see. But I'm pleased." He nodded his graying head and put out his cigarette.

"I was terrible!" The words were out of her mouth before she could stop them. She had fully expected to come to Mr. Lardner's office to hear that her screen test had been a major disappointment. She had left the studio wanting nothing more than to escape into some dark hole where she might quietly die of acute embarrassment.

Phillip Lardner brushed aside her objection with a wave of his diamond-and-gold-studded hand. "Not at all. Olivia, let me explain what a screen test is all about. Most people outside the industry don't understand." He got up and came around the enormous desk. He eased the back of his legs against the desk and folded his arms over his suited chest.

"A screen test is designed not entirely to see how well a person acts. In fact, that's the least of it. Not to strip the glamour from it, but acting is often more a craft than a talent." He held his hand out to stop any objection she might be thinking of making. "A handful of geniuses grace the screen, let me assure you, Olivia. What you see far more often—and more importantly—is the combined work of many talents, from cameramen to directors to writers. I'm not concerned with your ability to act. Later we'll take care of that. The best teachers . . . time. . . ." He shrugged.

"Beauty!" he thundered, startling Olivia. "The kind of beauty that projects on the screen! There are thousands of beautiful girls out there, but on the screen . . . nothing. And I'm talking about a certain kind of beauty now, Olivia. A . . . a . . ." he grabbed at the air as if to capture his thought in his hand, "star material. That's what I'm talking about. That's what a screen test is all about! To find that certain nameless something that magnetizes the eye. It's more than beauty. Even at your young age you have a certain poise, a special dignity! That's what we're looking for right now."

For the first time Olivia heard herself likened to a youthful Grace Kelly. She listened closely to Mr. Lardner's words, wondering why they left her so oddly depressed.

". . . a potential princess to fill a gap in Hollywood's royal court! I see a brilliant future, Olivia."

"I was like lead in front of that camera," she said woodenly. "Lead."

"You'll come along. Time and experience will fix that." He called in his secretary, a beautiful young woman who obviously lacked "star material," and she brought a hefty sheaf of documents with her.

Olivia listened while the producer explained the technicalities of contract negotiation. The eventual outcome of his speech was an invitation to attach her name at the bottom of a pompously worded legal document that all but assured Olivia of fame, fortune, and that place in the sun she had sworn someday to inhabit. There would be further meetings with lawyers and the producer. Yet something kept her from signing. She couldn't help but dwell on herself before that camera, her mind flashing stubbornly to actors she loved, whose performances brought words to life. In contrast, she thought about the others, the "star material" people, especially the inept beauties who pranced across the screen and left nothing of value in their passing.

She knew that heaven itself had opened its gates without her so much as tapping at the door. At seventeen, after five hard and demeaning years, she was offered a magic carpet that would take her wherever she wanted to go, even to the Beverly Hills that had cast her out and would now beg for her reentry.

At night her torment was all but unendurable. Why was she hesitating? She had lived for a chance like this. She had been patient. She had been true to herself. She had kept her blemishless pride, and now she was offered her golden reward. Any girl she knew would sign at once, would give anything to have this chance. What was wrong?

The answer was obvious, of course. She had known what it was from the first moment she had looked at the producer's gilt-edge calling card. The torment wasn't in not knowing, it was only in the pain of self-examination. At seventeen she was facing her first moment of truth. She was facing herself in a fashion that would agonize any serious, contemplative individual of twice her years and experience.

In the end she went alone to the office of the producer and humbly asked him the crucial, damning question.

He had looked at her with ill-concealed irritation, as if her question were of negligible consequence. "Can you act? What has acting got to do with anything? You think half those people out there pulling in the biggest box-office receipts can act?"

Her heart pounding in her heaving chest, Olivia stood her ground. "Can I act, Mr. Lardner?" she asked again, her eyes never wavering from his florid face.

He had glanced at her nervously, rustling the papers of her unsigned contract in his hands as if the sound of them carried more weight than what they promised. "Shit. Who knows? Maybe someday."

She hadn't signed, and as she walked out of that office for the last time, she thought with humorless irony that she felt none of the sense of self-satisfaction that she had supposed would accompany a virtuous decision. She felt terrible. Opportunity had hammered on her door, asking nothing but a realistic compromise of her integrity. She would not have been the first girl to make it on her looks. But she had to live with herself, and she had known all along that she would never, never become a great actress. Without that blessing of talent, she knew she could not attempt a less-than-serious career.

Olivia knew in the final essence that this, after all, had not been her first moment of truth. She had already faced moments that decided her fate. Once a phone call from her to her father could have restored her to a painfully lost world, and her pride had refused to allow her to grovel or compromise her integrity. When she had longed to go to Europe with Susan, she had only to disclose Marta's lie to get what she wanted; but again she had chosen personal dignity and sacrifice over comfort and pleasure.

In the same way she had known all along inside that she could not sign that contract and flaunt herself on the screen because of a fortuitous blend of genes that had produced a symmetry of features that others called beauty. To do so would have given her the world while poisoning the soul that wanted it.

CHAPTER 13

Nine months after Olivia turned her back on a screen career, she met Mark Lyman. He had not cared about the superficial beauty that all could see. He taught Olivia that love was a matter of soul. He read to her from Gibran's *The Prophet* with particular emphasis on the theory of work being love made visible. He shared his work with her, and she knew it was his ultimate gift.

She had moved into his studio with joy and humility. She was ashamed that she had surrendered her virginity to him just months before, and that curiosity had been the driving force. She was honest enough to tell him, and he had laughed at her. He told her it didn't matter how it began. What they had together now was what mattered.

These were days and nights of exquisite happiness, but Olivia learned that even spellbinding love lacked the magnificence to overshadow the promises she had made to herself. She wanted to be someone in her own right, and she wanted luxury and elegance as part of her life. She needed unshakable security, to be independent of the goodwill of anyone other than herself. She had not forgotten that love—even the pure love of a father for his only child—gave no more than an illusion of permanence. Mark loved her and swore that his love was eternal. She loved him in return but refused to deceive herself about eternity. Eternity was a single moment when worlds collided. Eternity was a phone that didn't ring. Eternity was also a kiss, here today but possibly gone tomorrow. Olivia was only nineteen, and eternity upon eternity had already been consumed by the dust of yesterday.

Thea Wallace, taller, more beautiful than ever, and still more sophisticated, blew magic into that dust, offering yet another vehicle of escape.

"I want to go to Europe, Olivia. Now! And I don't want to go alone."

They were lunching at an outdoor café, Thea ignoring her food in favor of consuming cigarette after cigarette while Olivia ate. "Europe!" The wonder of it took away Olivia's appetite. "But why? I mean why now?"

Thea tightened her lips, and her eyes were angry. "I have to get away. I can't take much more of my parents. I really can't! You have no idea how much Mother's riding me. She keeps throwing Everett in my face, Olivia. She has this absolutely tense thing about my future, which she is sure I'm going to ruin. She wants me to be like her, marry some nice, decent—and rich—boy and be done with it."

For all her habitual bursts of high drama, Olivia knew that Thea was authentically disturbed this time.

"I feel locked in a box! If I don't get the hell away—far enough away—they're going to railroad me into something I don't want. Damn it, Olivia, I want to live my own life! I don't know how yet, or what kind of life it will be, but it's got to be my choice, not Mother's."

"But Europe?" Olivia grudgingly acknowledged that the thought of her best friend being halfway around the world disturbed her. Even if they rarely talked the same language, they managed to understand each other in a special and precious way.

"Yes, Europe! And there's money enough to do it exquisitely." She reached for her friend's hand, the haunted look fading, replaced by an excited grin. "I want you to come with me, Olivia."

Olivia sat back. "I couldn't possibly afford. . . ." Her thoughts flew to Mark, not to her poverty. Leave Mark! It was a strange, painful thought. But she already felt pain in any thought about her relationship with Mark. No matter how much they loved each other, she felt as if she couldn't endure one more day living as they did. And Mark, knowing her discontent, was drinking again. The night before had ended miserably, with each of them wide-eyed in the dark, unable to sleep as the result of still another argument. To get away . . . To start all over. . . .

"Olivia, I don't give a damn about the money! It's my life that's at stake!" Thea's eyes filled with tears. "I have the money for both of us. To hell with the money! I need you! I can't do it alone. I really can't. If you want, you can pay me back when you have it. I don't care. But please say you'll come. It will be wonderful. Who knows what's waiting for us in Europe? Olivia, if you turn me down, I . . . I don't know what I'll do."

Olivia listened, and in her heart she knew this was one magic carpet she could ride without too much deliberation on the question of ethics. Thea needed to escape the pressures of her overpowering mother, and for all her outward confidence and composure, Thea could not go on her own. This would be the filling of mutual needs, and while it grieved Olivia to have to accept Thea's bounty to cover her own expenses, she knew that she would be repaying her friend with her encouragement and support long before she could repay her in money.

"Yes. All right, Thea. Yes! Let's do it!"

They hugged each other across the table, knocking over condiments and then laughingly repairing the damage.

There was no laughter, however, when she told Mark of her plans. Surprisingly, there was also no fight. Their mutual pain was too intense for an argument.

"Why?" His eyes burned into hers.

"Because I can't live like this!"

He followed her eyes around the bare studio, sweeping over the clutter and disorganization that resisted her most valiant attempts. His expression conveyed a suggestion of surprise, but his voice was tired. "*This,* as you put it, matters more than we do?"

She looked back at him. "It shouldn't," she said sadly, "but it does. There's never enough money . . . the *squalor* of it all! Mark, don't you see?"

"No, I don't see. I don't see at all, Olivia. Not what you see. I'm working for something. That's what you can't see. You think it's going to be like this forever! You lack faith in me—you make me question myself when you talk like this." He walked slowly to the canvas on which he was presently laboring. It was bold and exciting even in its partially completed state. "This will someday give you everything you want!"

She felt raw inside as she looked not at the painting but at the artist. "I don't for a minute doubt that, Mark. And I don't lack faith in you or your talent. But—please hear me, Mark—I can't wait! I can't. I've had too much of this. The ugliness, the dreams, the cheapness of always doing without, being behind, wanting what everyone else already has . . ." She hugged her arms tightly to her body, a body draped in bargain-basement clothing, a body that had once known the texture of fine cloth, the comfort of perfect fit.

"You don't love me, Olivia." His face was a protective mask, his eyes veiled, refusing to show his pain.

"I do love you!" *But not enough?* The question hung in the linseed-scented air.

"Then why are you leaving?" After a brief struggle with himself, Mark crossed the room and took her into his arms. "Why?"

She took refuge from her agony in his strong arms. "Maybe because I do love you," she admitted softly, wrestling with feelings even she didn't completely understand. She met his dark eyes with difficulty. "And I can't bear to see the way we're draining each other. We are. For a long time now. You know it, too. You can't live the way I want, and I can't live your way."

"Won't, you mean," he countered, stepping back, his arms falling heavily to his sides. "Damn it, say what you mean!" But there was no anger in his tone, just a trace of resistance to the defeat that was already in the air.

"I said can't and I meant can't," she insisted quietly. "You can't possibly know what it's done to me, living as I have, seeing my world blown apart. I feel as if I've been shanghaied aboard a sinking freighter, Mark, and the only way to get off is to hold my breath and take a leap into the sea. It has nothing to do with you or my feelings for you."

"What in God's name are we talking about if not feelings? Our love for each other! I don't know what the hell you hope to find out there, Olivia, but can it compare to what we already have?" He put a hand on her long neck, slid it down over her throat, stroked her body intimately, lovingly.

Gasping, she pulled back, beyond his beautiful, sensitive fingers. "It's the wrong time for us. Mark, please, try to understand. I'm not ready. I can't accept what you have to offer. Not now. Not yet!"

"I do understand, Olivia. Damn it, I do." He turned to the door, grabbing his jacket with one hand, the knob with the other. "But I don't accept. I'll never be able to accept losing you."

She waited until the door was closed behind him before sinking onto the old bed in which they had shared so much with each other. "God help me," she said to the space he had occupied, "I do love you."

Leaving Mark was a wrenching agony, yet because of her very ability to do it, Olivia knew that she had made the right decision. It was Mark himself, that wonderful teacher of the art of living, who had made her understand ultimately that any decision made and acted on is inevitably the right decision at the time.

CHAPTER 14

Europe was the biggest, most brilliant toy of all, and Olivia gobbled up every new experience like a starving kitten at a bowl of heavy cream. It was almost eight months before their innocently aimless wanderings brought them to Meiringen, Switzerland, where destiny in the admirable shape of Jean-Pierre DeSante waited for Olivia.

When Jean-Pierre, after a proper introduction by friends of Thea's family, began seriously to court Olivia, she hesitated, as if knowing from the first that her life hung in delicate balance. It was not lingering thoughts of Mark Lyman that kept her from encouraging the spectacularly handsome and charming architect and multimillionaire. Mark had never left her mind, of course. Her hesitancy came instead from a familiar source.

Just as Hollywood had tempted her with potentially empty riches, Jean-Pierre's enormous wealth activated the flashing of warning signals in her brain. She was terrified of responding to what being the wife of a very rich man could do to her. She was equally afraid that try as she might, she would find it impossible to locate the person behind the facade of Jean-Pierre's charm and opulence.

Thea, wide-eyed with disbelief, thought Olivia had taken permanent leave of her senses. She did her best to blast through her friend's resistance.

"Darling, the man is everything you could possibly want. He's all any woman with half a mind could want! And he's obviously wild for you, little idiot! You're actually holding his assets against him. I see it, but I don't believe it! The man is gorgeous, he's embarrassingly rich, he's charming enough for a fairy tale, and he also happens to have a very lovely head on his marvelously broad shoulders. Tell me, old girl, does a man have to be soaked in turpentine and starving in an artistic slum to reach you? The time is now, Olivia, my sweet. Your ship has finally landed. In Switzerland, yet! At least give the poor sucker a chance. Or are you afraid life might be too perfect for a change?"

As always Olivia had to do her own thinking and reach her own conclusions. However, Thea's words had hit home. Was she secretly afraid of the success she had claimed to want so badly? She had dated other men since leaving Mark. Jean-Pierre was indeed a prize above all others. Was she holding his perfection against him? Had she become enamored of the struggle to overcome defeat to the point of not allowing herself to attain happiness? She decided to keep seeing Jean-Pierre to find out.

It was three months of the stuff of dreams. He took her everywhere, flying her across the continent at a whim. He was also marvelous company, quick-witted, impossibly gallant, and so sexy that her body responded to his kisses long before her mind wanted any part of him. At the same time he was mature and patient and never pushed her into the slightest intimacy. He did not insist on taking her to bed, and his deference to her wishes had the effect of making her climb the walls with desire for him.

They had dined in the fabulous house he had built just at the edge of Meiringen, a monument to his genius and originality of design. After he had sent the servants to bed, he had taken her out to the rear terrace, which overlooked miles of flower-speckled grasslands. She suspected he would ask her to marry him in the romantic setting. They had lunched with his widowed mother earlier in the day, and Olivia had recognized the frosty approval of Jean-Pierre's choice in her eyes. It had been the final inspection, Olivia had sensed, more a formality than a deciding vote in her favor. She already knew that Jean-Pierre directed his own fate. She had found him to be forceful and decisive, clear-headed and forthright.

She looked at him searchingly after he made his declaration of love and asked her to be his wife. A part of her wanted to accept him. It was like a carefully worked play for which she had prepared her lines. She certainly felt something for him.

It was not the same thing she felt still for Mark, but in many ways it was a cleaner and more respectful emotion.

But how much of what she felt was influenced by the accomplishments he had accrued in his thirty years of life? Was it love she felt? In so many ways she didn't know him at all. She had seen him perform, had laughed at his wit, had quickened under his kisses. She had seen him use good taste and the correct degree of decorum in dealing with the townspeople, to whom he was a god. She had interacted with him among her friends and his, had seen him easily take command in emergencies and be gentle yet firm with animals and children. But what did it all mean? Who was he, down deep where no one could trespass?

With a pang of genuine regret, she gently refused his offer of marriage. She was truthful about her reason: the suspicion that they were still strangers.

He recovered with his usual charm and wit, kissing her lingeringly on the lips, his strong hands moving sensuously over her nearly naked back. "If you must reject my proposal, will you also refuse a proposition? Let me take you to bed, my beautiful angel. Let me make love to you. If I must be denied a lifetime, allow me to condense a life into one precious night."

Now that she was free of the strain of considering him as a mate, she could indulge her desire to go to bed with him. With genuine relief she laughed against his thick, nicely scented neck. "Prince Charming has changed into the prince of darkness. And the angel will shed her wings, just for a little while. Make love to me, Jean-Pierre. Make wild, fierce love to me. I do love you, you know," she admitted, surprising herself far more than him. "I just don't know who you are."

His bedroom was worthy of a palace, and in bed he was a king, a lion, a ferocious and voracious beast who knew the secret of evoking a like animality in his mate. He was not devoid of tenderness and consideration, but his lovemaking surpassed those commendable sensitivities to ravish Olivia's flesh while glorifying her spirit. She writhed under him victoriously, forgetting all else in his embrace. She discovered that Jean-Pierre had that one outstandingly masculine trait all but lost in many other men; the ability to conquer and subdue a woman in bed while imparting to her a sense of ultimate triumph. Olivia felt triumphant because she had driven an otherwise completely self-controlled being to the depths of his uncontrollable masculinity. He conquered her over and over, and each time she was the victor, the unquestionable winner in a competition for sensual magnificence.

Afterward, weary and yet too stimulated after their hours in bed to fall alseep, they had gone hand in hand to Jean-Pierre's fabulous sauna. In the cedar walls that smelled like the forest, half-draped by cloudlike veils of moist steam, they gave themselves up to the oppressive heat from the glowing coals and talked.

Actually it was Jean-Pierre who talked, and Olivia, drymouthed and limp, who listened. This was a different Jean-Pierre, relaxed by the hours of passion, body and limbs drained after rare multiple orgasms. His mind seemed less sharp and more introspective, and the scent of the sauna evoked memories of childhood, of his life with his parents, of the awesome responsibility of being an only child born to a prestigious and tradition-seeped family.

At first Olivia listened with a twinge of jealousy for a life unblemished by denial of anything material, but as he talked on, her feelings began to change. Without a trace of self-pity or even a hint of awareness of the acute loneliness he must have suffered, he told of a little boy who had everything but love; everything but understanding, kindness, or compassion; a boy who had never known a mother's kiss, a father's hug; a boy who had been shuffled through continents in search of the best schooling, dressed in the most expensive clothing, heaped with the greatest responsibilities and expectations. Jean-Pierre remembered entering his own home after years of formal education in a haze of panic that he might not be able to pick out his own mother and father from the masses of servants and relatives he knew not even by sight.

When he was permitted to live at home, his days were a regimen of disciplines administered by a staff of tutors brought from all over the world for the express purpose of creating a nearly flawless example of genteel magnificence. Every instance of his life was documented and observed, every function of existence was manipulated and utilized to shape him into the man they wanted him to be. Punishments were severe and delivered without a sign of emotionalism. Food not eaten properly was taken from his eager mouth. Laxity in application to his lessons was treated with spartan severity.

As Olivia listened she felt something inside her stiffen and then crack. Her lovely eyes filled with unnoticed tears. Most touching of all was Jean-Pierre's complete and devastating lack of awareness that in another, less-grand society he would have been considered a badly abused child. He had learned his lessons well—self-pity was intolerable, and because he had been given everything, he had been raised laudably, with fortune spilling its sunny rays on his handsome head.

He didn't notice the compassion on her face, nor did he understand the effect of his musings on her heart. In her silence Olivia was more completely his than she had been before or would be again. When he had finally finished, she had gone into his arms. She could do no more than hold him tightly to her naked flesh, could not be the mother he had never really had; but when she was finally able to speak without dissolving into tears, she huskily asked him if her acceptance of his proposition had canceled out his proposal.

Caught up in the memories of the distant past, he did not immediately understand. Then a slow, sweet smile altered his lips. "You have changed your mind, my darling?" His eyes told her she had the power to change his life with a word.

"I'll marry you," she had promised softly.

And I'll love you forever, she had thought but found herself unable to say.

CHAPTER 15

As always after confronting her staff with a flawed report, Marlissa Deloffre felt terrible.

She nodded formally to each of them as they filed out of her office—Bob Bernstein from histology; Kurt VanDeGenocter, who was in charge of the radio autography department; Barbara Simons, the aggressively masculine woman who headed the physical-evaluation lab; the rather morose young man, Dave Lewis, who normally ran his product-research section with more competence and efficiency than this report indicated, and the others. Rita Vanalden was the last one out, her plain, intelligent face shyly averted, her entire demeanor an apology for work that really hadn't reflected any discredit on her micropathology department, which consistently performed with professional excellence.

Feeling especially guilty, Marlissa smiled encouragingly at Rita, whom she rather liked, or toward whom she felt at least a certain empathy. She would have liked to know the woman better, sensing in Rita an unaffected gentleness that reminded Marlissa of the farm women at home. She hadn't met any women in San Francisco with whom she felt completely comfortable. On the other hand Rita was an employee, and Marlissa supposed it would be a tactical mistake to befriend someone she might have to reprimand or even discharge someday. Such an eventuality seemed remote—she wished all her staff were as competent as Rita—but it was still a consideration.

At once Marlissa felt a stab of personal irritation. Her real reason for needing to keep people like Rita at a safe distance had nothing to do with work or her responsibility to Magnifi-Scent. She couldn't afford to allow herself closeness to Rita, because in Rita and the others like her, she saw herself—or rather that side of herself she hated—the humble, insecurity-driven mouse who minimized her achievements and maximized her failings. At thirty-one, with two degrees in chemistry and biophysics, a long string of major accomplishments and awards to her credit, a piece of a fantastically successful business, a highly respected position that paid her more in a month than she had ever dreamed of making in a year, she was still a mouse.

She went to her desk and picked up the report, aware that its imperfection wasn't as flagrant as her irritation with it. She understood the thinking behind it perfectly. She skimmed over the pages quickly, mentally checking out a few details that particularly bothered her. It was difficult for Marlissa to understand why no one in her department seemed to grasp the incredible importance of flawless research. But on reflection she knew that the painstaking exactitude she demanded was not stressed in school. She had her father to thank for her own meticulousness. This report would probably pass without a moment's hesitation anywhere else. After all, this new facial mask varied only slightly from the one they had already merchandised with complete success. The likelihood of its being an inferior product or in any way harmful to the consumer was extremely remote.

She put the report in her top desk drawer, locked it

securely, then put her ring of drawer keys in a niche under the desk. Coming from a little Swiss village where few doors even had locks, Marlissa had to remind herself that such security measures were essential in big business. It was another of the alien concepts she found she had trouble absorbing. She doubted if even Olivia knew how much of a strain it was for her, adapting not only to a new country but conducting her work on this gigantic scale. She frequently longed for the simplicity of the lab at home, the way it was when she and her family ran a dying but enjoyable business. Then she was a cook in a kitchen, creating her cosmetics and perfumes almost singlehandedly, happiest when she was at work. And yet here she had everything—unheard of instruments and conveniences, to say nothing of a huge staff and an almost unlimited budget.

Olivia had spared nothing on this most vital part of her operation. Beyond her fantastically beautiful office and hidden by a paneled wall for absolute privacy was the most elaborately equipped lab money could buy, all for Marlissa's own use. There she could experiment to her heart's content, and in this room the very best of MagnifiScent's line was born, the finest compounds that gave the company its reputation for unparalleled excellence.

The tragedy was that the demands of her vast department made it almost impossible for Marlissa to spend the time she would like in her lab, and by necessity most of the line was created by her staff. At best she might develop a basic cream or eye shadow, a lipstick or a scent, and her staff would analyze what she had done and create variations on the theme. But she had been forced to relinquish her complete control over each and every product. She recognized that this was the reason she was such a tyrant about the work that came through, if not out of, her hands.

The keys dropped from their hiding place as she sat down at her desk to write herself a few notes about the facial mask. She cursed under her breath, but she understood that now more than ever she had to be careful. While no one had officially said anything to her about Riviera's new line, news of it was raging through the laboratory. She hadn't talked to Olivia yet. It had been too frantic a week for direct communication. Olivia had scheduled a meeting for Monday morning, but Marlissa suspected she would hear from her dear friend and boss sometime during the weekend.

Well, perhaps she could be reassuring at such a meeting. To

Marlissa it was not overly astounding that another line could closely match their own work. MagnifiScent had set a standard in the business that every other company was killing itself trying to duplicate. It was inevitable that one should succeed. It was surprising that Riviera had been the one. It was an established company that had never been known for its creativity or quality. Still, Marlissa was almost certain the similarity to her own compounds was a freak accident that would not be repeated.

Even so, she got up carefully, checking to see that the keys were still in their hiding place. Not that a dedicated formula thief couldn't find them in a minute if he or she had access to Marlissa's office. But the whole idea was just so much foolishness to the practical, unfanciful chemist from Switzerland. The lab was closed all weekend, and the only people who had entry to the building were her department heads. And each was a trusted employee, who, it was true, had complete access to the labs on his or her own time if there was some work that needed checking. But strangers and less important personnel would have to pass through MagnifiScent's excellent security department, and the odds were infinitesimal that her office, which housed the actual compiled reports and formulas, would be disturbed in her absence.

Because, almost in spite of herself, she was daily growing more sophisticated about the workings of big business, Marlissa knew about industrial spies and the stealing and buying of secrets between less scrupulous firms; but in many ways MagnifiScent was still a family business.

But not her own any longer, she thought with a surprising trace of bitterness.

At once she negated her traitorous thought. She had no cause for lingering regrets or hostility. If Olivia hadn't bought the business from her parents, they would have had to close their doors many years ago. What would her family have done then? Certainly she and her father could have found jobs elsewhere, but then nothing would have been left of the company the family had nursed from infancy. Instead, Olivia had appeared like an angel out of nowhere, and because of her brilliance and vision, MagnifiScent and the Deloffres were scooped out of nothingness and elevated to a fairy-tale life.

Marlissa thought of the wonderful house her parents had had built a stone's throw from the six-hundred-year-old farmhouse in which she had been born and lived until so recently. Her brothers and little sister had everything now. Her mother, who had never been strong, was healthier and happier than she had ever been. Her father, that sweet, quiet man of genius and humility, was a king today, reigning over their European laboratories. No, she had nothing, absolutely nothing, to feel toward Olivia but gratitude and respect.

She glanced over at the face of the starkly modern stainless-steel grandfather clock in the corner. She had never ceased to be vaguely affronted by the clock, with its modern lines and stunning impact on the eye. Not that it wasn't a masterpiece and outrageously expensive. Her entire office was the working room of a queen rather than a basically simple girl from the Alpine country. If it wasn't a reflection of her personal taste, she had no one to blame but herself. She could have had it decorated any way she liked, but at the last moment she had left its entire creation up to Grey Bertolli, an important new decorator. Bertolli had made his reputation by doing the foyers, salons, auditoriums, conference rooms, and executive offices of MagnifiScent. It was presumptuous of her to think she could have approached the striking beauty Bertolli had achieved. True, an office she had decorated herself would have been more comfortable, less overbearing, but if she had any doubts of her own importance to Olivia and MagnifiScent, Marlissa had only to open the door to her office and take a swift look around.

The thought brought her back to her musings about Rita and why she couldn't afford to encourage friendships with those who reminded her of her modest beginnings. Why else had she left Meiringen in the first place? Of course, Olivia needed her, but once the lab complex had been set up, Marlissa could have hired one of several outstanding people to run the complex. She could have gone back home and devoted herself to the work she loved best. She would now be enjoying long, fulfilling days creating compounds and blissful nights as Ernst Ooboron's wife. Life would have gone on being the simple, undemanding thing it had once been.

But much as Marlissa yearned for the life she had known, where musicians still played in the cobblestone streets and the measure of a woman's worth was the smile on her husband's face, she also had pined for a fuller, more glamorous life. It seemed to her that America was an enchanted land and San Francisco the fairy kingdom she had always sought, with exotic strangers moving at a brisk pace, the clamor of constant activity everywhere, the world of live entertainment, fabulous places to eat, and marvelous shops that sold everything imaginable.

The vision of Ernst stuck momentarily in her mind. It was surprising how clearly she could remember every expression on his remarkable face, the soft, low-key throb of his voice—Ernst, the carpenter whom she loved.

Once loved, she reminded herself firmly. If she had still loved him, how could she have left him behind in Meiringen? It was absurdly easy to put Ernst in perspective when she used logic instead of emotion. Her life with him would have been uneventful and unexciting. They had been quietly comfortable with each other, but as lovers they had created an undeniable magic. But Ernst was content with the life they had always known. He had no interest in new and exciting things. He could not possibly fit into her new world. She couldn't imagine him at the concerts, the parties, the lavish dinners she had attended since coming to San Francisco. He would have stood out among the new people she had met like a poor country cousin, gaping in confused disapproval at all he saw.

A sense of fairness interjected itself in her thoughts. Marlissa didn't believe she yet fit into this exciting new existence, either, but she had a way of managing to stand back and be an unobtrusive observer. She had not yet developed the style and sophistication to be boldly individualistic, but in her quietly dignified way she was just able to pass, to let others interpret her silences and lack of participation as the thoughtful attitude befitting a woman of success and genius. She was rapidly becoming a woman of importance, the wizard behind Olivia, and she was quick to see that all that was required of her was to dress in simple but expensive clothing, say little, and allow others to fill in the gaps that were caused by her own basic insecurity.

Sometimes the complexities of her new life threatened to overwhelm her. She still had to watch others at dinner to make sure she reached for the correct fork, and she was at a complete loss as to how to make the most of herself physically and socially. She thought of herself as an unremarkably plain woman. She knew that her lean body had a certain grace and beauty and that her face could be transformed into an arresting one by intelligent use of the very products she devised for the glorification of other women. But she hadn't yet developed a sense of personal style, and she lacked the boldness to present herself as a definite character who would stand out. She settled, therefore, for an unassuming facade that threatened no one and made her the one of the three brilliant forces behind MagnifiScent whom people could not quite remember. Yet those who recognized her held her in the same awe as the flawlessly elegant Olivia and the strikingly self-sufficient Thea.

Marlissa turned to a beveled wall mirror across from her desk, studied her neat figure in the lab coat, the faintly made-up, bland face that just avoided being pretty, the severely pulled-back dark brown hair, and felt, if not comfortable with the image, safe to be hidden behind it. Only her eyes came close to giving her away. They were a deep hazel and unflinchingly individualistic.

Another glance at the clock reminded her that it was now past the time she normally left for home. The thought of home made her relax. It would be good to get to her house in St. Francis Wood and luxuriate in a long and tranquil weekend. She had nothing planned, for once. She had known she would need the rest.

It had been an exceptionally rough week, which partially explained her brusqueness with her staff. Riviera's new line had motivated some of the increased frenzy of the work schedule. Olivia was pushing hard for Marlissa's department to finish the next line, an especially innovative one with a daring emphasis on seductive hues of gold. Working with this color was tricky—metallic cosmetics were always tricky. Everything had to be extremely hush-hush as well, which was the normal procedure when any company was launching a completely new look. The one that got there first got the credit and the sales.

Most of the reports and formulas were in her massive top drawer, along with the one on the less important facial mask, and Marlissa was generally pleased with them. Most of the initial compounding she had done herself, and she was particularly pleased with the basic skin makeup, a creamy foundation that contained a powder that imparted a very subtle golden hue to the face. It would be wonderfully effective with the new blusher, a marvel of bronzed reds, and the eye shadows that would carry the theme to this most important area of the face. Only the lipsticks were coming along slowly. These had to be particularly spectacular. So much had already been done with lip makeup that it demanded all of Marlissa's creativity to conjure up something really different in this department. Most of the variation in other companies came from the clever naming of the lipsticks. Marlissa wanted the new line to be distinctive in the product as well as the advertising.

Abruptly aware that she was still immersed in business not two minutes after comforting herself with delicious thoughts of a long, lazy weekend, Marlissa reached for her purse and started for the door. The phone rang just as she was reaching for the brass knob.

Hoping it wasn't Olivia, who might want to have that meeting immediately, she put the receiver to her ear. "Hello?"

"Marlissa? This is Brad Cavell. Do you remember me? We met at the Tremains' dinner party two weeks ago."

She held the receiver tightly and was surprised to find that she remembered the caller immediately. He had been sitting at her left at the dinner. Tall and very blond. Perhaps late thirties, even forty. Very definitely handsome and suave. Had he been with that exotic, dark-haired girl seated next to him? "Oh, yes, Brad, I remember." She felt acutely self-conscious and had no idea why he was calling. "How are you?" she asked for lack of anything else to say.

"Busy." His laugh came easily. "Or at least that's my excuse for calling at the last minute. Look, by any chance, do you happen to be free tonight? I have tickets to the ballet at the opera house. It's the New York City Ballet; I've forgotten which one they're doing tonight."

"*Swan Lake*," she said softly. She had tried to get a ticket herself but found none available. She was surprised and flattered and suspicious. Why would a man like Brad Cavell ask her out, and to an event for which any man could be assured a fascinating date? But the fact that he was asking at the last minute implied that he was perhaps turning to her for a quick fill-in date. It made the offer less flattering but more realistic.

"Yes, of course." Brad said quickly. "I see you follow the ballet. Wonderful. I apologize for calling so late, but frankly I was out of town all week on business and didn't think I would make it back in time. Will you forgive me for not calling earlier and come anyway?"

He was charming. And handsome. In fact, he appeared to be exactly the kind of man any girl from a small town would dream about dating.

"Well, I don't know, Brad," she said haltingly, her thin accent sounding more pronounced in her own ears. "It's been a difficult week, and I was just contemplating a quiet evening at home. Still, I did want to see the New York City Ballet before they left San Francisco . . ." She hoped she sounded more drawn to the offered entertainment than Brad Cavell himself.

"I absolutely promise a relaxed evening. The ballet and supper afterward. How does that sound?"

Marlissa thought it sounded like a miracle. But she was frightened, too. What could she say to this sophisticated stranger? How could she hope to hold his interest? What did she know but her formulas and small-town customs? But then she caught herself being that frightened little mouse again. This last-minute date was an omen, a challenge that she could either boldly take or safely reject. Either she was going to start living the glamorous life of her dreams or she might as well go home to Ernst's predictable future.

"It sounds wonderful. I'd love to go, Brad." She gave him her home address and phone number and agreed to be ready by quarter to eight.

Yet oddly, considering how quickly Brad Cavell's image had come to her mind before, she found the image of him fading once she hung up. Only Ernst's homely face, with its patient sad eyes, hung in the coolly filtered air.

CHAPTER 16

Rita stood in front of the open refrigerator indecisively, her eyes lovingly caressing the eggs and wedges of hard cheeses, the carton of thick, chilled sour cream. With a weary sigh she wondered why a year of happiness had added more unwanted pounds to her plump figure. She had been taught to believe that overeating was a symptom of boredom and emotional unfulfillment. Yet here she was, content as a purring kitten, with her same old murderous appetite.

"Blast it," she muttered aloud, reaching for the eggs,

cheese, butter, and sour cream. Unloading these on the counter, she went back to the refrigerator for fresh white mushroom caps and an open can of mild green chili peppers. She would make a tangy gourmet omelette topped with sour cream and accompanied with hot-from-the-oven baking-powder biscuits. Stephen loved a substantial breakfast, and weekends were the only time she had to prepare anything special. She would start her diet on Monday. Mondays were good days to start diets. Another pound or two wouldn't matter at this point.

Having rationalized her desire, Rita got out a half-dozen oranges and the juicer and went to work. After putting the juice in the refrigerator to chill, she decided to use the rinds in a breakfast bubble cake. Her hands moved as deftly in the kitchen as they did in the laboratory, and soon the pan of biscuits was in the oven and the coffee cake was rising under a clean kitchen towel near the stove.

She left the kitchen and walked quietly through the living room to stop at the door to their bedroom. Stephen was still asleep, his long lashes casting shadows under his closed eyes. His mouth was parted like a child's, and he was snoring faintly, his perfect body relaxed in sleep and taking up the lion's share of the king-size bed she had bought just before their wedding. The only indication of tension was in the straining cloth at the crotch of his ivory cotton pajamas. He almost always woke up with an erection in the morning, even when they had made love the night before, and sometimes the tenting of his pants would be noticeable as much as fifteen minutes before he actually opened his eyes.

Rita turned away from him with a shiver of desire and discomfort and went back to the kitchen. Stephen sometimes liked to make love to her in the morning, especially when he was still half-asleep. But she was awkward with him during those times, acutely conscious of her body under the unkind harshness of daylight. She much preferred the night. In the darkness she didn't feel so aware of her imperfections and was freer to respond to her husband. She didn't feel as if she was being an inadequate wife by making herself unavailable in the mornings—very often the eye-catching bulge would be gone when he returned from his first trip to the bathroom. Stephen was easily distracted by an attractively served breakfast and a steaming cup of freshly ground coffee.

She heard the flush of the toilet from the other room just as she took the biscuits from the oven. The sound made Rita think again of her desire to buy a house and move out of this apartment. She had been raised in a house, and it still seemed the proper home for a family. For the outrageous rent she was paying for this apartment, it was disgusting the way sounds carried through the paper-thin walls. She was still slightly nettled that Stephen had come out so adamantly against her suggestion that they buy a house. After all, they might have children, and as a real-estate man, Stephen should know that the money they were throwing away in rent could be building equity for their future. And since he *was* in real estate, however halfheartedly, he could undoubtedly find them a real bargain and save them money by using his seller's commission as part of the down payment.

She silently bolstered her side of the argument as she set the kitchen table. She was making enough money so that income tax was a problem, and everyone said that owning a house was a real tax advantage, particularly for childless couples. It would be nice to have a bigger place with extra bedrooms. Then she could invite various members of her family to visit comfortably. And Stephen had some family back East who might come if they had room, perhaps. Animals were forbidden in this and most apartments, and Stephen should have a dog. He looked like the kind of man who would look good with a great big shaggy-haired sheepdog or a sleek shepherd by his side. That was another thing—apartments were too restrictive. In a house you could live more expansively.

She had just poured the coffee when he came into the kitchen, his hair still uncombed, the nice blue cord robe she had bought him loosely tied over his pajamas. "Hey, a feast!" He drooped one eye and pointed his index finger at her like a gun. "Pow! Pow! I got you, you little killer, you." He sat down on his chair and picked up the orange juice.

She smiled. He always accused her of trying to kill him with an overdose of calories, while in truth he hadn't gained a single ounce while she, on the other hand, was wearing a whole dress size larger than when they were married.

She checked the bubble cake, brought the coffee pot to the table, and returned to the stove to carefully slip the omelette into a serving plate. The home fries were just right, and she dished them out before sitting down. Before she touched her own food or coffee, Rita took a gratifying visual scan of the table she had set. Everything looked and smelled beautiful. Her own homemade fig preserves were sparkling like amber jewels in the cut-crystal jelly pot, and the aroma of the about-ready bubble cake in the oven added a touch of clove and cinnamon. "Hope you're hungry." she said.

Stephen looked at the array of food and groaned. "I'll give it my best shot," he promised, cutting through an edge of the omelette while she buttered him a biscuit.

She began to eat eagerly, as always her own best customer. Her thoughts returned to her desire to buy a house. "You know, Stephen, I was just thinking . . . wouldn't it be nice to have a dog?"

He looked at her in surprise. "A dog?" He looked around as if he expected one to pop out of the oven. "Here?"

She brightened at the perfect opening. "No, darling, of course not here! Dogs aren't allowed in the building. But if we had our own house we could have a dog."

Stephen eyed her warily. "Who the hell wants a dog?"

She reached for her coffee cup, instantly defeated by the irritation in his voice. She wondered if she was taking it too personally, as if purchasing a house somehow meant deepening their commitment to each other in her mind. It was a crazy thought, she reasoned. After all, he had married her, and that was a far bigger affirmation of devotion. No, she thought she could guess the reason for Stephen's reluctance. It had to be the fact that it would not be them buying a house but Rita buying the house for them. And that, to a man, would likely be humiliating.

She watched Stephen as he returned to his breakfast, his eyes glued to his plate. Why hadn't she been more sensitive to him? Their money arrangement was, she supposed, a strange one for a married couple. She paid for everything connected with their home, the food they ate, their clothing and laundry. They had a joint checking account, but she was the one who wrote the checks, and she was the only one who made deposits into the account. After a year together she still had no idea what Stephen made at his real estate, but it couldn't have been much because she had had to pay the yearly fee for the renewal of his license. There was also a marked absence of the phone calls at home that seemed to be a part of any realtor's work. He also hadn't put much mileage on her new Buick, even though he drove it far more than she did, and supposedly for business. It made sense—a realtor needed a respectable-looking car, and his old Chevy looked down-at-the-heels. She was only a mile or so from work and really needed to walk off some calories. Of course, the way it ended up was that Stephen drove the new car and she took his old one to work. It didn't matter to her all that much, and Rita was more than willing to do anything she could to help him with his career.

But for all their avoidance of the subject of money, the facts would speak for themselves when they got down to the serious business of buying a house. It would evoke an image of the money box, as she called it, the cigarette box she kept in the bedroom and made sure was stuffed with bills all the time. It was supposed to be for emergencies, when pocket money was needed, and it had been the only way Rita could think of to leave money around for Stephen so that he wouldn't have to ask her for cigarette money. It was supposed to be a face-saver.

Rita suddenly recalled that it had been a good while since she had had to refill the money box. Until perhaps three months ago it had always been empty when she peeked into it. Now the crisp bills she had put in there hadn't been touched in a long time. That must mean that Stephen had made some sales and hadn't mentioned them to her.

"I see *A Chorus Line* is coming back to town again," Stephen said from behind the paper.

"Should we see it again?" she asked eagerly, getting up and clearing the table.

"Maybe. We'll see." He turned the page.

She caught a glimpse of his beautiful features before the newspaper blocked her view again, and her love for him turned like a heavy weight in the pit of her chest. How could she have been so tactless about the house? How could she ever hurt the man she adored, no matter how unintentionally?

Bending to put the plates in the dishwasher, Rita tried to think of some way to make it up to him. She had envisioned a quiet day at home. She was tired. But she would be happy to spend the day however he wanted. Just being with Stephen was satisfying to her. "What would you like to do today? You name it. Anything you want." He was like a little boy in so many ways, and she liked babying him.

"Anything, huh?" His voice sounded amused, but he didn't put down the paper. "I thought you were wiped out and wanted to stay home. Sounds like you had a hell of a week, what with the new line and all."

"I had a good sleep." She smiled at his knees, all that she

could see of him at the moment. "Would you like to go for a drive? Maybe to Sausalito. Or maybe we could go to Mt. Tamalpais." She crossed her fingers at the last suggestion, knowing he would want to hike up to the top. "Or let's go shopping. You need some new shirts. My treat."

He lowered the paper to his lap. "How about Muir Woods? I'd like to see those redwoods again. Maybe we can run down some deer." He made a comically evil face. "How about it? We could eat at that place in Sausalito afterward, the one you like."

"That sounds wonderful. If we have the time, we could get those shirts, too. But I have to stop in at the lab for a little while first, okay? I won't be long. We could go by on the way."

He put the paper down and frowned, but he didn't look annoyed at all. "Really? They work you too hard. You won't be too tired afterward?"

Rita felt a tug at his consideration. Other husbands would hate the thought of hanging around while their wives worked, but Stephen never complained when she asked him to go in with her on Saturdays. He was really unbelievably sweet.

He got up, walked across the room, and kissed her lightly on the cheek. "Give me five minutes to get ready."

She heard the hiss of the shower and finished cleaning up. The cooling coffee cake was still sitting on the counter, forgotten.

Knowing she'd feel a queasy protest from her stomach later, she cut out a wedge and began to eat.

CHAPTER 17

Thea put down her fork and looked at Olivia over a centerpiece of white roses and slender green ferns. She was about to speak when the waiter appeared with noiseless efficiency to refill their coffee cups.

Olivia smiled a thank-you and sipped at the hot coffee gingerly. The muscles in her sculptured face felt tense from betraying none of the emotions she was experiencing. The week had seemed to last forever. Thea hadn't returned to San Francisco until late last night, and both of their schedules were too full today to stretch out this lunch break as long as Olivia would have liked.

She felt her friend's disturbed eyes on her and dropped the polite smile she'd held for the departing waiter. "I feel like hell, but I'll live, Thea. Don't look at me that way."

"Actually, you look marvelous. A little red at the eye to the discerning observer, but quite wonderful."

Olivia felt a smile forming again. "So Mark told me. Before he left, that is." She looked away briefly, reliving the moment when he had walked out of her house so firmly.

Thea shook her sleek head and patted her brown hair, held fast by the inevitable clip at the nape of her neck. "No, I mean you look unusually stunning. Better than you looked when I saw you last Friday. You're absolutely glowing, darling."

Olivia passed a hand over her eyes. "Like a woman in love, right?" She brushed nonexistent crumbs from her blond-on-blond silk and cashmere separates. She had been photographed for *Newsweek* earlier that morning in her office, and she knew she looked good. Looking good was her business, with or without Mark Lyman.

She set the coffee cup down carefully in its saucer, bitterness tightening her lips. "Damn it, Thea, after waiting so long for that man, I had to push him. I couldn't seem to help myself. We could have had the whole weekend together, and if he got his show, at least another beautiful, delicious month. But I couldn't wait. I couldn't let things develop naturally. I wanted to know that he was there to stay."

She stared at her friend, pausing long enough to control her voice. "And damn Mark, too," she hissed softly. "Damn his stupid pride!"

Thea took out her cigarette case, helped herself, and started to offer a cigarette to Olivia. Then, remembering that Olivia had quit, she apologized. They had both tried to stop so many times. In the years that they had known each other, close to a thousand dollars had changed hands in earnest bets over who had the greatest self-control. Thea didn't mind losing; Olivia looked as if she could use a cigarette. "Will it bother you if I smoke?"

"No. I'm used to it now. Go ahead."

After exhaling deeply, Thea plunged on with what was uppermost in her mind since Olivia had finished recapping her night with Mark. "But why does it have to be everything or nothing at all? Why can't you simply go on seeing each other on a more-or-less casual basis? He's got things to do. You've got things to do. You can weekend in New York with him, if he's going back there after his show. He can come out here. It doesn't even have to cost him a dime. Miles takes the company jet to New York frequently. Mark could catch a ride with him. What's wrong with that? Frankly, it sounds perfect to me. Who needs a man hanging around all the time?"

Olivia shook her head, her blue eyes flashing ice and pain. "Because that's not the way things work with us. It's always been everything or nothing at all. Don't you remember? When I went to Europe with you, there was no question that it was only a vacation from him for either of us. Either I was going to live on his terms, or we were through."

"So it's become a contest of wills, is that it?" Thea asked, not pretending to understand but probing for an explanation. "Live his way or yours?" She laughed shortly. "Well, darling, I say he's a bit of a fool not to choose your way, if that's what it's all about. I suppose he's still living in some ghastly slum, in the name of art?"

Olivia refused to be drawn into any side issues. She and Thea had to be back at her office in less than an hour. Marlissa was coming up to discuss the new line, and Olivia had yet to work out a way to approach her other friend about the possibility that someone in Marlissa's department was stealing and probably selling their all-important formulas. She still found it impossible to believe that Marlissa herself was in any way responsible. But the scan of the final laboratory analysis on her desk this morning had confirmed her fears—Riviera's latest line was a carbon copy of their own. Olivia felt exhausted. She was finding that there were some things that money couldn't buy, not any amount of money. Time, for one thing. And love, for another.

"It's more than a contest of wills, Thea," Olivia said hurriedly. She felt an urgent need to unburden herself about Mark, only now aware of how much she had depended upon the Friday-night meeting to bring them back together permanently. But the confusion in her own mind kept the words from flowing easily. "Mark is death on compromise about anything that's important to him. You know that. When I left him to go to Europe with you, I had no reason ever to expect to see him again. He understood why I had to go, of course. But understanding isn't the same as accepting. All he ever accepted was that I didn't love him enough to go on living like that. At the time I thought he might be right. What the hell did I know? I was barely twenty-two at the time. Mark was the only man I'd ever loved, and I'd read all the romantic novels. If you love someone and it's the real thing, you live on love and your hovel becomes a palace. Well, his studio was a nightmare, and I hated being broke as much as I'd hated it when I was living with my mother and stepfather. With Mark, I was happy at moments and miserable at other times." She watched Thea snuff out what was left of her cigarette and tasted the smoke with acute longing, remembering her regretted moment of weakness in her office Friday, and looked away.

"Go on," Thea said encouragingly.

Olivia watched a waiter cross the room with a silver tray laden with delicate pastries. "I suppose I thought that if Mark was willing to let me go without a fight, if he wouldn't promise to compromise his art just enough to get a job so we could live decently, he didn't really love me, either. That's where I was when I went away with you, Thea." She looked directly at her friend. "I'd already turned down a chance to have a shot at the movies, and I had one serious love affair under my belt. I thought I knew what love wasn't.

"When I met Jean-Pierre, all those romantic novels came

crashing back at me. He had it all. More than beauty and enormous wealth. He seemed to have a purpose, to know exactly who he was and where he was going. He seemed to have the same burning passion for his work that Mark had, but he already had reached the pinnacle of success. He was beyond compromise, for either of us. And I did love him." She shot a quick, defensive glance at her friend, whose face betrayed a faint cynicism. "For a while I did love him. It took me a while to realize that I didn't know Jean-Pierre at all. He never wanted me to know him. It wasn't necessary that I know him to fulfill his needs. And for myself. . . ." She shrugged. "I suppose I was simply filling in the blanks in our relationship so that I could live out a beautiful, lovely dream.

"I can't tell you what it was like, living in Meiringen after that first year or so." Olivia glanced at her gold braided watch. "It doesn't matter. Not now. The important thing was that once I saw Mark in New York I knew that whatever I had had with Jean-Pierre was going to be over if I stayed in Mark's studio five minutes longer. He was hurt when I left him again. And again he understood my going but couldn't accept it. Thea, I swear to you that I returned to Switzerland determined to make my marriage work. I had no illusions then about being able to keep Mark on the side. Mark wouldn't have tolerated it, even if I were able to keep an affair from Jean-Pierre."

Thea tapped another cigarette out of the pack. "But none of that matters now. Jean-Pierre died. In a plane accident, remember? No fault of yours. You're a free woman. Mark isn't married. And here you are, after so long, still apart because neither of you can live with the other's assets or limitations. What are you going to do? Try to forget him again? Or live like a nun in the slim hope he'll someday make it and he won't be reduced to living off you?"

For the first time since they had met for lunch, Olivia's whole face eased into a real smile. "Exactly."

Thea looked at her dubiously. "Another beautiful, lovely dream?"

The smile became more radiant. "More than that." She had planned to reveal her strategy to Thea, had been leading up to this point from the time they had entered the restaurant. But suddenly she felt a great reluctance to tell Thea about the phone call she had made earlier. There was time to talk about it later, when things started moving. It had proved to be absurdly simple, after all. On reflection through her lonely weekend, she had remembered that she had a name and a fortune at her disposal. There were great numbers of people in important positions who would welcome the opportunity to please her.

The Dakota, while it was not insignificant, was not the finest showcase for an emerging artist with a brilliant future. If there had been the slightest doubt in Olivia's mind about the quality of Mark's work, she wouldn't have dared the most subtle, skillful manipulation. But Mark was a genius, with freshness and creativity, a master craftsman who had reason to have confidence in his talent. She was certainly not the only one to realize that.

She had met James Lacy a long time ago, in Los Angeles. Mark had prepared some paintings to show him at a starving-artists' show in Westwood Village, near UCLA. Lacy had commented on Mark's work, quite favorably. She had begged Mark to pursue the contact as Lacy became more and more recognized in the art world. But Mark had insisted that he was only scratching the surface of his potential at the time and had nothing yet to show the great man. Olivia knew now that Mark had been wiser than she, but she also suspected that Mark would never himself make use of the brief encounter to further his career. He wanted the world to come to him, to recognize his talent without his intervention.

But since then Olivia had met Lacy on a number of occasions: benefits, charity drives, the dinner celebrating the opening of the new Dali collection at the San Francisco Museum of Art. He was a discreet and sophisticated man, and he had approached Olivia twice on donating a wing to the Impressionists' museum he wanted to build in Sausalito.

Lacy had been delighted to hear from her. The conversation had gone perfectly. They discussed the possibility of her contribution, Olivia pretending confusion about whether to name the wing after herself, MagnifiScent, or perhaps Jean-Pierre, who had already donated large sums of money to art museums in Europe. When Mark's name was mentioned, Olivia did it with cunning and tact. There was no more than the hint of a suggestion that a one-man show in the best San Francisco gallery would affect Olivia's decision to contribute to Lacy's cause in the least. Yet by the time she had replaced the receiver of her silver phone in its cradle, she knew that Mark would soon be a happy man. It was a step—a small step, but one that she was sure would lead him back to her door. This time to stay.

"Olivia?" Thea stared at her friend with a troubled expression.

Again Olivia hesitated. She wanted to talk to Thea about what she had done, even ask for Thea's help in mapping out a campaign to elevate Mark to worldwide recognition swiftly and without the slightest possibility of being accused in any way of participating in his change of fortune. That was the one part in her plan that terrified her. If Mark ever suspected. . . . She brushed the fear away. She'd see to it that he never did. "Forget it, Thea." She shook her head. She realized she couldn't afford to reveal herself, not even to her closest friend. In fact, Thea could be her safety guide, could unknowingly play the role of a miner's caged bird. If Thea suspected Olivia's manipulations at any stage of Mark's growing popularity, Olivia would know quickly to cover her tracks still more.

She glanced at her watch more significantly. "It's all right, really. I feel better already. I found out the one thing I needed to find out. Mark still loves me. Nothing's changed between us. He'll have his show at the Dakota, it will be a huge success, and before you know it, he'll be hanging on all the best walls and I'll be wishing for more closet space."

Thea laughed. "I see you have it all figured out. And what if he has the show and nobody shows?" Her face lightened with understanding. "But that couldn't happen, could it? I myself have a wall or two that's screaming out for the work of a dedicated artist." She speared a wedge of her forgotten tart. "You get an *A* for patience, and we'll grade you on luck later on."

CHAPTER 18

Tugging the collar more tightly around her neck, Thea huddled inside her camel's-hair coat and dashed across Market Street toward her pale yellow Rolls Corniche.

The street was mobbed with shoppers on their way home to prepare dinner. Thea noticed a sullen-faced young man in a leather jacket and faded, tight jeans leaning against a shop window not far from her car. His thick black hair was wind tumbled and his hands were deep in the pockets of the jacket. He was eyeing the convertible steadily. Thea fumbled for the car keys as she reached the door on the driver's side, trying at the same time to balance the box and the bag she carried.

For a moment their eyes met, and Thea felt a familiar tightness in her throat. He was a handsome boy, a touch too lean and hungry for her tastes but with an arrogance and masculinity she had come to equate with sexual appeal.

Thea unlocked the door, put her packages on the backseat, and eased behind the driver's seat. She looked again at the leather-jacketed youth, annoyed to find that a part of her wanted to throw caution to the wind and invite him home with her.

She started the engine, waited until the light changed to green, and drove past the boy with a last hungry glance. She felt deflated. This unneccesary shopping trip had been largely motivated by a need to distract herself from just such temptation. It had been a hell of a week—a hell of a month, actually. She was up to her ears in problems that basically should have been none of her concern, and she had yet to sit down and figure out her puzzling weekend with Everett in Los Angeles. Some people drank at such moments, others took pills or overate, and she. . . .

In the rearview mirror she could see the boy still standing against the empty storefront. He had turned his head away, looking, no doubt, for new prey.

Thea held the wheel steady and followed Market Street all the way to Portola Drive. As she neared St. Francis Wood, where Marlissa lived, she slowed and impulsively took a left turn.

Part of her sudden decision to visit Marlissa stemmed from a desire to settle once and for all the question of whether Marlissa was in any way involved with the espionage at work. But the greater motivation came from a need to distract herself a little longer in the hope that her terrible temptation to find a man for the evening would eventually pass. She didn't completely understand why she was so controlled by these urges, which she was beginning to classify as self-destructive and exceedingly dangerous. Why, for that matter, if the longings were simply sexual, couldn't they be satisfied by Daniel or other men she dated? The term *forbidden fruit* crossed her mind, but she didn't care to ponder the meaning of that, either.

After Beverly Hills, St. Francis Wood was only moderately obvious about being an exclusive, expensive area in which to live. The homes were rather close together. Land had a different meaning in San Francisco than in L.A. It was more precious here, and less of it was allotted to even the most costly dwelling.

Thea turned left at The Circle, the small park on San Anselmo, drove past the fountain, and made another left on Marlissa's street. She had only been to the house once before. Marlissa was somewhat reclusive about her home life.

Thea had no trouble finding the house. It resembled a small gingerbread cottage from the street, with bushes and vines and one or two massive trees obstructing the view of the rest of the house beyond the small thatched roof. To the casual stranger driving through St. Francis Wood, Marlissa's house looked tiny, but beyond the confusion of greenery it was large and elegant and had a rare air of privacy.

She parked in the driveway behind Marlissa's car, both gratified and vaguely disturbed to see that her friend was at home and apparently alone. Now that she was here, she had no idea how she could conduct this interrogation.

In Olivia's office earlier that week, nothing had surfaced about the theft of formulas, the subject uppermost on Olivia's and her own mind. It was a sticky subject, and Thea was tempted to get back in her car and leave before she was noticed.

To nurse any suspicion about Marlissa was hideous and unworthy of the threesome who had been friends throughout the entire development of MagnifiScent. There was something about Marlissa that forbade so much as the suggestion of dishonor. In many ways Marlissa Deloffre was an anomaly in business. She retained the straightforward, simple, puristic intellectualism of a scientist and the quiet, somewhat humble demeanor of the farm people of her homeland.

Marlissa was also human, and a woman, and Thea was sophisticated and even bitchy enough to understand the multitude of factors that motivated people to do despicable things, deeds for which they would never be suspected. There had to be a part of Marlissa that resented Olivia deeply, however unfair and illogical such a resentment might be. After all, Olivia had walked in and taken over. No one really appreciated being taken over, not even when the act brought everything someone thought she wanted. Without Olivia there would be no MagnifiScent, and Marlissa would be just another bright young chemist working for someone else, drawing a modest salary and most likely still living with her family or perhaps with that boy she had been going with in Switzerland. Now she had power, prestige, money, and an enormous laboratory over which she was completely in charge. As a scientist alone, this had to be a paradise for Marlissa. Her slightest creative whim was catered to immediately, and she was free to draw from a bottomless well of money to make certain that any tool of her trade was instantly available to her staff and herself.

Thea got out of the car and took a moment to light a bracing cigarette. She stopped herself from silently enumerating what Marlissa had because of Olivia and put her attention on what the girl didn't have because of or in contrast to Olivia DeSante.

Okay, she didn't have the company that had once belonged to her family. Regardless of the overall improvement of everyone's situation, the company was definitely Olivia's. Would that possibly grate on Marlissa at rare moments? Wasn't ambition a part of the girl's great motivation to have worked so tirelessly in her shop at home? Why wasn't it possible that Marlissa had once dreamed of being where her own efforts had instead put Olivia?

And there was more, if one could manage to be objective enough to study the facts. Olivia was an extraordinary woman. She was unquestionably beautiful. She had enviable style and charm. She was sophisticated and witty. The public had made her one of their golden idols. Millions knew her name, her face. Television and the press clamored for her image and words.

In comparison Marlissa was a rather plain girl who hadn't even made good use of the very products she had created. She was not sophisticated in the least, and shyness masked her natural wit. She was relatively unknown outside of the business. When information was sought regarding Marlissa's own masterpieces, Olivia was the one who was consulted. In a way Olivia fronted for Marlissa and therefore reaped the rewards of fame that Marlissa might have felt were rightly her due.

On the surface Marlissa would not be suspected of such resentment. She seemed instead to have her thoughts centered on solving the problems raised by her work, without a trace of personal ambition or avarice. But who knew? As well as Thea thought she knew Marlissa, did anyone ever really know anyone else? Would Marlissa or even Olivia look at her, for example, and know or even suspect the sick desire that clawed at Thea's insides, the secret life that thrilled and shamed her so deeply?

Thea crushed the cigarette under her foot and started for the house. She was about to knock when the door flew open.

For a moment Marlissa's face wore a glow and excitement that elevated it to near-beauty. Then, recognizing her visitor, the face lost a trace of its unusual animation, although the younger woman smiled with surprise and welcome.

"Thea! I thought you were . . . no matter. What a surprise. Do come in."

Wondering who it was that Marlissa had expected at her door, Thea walked into the living room and sat down. "I hope I haven't caught you at a bad time, Marlissa. I was just driving home and had this utterly desperate need for a drink and a friendly face. In that order. Do you mind?"

"Not at all. What may I bring you?" Marlissa started for the bar, took a quick, discreet look at Thea, and then glanced just as discreetly at the clock on the solid oak mantle.

"A Scotch on the rocks would be lovely." Thea caught and considered each of Marlissa's glances. Much as she liked Marlissa, once again Thea found herself somewhat uncomfortable with her. There was something shrewdly analytical about this woman from Switzerland that made Thea feel naked before her. If anyone at all suspected her own depths of despair, Thea thought it might be Marlissa. She instantly regretted her use of the word *desperate* in connection with her need for a drink and a friendly face. Then she wondered at her own need for secrecy—wouldn't it be a relief to blurt out her troubled emotions to a sympathetic ear? Yet she couldn't imagine baring herself that way, saying, "Marlissa, I'm lonely and frightened. I run to strangers to escape myself, and why did it feel so damned, irritatingly good to be with Everett last weekend? Have I gone the long way around only to come home again?"

Marlissa brought the drink and silently handed it to her friend, her eyes watchful and mutely concerned. "Is everything all right?" she inquired softly.

"Yes, of course." Thea smiled, took a drink, and felt the panic fade away. What was wrong with her? She reminded herself why she had come to Marlissa's house and forced her mind back to the woman who was settling down on the lovely Victorian couch next to her, a pale amber cordial in her hand.

Her first thought was that Marlissa looked unusually attractive. She realized that she had almost never seen her wearing a noticeable amount of makeup, and that she was very nearly pretty with it on. She was also quite appealingly dressed. The simply but beautifully cut black wool dress looked like a Dejac or perhaps a Pierre Cardin creation, and it brought out Marlissa's good, lean figure. She was also wearing one of her perfumes rather heavily, and the silver and turquoise jewelry at her wrist and neck lent an exotic, feminine effect.

Again Thea felt curiosity about whom Marlissa had hoped to find at her door. "I do like this house, Marlissa. It looks like you." She glanced comfortably around, evaluating the European furnishings she suspected had come across the ocean with Marlissa. They had the look of family heirlooms, many of them handmade. It was a superb room with a home-spun richness that combined elegance and quaint individuality. Thea found herself thinking that if Marlissa would just loosen up, be unashamedly herself, the personal style that would emerge would be positively marvelous and chic. With more force than she had said it the first time, she repeated her comment. "It looks like you."

Marlissa's face struggled between showing shy pleasure and

an adolescent self-consciousness. "Thank you," she said faintly.

Now that she was here, Thea knew she would never, never state the suspicions on her mind. She knew she was neither clever enough to do it well nor cold enough to be indifferent about her lack of tact. So she ingeniously invented a reason for her unexpected appearance. "Olivia saw Mark last weekend. Did she tell you?"

Marlissa nodded, her sharp eyes displaying concern. "We've hardly had more than a moment alone in weeks. This new line is taking away all our time, especially with the possibility that someone has access to our formulas. She did mention seeing Mark, however, and I noticed that she seemed reluctant to talk about the meeting."

Thea let the perfect opening for some careful questions about the theft go by, silently cursing herself for her timidity. But now that she had broached the subject of Olivia and Mark, she welcomed the opportunity to pursue it further. "She wanted him to stay—permanently, I mean—and the bastard walked out on her.

"It was that old thing between them, I gather," Thea continued angrily. "If you love me you'll give up all this and live on my level. Actually, darling, in all fairness, I suppose that's the position of them both. Of course it's utter nonsense to imagine that Olivia would go back to his standard of living, but Mark seems just as adamant about not being elevated to a little basic comfort until he can afford it himself. What a primitive attitude! I don't understand him. Not all men would be so foolish. I know rather a few who would appreciate nothing more than to live in the comfort Olivia would gladly supply, and I don't mean gigolos, either. Why should an artist have to suffer to do good work? Many of the best artists had their patrons, and who knows what Rembrandt would have turned out if he hadn't had a wife who cooked him hot meals and fluffed his pillows for him at night?" Having run down for the moment, Thea took a swallow of her Scotch and lit a cigarette.

Marlissa smiled. "I don't think, perhaps, it is quite so simple as you would wish it. I know many such men, men who would be destroyed by living in such an arrangement. Women as well: it is not truly a sexist issue, I do not believe. But society has made it more acceptable for a woman to live on the earnings of her husband, sometimes even to rest on his accomplishments. One is introduced as the wife of the doctor or the wife of the bootmaker, and she assumes the status his profession elicits. Women have accepted this role for centuries and it is only very recently that they have objected to it as demeaning to themselves as individuals." Marlissa sipped at her amaretto and took another almost-imperceptible glance at the mantel clock.

"For a man it is quite different, even today," she continued. "To live in the shadow of a more successful woman is beyond a humiliation, it is a daily reflection on his inability to provide for her in the manner to which she is accustomed and that she obviously requires. It has often occurred to me that an artist must, by the nature of his chosen work, have a strong, seemingly impenetrable ego. He must confront a canvas or a piece of marble—or a blank page or whatever his medium demands—with a solid conviction that he alone can bring to it a presence, a statement that will have meaning to others. In the face of such an endeavor, it is not unreasonable that he dare not surround himself with the evidence that he has so far, in the eyes of the one he loves, been in any way less than successful."

She paused to put her glass down. "I have never met Olivia's Mark, but from all I've heard, he takes himself and his art with the utmost seriousness. I would suspect that he is completely unable to come to her until he has attained undisputed recognition. I find his position wholly understandable, if not commendable."

She smiled with that same characteristic shyness. "And only not commendable because perfection would be the ability to rise beyond all this and have the self-assurance to be unaffected by the wealth and success of anyone else. But few of us ever reach this ideal. One who has would earn my awed respect, but I would be terrified by his saintly aloofness."

Thea pondered Marlissa's words, unprepared for the response she had received to her hastily constructed excuse for appearing on her doorstep to beg a drink. She couldn't deny that Marlissa had made a great deal of sense, but she felt an almost childish resentment at having Mark's position so logically stated.

"I understand what you're saying, love, but I hate it, anyway." She finished her Scotch and grimaced. "Olivia's dying to be with Mark. It's too absurd for words that she should follow him barefoot to some artist's ghetto until he gets around to making something of himself, and everything would be so wonderfully simple if he'd just plant his shoes under her bed and his smelly paintbrushes in her greenhouse." She felt a tinge of surprise at her longing for a storybook happy ending for her friend. How deep, she wondered, did her carefully cultivated cynicism really go?

"That's not very heavy or psychological, I realize," she went on, "but God, Olivia deserves a little pleasure for a change, doesn't she? For all that she's got, what does she have, damn it? What do any of us have?" she asked in a rare moment of unconscious honesty. She smoothed her face at once, then drained her glass. She knew she should go. It was obvious that Marlissa was waiting for someone special.

A wave of curiosity replaced Thea's mood of outrage over Olivia's love affair. She very much wanted to know the identity of Marlissa's caller. He—because it had to be a man; one didn't look the way Marlissa was looking unless it was a man—had to be someone special. Thea knew that Marlissa rarely dated, that she probably still was suffering over her decision to leave that Swiss carpenter behind. True, Marlissa had not suffered alone, had in fact surprised Thea with an active social life since coming to San Fransciso, but men, to Thea's knowledge, had not been a significant part of that life. Or at least not a man who brought such an obvious sparkle to Marlissa's naturally rather somber eyes.

"Would you care for another drink?"

Thea was on the point of accepting the polite offer when her mood shifted again. It was just growing dark outside. Marlissa's date would be arriving at any moment, she was certain, and she no longer had the heart to magnify Marlissa's understated nervousness. Much as she admitted to a crude curiosity, she knew it was time to leave.

"Got to run. I'm already late." Thea stood up decisively, making the best of her noble sacrifice by giving herself a mental pat on the head. "I've got to take my horse for a run. I haven't gotten over there all week."

She was almost to the door when she heard a car pull to a stop in front of the house. Thea felt a quick moment of elation. She had done her best to be a good and sensitive friend, and now the matter was out of her hands. Even her best efforts to make a getaway would be detained by a mandatory introduction to the mystery man. She noticed the panicked look on Marlissa's face, then saw the intelligent features resign themselves to the inevitable. There was even the suggestion of pride on her face at the thought of the man she would be momentarily presenting to her friend. This, Thea thought, must be some hunk of man.

She stood aside while Marlissa answered the sharp rap at her door. She peered over Marlissa's dark hair and saw blondness, good shoulders. The greeting was warm and the voice nice and husky.

"Thea, I'd like you to meet my friend Brad Cavell. Brad, may I introduce my dear friend Thea Wallace." Marlissa stepped to one side, her face pink-cheeked and happy.

Thea stared at Brad Cavell mutely. Then, catching herself, she worked her features into a cordial smile and mouthed an appropriate greeting.

Brad smiled broadly, and if he understood Thea's connection with MagnifiScent, he didn't reveal his knowledge. "Nice to meet you," he said blandly.

Thea said her farewell hastily and started for her car. She knew her own cheeks were flaming as brightly as Marlissa's, but for a completely different reason.

She got into her car and backed it carefully to the street. She drove slowly out of St. Francis Wood, but at the corner, instead of turning left toward her home, she instead made a right turn, heading the car in the direction of Olivia's stately house in Pacific Heights. She had to see Olivia right away. She had known that the moment she had seen Brad Cavell.

She had recognized him instantly. Brad Cavell was Jason Blendes's nephew.

And Jason Blendes, Thea knew, was the sole owner of none other than Riviera Cosmetics.

CHAPTER 19

Alone in the roomy four-poster bed for the moment, Marlissa listened to the muffled hiss of the shower in the adjoining bath and wondered if what she felt for Brad was love.

Certainly she felt something.

It was really an odd question, she decided, considering this last hour when they had rumpled this bed so thoroughly together, this bed her own grandfather had carved for his bride more than a half-century before. Her next thought belied an unconscious prejudice—in this New World one did not have to love in order to perform the motions of love. Catching herself, Marlissa admitted that love wasn't essential in her old world, either.

She contemplated the structure of her thoughts the same way she studied formulas, taking them first in their individual parts and then studying them as a whole. Why had she raised the issue of love? Brad had not mentioned love.

"I want you," he had said earlier, kissing her lingeringly at the door he had not after all exited through.

Not *I love you*.

Love was a concept of her own that came naturally to a woman who had never before made love without feeling that emotion toward her partner. But was it love she had felt in Brad's arms, or simply need?

The shower droned on, and Marlissa imagined Brad under its splinterish stream. He was quite beautiful naked, with smooth skin pulled taut over a muscular frame, the fine hairs on his body glinting like white gold. There was no mistaking the fact that he excited her. Even now, while she was still warm from his embrace, Marlissa felt a rush of desire for him. She reached a hand to her other arm, rubbing the soft flesh harshly, wondering at the dichotomy of impulses that made a physical lust translate into an iciness in her skin. And how was it that she could possibly have disliked the sex she had just experienced and still want him again?

She examined her feelings briefly, wondering what it was she had disliked. Brad had been considerate, passionate, and skillful. He had invested as much energy in arousing her as in satisfying himself. He had been successful, too, and she thought she could still detect the faint echo of her own moaning acknowledgment that he was an adroit lover. Had she really disliked the passion he aroused in her—or herself for being aroused?

The tempo of the shower changed abruptly, slowing almost to a drip and then crashing down again furiously. So Brad liked to follow up with a cold shower. Would she come to know all of his little idiosyncrasies? A cold rinse meant he would soon be back. Should she cover her nakedness with a dressing gown and get out of the bed? Or would he expect her to be waiting under the sheets, naked and warm?

Annoyed with herself for worrying over the etiquette of their moment of intimacy rather than its meaning in her life, Marlissa pulled the covers up to her shoulders and turned on her side, facing the door behind which Brad still endured his cold shower. He had turned on the little rose-painted lamp next to the bed when he got up, and in its fanning light she took in the comfortable clutter of her bedroom.

Although larger and certainly more elegant, it still resembled her room at home. Most of the furnishings had come from that room, and they were things she loved, things that made her less homesick for the land of her birth. Even the little oval rug her mother had woven for her when Marlissa was a child was at the foot of the bed, its intricate pattern of the snow-capped Jungfrau mountains overlooking a slice of the Bernese Oberland where she had lived for so long. The massive and beautifully carved seventeenth-century south German armoire had been passed down through her father's family, and it was still another link with a past she never wanted to forget completely.

Even this house had been a concession to the stubborn part of her that longed for the old and familiar. Regardless of its overall size and value, each room seemed snug and cozy inside, European rather than American. She had originally looked for a much smaller house—she was still disturbed by the wastefulness of such space for one woman alone—but this cheerfully incongruous home had captivated her as soon as she had seen it, nestled in vines and bushes, hiding its opulence from the street.

Of all San Francisco, St. Francis Wood alone gave a hint of being in touch with nature. The houses here had a bit of breathing space between them at least, unlike Olivia's home in Pacific Heights. Marlissa was happy in her house, yet it faintly embarrassed her too—in it she was a creature of parts, clinging to the known, the familiar, the cherished, and yet aware that she was hiding behind an address and a large-enough investment to prove that she had moved on to bigger and better things.

The shower finally stopped hissing. She could hear Brad moving around the bathroom, working the faucets, flushing the toilet. In a moment he would be out, and she was not yet ready to deal with him.

Marlissa had no idea what they would say to each other or what he expected of her. Was she supposed to be casual and witty or bold and seductive? He was a stranger, really, and she was unused to taking strangers to her bed. Had he seemed a stranger earlier, when he had kissed her and whispered his need of her?

It had been a dazzling week. Starting with the ballet on Friday night, she and Brad had been together every free moment since. He had picked her up early on Saturday and taken her on a long ride through Marin County, to a charmingly terraced restaurant where they lunched outside under a bright red canopy that flapped in the wind. He loved to drive and was boyishly proud of his new white Excalibur, and Marlissa appreciated the masterful way he handled the car. She liked men who drove well, as if a man who controlled a car with style and ease might handle a woman with the same expertise.

He'd also taken her out on Sunday, for still another long drive and then dinner at a wharf restaurant. And Monday he had called again, suggesting an early dinner downtown and bar-hopping in North Beach afterward, to hear some live jazz, another passion of Brad's, one she happened to share.

Tuesday she had been firm about staying home and catching up on her domestic chores. Except for a woman who came in and cleaned once a week and a biweekly laundry service, she took care of the big house herself, and Brad's company, however charming and novel, had put her behind schedule. Wednesday night he had taken her to a disappointingly boring play and afterward to a lively disco for some energetic dancing and entirely too much drinking. Thursday it was a long dinner at an East Indian restaurant, where he spoke about his recent divorce and his children—Brad Jr., seven, and Kierra, almost five—for the first time.

Unlike Ernst, Brad liked to talk, and yet she felt as if she knew very little about him. It wasn't until a week of steady dating had passed before she had even known he had been married and was a father. While he seemed appealingly candid about the dissolution of his nine-year marriage, he didn't offer any real glimpse into the dynamics of the failure. He seemed far more determined about assuring Marlissa that the divorce, painful as it had been, hadn't soured him on marriage.

Something about the way he had stressed that point immediately changed the atmosphere between them. Marlissa knew that very young people arrived at the thought of marriage after finding themselves in love, but older couples considered the feasibility of permanency much earlier in their relationship. The suitability of a date as a marriage partner had to be established first. Marlissa knew that Brad had already done such thinking about her or he would have mentioned his divorce more casually. And Marlissa also sensed that she had been placed in the column of possibilities. This fact surprised her. She would have expected Brad to be attracted to a more glamorous woman. His tastes were not sedate. The car, his manner of dressing, his own handsomeness evoked the image of someone like Olivia or Thea at his side. She didn't consider herself completely unattractive, but she knew that she had not yet begun to bring out her potential. Marlissa wondered if Brad fancied himself the kind of man who could make a woman bloom through his love. She found the possiblity appealing.

After their conversation and an excellent curry dinner, they had returned to her house. She had known then that he wanted to make love to her, but she wanted time alone to think. His kisses excited her, but she gently pushed him away. He had accepted her excuses about a particularly difficult day of work ahead after she agreed to go out with him again the next night.

Marlissa hadn't exaggerated the work waiting for her the next day, but for once her attention was diverted from her job. She weighed her emotions carefully on a scale that automatically discounted that part of her that was simply flattered by being courted by a man like Brad, and measured what remained with the eagle eye of a chemist over an eyedropper. Leaving Ernst geographically had not been the same as departing from him emotionally. She had not broken down and responded to his frequent letters, but he was on her mind daily. For the first time since coming to the United States, she had met a man who pushed Ernst from the center of her mind. That had to mean something significant. Perhaps it meant that what she felt for Brad was the faint stirring of something that would eventually grow into love.

The thought was exciting. Marlissa knew that loving Brad, being his wife, would give her the very life she had dreamed of from the moment Olivia had asked her to come to San Francisco. Brad would teach her how to fully enjoy her new life. She didn't exactly know how he earned his money other than that he was vice-president of a small supplies operation that fed into a parent business, but she did know that he lived well. He had not yet spoken at any length of his work, nor had he allowed her to speak of her own. He seemed to be the type of man who preferred to leave work at the office, which suited Marlissa perfectly. She gave entirely too much of herself to MagnifiScent and was happy to leave that world at the end of the day.

She had sat at her desk, an unread report in front of her, for once indifferent to her work. She thought of Brad's lips, which were rather on the thin side but very finely shaped. More than once her eyes had been drawn to those lips. She liked the way they moved over hers, how his tongue had sought her own. She liked the feel of his arms around her, the hard pressure of his body against her. She couldn't deny that she wanted Brad Cavell.

Tonight she would know if she loved him. In his arms she would discover if at last she could make this final move from the safe harbor of home to a new love. Briefly she wondered if Ernst might be experiencing such a metamorphosis. Had he found someone else? She could not imagine Ernst with another woman and she found the image childishly disturbing. She brushed the consideration from her mind and thought instead of what to wear tonight for Brad.

She had left work in a frenzy of excitement, eager to get ready, half-terrified that he might not come at the last moment and equally hopeful that he would call with some excuse. She was certain that other women entertained no such confusion of feelings. Other women seemed to handle this aspect of their lives with remarkable calm and practicality.

To get her mind off her nervousness, Marlissa busied herself by conducting an elaborate toilet, bathing, dressing, perfuming, making up as if she were the person she would have liked to be rather than the simple farm girl she still believed she was at heart. For all of her painstaking ritual, she was ready and waiting almost an hour before Brad was due.

Her initial reaction to the sound of a car pulling into her driveway had been heart-pounding excitement. The thought that he might be early, a possible indication that he was no more casual about this date than she, elated her. In a state of happy anticipation, she had thrown open the door without waiting for his knock. At the sight of Thea she had been momentarily devastated but managed to recover quickly.

Actually, she decided later while waiting for Brad's return from the shower, Thea's unexpected arrival had been a blessing in disguise. In shifting her thoughts to Olivia's problems with Mark, Marlissa regained a drop of perspective on herself. She was really not so terribly removed from her more sophisticated friends in the final distillation. They were three women who were essentially undergoing the same agonies of life. Olivia, who had everything, was a woman alone struggling to find and keep love. And Thea . . . Marlissa had often contemplated Thea with a degree of concern. Thea gave every indication of being one of those no-longer-so-rare women who seemed to enjoy her freedom above all. She dated constantly, seemed never to spend a moment alone, played at her job as if it were a hobby and knew perhaps even better than Olivia how to enjoy money. Thea had the time to live as she chose, while Marlissa and Olivia were virtually tied to work at least five days a week. Thea was wealthy, had three houses and a glamorous life. But Marlissa sensed a very real sadness behind Thea's cool brown stare and worried about her often.

She had kept her silence, too discreet ever to approach Thea until such time as Thea might come to her. But Thea frightened Marlissa, reminded her of that famous poem about the man who had everything and yet, to the amazement of all, was found dead by his own hand. Marlissa sensed a terrible loneliness in Thea, a quiet desperation. She had watched Thea carefully as they talked of Olivia's problems with Mark, and in doing so some of her own panic had eased. All women had crosses to bear, and really hers was quite moderate. She had a marvelous new man who wanted to take her to bed, and she would now gladly resign herself to the inevitable.

It had gone with surprising ease. They had dined and returned to her house. She had thought that Brad might possibly suggest his penthouse apartment downtown, but she saw that he was sensitive enough not to push too fast or insist on a declaration from her. They returned to her home as if after any date, and his statement about wanting her carried a feeling of hope rather than an ultimatum.

She had taken him to her bedroom without a shred of outward awkwardness. She had been nicely distracted by an avalanche of pure sexual excitement. She glowed with desire, the workings of her personal chemistry factory turned to maximum efficiency by the stroking of his hands on her body, his lips on hers, his tongue moving with slow deliberation over hers. She felt her clothing on her as a burden, the beautiful black wool dress, the lacy underthings she had purchased for such a time as this. Her skin ached to be relieved of clothing, to rub with uninhibited joy against Brad's harder flesh. By the time she led him to her bed, she felt her entire body yearning with desire.

Waiting for him to come back to her after his shower, Marlissa knew that she could find no fault with Brad as a lover, that any schism in her feelings about him came from herself. Not even Ernst had thrilled her this way. What had Ernst known of the subtleties of lovemaking? He was an unworldly man with little experience outside of what they had learned in each other's arms. His lovemaking had always been direct, considerate, and simplistic, made exciting by their love for each other and the closeness they shared that encouraged experimentation and even humor in their passions.

But Brad had known many women, and it gave him an inarguable advantage. He understood what it took to rouse a woman to spectacular heights. He knew how to use just the tips of his fingers to play on her senses, the tip of his tongue, as well, tracing patterns over her skin, the corners of her lips, the undersides of her breasts. He had known when to hold her so tightly it took her breath away, and when to be passive, tormentingly passive once he had aroused her, in order to force her to do things she had had no idea she was capable of doing.

Faintly aghast at the memory, Marlissa relived the moment when his maddening game of intense stimulation had abruptly led to a teasing withdrawal. He had held her against him, not quite on top of her body but rather to the side of it. He had left no doubt of his readiness to penetrate her, and she had completely lost her reluctance to hide her own receptivity. And then he had simply lain there until she could stand it no longer. Marlissa had thrown her body against his in a paroxysm of urgent desire that shocked her sensibilities but was too great to deny. And then, before she could withdraw in confusion or even return to her habitual modesty, Brad had thrust himself between her trembling legs, giving her exactly what her hungry body had demanded. She had cried out then—the sound had filled the room, shattered her senses, and, in some way Marlissa did not fully understand, saddened her with the knowledge that her body had its own wisdom and, after all, the question of love belonged in some alternate universe.

That orgasm had come swiftly and with stunning force, and it was only the first. He had left her for the shower in the adjoining room, leaving her to the privacy of her own troubled thoughts, to the question of love, only after he had provoked her into two others of at least equal strength.

Brad came slowly into the room, the steam following him like a private cloud. The towel still in his hand, he closed the door behind him, and the room was darker again. He looked very large in the dim light from the little rose-painted lamp, a blond giant with damp, pale curls and pale flesh.

Marlissa forced herself to look higher, as shy before his eyes as she was of staring too obviously at his body.

"Did you leave any hot water for me?" she asked with an attempt at casualness, making no move to leave the protective shield of the blanket. She was not afraid to stand naked before him, knowing that her undressed body was far more attractive than it appeared in clothing. She had the kind of slender build that hid its soft curves in anything less than the tightest of garments, which she would never think of wearing. Modesty kept the blanket pulled to her throat.

He nodded, a small smile playing at his lips. He came to the bed and slowly peeled back the cover, his eyes exploring her body with the familiarity and interest of a satisfied lover. He bent over and kissed her shoulder with something more than tenderness. "Don't take too long, Marlissa," he said without the smile.

Then, without looking at her any longer, he circled the bed

slowly to give her time to make a graceful exit from the room as he slipped into the other side of the four-poster.

Marlissa adjusted the shower and soaped herself languidly. The question of love would have to wait for another time.

CHAPTER 20

Justine Brandon sat at her desk in a haze of excitement, so gratified by the news that she couldn't think yet of how best to put it to work.

"Justine, I'm leaving for the day."

She looked up at the sound of Thea's voice. "Oh, is there anything special you need done?" she asked ingratiatingly, sure her boss knew as well as she that Justine knew to the finest detail what needed doing.

"No, nothing you don't know about. I'm lunching with Olivia, but if anything comes up, darling, say I've died or something. Postpone or whatever you have to do. I'll be back in the morning. Not too early, of course." With a wave and leaving a delicious cloud of Oli behind her, she was gone.

Perfect. Now Justine had the whole rest of the day to implement her plan—once she had one firmly in mind. Now that she knew that Marlissa was definitely the weak link, she would proceed with caution. And to think her information had come through a friendly socialite, of all people!

So far, so good. For weeks now Justine had been putting out discreet feelers in all directions, tapping every possible source so that an entire network of spies was keeping an eye on Marlissa Deloffre for her. But never had she expected such a rich return on her investment of bribes and promises. It was almost too good to be true that Marlissa was dating Brad Cavell! Could the chemist possibly be innocent of his reason for dating her? Well, if Marlissa was, Justine was not.

It would be like knocking down a difficult split in bowling:

one ball and good-bye, Marlissa; a second—sometime, somehow—and farewell, Thea.

She reached for the phone to call Donna Alonzo, one of the private secretaries who had a special genius for planting a scrap of gossip in exactly the right places.

"Ball one," she said, smiling into the phone.

It had started as a trickle and was now a bursting dam, gossip spreading wildly through the various departments of MagnifiScent's executive branch and its subdivisions. Justine heard it from a dozen lips. The tension in the top three floors of the modern white building with the bronze-tinted windows and silver-imprinted, wide gold awnings was intense.

"Marlissa Deloffre? Why, she started this company!"

". . . jealousy, I suppose. Still I wouldn't have believed . . ."

"Well, someone did it, and from what I hear . . ."

Justine ate her yogurt-and-fruit lunches at her office, loath to spend any time at all away from her desk. The rumors were music to her ears, balm to her tired soul. It had taken time, but now even Thea's eyes revealed doubt. Justine, through her informer, had found the final link—Brad Cavell. To actually know who it was that was behind the theft of the formulas! It was like panning a stream and finding gold.

For once even her mother had been satisfied with her efforts. That in itself was a major win. Justine had done her work well. Marlissa would either lose her job or, at the least, lose her exalted position at MagnifiScent. All by herself Justine had made room at the top. While it was true that she couldn't very well slip into Marlissa's shoes, she had ample experience to understand perfectly that an important shake-up would result from Marlissa's fall from grace. Thrown into the bargain would be the emotional state of Thea and Olivia. They would be ripe for welcoming a new "friend," and this time they would want someone with experience and drive. Thea would spend her time commiserating with Olivia, and Justine would quietly take over. It would happen just the way she planned. Knock down the building, then efficiently pick up the pieces.

Olivia could continue as queen for the day, and Justine didn't give a damn if Thea hung around as Olivia's lady-in-waiting.

Not when she, Justine Brandon, with a title and salary befitting her talents, became the power!

CHAPTER 21

Rita Vanalden stared at the Normandy Apartments through a film of unshed tears. It was an impressive building overlooking the wharf and Ghirardelli Square, newly renovated but retaining the classic Victorian style that gave San Francisco so much of its unforgettable charm.

What did it prove? she asked herself fiercely, unable to tear her eyes away fearing the woman, whoever she was, might conveniently walk through the entrance guarded by a uniformed doorman and confirm her hideous fears.

The light changed, and the impatient line of traffic behind Rita started clamoring to surge forward. She depressed the clutch, shifted from neutral to first, let up on the clutch and began to bear down on the accelerator. Stephen's old Chevy immediately stalled, and the car behind hers sounded its horn.

All the unshed tears accumulated during the past two days spilled over, blinding Rita's eyes and scalding her cheeks. She got the car going on the next try and drove with the flow of traffic without the slightest thought of where she was going or what she was doing.

For almost two days Rita had carried around the receipt for the month's apartment rental in her purse. It had curled between her billfold and her glasses case like a venomous snake. She had found it in a chance moment alone in her own apartment, while Stephen was supposedly seeing a movie. Stephen had called about the movie, but she had to work late. By the time she had left her lab, she had been actually looking forward to a rare evening alone in which to tidy up and go through the laundry accumulating in the bathroom hamper. By the time she had finished sorting the laundry, she was feeling less tired and reluctant to crawl into their big bed alone. Stephen wouldn't be home for at least another hour.

Usually she never invaded the privacy of his side of the oversize dresser they shared. The maid had instructions not to disturb any of Stephen's clutter and to leave his cleaned laundry out for him to put away. Stephen kept his drawers in an untidy state of confusion, but that was how he liked it. Rita was by nature orderly, taking pleasure in neatly stacked blouses and precisely folded sweaters. The odd bits of shirttails and socks caught in the almost-shut drawers captured her roving eye, and impulsively she opened Stephen's top drawer and almost guiltily went to work pairing compatible lengths of nylon and wool. She didn't dare make her intrusion too obvious, so she resisted her urge to bring order to the chaos she discovered.

The second drawer was even more cluttered. About to close it and conceal the eyesore, she happened to notice the cuff of one of her own plaid turtleneck shirts she liked to wear under a sweater on cold mornings. It nettled her that the maid hadn't noticed that it was her shirt when dividing the laundry. It was the size, of course, that had misled the woman into assuming it was Stephen's garment. Chagrined, Rita imagined it would be safe to remove the turtleneck—if Stephen hadn't noticed it when he had haphazardly stuffed his shirts away, it was unlikely he would notice its disappearance.

She had found the receipt under the shirt. It was crumpled but new-looking, and she had seen that it was a receipt at once. In her usual methodical fashion, all receipts went into a special file to be examined at tax time. She picked it out of the drawer with no special intuition.

At first she had stared at the bit of smoothed paper without comprehension, seeing that it was a rent receipt in Stephen's name for an apartment across town. It took a moment to go through the mental stages that began with noncomprehension and moved swiftly to frantic suspicion. Stephen—her Stephen—was obviously paying for an apartment near Ghirardelli Square. Paying an enormous price for this apartment, from the scribbled amount on the receipt. But why? Why did he need another apartment? How, for that matter, could he possibly afford to pay $1,400 for an apartment for any purpose?

She had sat down heavily on their bed, the scrap of paper balling in her fist, her face crumpled as she made an effort not to cry. Stephen—her Stephen—was keeping another apartment for the only possible reason men kept secret apartments. Stephen had a mistress.

She tried to talk herself out of the terrible suspicion. There must be some other reason. Perhaps Stephen had rented the apartment in his name for a client who was in transition between one house and another. Or . . . she searched her mind for an explanation, any explanation, but logic eliminated the jumble of possibilities one by one, until she was again left with only the first: that Stephen had another woman.

In an odd way Rita felt something akin to a perverse satisfaction at her conclusion. It was like wrestling with a difficult equation for a long time and feeling relieved at finally arriving at the correct answer. It had never completely made sense to her, Stephen's apparent love and devotion to her. Like a decimal in the wrong place or a figure in the wrong column, their relationship hadn't quite added up. This new revelation brought, in spite of a torrent of agony, a clarification that her pragmatic mind had previously sensed was lacking.

Stephen had married her because she represented security and comfort, was undemanding and generous. She offered the safety of mother and home and only the minor inconvenience of marital demands and insincere devotion. For love and excitement he had some beautiful sexpot installed comfortably close at hand, undoubtedly a woman who matched his perfect face, his spectacular body. She had to be lovely and cold, and perhaps they shared the joke that was called a wife, the joke that hid behind the respectable title of wife.

She hadn't cried then, had instead held it all inside, dropping the receipt into her purse as if hiding it away would erase it from her mind and therefore from reality. For two long days she had resisted the impulse to look at it again. She had feigned sleep when Stephen came home, supposedly from his movie, and other than to stumble over her tongue when they were together, she had not revealed her knowledge to Stephen in any way.

This afternoon she had given in to compulsion and driven by the Normandy Apartments on her way home. Perhaps her outbreak of tears was healthier than her previous control.

She studied her face in the visor mirror before parking in front of her own apartment building. Her eyes were a little red rimmed, but she doubted that Stephen would notice. Her feet felt leaden as she walked from the elevator, but her voice was normal as she stopped to pass a few words with Milton Bannerman in the hallway outside her door. Mrs. Bannerman had died several months earlier of cancer, and Rita effortlessly transcended her own unhappiness to speak to this nice man's sorrow. She had been promising herself to ask him over for dinner some evening, and impulsively she asked him to join them for the roast she had put in the oven earlier. She didn't really want to be alone with Stephen.

Rita unlocked her door slowly after suggesting Milton give her an hour to throw things together. She watched him walk back to his lonely apartment, sympathy for him blending with pity for herself. Time would solve Milton's problem. He was nice-looking, younger than his wife had been and comfortably fixed. Eventually he would remarry. Rita judged him to be no more than fifty, not even too old to begin another family, really. The world was filled with women looking for husbands. It was different for her. If she divorced Stephen—how long could she live with him, knowing what she knew?—there would be no one for her. She would be alone again. Older, fatter, and so very much more bereft after having known this year of ecstasy.

Instead of Stephen, she found a note waiting in the spotless kitchen, which smelled deliciously of half-done roast beef. She skimmed over the lines about having to show property across the bay to a potential customer. This was not an unusual note. Other evenings she had returned to the apartment after work to find him gone on the same mission. She had never questioned his absences before, not even when he had returned long after she had gone to bed. She had imagined that the showing of property could be time consuming, followed by a session in his broker's office going over figures and interest rates. People worked during the week, and evenings were a reasonable time to show houses. She had never objected, eager to encourage him in his job.

But now she wondered where he really was. Had her new car been parked in the subterranean garage even as she had driven by the Normandy Apartments in Stephen's old relic?

Scarcely aware of the purposeful step of her feet, Rita marched into the bedroom and began to go through Stephen's dresser drawers. She ignored the clutter and disturbed nothing until she found a handful of bills and paper scraps at the bottom of his underwear drawer. She went through them one by one, her lips compressed. There were two other rent receipts for previous months; not consecutive ones, but one was more elaborate, showing that Stephen had rented the apartment four months earlier with a hefty deposit. The others were stubs, from expensive restaurants and bills from fancy men's shops for the purchase of clothing and accessories, none of which Rita recognized as belonging to Stephen. He not only had the apartment and the woman, then. He also maintained a wardrobe there.

She put the bills back where she had found them and wandered slowly back to the kitchen. If the mystery of Stephen's love had been unhappily solved, this new data about him raised all sorts of new questions. Where was the money coming from? She had always been generous with Stephen, keeping the money box full and giving him access to her credit cards. But this secret life was not paid for by her generosity. There was absolutely no indication that Stephen had suddenly become successful at selling real estate. In fact, the field had been suffering serious setbacks lately. The economy being what it was, realtors who had been successful in the past were finding themselves with an abundance of listings and a lack of serious buyers. Stephen had not done well when business was brisk. She had no reason to suspect that he was now pulling in a phenomenal amount of commissions.

The dinging of the little bell on the oven timer stopped Rita's train of thought. Quickly she began to prepare a salad and make gravy. It wasn't Milton Bannerman's fault that her life had been shattered. In a way she was grateful that he was coming for dinner. She didn't want to be alone, didn't want to have to think. Perhaps together they could mask their personal grief behind light dinner conversation. There was time later for thinking, for the decision she had, in her heart, already made.

Impulsively Rita dabbed on a coat of Red Fox, Magnifi-Scent's newest lipstick, and started to spray herself lightly with Oli just as she heard Milton's knock at her door. She fixed a smile into place, the sides of her face aching from the effort.

CHAPTER 22

From where Olivia sat in the atrium of the Hyatt Regency, she could watch Mark by looking across the tree-lined walkway. She smiled, enjoying the spectacle of Mark getting the full deluxe treatment from Maestro Gerhard's staff.

He was sprawled on a barber chair, with a manicurist at one hand and a hairstylist working on his head. His smile was almost comical, so broad it took years from his face. From her distance Olivia thought he looked younger than the boy he had been when they first met. He was having the time of his life, and it showed.

The barber finished, and a pretty young woman closed in to begin shaving Mark. His look of delight deepened to absolute rapture as she began to lather his wonderful face.

Olivia had to touch her lips to restrain a laugh. Vicariously she was having at least as good a time as Mark. It was shameless luxury for her to take the afternoon off on a day no less hectic and demanding than any other. But she had not been able to resist joining Mark on his splurge, sharing his moment of childlike self-indulgence. His show at the prestigious Neftale Gallery had been an enormous success. He had sold with spectacular ease, at José Neftale's outrageous prices, and the event of his opening had exceeded her wildest hopes and his most grandiose dreams.

James Lacy had not failed Olivia. His far-reaching influence crossed the continent, perhaps the world. The night of Mark's opening at the prestigious Neftale Gallery had been a star-studded affair. Champagne had flowed, the guests were dressed to the teeth, and Olivia, who had insisted on arriving on Mark's arm, had been in a state of artfully concealed panic. Cameras had flashed as they stepped from her black

Rolls and had not stopped snapping pictures of Mark and her for the entire evening.

The response to his work did not surprise her. Olivia had been almost smug about his success, knowing that her hunches about his talent and skill had been justified. Both his sculptures and his paintings were highly praised by the art critics the next day, and the caliber of those who attended— and even better, bought—made the event a social success as well. He made all the San Francisco newspapers and would highlight the art section of several other big-city papers in their Sunday sections. Already there was no doubt that an important new artist had been discovered and that Mark Earl Lyman, long ignored, was on his way up.

Olivia finished her drink as Mark was getting out of the chair, his handsomeness now polished to perfection. She thought of his excited voice when he had called to tell her of the unexpected call from José Neftale's secretary, which had resulted in a meeting with the man and the contract. She and Mark had been together almost constantly since, and although at the last minute Mark hadn't wanted her to come to the opening with him, in terror that it would be a flop and she would witness his embarrassment, he had gotten over his stage fright enough to relent.

Soon Mark would leave on a tour of other cities, to put in a personal appearance at the opening of each show. Afterward he would fly back to New York to close his studio and see to the moving of his supplies and tools to San Francisco, to her greenhouse, which was even now being renovated for him. He would also have a wing of the house for his work. As soon as they could organize it, they would have a wedding that would rival a royal coronation. Olivia wanted to encompass all of San Francisco in her happiness. They had not yet spoken of marriage, but in the way they had of understanding each other's deepest feelings, she knew he was as eager to ceremonialize their love as she.

But first they had more immediate things to do. She was taking him to Pappagallo for shoes and to Galletti Brothers for Birkenstock sandals, and then to Roos-Atkins for formal wear, of which he presently had nothing and would badly need on his tour. Then they would dine at home and go to bed early and sleep late, as they had been doing frequently for the past month. He was still officially living at his hotel, but he spent most nights with her in Pacific Heights. He would not bother with the formality of having his own hotel room after his return from New York.

Olivia left a large tip on the cocktail hostess's tray, smiled remotely at the next table of drinkers who had obviously recognized her but were trying not to gawk, and got up to meet Mark as he left Maestro Gerhard's shop. She was ecstatically happy, happier than she had ever been in her entire life. Crossing the lounge, she prayed for eternal happiness. She knew how vulnerable the happiness she had found really was. Mark must never know the hand she had had in the manipulation of his career. Never.

He was crossing the artificial boulevard to join her as she passed the shadow of a tree where a caged bird sang, his hand raised in greeting, his face wreathed in smiles. The shadow left her heart as the tree's shadow fell behind her hurrying figure in a cap-sleeved white dress and matching cardigan, a fur-lined raincoat trailing over her shoulders. Once she had thought eternity to be a word of fairy tales. Well, finally she had turned her life into a perpetual fairy tale. She grinned fully and lifted her hand to return Mark's greeting.

CHAPTER 23

Thea drove through the Presidio slowly, barely glancing at the lovely, tree-shrouded grounds, her mind very nearly a blank since leaving Olivia's house.

She had been foolish to go to Olivia's place without calling first. It was getting to be a habit of hers, dropping in on people without so much as a courtesy call first. Her mother would be horrified at this further proof of her deviation from good manners. She should have known that Olivia would be out with Mark, as usual. They had been together constantly since his brilliant opening at Neftale's gallery. As happy as she was for her friend, Thea felt especially lonely now that Olivia was less accessible to her. For that reason alone she had turned the convertible into the Presidio, lengthening her trip back home simply to fill the time.

She had felt especially edgy all week, ever since Everett had called on Thursday night. It had been a long phone call, intense and somewhat frightening. The weekend they had unexpectedly spent together in Los Angeles, when Thea had gone to visit her parents, had been as unsettling for Everett as it had been for her. Perhaps he had also been surprised at the reversal of the cat-and-mouse game they had played since childhood.

The weekend had been a delight and a revelation. Thea had amazed both of them by finding him wonderful and welcome company. Late drinks after her flight had led to a conversation about life that had kept them up until sunrise. She had agreed to meet him for lunch the next day, and that had extended late into the afternoon. He had teased her about being a stranger to her own city and proved he was right by showing her a Los Angeles she had never known—and an Everett she had never imagined. They had gone to the Watts Towers, a gaudy and yet stunningly original, whimsical monument that immortalized a poor Italian immigrant who had loved his adopted country enough to spend thirty years making it a present. Everett knew a great deal about local history, and after he had taken her on a refreshingly interesting tour of Los Angeles historical landmarks, he had told her quite a bit about the legends of San Francisco, also a city he enjoyed and had bothered to investigate in depth. She had begged off dining with him in order to spend some time with her family, but spent all of Sunday with Everett, again wandering around the city and talking.

On Sunday their talk became more personal. Everett spoke of his marriage and its end with honesty and feeling, but he was never maudlin or self-pitying. He seemed to have an unusual capacity for candor, and he left no doubt in Thea's mind that he had always loved her and had shared her mother's dream of eventually making her his wife.

Ordinarily Thea would have deflected his efforts to speak so frankly or at the very least minimized his words by responding with her usual highly stylized, cynical banter. But there was something so dignified and trusting about Everett that she held her tongue in check, and she found herself answering his questions honestly. She was careful to conceal that part of her life that had to be kept secret, but she had found it almost impossible to mask her loneliness and unhappiness from Everett. Much as she wanted to make him believe her life was the glittering jewel others thought it to be, he had a way of evoking truth from her, making her want very much to abandon the games she played even with herself. She had felt very close to Everett by the time he left her at the airport for her return flight to San Francisco, and he had remained in her mind since.

Once home, of course, she had managed to put him in realistic perspective. He was still Everett, that supremely perfect mate of her mother's fantasies, and she wasn't about to forget that she had spent a lifetime avoiding him. And yet she had found herself comparing him favorably to Daniel and the other men she dated. She had not been able to stop herself from returning to the third-rate bars and taking men to her apartment in town, but surprisingly, she had been unable to resist a temptation to allow her mind to drift to him as she was having sex with these strangers. Afterward, too, alone in her bed at home, she would think of Everett and wonder how he would be as a lover. They had never so much as kissed with passion. She had not allowed it, even though he was not unappealing.

In fact she rather liked the way he looked. He was tall, with sandy brown hair just beginning to gray at the temples, and he had nice eyes, a firm jaw, and an adequate body kept trim by vigorous bouts of handball three times a week. He was the head of a large corporation he had taken over from his father and made still larger, yet he didn't let his success overwhelm his perspective on life. And although he made frequent trips to San Francisco, where he maintained a branch office, he had never once invaded her territory by so much as a phone call when he was in her city. Even now, since their weekend, he called her only from Los Angeles and never when he was in The City.

She was not thinking of Everett as she drove through the Presidio, not directly. She had not allowed herself to wrestle openly with the proposal he had made on the phone. It was safer to drive aimlessly, thinking of nothing until she noticed the muscular young soldier at the side of the road.

It wasn't so much that he was particularly handsome, though he had good features and a nice body. But his eyes had a restless light, and the way he idled by the curb suggested that he was off duty and eager for a little entertainment.

Without conscious thought, almost as though she were

suspending personal involvement in her actions, Thea slowed the car and smiled at the soldier. She brushed aside a momentary reentry into reality: the knowledge that she should not be doing this in the Rolls. "Need a ride, soldier? I've lots of room."

He looked stricken, first by the opulent car, and then by the classy-looking female driving it. But he was quick on the uptake and obviously a fellow who believed in unexpected good fortune. "You bet, baby. I sure am going in your direction, whatever that happens to be."

He got in, and she gunned the motor as she jiggled two cigarettes out of the pack on the seat next to her. "Light us up, okay?" Up close he really was a kid, and a good-looking one.

She took the smoking cigarette still damp from his lips and puffed eagerly, conscious of his eyes on her lean body under the split-neck jumpsuit she wore. As always at such times, she was in a hurry now that he was in her car. She didn't want to waste time on conversation. "I've got a place in town. Not too far. I think there's some Scotch. And beer. Want to come?"

Grinning widely, he said, "You bet I want to come, honey! Hey, this car is out of sight!"

"It belongs to my boss," she said shortly.

Those were the last words they spoke until they were in her secret apartment and rapidly undressing, the drink forgotten.

"Hey, sweetheart, what's your name, anyway?" he asked staring at her firm breasts as she tossed her bra on a chair.

"Cinderella." She skinned out of her panties and got on the king-size bed.

It started out much like any other similiar experience. This soldier liked to kiss, and some of the men she had brought here didn't. He had a beautiful body, and he touched hers knowingly, a practiced sensualist, good at what he liked.

But after they had been on the bed for less than a minute, as suddenly as Thea's desire had begun, it abruptly ended. She looked into his heavily lidded brown eyes and knew she didn't want him at all. Where she hadn't allowed a single conscious thought of Everett Hamlinton to enter her mind, she now, absurdly, almost embarrassingly, found he was so completely there that she couldn't bear to be with this stranger. Her change of heart shocked her so much that she almost pushed the soldier off the bed. She caught herself in time, grimaced and let him continue to manipulate their bodies. Thea had never before been turned off to a good-looking man at this stage of the game. She could feel herself dry up as if something in her body's machinery had stopped working.

She wanted Everett. She didn't give a damn how absurd the whole thing was. She wanted only Everett.

"Come on, baby. Let's go." The soldier, impatient now, wanted to bring them to a climax.

Thinking of the fate of the girl in *Looking for Mr. Goodbar* and also reminding herself that a woman didn't go to this point and then cry wolf, she let him have his way, but she was dead inside. She only wanted Everett, and this was not Everett. She went through the motions of passion by rote, feeling dirtier than she had ever before in her whole life.

Afterward, long after he had left but before she could drag herself out of the soiled bed, Thea contemplated suicide. She snapped out of her mood quickly once she realized that it hadn't been death for which she was longing while she had been with the soldier. It had been Everett. And, she reminded herself, Everett wanted her.

Thea got up, showered quickly, and with a towel wrapped around her, went to the phone.

"Everett? Everett? Is it really you?"

"Thea?"

She heard the surprise and pleasure in his voice. It was a nice voice, not too deep, but rich and cultured.

"Will you come to San Francisco, Everett? I think . . ." she took a long, much-needed breath. "I think we should get married, Everett. Are you there?"

"Not yet, Thea. But I'm on my way!"

She hung up, dressed quickly, and left the apartment knowing she'd never be back.

CHAPTER 24

It had not been easy to do what she had done.

Marlissa had called Brad Cavell to her home for the express purpose of ending her relationship with him. But she delayed making the announcement in spite of the fact that she had already made up her mind about the necessity of it.

The past month had flown by, and if it hadn't been an altogether perfect month, it had nevertheless been a stimulating, significant time in her life. Brad had been a competent and inventive lover and an even better teacher. In a few short weeks Marlissa felt as educated in the finer points of the good life as if she'd gone through a crash course at a charm school. Brad had taken her everywhere, and with infinite tact and sophistication he'd shown her the ins and outs of a world he knew so well, a world that Marlissa had felt she might never touch except as an outsider.

Under his encouragement she had grown more daring, had allowed her individualistic tastes to emerge. She was also growing more sure of herself. Brad had done that for her, as well. Just the comforting fact of having a good-looking, worldly man at her side had done wonders for her self-esteem and confidence. By imitating his use of utensils at dinner, she had learned how to handle her silver in the proper American fashion. By hearing him order, she had learned a great deal about food and wine. She already had a good background in music and art, learned at home from her parents, but she had learned subtle distinctions so that a glance at a painting or listening to a few bars of music now could be filtered through her own acquired eye and ear, understood, and then judged by finer standards. Through Brad's coaxing she had also risked active participation in conversation with the people she met through him.

Perhaps that had been the biggest revelation of all, the reaction these people had to what she said about a variety of subjects. Before she had been content to listen quietly, to remain safely on the fringes of a discussion. It was a strange insecurity she had unknowingly shared with many bright and successful people, a social ineptitude, an inner conviction that she was uninformed outside of the tiny sphere of her own specialty. But she had strong feelings and opinions on everything from the arts to politics, and under Brad's encouragement, she had begun to open up. When she found out that others enjoyed listening to her, she opened even more, happy to be an active participant in society.

None of this, however, had done anything at all toward convincing Marlissa that what she felt for Brad Cavell was love or even its close cousin.

In bed he had also helped her find herself as a woman. While he did not continue to excite her after the first few times, Brad taught her that she did not have to be vastly stimulated or emotionally overwhelmed to find pleasure in bed with a man. And if he suspected that he was the first person to instruct her in this truth, he never mentioned it or questioned her about it.

As a result, she thought of him as something of a friend and liked him, and more than once wished she could forget Ernst and love Brad instead.

He was not perfect, of course. He had a basically secretive nature and something of a hot temper. He was also vain and overly involved with himself. He was not democratic toward household help and waiters and others in the service professions, a fact that had disturbed Marlissa continually during dates. He was also not innocent of taking gratification from Marlissa's personal and social growth, recognizing his hand in it and showing his self-satisfaction in a wry smile or a chance remark.

Still, none of that altered the fact that he had been good to her, and she was not without regret at her determination to end the relationship. She wished that he had told her in the beginning that he was intimately connected with Riviera Cosmetics. The theft of key personnel from one company to another was common in every industry, and Marlissa had no illusions or humility about her value in her own field. It seemed more than possible that behind Brad's constant attentions was the hope that she could be persuaded to work for Riviera. She had no idea how far Brad might have planned to go; she understood that few people operated on only one level. He might very well want to continue the relationship indefinitely, or even to marry her because he sincerely enjoyed her company and thought she would make an adequate wife; and the knowledge that, as his wife, she would owe her loyalties to her new family, would simply be an added bonus. If he was simply a man who was determined to get ahead at any price, his prime motive could be nothing more than capturing her for Riviera, and such a man might go even as far as marriage to get what he wanted.

She had puzzled the whole thing out for over a week before making up her mind and inviting Brad to her house for this confrontation. She was not one to act impulsively, the scientist in her insisting on taking the time to weigh all factors and aspects carefully.

In the end she had known that whatever his motives, a liaison between herself and a top executive at Riviera was out of the question. It confused the clear-cut issue of loyalties on both sides and would be destructive to morale.

She had waited for Brad to finish a story he was relating about a friend she had met recently, then quietly told him her knowledge of his family and business ties and that she deemed it necessary to terminate their relationship. She did not directly accuse him of hoping to steal her away from MagnifiScent for Riviera, but she implied a possible base motive for his initial attraction.

Brad listened wordlessly until she was through, his face revealing nothing until it was his turn to speak. Then his features hardened and his lips curled.

"I'm going to tell you something funny, Marlissa, something to amuse you on those cold nights when you're alone in that bed of yours, regretting tonight." He stared at her a moment, a slow, cold smile on his lips. "I was thinking of asking you to be my wife. I wanted to marry you. Not because of your beauty," he raked his eyes over her deprecatingly, "but because you're not beautiful. Not because of what you are, but because of what you aren't. My wife was a beautiful bitch. She knew it, too. She destroyed my home, took my children from me, and knocked over years of building our relationship because she was too beautiful to be content with only one man. I imagined I would find contentment with a less glamorous woman who would remain loyal. I never mentioned the fact that I was connected to Riviera because I was afraid you would think that was the basis of my interest in you. I didn't give a damn about your company or mine! And you threw it all away because you think I'm trying to steal your formulas for Riviera Cosmetics." He laughed derisively.

"Steal the formulas?" she repeated in confusion.

He nodded. "It's written all over your face." He turned to leave, but an impulse to wound made him turn back to her for one last stab. "As if Riviera had to steal them from you personally. Isn't it obvious we already know what you people are up to over there?"

After he was gone, Marlissa had a stiff drink and went to the phone. She apologized for disturbing Olivia at home and related the night's events directly and with no show of emotion. She could tell from Olivia's voice what she had already suspected, that Olivia and likely Thea had both known who Brad Cavell was. Yet her friends had been tactful and trusting enough not to mention a word to her.

"I have an idea now about how the formulas have been learned. I'll come to your office tomorrow, if you've a free moment, and we'll talk about it." She paused. "And Olivia . . . I want to thank you for your discretion. For not telling me about Brad's connection with Riviera Cosmetics. It was best to learn of it on my own. I feel foolish, but less so than if you and Thea had opened my eyes."

Olivia's voice sounded ecstatic but relieved. "I must ask. How *did* you find out?"

An impish grin spread across Marlissa's face. "I read about it in a gossip column. In the society column, that is. In a paragraph about interesting twosomes in town. Imagine! Marlissa Deloffre from Meiringen in the society pages!" The smile was replaced by a look of wonder. "Does that mean I have, how do you say, made it?"

CHAPTER 25

For five days Rita Vanalden tried to find another answer to the question that plagued her relentlessly. In a way she knew that her preoccupation with where Stephen had gotten the money to keep his mistress was a device for keeping her sane. Why did it matter where the money came from, when what it had gone for was the real issue?

But there was another reason she had to know. It was one thing to be destroyed personally and another to be ruined professionally. Rita was an ethical woman. She would never tolerate being an accessory to a crime like the one she suspected Stephen of perpetrating.

Yet every time she examined the facts, she came up with the same answer. From the start he had shown an excessive interest in her job. Why would a man unconnected with the cosmetics industry be interested in her work? Those times he had gone with her to the complex—wouldn't he have leaped at the chance to be with his mistress? She tried to remember how he had filled the hours while she worked. He had wandered around the complex with seeming aimlessness, popping in on her to inquire how long she'd be but displaying no impatience. Marlissa was a meticulous woman in almost every way, but Rita knew that she was careless about security and rarely locked her office door. She supposed she kept the all-important formulas locked in a safe somewhere in her office, but on closer examination she began to wonder even about that supposition. People were amazingly consistent creatures. The woman who double-locked her door was the one who kept valuables in a safe. The one who never locked the door might well be as careless about her diamonds . . . or her formulas. Marlissa had lived most of her life in a tiny Swiss village where there was no need for locks and safes. She would not have the typical city dweller's lack of trust. And because of MagnifiScent's tight, professional security system, especially in the lab, Marlissa would think her formulas were perfectly safe. Even when Olivia herself came to the lab complex, she had to wear a special badge. Visitors were escorted through the complex, and while there was no hesitation about allowing the various department heads to come and go at will after hours, they were first checked by the security people for identification, and Rita had to wear her own badge and get a visitor's tag for Stephen. She had had to use her own keys to get into the complex proper, although the separate labs were never locked. She was not the only one to bring a mate or other relative to work on occasion. Barbara Cantor, for instance, frequently brought her eldest daughter to help her with paperwork.

"Stephen?" It was almost time for bed on Friday night.

He looked up from the television set.

"I meant to tell you: I have to go to work again in the morning. We're really piled up this week."

"Again?" His forehead was wrinkled. "I thought you guys finished that new line."

"We did, but we've begun a new one for the autumn collection, and I want to get a jump on next week by cleaning up a bit from the last rush." She watched him closely, suspicious of the disappointment in his expression.

"Well, you know best." He turned back to the color set and his favorite show just as Bill Bixby was undergoing the metamorphosis from man to Hulk. "You won't be long, will you? Tomorrow?"

She kept her eyes on him. "Most of the morning." She waited while the green giant overturned a car. "Do you want to come along? To work?"

Without looking at her, he shrugged. "I don't think so, baby. I better stick around in case there's any calls."

She nodded thoughtfully. "As you wish. I'd better get to bed."

"I'll be in as soon as this is over."

Rita took a long shower and turned away from the wall mirror as she slipped into a nightgown after hastily drying herself. But the gown, an old one, was tight under the arms and told her what she hadn't allowed the mirror to reveal, that she had put on a few more pounds again. It was an old pattern, the crazy eating when she was upset, and never had she been more upset than since that night she had found the first rent receipt. How then did she justify the weight she'd gained during the year, when in her stupidity she had believed herself married to a wonderful man who loved her?

She got into bed after changing to a more comfortable gown, thinking that however gross her body, it still had the ability to desire love. Inside she was a woman like any other, with the same needs and feelings. And like any woman, in spite of her bulk she sometimes had the power to be attractive and let her earthy female nature show. She recalled that Milton Bannerman had flattered her repeatedly at their dinner, insisting that she was a warm and lovely woman.

Rita didn't allow herself to hold onto the pleasure that memory elicited. Milton was terribly alone, and in his grief he would naturally respond to her sympathetic warmth. She had sincerely enjoyed him, too, particularly with the knowledge of Stephen's betrayal in her mind. By contrast Milton's sincerity was a balm, and she felt herself almost jealous of whatever woman would come along and get him.

She heard Stephen turn off the set and begin to lock up and douse the lights. She thought of his seeming disinterest in coming to work with her in the morning. It had admittedly surprised her, taken her off guard. Tomorrow, if ever, he should be frothing to have an excuse to get into the complex. The new formulas were done and waiting, and she had allowed that information to fall on his ears. Yet he had rejected her invitation.

Rita knew she was a poor detective. Her mind, good as it was, didn't go in that direction. She tried to reach for intricacies and was lost, having instead no choice but to study the surface data. In fairness she remembered that he had never shown undue interest in going to the lab with her. He had gone, however, claiming that he'd rather be with her than alone. Was he so devious that he had deliberately planted the idea that his presence was at her request rather than his own desire? Or was she completely wrong about him? If he wasn't stealing the formulas and selling them to Riviera, could it be possible that there was no woman at the Normandy Apartments? That the whole thing was a fiction created by her own insecurity?

Then she remembered the rent receipts in his name and the other damning bills and receipts. The woman was real. Wherever the money was coming from, the woman was real.

Even so, it soothed her just a little to have a reason to hope that in his betrayal he hadn't also compromised her integrity. She was fiercely glad that he had decided to stay home in the morning, even if "staying home" meant running to his mistress.

Stephen had already changed into his pajamas, the dark red ones she had bought him only a few months ago. They were silk and very sexy, and until recently the sight of them on his firm body was enough to set the juices in her body running.

He flicked off the light but left the bathroom door ajar, with its dimmed light spilling into the bedroom. Stephen didn't like to sleep in total darkness, although Rita preferred it, especially when they had sex. He pushed back the electric blanket and fiddled with his control box. The blanket with the dual control was perfect for them. Stephen claimed she liked the bed too warm for his comfort, and though she had always been more than happy to do things his way, she was unable to sleep in a cold bed.

With a yawn he stretched out next to her and turned on his side to face her. The bathroom light made his face easily visible while throwing hers in darkness when they were turned toward each other. "Good show tonight. You should have watched." He turned and reached out for her.

A heavy lump formed in her throat as she cringed from his groping hand. It had been weeks since they had made love, and her body reacted to his gesture while her mind was horrified by it. Yet since finding the rent receipts, she hadn't wanted him to touch her. She supposed it would have been inevitable for him to compare nights of love with her to those with his mistress and she cringed from the thought.

"Don't," she protested, trying very hard to act natural and unoffended. It wasn't as hard as it might have been, simply because her body was betraying her again, and an edge of uncontrollable excitement made her voice rather coy and breathless. "I . . . it's the wrong time of the month," she lied, knowing that unlike some husbands, he kept no calendar of her cycle.

"Can't go against the clock, I guess," he complained with an exaggerated sigh. He patted her lightly on the shoulder, then turned onto his other side and went to sleep.

Rita was extremely tired herself, and the one pleasant thought in her mind was that she could sleep late the next morning. Then she remembered that she had claimed a need to work and would have to get up at the usual time because of it. She willed herself to a deep dreamless sleep.

When she got up in the morning, she found him already dressed, with freshly brewed coffee scenting the apartment.
"What the hell. I thought I might as well go on in with you. I hate sitting by the phone waiting for it to ring."
She stared wordlessly at his blandly smiling face.

CHAPTER 26

He had loved her house, the Marina, her beautiful Arab gelding Legacy, and the sailboat she hardly ever used anymore.

After a delicious lobster dinner at Castagnola's on the wharf, they had returned to her house to drink and talk. Thea sent her maid to bed and changed into a silk crepe de Chine lounging suit that did wonderful things for her figure and brought out the red glints in her long brown hair. She wasn't trying to look deliberately sexy for Everett, but she thought it only fitting that they end this long-awaited discussion about their marriage with a more intimate knowledge of each other. They had kissed for the first time with any intensity at the airport, and she found that she was actually impatient to take him to her bed. But this was a comfortable impatience, so unlike the way she had felt with other men. For the first time since she was a girl, Thea looked at the remainder of her life as a long, lazy country road that she could explore at her leisure.

It was a delightfully alien sensation, to be happy at last. And looking at the man she would marry, she knew she was indeed happy.

He had loosened his tie and removed the jacket of his suit.

The graying hair at his temples gave him a distinguished look, even though the rest of his sandy hair was slightly rumpled. He smiled as she reentered the room and poured her a brandy. His own glass was nearly empty, so he refilled it at the same time.

"To us," he saluted, raising his glass. "To our marriage."

She drank, enjoyed the warmth and smoothness of the superb brandy. She grinned at him. "Won't Mother be surprised?"

"I doubt it. She always knew you'd see the light." He looked at her a moment.

Now that they were alone in the privacy of her house, Thea sensed that a slight uncertainty had crept over Everett. His jaw was less firm and yet more determined, as if he had come to some decision after a concentrated struggle.

"I don't want you to think that marrying me is going to destroy your life, Thea," he began after another sip of the brandy. His eyes met hers but seemed not to penetrate beneath the surface. He held up a hand as if to stop whatever she might say. "I understand your reluctance about settling down and that monumental fear of boredom that kept you from considering marriage to me years ago. We'll have a good life together. I promise you that. We're both adults now. I think the first burst of idealism has left us both, thank God. We can still keep our independence. You won't have to feel chained to one man."

Thea put her brandy down on the starkly modern glass table in front of the couch on which they sat, her face expressionless, her mind working at a furious pace. Something was wrong here, but the wrongness had come from out of left field and she was lost. "Chained?"

He nodded. "Yes. We'll keep this house and mine in Beverly Hills. I have to be in San Francisco a good deal of the time, but I'm also needed in Los Angeles. I make frequent trips to Rome and Paris, sometimes London and Hong Kong, as well. You have your work at MagnifiScent, and I know you travel often, too. None of that need change. When we're together I think it best that we *are* together. I don't think things work very well otherwise. But when we're apart I have no objection to an agreement of mutual privacy. As long as we both maintain absolute discretion, of course."

What Everett was saying was beginning to fit together like pieces in a puzzle. He was outlining the conditions of their life together, telling her that this marriage she had been so certain he had ardently desired would be one without even so much as the pretense of fidelity.

Thea realized that she could not have been more shocked if Everett had told her he was a closet transvestite.

She took a steadying gulp of her brandy and lit a fresh cigarette from the glowing stub of the last. The effort to keep herself from outwardly reacting to his words was monumental. "You're not . . . concerned with any affairs I might have, then?"

He did not avoid her eyes but rather continued to consider their surface. "As I said, we're both adults and accustomed to our present lives. I'm sure we can both be discreet, however."

Thea looked into herself and found pain and disappointment. How strange it was. If Everett had suggested such a marriage years ago, she might have considered his proposal seriously then. It was what she had always hoped for, a marriage to a stable, acceptable man that would allow her guilt-free affairs on the side. She could have all the advantages of a solid relationship, gratify her parents, ease her acute loneliness, and still enjoy a variety of men, still satisfy that need for constant change and excitement. Why then did she now feel like crying?

Part of it was Everett, of course. He was the last man from whom she expected to hear such a proposal. She felt as though the breath had been knocked out of her. Not only wasn't this the Everett of years before, but the man seated next to her in his shirt sleeves was unrelated to the man she had begun to know in Los Angeles so recently. Yet it *was* Everett, and he was offering her what she had always wanted. *Careful what you wish for lest you get it,* she thought to herself. Was it always this way? Yet Olivia had finally gotten what she'd always wanted, just the way she'd wanted it. When Mark returned from New York any day now, they would plan their marriage, and Thea had never seen her friend so ecstatic. Thea pictured Olivia's beautiful face under the perfectly arranged platinum hair when she broke her good news over lunch the week before. Remembering, Thea realized that for all of Olivia's great joy, there had also been an edge of nervousness in that flawless face, in the clear blue eyes. Was it true, then, what she had long suspected? That no one ever completely knew anyone else? She looked at Everett, who had just finished mouthing words she would never have expected to come from his lips.

He was suggesting a wedding large enough to gratify their

myriad family and social obligations, unaware of her tortured thoughts. For one wild moment she considered interrupting his monologue, running out of the room, something, anything. This travesty of a marriage he was describing a ceremony for would never take place.

But Thea kept her lips compressed while she recalled that terrible moment in the apartment in town, with the warm young soldier and her own cold body. She thought also of the pills on which she depended for sleep, the alcohol she used like medicine, and, most of all, her fleeting brush with the serious thought of taking her own life after the soldier had finally gone. Unshed tears burned the backs of her eyes.

What Everett was suggesting wasn't exactly what she wanted, wasn't her idea of marriage at all. But what was the alternative? Her past frightened her seriously. A future containing more of the same, and worse, was truly terrifying. Everett was a good man. Everett would save her.

She reached out and touched his hand, trying not to tremble. "Everett? Do you love me?"

For the first time since they had come back to her house, he looked deeply into her eyes. His voice was serious and tender. "I have always loved you, Thea."

It would have to do. "Will we have the wedding in Beverly Hills or here?"

CHAPTER 27

It had been absurdly easy once Marlissa had put her mind to the problem. Since the only people who could be involved in the theft of the formulas were her own department heads—they were the only people with keys to the complex itself other than the scrupulously checked security staff—she had merely to wait and watch.

With Olivia's approval, Marlissa had worked out a simple

but foolproof scheme for catching her thief. Unknown to her staff, the conference room adjoining Marlissa's office had been supplied with food and a comfortable bed late Thursday night and carefully locked from the hall. On Friday, after her typical cool farewells to Barbara Cantor and anyone else she encountered at closing time, she slipped into the conference room unnoticed. She had planned it carefully, leaving her car at home and taxiing to work that morning, and making it no secret that the completed formulas for the new line were piled up in her office. All that was left was to wait it out. When the culprit entered her office, she would know it and would have only to press one button on her phone to bring a guard quickly to the door of her office while she confronted the thief. Neither Olivia nor Thea had cared for that part of her plan, fearful that Marlissa would be in danger. But Marlissa had reminded them that the thief would have gone through the metal detector at the entrance to the complex, and anyway had no need for any weapon other than a good pen, some scratch paper, or, more likely, a small, easily concealed and harmless camera. This sort of espionage had been done before many times in industry, and the thief was rarely someone out of a James Bond movie, weighed down with guns and other movieland artifacts.

Marlissa was glad to have the time alone for other reasons. She needed time to consider the fact that Brad Cavell's exit from her life had left her with a tremendous sense of relief. Yet it had been wonderful to have a charming man around, and already her body was missing the lovemaking on which she had come to depend. Since she had had her scene with Brad, she found her thoughts returning over and over to Ernst. She had not heard from him in a long time. Not that she wanted to let him back into her life. He stood for everything she had moved away from, and even the fact that it was still possible for her to love the simple carpenter mocked and embarrassed Marlissa.

She was thinking of Ernst Saturday morning when she heard the slight but distinctive sound of the door to her office opening. She waited soundlessly, giving the intruder ample time to go about the job. While she waited she considered for the first time her feelings if she should open the door and find herself staring at one of her trusted employees. She had hand-picked her staff, taking into consideration not only their education and background but the kind of people they were as well. There was not a single person in her entire complex whom she did not respect and trust. Mentally she went through her people one by one, excited at what she was about to do but saddened by what she would find out. Her hand had automatically reached for the phone at the sound of the door being opened and pushed the button summoning the guard, and she knew that already he would be posted outside the office door, waiting for a word from her to burst into the room.

She pushed open the closed but unlatched adjoining door and saw the man at her desk, caught in the act of going through her thick folder containing the formulas for MagnifiScent's brilliant new line. Actually it was a dummy case consisting of old and discarded formulas, on the outside chance that her thief would somehow outwit her. But this man didn't know. That was obvious from the way he was snapping pictures of the reports one after the next with a small, complicated-looking camera.

In the split second before he realized he was no longer alone, Marlissa made a concentrated effort to identify the thief. She thought the handsome profile was familiar. Marlissa had an excellent memory for faces, a less-impressive one for names to put with the faces, but still she had often astounded near-strangers with her quick recall of their identities. She felt she hadn't met this man before, and yet he looked familiar, as if she had seen him in a movie or his picture in a magazine. He was certainly handsome enough, in his way, to be an actor. Then she had it. His picture. On one of the lab walls. A really clear, excellent likeness, a portrait.

Marlissa made the connection and felt a deep sadness for Rita, so nice, so good, so plain, whose work was always so impeccable. However her husband had come to be in her office, Marlissa was certain it was not with Rita's approval or knowledge.

"Find what you are looking for, Mr. Vanalden?" As always when she was excited, her accent had become more noticeable, the only indication of her emotions.

He lowered the camera slowly, his face chalky. With satisfaction Marlissa noticed that he didn't look quite so handsome anymore. She let him drop the papers and start for the door, a common thief reverting to the impulse to run from detection.

"I would suggest you stay where you are, Mr. Vanalden.

There is an armed guard on the other side of that door. You have nowhere to go."

His eyes fascinated her. They darted from side to side as if considering alternate escape patterns, when it was so obvious that she was right. Marlissa saw the slowly dawning realization that his undoubtedly profitable game was over.

Like a moody child he slumped down on a chair. "You going to bust me, or what?" He spoke in a sulky tone, angry more than frightened. Marlissa suspected that he had been in trouble before.

"Bust?"

He gestured impatiently. "Arrest me. Tell my wife. The whole bit." As if only considering the possibility of his wife knowing for the first time, he shook his head. "Man, this will kill Rita."

Marlissa couldn't think of a single thing he could have said that would have affected her more. She had been right; Rita Vanalden had no idea of her husband's activities. Marlissa remembered when Rita married this man, the excitement and happiness that had shone from her bemused eyes. Rita was not the sort of woman to speak her heart to others, but her joy had been so apparent that the entire lab complex had felt happy for her and had wished her a long and happy marriage. But Marlissa knew that people, even the best of them, had contrary natures. Much as they had shared Rita's happiness at the time, they would titter among themselves at the revelation of her handsome husband's crime. That sweet, basically simple woman with a heart as big as her body would feel humiliated before every single employee at MagnifiScent, from the highest to the lowest.

She allowed herself a moment to think of her choices. As long as there would be no further stealing at the lab, Marlissa knew Olivia would agree to whatever she decided in the matter of Mr. Vanalden. Arresting him would serve little useful purpose. The previously stolen formulas would not be lifted from the minds of the chemists at Riviera. The ordeal of a lawsuit would involve first proving that this man had indeed placed the formulas in Riviera's hands, a tricky job because Marlissa had no doubt that the man would hold his tongue, especially if Riviera made it worth his while to do that much.

Relieving all the department heads of their keys would require a change in work habits, but one easily accomplished. She could make sure that Mr. Vanalden and others of his ilk couldn't repeat his crime in the future. Marlissa had also learned her lesson and would lock all important data away carefully from now on. No, she finally decided, having this poor excuse for a man incarcerated would satisfy nothing more than a desire for vengeance.

She also forced herself to consider the other side of the issue. What, in the long run, would she be doing for Rita if she kept her silence? Her father had long ago taught Marlissa the ultimate kindness of inflicting temporary pain for the eventual and longer-lasting good of the individual. By not letting Rita see what sort of creature she had married, wouldn't that be setting her up for even greater hardship in the future? A man who could do what this one had done was capable of other forms of evil. Wouldn't it be an actual kindness to expose him and be done with it?

While Vanalden sat heavily in the chair, sullenly watching the face of the woman who held his future in her hands, Marlissa searched her soul for the right step to take. She recalled the way Olivia and Thea had let her discover for herself Brad Cavell's connection with Riviera Cosmetics. While it was true that Marlissa would have severed the relationship sooner had she been informed, she had appreciated her friends' discretion. They had granted her the dignity of handling matters her own way and in her own time.

She thought also of Rita attempting to work among people who would be at best pitying her, could see her quickly quitting, perhaps retreating to that small town from which she had come. There, at last, Marlissa had a motive she could place on the side of the good of the company. Rita was an excellent chemist and ran her department most competently. MagnifiScent would lose a valuable employee.

Rita would soon enough find out the kind of man her husband was. She deserved privacy in which to do it.

Marlissa went to the door, opened it, and gestured for the guard to follow her back inside. She had already placed him in her mind: an older man, close-mouthed, sensible.

"Mr. Wittaker, will you remember this man?"

The guard observed him at length. "Anytime, anyplace, Dr. Deloffre."

"Would you see to it personally that all the other security guards see his photograph? You'll find it on the wall in the Analytical Biochemistry lab. After closing hours only, please. With discretion."

"Yes, ma'am. The boys know how to watch their tongues. It will be taken care of. You have my word."

She nodded. "Mr. Vanalden is never to be permitted on the premises again. Ever." She turned to the still-seated man. "You are very fortunate, Mr. Vanalden. I suspect that not for the first time you owe a debt of gratitude to your wife. You will return to her now, make your excuses, and be out of this building in five minutes. Mr. Wittaker will wait for you in the hall to see that you don't dawdle. Do you understand, Mr. Vanalden? I suggest you don't ever try this again. There will be no second chance."

Stephen Vanalden looked up, the anger in his eyes lightening as his mouth curved with an unconcealed smirk of satisfaction. He walked out of the office, the security guard behind him, but his step was not leisurely.

After he was gone, Marlissa sagged into her desk chair, drained. She fervently hoped she had made the right choice. And her heart ached with sadness for Rita Vanalden.

Her fingers idly rummaged through the mail that had been delivered to her desk after she had left her office the previous afternoon. Because she wanted to be sure the man had left the building before she went home, she disinterestedly scanned the mail to pass the time.

One letter stood out from the others. She recognized the Swiss stamps instantly, Ernst's broad scrawl a moment later. She read the note inside quickly, then let the page fall to her desk.

Ernst was at this moment on his way to San Francisco.

CHAPTER 28

Rita sat tensely on the hard rear seat of the taxi, her eyes blind to anything other than the tail of her own car as it moved through traffic in front of her.

The whole thing had gone like a movie. No, she amended, like a nightmare. Stephen had gone with her to her lab, then wandered out into the hallway. She had watched him out of the corner of her eye as he casually sauntered through the glass maze, unaware that she was watching his every step. She was an expert at this game, had played it so many times in the days when she had desired her lab assistant from afar.

When he had rounded the corner in the direction of Marlissa's private office, Rita had put down the tools of her trade with her habitual care and crept into the hall after Stephen, moving slowly on the balls of her feet, making not a sound. There was a place by the water fountain where she could watch without being noticed, under the white sign with the red bold-faced letters proclaiming that the water was unsafe and not to be used for drinking. The complex had the required number of these fountains of deionized water in case of contamination with certain chemicals. This one had a closet next to it, and within its shadow she would be undetectable.

She reached the fountain just as Stephen was almost soundlessly letting himself into Marlissa's office. Rita felt an unreasonable flash of irritation toward her boss. Even after Riviera's new line had stunned them and told them all that somehow the rival company had access to their formulas, Marlissa had continued to leave her door unlocked.

Immediately Rita knew her initial reaction was unreasonable and defensive. Even now she could try to find excuses for her husband, somehow try to justify his inexcusable actions.

After little more than a minute, two at the most, Rita heard the sound of footsteps walking lightly down the hall. She flattened herself against the wall, cursing her extra fifty pounds but not overly worried because the steps were coming from the other way and it was improbable that she would be noticed.

It was one of the security guards, and Rita's heart almost stopped when she saw the good-sized man plant himself quietly outside Marlissa's door.

Afraid that the thundering beat of her heart would give her away, Rita watched for several minutes more. The door opened softly, and Rita could see Marlissa Deloffre just inside. Marlissa gestured wordlessly for the guard to come into the office. When the door had closed behind both of them, Rita tiptoed back to her own lab. She kept quiet because she had programmed herself for caution, but she knew it no longer mattered. The three of them were together in the room: Marlissa, the guard, and Stephen.

She sat down in front of a microscope because her legs refused to hold her any longer. In a strange way she felt almost at peace. Now it was over. Finished. Marlissa would do what she had to do, and Rita would finally face the consequences of her foolish choice of a mate. Dully she waited for the wail of a police siren. It seemed the logical next sound.

Instead, only moments later she heard familiar footsteps coming her way. She looked up and into Stephen's face.

Shock was etched through his eyes, but his lips wore a casual, almost jaunty smile. "Are you done yet?"

She swallowed, found her vioce. "Almost." She could not meet his eyes. What had happened?

"Listen, babe, I'll meet you back at the car, okay? I want to grab some smokes."

She nodded, not trusting herself to speak. His Winstons were sticking out of his shirt pocket.

As soon as he had gone down the hall, Rita hurried to the lab on the other side. It had a window that looked out on the enclosed hallway that led to the exit. She arrived just in time to see the stern-faced guard escort Stephen out the door. The guard's stance was clearly disapproving and seemed to carry a mute warning.

Rita walked back to her office and slowly put things in order. Now she was clear about what had happened in Marlissa's office. Stephen had been warned and dismissed. If there were to be criminal actions they were being delayed, and the only reason for that would be concern for Rita. Under Marlissa's businesslike coolness was a compassionate heart. Blinking back tears, Rita was mildly surprised that her strongest feeling was of gratitude for Marlissa, and other than that she felt no emotion at all.

But she did feel a sense of business still unfinished.

Now Stephen was in the car smoking a cigarette, and he even wore a smile of greeting for her as she approached, as if nothing had happened.

Rita found she had a talent for duplicity herself. "I just got a call from my sister Phyliss. My brother Ray and his wife Edie are taking a trip to Hawaii, and they'll be held up at the San Francisco airport for an hour or two. I'm going down to visit with them until their plane takes off. There won't be enough time to bring them home and get them back in time. Do you want to come?"

He hesitated, then slowly shook his head. "Would you mind if I pass, baby? They didn't exactly give us a hell of a lot of warning, and I thought maybe I'd check in at my office. I was going to ask you if you wanted to go with me."

It was almost funny, the way Rita could watch the wheels turning in his mind. Had he always been this heavy-handed, this obvious? She had felt safe in asking him to come to the airport, though she had no intention of going there herself. After his shock she had imagined he would want to run to the arms of his mistress, perhaps to plan other horrible ways of making money to support their love nest. Pretending a phone call from her sister was a stroke of on-the-spot genius— Stephen would believe he had hours of freedom from her. And his counteroffer to take her to his office for the first time almost amused Rita. He knew that any other time she would have accepted with pleasure. Stephen had never included her in the rest of his life. Now she knew why, of course. Probably all his friends knew about the beautiful woman he kept on the side and laughed about his drab, fat wife. The people at his office might know, as well, though she had begun to doubt that he even had an office.

She had him drive her to a downtown hotel, where she could get limousine service to the airport, insisting he take the car to the office. She protested that she didn't feel like fighting traffic all the way out there. Since Rita had no idea of what could be seen from Stephen's secret apartment, she didn't intend to chance giving herself away by driving up in one of their cars. Having checked her purse to be sure she had the taxi fare, she felt a grim satisfaction in the completeness of her plotting.

To be on the safe side, she'd bought herself a cup of coffee in the hotel coffee shop before hailing a cab. She gave the driver the address, and she was distressed to catch sight of her own car just ahead. Stephen should have been already with the woman, likely in her arms, long before now. She refused to be cheated out of her moment of truth, when she would knock on the door of the apartment and see them together. More, let them see her and know that their whole house of cards had come down on them at once.

But the car was only one like her own, and the driver turned out to be a gray-haired woman with a small poodle by her side. The cab caught up to the car at the light, and Rita sat back in her seat once again, her heart pounding.

She directed the cab driver to let her off at the corner and walked rapidly to the building with the fancy awning with THE NORMANDY APARTMENTS scrawled in red on a white background. Apartment 109. The number was emblazoned on her memory. She had long ago destroyed the pink slip of paper on which she had found it.

She listened for a moment outside the heavy door of the apartment before knocking. Her firm rap on the door seemed to echo in the silence. Rita felt the blood freeze in her veins as a strange voice called out, "Wait!"

Now it would be over. After she had seen the woman with her own eyes, she would be through. She would go straight back home, pack Stephen's bags, then line them up in the hall. Then she just might invite Milton Bannerman to dinner again. The door swung open and her teeth unwittingly dug into her bottom lip.

Oddly, she noticed Stephen first. He was standing by what was likely a bedroom door, shrugging into a bathrobe, tousled, his hair disordered in the way it became when he made love. His lips had that same swollen redness, too, as if he had bitten into a ripe purple plum. He had been looking at his lover, not at the door, and his face was cranky. Stephen always hated to be interrupted once he was in the act. "Who the hell . . . ?"

That was when he turned toward the door to see who had disturbed his pleasure.

But Rita wasn't looking at her husband any longer. Her eyes were instead fixed on the creature who had taken Stephen away from her.

At least she had one thing right . . . *he* was indeed beautiful.

CHAPTER 29

Supremely confident, her face contorted with all the subtle elements of tragedy, noble determination, and acute sympathy, Justine stood before Thea to deliver the kiss of death for Marlissa.

"I feel really . . . uncomfortable, Thea, butting into this thing," she began. She lifted and dropped her thin shoulders in what she hoped was a gesture of dramatic proof of her distaste for the news she was bearing, aware that her news was already heavily on Thea's mind. "Someone has to come right out and say something, and I guess the job has fallen on me." She made her smile apologetic.

Justine's mother had advised her against this scene the night before, cautioning her to sit back and wait for Olivia to act on Marlissa's unintentional betrayal. But Justine's instincts told her that she was not in a position to assess the value of the friendship that existed between these three remarkably unbusinesslike women who had somehow managed to put together and operate this immensely successful company. The gossip about Marlissa dating Brad Cavell and his relationship to Riviera was open knowledge in every office and hallway, and still nothing had been done. It was remotely possible that Thea had indeed missed the rumors or was even shielding them from Olivia's ears. Now it was time to deal directly with that eventuality. By bringing the gossip into the open, Justine would be sure Thea had the information, and if the woman was actually covering for Marlissa to Olivia,

Justine's aggressive disclosure would give Thea the realization that Olivia would be the next to know.

"I wouldn't speak at all, but my loyalty to MagnifiScent, and of course to you, forces me to speak my mind."

Thea indicated a chair, and Justine sat stiffly on its edge. The younger woman looked drawn and pale, the residue of her tan covering her skin like an ill-fitting mask. Even so there was tremendous charm to Thea's face, that same polished prettiness that came through whatever the woman's mood. Justine felt a fresh wave of resentment, of bitter jealousy. *What could business mean to a rich and beautiful woman like you? Step aside, Thea! First Marlissa, and then you!*

"What is it, Justine?" Thea pulled a cigarette from the box but didn't reach for her lighter.

"This thing with Marlissa . . . what's going to happen now?"

"Marlissa?"

So that's the way it was going to be, she thought grimly. Justine froze the concerned look tightly to her features, prepared to spell it out for Thea. "About her dating Brad Cavell. It's so unfair to the company . . . isn't Olivia going to do anything?" She took a deep breath.

Thea's eyes studied her speculatively. The corner of her mouth quirked in what might have been a very faint smile. "Certainly you don't listen to rumors, Justine?" It was a chiding voice, but behind it was something not unlike a threat.

Justine caught the implication but refused to be stifled by it. She felt a quick thrill of surprise and excitement, like a hunter coming upon unexpected game. Until this moment she hadn't believed that Thea had it in her to protect Marlissa this way. But now it was obvious: Thea, perhaps for some antiquated principle of friendship, had kept Marlissa's relationship with Brad from Olivia! "I'm talking about fact, Thea, not rumor. It's obvious that Marlissa has violated security through her relationship with this man. Olivia must be told about this before our new line shows up in every cut-rate drugstore in America!"

Now the smile on Thea's tense face was real and rather frightening. "Oh, let's not bother Olivia with such trivia, darling," she said almost lazily.

Enraged and close to showing it, Justine got to her feet. "I think Olivia needs to be bothered with this." Her voice made it a challenge rather than a statement. "And right away."

Thea said nothing at first. The infuriating smile was fixed in place, but her eyes were hard and bright. Finally she spoke. "I can see you've put a great deal of energy into this, Justine. Perhaps you've also put out energy to circulate this demeaning story? Hmm? I'd rather wondered who was behind it. Ambition is a wonderful character trait—used wisely, that is, and coupled with a little real loyalty." The smile died. Thea put down her cigarette and squared her shoulders.

"My loyalty is to Olivia DeSante and MagnifiScent," Justine countered coldly. "I'm going to see her now."

"I think not." Thea found her lighter, calmly maneuvered the cigarette between her lips, and lit it with the same hand. "You know, I've grown rather fat and lazy lately, letting others do my work. I've suddenly decided, darling, that I won't be needing an assistant after all. I'm afraid that means you'll be joining the ranks of the unemployed." It was Thea's turn to smile sweetly. "And before you go disturbing Olivia—did I forget to tell you? The formula thief was discovered Saturday. A rather nasty man, I'm told. Security has taken care of the entire matter."

Justine gasped and took a step back blindly.

"You will remember to shut the door on your way out, won't you?"

Justine, her expression for once entirely her own, did as she was told.

CHAPTER 30

Rita worked quickly, her habit of neatness and efficiency allowing the transfer of Stephen's clothing from dresser and closets to suitcases to happen faster than she expected. She resisted the urge to bring order from chaos, folding only when essential to fitting a garment into the suitcases. It was really an easy task, because other than his clothing—most of which she had bought—Stephen owned nothing. Even the suitcases were hers, but it would be a final present, one she gave willingly.

As she packed, she kept expecting to be overwhelmed with grief and pain. Now, if ever, was the appropriate time for pain. But she had agonized over Stephen for so long, that now, when the end was at hand, she could feel nothing but repulsion for the man she had loved so long and so well, and a strangely soul-lightening sense of relief.

She was surprised at her own understanding of the relief she felt. She would have expected that to come later, much later. But somehow she knew.

Calmly she closed one suitcase and looked through the apartment for stray bits of Stephen's belongings. There was still room in the second bag. From a great emotional distance Rita found it poignantly sad that a man of Stephen's age had so little to call his own.

A man. Her mind still shied from her new knowledge of whom Stephen had been keeping in that luxurious apartment. But the meaning of what she'd seen was filtering through the layers of shock as cleanly and quickly as the elimination of Stephen from her apartment was progressing.

Was that really the source of my heartache from the moment I found the evidence of Stephen's infidelity? she asked herself wonderingly. *That the failure had been mine as a woman? That I was not woman enough to keep a man from another woman?* And now, understanding that the flaw was in Stephen, a deep, twisted flaw she had neither the experience nor the wisdom to understand, she was oddly at peace with herself. Her only failure lay in being a woman, not in the kind of woman she was.

She brought the closed suitcases to the door, pushing away the memory of what she had seen at the other apartment.

The door opened just as she reached it.

Stephen walked in, his eyes wild, his hair still tousled. "Rita! We have to talk!"

She took a deep breath and resolutely marched past him, the suitcases weighing down both arms. She put them in the hall, just beyond the door.

Rita waited until she was back in the apartment to issue the words she wanted to shout. "There's nothing to say. I want you out of here."

He took a step toward her, an arm extended as if to touch her.

She refused to back down an inch, not in determination and not in gesture. But she turned her head to avoid his touch.

"Look, baby, you don't understand . . . That wasn't what you thought . . ."

"I don't want to talk about it! I don't want to *think* about it! I just want you to leave now!" Her insides tightened with disgust, with the shame he seemed unable to feel. "Now!"

He stared at her silently for a moment. Then, looking more like a child than ever, he bit down on his bottom lip. When his mouth relaxed again, his eyes hardened. "All right! I don't need you! I don't need any woman!"

Rita looked at his face, the face she had adored. In it she now saw only weakness and petulance and a dawning of the realization that he was again being forced to take care of himself. "You're right, Stephen. Leave now. I'd rather not make a scene, but if you aren't out of this apartment in one minute, I fully intend to call the police."

She walked to the phone, and by the time she reached for the receiver, he was gone.

Rita closed her eyes and again waited for some violent emotional reaction. Still there was only relief. When she thought he'd had time to remove his belongings, she went to the door. She cracked it enough to hear the familiar strain of the nearby elevator. She let the door widen and closed her eyes to fully enjoy the wonderful aloneness she had feared before.

"Rita?"

Startled, she opened her eyes to see Milton Bannerman looking at her with concern on his face—what she could see of it behind two sacks of groceries.

"Are you all right?" He shifted the bags awkwardly. "I was going into my apartment and saw . . . *him* . . ." he said the word with apologetic distaste, "leaving. Suitcases." He shrugged and nearly spilled huge oranges from the bag on the left.

Rita grabbed for the oranges and smiled. "Here, Milton. Let me take that." She struggled with him briefly but ended up with one of the heavy bags. "Oh, ice cream! It's melting! Let's get it into your freezer."

She followed him down the hall and waited while he found his key and unlocked the door.

Not since the night of the party so long ago had she been in the Bannerman apartment, and she looked with approval at the perfect order of each room they passed on the way to the spotless kitchen. She liked that. Most men, she imagined, let themselves and their homes go after the death of a wife. She realized that everything about the older man pleased her and couldn't keep from comparing Milton to Stephen in her mind. The tally sheet was embarrassingly disproportionate—Stephen's only asset was his physical appeal, which had recently lost its allure in Rita's eyes.

"I should be carrying your groceries, not you mine," Milton said lightly, taking the sack from her. He put it down and, ignoring the melting ice cream, put a gentle arm around her shoulders. "You're all right?" His kind eyes caressed her face.

The way he was looking at her made Rita feel dainty and young. "Yes, I . . . You know, Milton, yes, I really am fine." She even smiled. "Oh, the ice cream!" She plucked the box out of the sack and put it in the freezer. It fit nicely between orderly stacks of frozen vegetables and a neat line of assorted juices. "I'm actually feeling fine!" She turned back to him. "I can hardly believe how good . . ."

And then, to her surprise and horror, she was crying!

"Here . . . it's all right. . . ." He held her closely and patted her back, riding out the storm with patience and concern. "Let it all go, Rita . . . that's right . . . good. . . ."

Later, when they were drinking the coffee she had made and sitting at his comfortable kitchen table, she told him the whole story. Not because he pried, but because Rita somehow knew that it was safe to tell this man anything. She found it surprisingly easy to tell him even what she had found at the Normandy Apartments.

"Rita, this is not a man to condemn," he said, touching her hand and looking deeply into her eyes. "This is a man to pity. I pity him very much."

"Because . . . because he's a . . . a. . . ." She could not say the word even now.

He smiled. "No, not because of that. I pity him because he had a woman like you and was fool enough to lose her."

Rita felt the quickening of her heart. Part of it was what this good man had said, but more was due to the special way he was looking at her. She felt pretty in his eyes, slim and graceful, young. She tried to return his smile.

"And now," he said, suddenly all business, "I'm going to make you such a dinner—"

"Oh, I couldn't," she protested.

"And why not? You don't trust my cooking? Wait, I'll surprise you with my great talent."

He had a wonderful grin.

He leaned toward her. "Please. You need your strength. For the tomorrows. The new days ahead." His hand moved gently over hers. He looked at her shyly, but with determination.

Slowly, basking in the warmth of his loving gaze, she returned the pressure of his hand.

CHAPTER 31

Olivia hadn't expected Mark back for at least another day. She had unlocked her front door, crossed the foyer, and was about to turn toward the stairs to change when she saw him standing in the middle of the living room, staring at her.

"Mark!" Her face broke into a smile and she began to hurry to him, her arms extended for an embrace.

Something about the way he was looking at her stopped Olivia cold. She stood where she was, in the shadow of the archway. "I didn't expect you so soon," she said softly, frightened by the quiet fury in his eyes.

"I saw Lacy in New York," he said without preamble. "Don't worry, I didn't hear it from him. So feel free to go ahead with your gift of the museum wing and anything else you promised in return for the favor of promoting me." He paused to let his words sink in. "Lacy doesn't have a big mouth. You were right about that. But he has a bitch secretary who drinks a little too much."

Olivia came all the way into the room, her step infinitely more restrained. She didn't say anything until she had poured herself a glass of brandy and tasted it. She almost fixed a drink for Mark but saw he had his own. Gin.

She held her glass with both hands, her face flushed from the wind, her hair perfectly in place. She looked breathlessly beautiful in a soft, pure-white angora suit. She sat down on a straight-back chair and stared at him, fighting for composure. "Mark, we have to talk calmly about this. I know you're upset, but I think I can explain."

He rested against the far wall, his legs crossing at the ankles, looking unconsciously devastating in his well-made trousers and the velour shirt they had bought together on that wonderful shopping spree only weeks earlier. "Oh, can you? Go right ahead. Don't let me stop you." He took another drink from the glass in his hand.

Olivia saw that this was not the first glass he had emptied in the last hour. She could hear it in his voice. But he was far from drunk, and she knew this might be her only chance to reach him. "I did talk to Lacy. The wing . . . that was something we had discussed before. It really had nothing to do with you."

He closed his eyes and spoke so softly she had to strain to hear him. "Don't lie to me, Olivia. That's the one thing you never did. Before . . . all this." He gestured eloquently with the hand that held the empty glass.

She started to protest but stopped, knowing he was right. The wing had been mentioned, and both she and James Lacy had understood its connection with Mark getting his show at Neftale's and much of what came afterward. Desperately she raised her voice. "Why are you making such a big deal of it, Mark? My God, so I helped you a little! It's in the best tradition, you know. I'm not the first person in my field to help artists! Rubinstein did it a long time ago. She gave several of the greatest artists of the century their foot in the door. Does that take something from their art? Is she guilty of something terrible because she used her money and influence to wake up a blind and indifferent world?"

He was nodding with her words, as if it were music she was making and he was trying to catch the beat. He opened his eyes and looked at her. "You really don't understand, do you? I rather imagined you wouldn't." He crossed the room quickly to stand over her. "I wanted to do it myself! Why is it so hard to get that through your beautiful head, Olivia? All I asked is that you let me do it myself, whatever the hell I'm meant to do. I never wanted your help. I detest your helping me! You're not my mother, and I'm no one's child. I never asked a fucking thing of you, Olivia. I didn't even ask you to wait until I'd made it! I was going to come back to you when I'd done for myself what you've done for yourself. I would have returned with pride, Olivia. And if you had something better going at the time, I'd have walked away." He paused, almost smiled. "But you know something funny? I always had so much faith in us that I thought you'd be there waiting, ready, that day, whenever it came." The half-smile died.

"But you couldn't wait, could you? You couldn't leave me alone. You had to get in there, twist and manipulate, bribe and plot. You wanted me at any cost, even at the price of my self-respect! And what of your self-respect? Or your respect for me? For me, Olivia, as a man. As an artist!"

She stood up, tried to reach out for him. She felt as if her life was being torn to bits, and she was not sure who was responsible for the tearing. Through a haze of hot tears she saw him step back outside her reach, as if her touch was now repugnant to him. "Mark! I never meant to hurt you! I only wanted to help!"

He nodded and reached down for his jacket. "I believe you mean that, Olivia. I believe you don't realize what it is you've done." He'd not once raised his voice, and now he lowered it still more. "You've robbed me of a lifetime of work—that's what your manipulation of my career has done. Now I may never know if my recognition has come through my work or your name. Damn it, Olivia, if I'm ever to make it, I'll have to start all over again! Do you understand? *Start all over!* Either that"—he put on the jacket and started for the door—"or quit. That's what you've done to me."

She watched him go, remembering the last time he had left, trying to tell herself that as before, he would come back. He would have to come back. "Mark! My God! You don't understand—I did it all for you! Please . . . don't go," she cried out. Somehow she knew that this time was not the same. He would leave, and he would never come back.

She couldn't help herself—all the pain inside demanded immediate release. She would not even have the dignity of crying alone. She pressed her hands to her face and allowed the tears to push through the edges of her shaking fingers. Even then some faint voice inside reminded her that Mark could never resist tears.

"I once heard a quote, I don't remember who said it," he said almost conversationally from the archway on his way to the door. "It went something like this: 'I climbed upon his back and told him I loved him. I said that everything I'd ever done had been for him. I told him I would do anything in the world for him. Except get off his back.'

"The only way to get you off my back, Olivia, is to get out of your life. Good-bye, Olivia."

She didn't see him leave.

BOOK TWO

Let the long contention cease!
Geese are swans, and swans are geese.
—*Matthew Arnold*

CHAPTER 32

It was one of those rare, spectacular days in San Francisco, a true summer day with the temperature in the high eighties, the wind for once only a gentle breeze and the sky unblemished by haze or clouds. Because the weather was so good, Olivia's spirits had risen with it, and the day had flown by quickly, productively. At six o'clock, and with only two hours left until she had to meet Howard Thomas, she still lingered at the office with Thea Hamlinton, contemplating a third martini.

Olivia hesitated before refilling Thea's glass. "You *are* still capable of driving home unassisted, aren't you?" she asked, smiling but a little concerned. Thea's drinking had lessened greatly since she'd married Everett almost a year and a half ago, but today she'd quickly downed three martinis to Olivia's two.

"Perfectly." Thea giggled, held her glass out, and glanced down at the scribbles she had made on her pad. "I keep wanting to change the word *line* into *lion*. You know, 'MagnifiScent has tamed the lion of time.' The lines of time, actually, but that sounds so . . . unromantic."

Olivia shook her head. "Not tamed. Merely smoothed out for a few hours. Now if Marlissa could come up with a cream that would remove lines entirely. . . . Not that I'm not ecstatic about what she has done. This is without a doubt the best product of its kind. We'll wipe out the market. Imagine it—one application of this cream and a woman loses years from her face. If only for the night."

Olivia allowed herself to be momentarily distracted by the miracle of product development. She was awed by the knowledge that in a relatively short time the application of cosmetics had progressed from the stage at which women had whitened their faces with zinc-based solutions that ruined their skin and often their health, to now, when creams and paints added beauty while actually repairing damaged tissues. She scanned her list of possible names for the new product.

"You're right," she said, leaning back in her chair. "We need romance, but not at the sacrifice of honesty." She took a sip of her drink and basked in an all-too-rare sense of well-being. This was one of the moments she liked best in life, idling over a cocktail in her office at the end of the day waiting for inspiration to hit. While she employed a whole department of people to create names and publicity for her new lines, often Olivia came up with the best names herself. "Hmm . . . Magic Moment . . . or . . . Time Stop . . . no, I suppose honesty won't stretch that far. . . ."

Thea put down her glass and pressed her fingertips against her temples as if to provoke a brilliant idea.

Olivia smiled at her friend fondly. "You look as if you've swallowed a mouthful from the fountain of youth yourself." She held her hand out. "Forget it," she said as Thea looked up hopefully. "Label this Fountain of Youth and customers will wake up the next morning hating us as they count the same number of wrinkles." She returned to her study of Thea, thinking she had never seen her friend look so radiant. She'd had her hair cut and restyled. The new scattered bangs gave her a feminine girlishness, accentuated by a natural streaking from her hours in the sun. The bleached gold went well with the light brown of her hair, and her good, clear skin was tan, intensifying the darkness of her eyes. But it was more than the sun and a hairstylist that had made Thea look so wonderful. "Marriage must agree with you," Olivia commented.

For an instant Thea looked away from Olivia. When she looked back, her lips were smiling. "It's not bad stuff. You should try it sometime." It was Thea's turn to study Olivia. "How are things going with Howard?"

"Perfect. But don't you start on me. Just because Howard is wonderful, brilliant, and probably the best thing that's ever happened to me doesn't mean I'm ready to get married." She laughed at herself. "I'd make a hell of a lawyer, wouldn't I? I'd convict my own client."

Thea's shrug was eloquent. "I didn't put those words in your mouth, darling. So why don't you marry him? I thought he was rather perfect myself." She sipped from her glass. "Perfect, but not Mark, is that it?"

Olivia sat absolutely motionless, seeming more a lifelike portrait than a flesh-and-blood woman. In the nearly two years since she had last seen Mark, her wonderful face had altered subtly—not aged, really, but matured in some undefinable fashion. The classic lines and angles were all there, but now there was a softness that had been missing before, a depth to the ice-blue eyes, a reflective melancholy.

"Mark," she repeated softly, echoing Thea dreamily. "No, he's not Mark." She looked at her friend sharply. "Where the hell is he, Thea?"

"I don't know, darling." She hesitated only a moment. "Don't you?"

They hadn't talked about Mark for a long time. Olivia fought the temptation to change the subject. The calm pleasure she had felt minutes before was gone now. "No, I don't. Not one word, Thea. In all this time, not one word! I've asked everyone. You wouldn't believe how hard I've tried to find him." She looked up to meet Thea's incredulous eyes. "It's as if he's disappeared."

She got up and walked slowly to the windows. She stood with her back to her friend, staring at but not seeing the Golden Gate Bridge in the distance.

"You haven't mentioned Mark for ages, love. Are you thinking about him now because Howard's asked you to marry him?"

Olivia nodded without turning around. "Yes, I suppose so. He wants an answer, and he won't wait forever. The insane thing is there's no reason not to marry him. He's wonderful company, I adore Kevin and Jennifer"—she thought briefly of Howard's teenage children, who were ardently in favor of their widowed father marrying her—"and I adore Howard, too. He's been good to me, Thea. And good for me."

"I thought you were the one who always said that five-letter words like *adore* are used by people who want to cover the fact that they can't say *love*." Thea smiled gently. "Do you really love him, Olivia? The way you've always loved Mark?"

"I'll never love anyone the way I love Mark." Olivia felt a sharp pain inside her chest. "But what the hell does that have to do with anything? I'm thirty-four years old, and I'm sick to death of waiting, and I'm so damned lonely—" She broke off her sentence and walked firmly back to the desk and the rest of her martini. "Why are we talking about this?" She picked up her note pad. "How did we get from a name for the face smoother to Mark?" Olivia stared hard at the pad.

"You know," Olivia mused, "most people don't realize the enormous difference the name of a product has on its popularity. Marlissa herself can't understand it. She thinks that if a product is good, that should be enough. It certainly is true that the best name in the world won't help a bad product, but the wrong name can destroy a perfectly good one, too. Especially in cosmetics. I don't think it was until Charles Revson came along with his *Fire and Ice* campaign in 1952 that this point really hit home. What was that he once said? Oh, yes, and I quote, 'In the factory, we make cosmetics; in the store, we sell hope.' And hope, Thea, means a name that evokes romance and excitement. So what do we have here? A marvel, really. Something that can turn back the clock for a little while, can make a woman appear younger in minutes. We need a name that will make women think about what that can mean to her personally . . . it's a brief second chance, a. . . ."

Thea, watching her friend carefully, reached over and touched Olivia's hand. "Look, darling, I know what you're going through with the decision to marry Howard or not, I know you can't give up the hope that Mark will show up again. Do you want to talk about it? We can work on a name for the cream in the morning, at the meeting. I think Howard's proposal is heavy in your mind. Won't it help to talk it out?"

Olivia put down her pad and sank into her chair. "I don't see the point of it, but thanks, Thea. What is there to say? You know as much as I do. Mark simply disappeared. At first I didn't worry. He'd done wonderfully at his shows, so money wouldn't have been a problem for a while. But when a year passed and I hadn't heard anything . . . I . . . well, I had to try to find him. Discreetly, of course." She grimaced. "By then I knew a great deal about discretion."

She didn't bother to tell Thea about her efforts to locate Mark, the detectives she'd hired or how she had had her salon director, Miles Holbrook, pretend to be a collector willing to pay anything for a Lyman original from the artist himself. "But no one seems to know where he is. It's as if he vanished the night he stepped out of my house. That's the way he wanted it, so I suppose I was a fool to try to find him."

Then a shadow seemed to leave Olivia's eyes and she smiled at Thea. "You know, I really can't blame myself for what happened. I was doing the best I could at the time. More than friend and lover, Mark has always been my greatest teacher. He believes everyone does the best she can based on who she is and what she knows at the time, and he considers guilt a waste of time. Angry as he was the night he left, I'm sure later he understood that I really was trying to help. Only at the time I didn't know that the one I was most interested in helping was myself, not Mark."

"But everything you did, you did for him!"

Olivia smiled as if at a private joke. "I did everything for him except get off his back."

Thea looked up from the cigarette she was lighting. "What?"

"Nothing. But Mark was right. He had to make it on his own. Because he knew I would never have respected him fully unless he did. Don't misunderstand—I'd have loved him in any case. If he had never made a dime as an artist, I would have respected him for trying. Don't you see? But if he didn't do it alone, I would always have had a little element of doubt about how good he was, about what would have happened to him if I hadn't been pulling the strings. That's what's good about my relationship with Howard. He has been completely successful on his own. He doesn't need anything from me—except love."

"Which might be the only thing you can't give him. Did you ever think of that?"

"Unfortunately, yes. Only I'm not sure what love is exactly anymore. If it's not the variety that acts like a fatal disease. How can I say that what I feel for Howard isn't love?" She shot a steely glance at Thea. "Don't say it isn't love. It just isn't . . . violent love. I'm not sure the violent kind is what I want any longer. It hurts too damn much. And it takes too much energy. I could be happy with Howard. We could have a good life."

Thea put out her cigarette. "I hear what you're saying, Olivia, but I also hear you trying to talk yourself into something you might not want. You've had one less-than-satisfying marriage, and I'd hate to see you try another. God knows you've given Mark every chance in the world, and maybe Mark won't be back. Maybe he has disappeared. Maybe he has married someone else, and has a family." Thea kept her eyes on Olivia's face as she lit another cigarette. "I wish you could see your face right now. You look as if I'd stabbed you and twisted the knife. No, don't deny it," she added quickly as Olivia opened her mouth to protest. "It was a calculated thrust, darling. Maybe someday you might be ready to settle for less than you want, but this isn't the day."

Thea had hit home, and Olivia was too honest to deny how much the thought of Mark being with another woman disturbed her. "Do you want to hear the ultimate in selfishness? I would rather Mark be *dead* than out there somewhere in space. At least if he were dead I could have mourned and forgotten him! I wouldn't have to go on waiting, wondering. . . . Oh, damn it, Thea, see what you've done to me? I don't mean any of this. After Mark left, I worked it all out. At first I couldn't understand why he was so upset. I played a lot with the word *manipulation*—an unpleasant word, but in the real world it's as necessary as breathing." She gestured toward her pad. "When we come up with a name for a product, for example, we're manipulating the public. Social tact is manipulation. Parents manipulate their children, children their parents." She smiled. "Believe me, I played with that concept until I'd managed to make Mark the villain instead of me. And do you know what the final truth is? I simply didn't trust Mark or myself enough to let his career move at his own pace. I wanted him that minute. I made everything else in my life work the way I wanted it, so why not Mark?"

"So now you're finally giving up? You've waited long enough, and you're calling in the second string?"

Olivia looked at Thea levelly. "Yes, I suppose you could say that." She paused thoughtfully. "That doesn't sound quite fair to Howard, does it?"

"No." Thea's face revealed an internal struggle. "Look, Olivia, I didn't want to say anything until I was sure, but—"

The phone's loud ring startled both women.

Olivia answered it quickly. "Yes?"

"Mrs. DeSante, this is Clyde Williams. Security. I'm sorry to disturb you, but there's a man here who insists on seeing you."

Frowning, Olivia glanced over at Thea, her thoughts going again to Mark. She brushed the foolish hope out of her mind. "The offices are closed, Mr. Williams," she reminded the security officer gently, surprised that he would disturb her. People were always wanting to see her, wherever she was. "Perhaps you could advise him to contact my personal secretary Monday morning about a possible appointment." Myoko was a genius at discouraging unwelcome callers.

The security guard's voice was hesitant, uncomfortable. "Oh, yes, Mrs. DeSante. Normally I would have done that first thing. But he . . . the man says he's your father, and I don't have his name on my—"

"My *what?*"

Thea looked up from her drink at the sound of Olivia's voice.

"Yeah. Name of Nash. Let's see . . . James Franklin Nash. That's it. Should I bring him up?"

Olivia nodded, realized the guard downstairs couldn't see her gesture, and weakly instructed him to do so at once. She hung up woodenly. "My father is on his way up here, Thea. My father!"

"Is this some sort of joke?" Thea suggested dubiously, knowing that Olivia hadn't seen or even heard from her father since she was twelve years old. "Should I stay?"

"Yes. No. No, you'd better go. If it's some grim joke, security will be here." Her face was paler than ever. "How could it be a joke?" She tried to analyze her feelings but drew an emotional blank. It had been too long; too much had happened. Her father was like a character in a barely remembered book. "This should be . . . interesting. Thea, I thought you said your mother told you he'd remarried about ten years ago and sold the house in Beverly Hills."

She nodded. "Mother said his second wife died a few years ago. They were living in Florida after he retired, I believe. Why in hell is he here now?" She got up and buttoned her brown velvet blazer. "Call me later, will you? I'll be home." She glanced worriedly at Olivia's face, which was perfectly composed. "Call me even if you don't need me. I simply can't wait until tomorrow to hear about this."

Olivia nodded and watched her friend go to the door. "I promise. Before I go out with Howard."

The mention of Howard made Thea hesitate. "Olivia?" She opened the door and peered into the empty outer office and the silent hallway beyond. Then she turned back to her friend. "Listen, don't say yes to Howard tonight, do you understand?"

"What?" Olivia was thinking of her father, musing over the troubled past.

Thea took a deep breath. "I didn't want to say anything until I was absolutely sure, but I think I might possibly know where Mark is. Just don't agree to marry Howard right this minute, okay?" She laughed at the quizzical expression on

Olivia's face, at the flash of hope just underneath. "You never were one to settle for second best."

"Thea!" But Olivia was talking to an empty space. She half-rose to go after Thea and then sank back into her chair. What had Thea been saying? But she couldn't afford to think about Mark now, because for the first time since her twelfth birthday she had her father to contend with.

"One disaster at a time," she said with a trace of nervous humor. Then she bent over and began to scribble on her pad, wanting very much to look preoccupied and undisturbed when her father walked in.

In a way it was almost funny. Her father had prided himself on always being on time. He had been fastidious about punctuality.

And now he was twenty-two years too late.

CHAPTER 33

Stepping from under the cool, dim shade of MagnifiScent's awnings to the uncovered patch of sun-struck concrete walkway leading to her parking space, Thea felt a trifle giddy. She good-naturedly cursed the last martini and craned her neck for a glimpse of a uniformed security guard escorting an elderly man.

She reached her car without seeing any twosome fitting this description. She barely remembered Olivia's father, had only caught fleeting glimpses of him even when she was a guest at the Nash house as a child.

Deciding that Nash was already in the building, Thea got into her convertible and started the engine. She pushed Olivia out of her mind as she drove onto the street. Olivia could handle anything, even a meeting with her long-lost father. But Olivia was human, too, and that was why Thea had blurted out her hint that Mark might not be somewhere in oblivion.

Thea pushed that line of speculation away as well. She and Olivia could talk about it later. Right now she had to concentrate on getting through traffic. She had less than fifteen minutes to get to Klaus Murer before it closed if she wanted to get the ring she had ordered before Monday. She was eager to get home. Everett would be flying in later that evening, and she had a million things to do first. His birthday was Sunday. The ring had been a sudden inspiration, and she'd barely given the famous jeweler time to work on it. If she had to, she'd double-park and risk a ticket. She was uncertain about the inscription she'd ordered on the inside of the band, and she might have to have it changed.

A car changed lanes in front of her without signaling. Thea braked hard, but nothing could dampen her spirits. It was always this way when she knew she would be with her husband within hours. This would be a short weekend for them, however. Everett had to be at his San Francisco office for a meeting the next morning, and she also had a rare Saturday meeting with Olivia and the executive staff at MagnifiScent. They would meet immediately afterward at the airport and fly to L.A. For fun, they would be going to a party at Hugh Hefner's celebrated Playboy Mansion in Holmby Hills on Saturday night. Then Sunday morning she would return to San Francisco, while Everett flew to Rome. Then it would be a solid two weeks before they would be together again.

Thea breezed through a yellow light and began a zigzag of turns that would eventually bring her to the jeweler's shop. She was finally over resenting The City's confusing one-way streets and was finding a certain amount of pleasure at plotting her course. She liked San Francisco. It kept her on her toes. Los Angeles was too relaxed, too agreeable. Easy, wide boulevards; calm, generally balmy weather; a lazy, let-your-hair-down style. Here everything was brisk and challenging, and it made her feel more alive.

Have I changed? Thea wondered. Was she simply trying to convince herself that she had the best of all possible marriages in the best of all worlds?

I'm happy! she told herself, impatiently waiting for the light to change. But couldn't she be happier? Thea sighed, glanced at her watch, and saw that she had a scant five minutes to find a place to park and dash into the store. She gunned the motor, edged a large Mercedes out of the other lane, and made the next light easily. All right, it was possible to admit to herself that she had hoped for a long time that Everett would insist she give up her position at MagnifiScent and live with him permanently in Beverly Hills. They would have kept the house on the Marina for their frequent business trips, of course, but without her job there was no reason they couldn't live together like most couples. She would have acknowledged that the times they were apart were difficult for her. Not unbearable, because she always had the next meeting to look forward to, and Everett called almost nightly. But she hadn't even been able to tell him how much she missed him, because he had never implied that their life-style bothered him in the least.

The irony of the situation was not beyond Thea. That she of all people would end up ardently desiring the most conventional of all marriages, and wanting it with Everett . . . yes, it was amusing. Only it didn't *feel* amusing. She only knew that being with Everett gave her all the excitement she had ever wanted, and that being away from him left her hungry and tense. It wasn't sex, either. How could she find in the arms of any other man what she had found with Everett? How could she ever have suspected the sensual depths of the man? Where had he learned how to please a woman so completely? Thea shivered deliciously, remembering the time after time he had slowly and skillfully aroused endless passion in her, leaving her breathless, exhausted, and completely fulfilled afterward. Incredible that after a year and a half of marriage, she still felt the same wild urge at the thought of a night alone with her husband. Everett, who had once left her cold—no, even worse, had actually been so unappealing that she had left the country to avoid him. She could barely acknowledge the girl she had been then, blind, stubborn, defiant, looking in all the wrong places for what she already had. *What a lot of wasted years,* she thought wistfully.

There was a parking space right in front of the jeweler's shop. Thea slid into it and was back in her car ten minutes later, less frantic now that she had her prize. She lit a cigarette and opened the velvet-lined box to look at Everett's present again.

It was perfect, and it had been her design. She looked at it in its black velvet nest with a glow of satisfaction. The idea of having it made had come out of a light conversation she had had with Everett the last time they were together. The subject of wedding rings for men had come up. It had bothered Thea that he hadn't wanted a double-ring ceremony, and his naked left hand was a constant reminder that he was not committed to her on all levels. They never talked about their relationships with other people, of course. That was part of their agreed-upon discretion. But Thea thought about the other women in Everett's life constantly. It was the fly in the ointment, the one bone of contention that had become lodged in her throat. He never gave the slightest indication that he ever thought about the men she must be seeing. And the ultimate irony was that there were no other men in Thea's life.

She put out her cigarette and took the ring from its cradle. She turned the ring over. *E now and always T,* it read in thin script. The weight of the ring felt good in her hand, comforting, reassuring. It would make her a part of him wherever he went, whoever was at his side.

Thea returned the ring to its box, put it carefully into her purse, and started the engine. Her thoughts kept returning to the ring. The picture of Everett wearing it comforted her. It seemed to Thea the ring was a talisman that would bind him to her with more power than the legal papers that had made them husband and wife.

She glanced at her watch. She would have to hurry again to keep the next appointment. Her brief happiness over the ring was dulled by a sense of apprehension, and nervously she fumbled for another cigarette as she melted into the slowly moving traffic. She dared not be late for this hastily made appointment, the outcome of which could alter her entire life.

The ring's symbolic importance dwindled as she drove tensely to the doctor's office.

CHAPTER 34

Marlissa Deloffre dawdled a moment in her office, enjoying the quiet and sorting the papers she had prepared for her meeting in Olivia's office. She rarely minded working on a Saturday, and today the intrusion into her weekend was a blessing.

She leaned back in her chair and glanced around the office. As she herself had, it had changed in the last year and a half. Interestingly, the changes had been somewhat parallel, and both she and the room looked better for them. She had once been rather drab and anonymous in appearance, but she now had a decided style of her own, tested and enlarged by experimentation. The room had also become more distinctively hers, her personality no longer hidden by the heavier, more decisive hand of an interior decorator.

It had always been an impressive office, with its well-chosen paintings and prints on the walls, an Epstein reproduction on its own stainless-steel pillar, the matching modern grandfather clock. Before, it had been the office of any top executive, but now it was stamped with the personality of its mistress. Marlissa had hung a lovely tapestry on one wall, a small and finely detailed collection of Japanese plates on another, and scattered mementos from home on tabletops and on her desk, unashamed of their honest sentimentality. There was also a favorite picture of her parents framed in Florentine leather, and a few of her degrees and awards behind her desk. The touches she had added lent warmth and interest that was previously lacking.

She glanced into the beveled-glass mirror across from her desk and studied herself without vanity or illusion. She was still not the flawless beauty that Olivia was, nor had she approached Thea's high level of sophistication. But her dark brown hair had been smartly cut and styled to emphasize her good cheekbones and lower jaw, which was prettily tipped at the chin. The judicious use of the cosmetics she had created polished her face and let its character show. Her natural good taste had led her to buy a wardrobe that was an attractive reflection of Marlissa in her entirety, still basically European but contemporary. She had an eye for quality and a nose for a new style that would not be ludicrous by the next season.

Marlissa knew that there had been internal changes as well, but on that score she felt less settled, less sure that the alterations had been entirely positive. She well remembered the insecure woman she had been when she had started seeing Brad Cavell. Becoming involved with Brad had initiated the change, certainly, and since then she had dated a fair number of men like him, all worldly, accustomed to living well, clever with women. She was supposed to go sailing with one of them today, in fact, but this meeting had taken precedence.

Marlissa folded her arms on the desk, rested her head on them, and mentally began lining up the men in her life. First Matt Douglas, the eternal preppie, who clung to his memories of college days and was an inveterate football-game goer whenever his alma mater was involved. Matt, a stockbroker by trade, was entertaining, rich, and uncomplicated. He was recovering slowly from his second divorce in ten years and wanted nothing more than an intelligent, undesigning date and, from time to time, an equally uncomplicated, energetic romp in bed.

Then there was Phillip, also divorced and a spectacularly talented violinist, who made his living as vice-president of an insurance company. He took her to concerts and operas, and since he was terrified of a deep involvement with any woman, never suggested sex. He was no doubt waiting until his wife came to her senses and took him back.

Alec Van Der Mere, another displaced European, was married, but his work as the head of an import business kept him from spending the majority of his time at home in Holland. The fact of his marriage would have bothered Marlissa, but he told her that he and his wife had worked out an arrangement that allowed both to act as free agents. He adored Marlissa but he did not love her and always treated her with respect.

And then there was Ernst.

Not for the first time in the year and a half since Ernst had come to this country, Marlissa was conscious of a heavy weight in her chest at the thought of him.

He had arrived in New York even before she had received the letter stating his intention to come to San Francisco almost a year and a half ago. But he had lingered in New York, visiting relatives and friends of his extensive family there. He had negotiated the sale of his carpentry business in Meiringen by mail, to an uncle who wanted to retire in the town of his birth, and the sale had involved a transfer of bonds that further delayed Ernst's departure from the East Coast.

Ernst had called her at her house the first night after he arrived in New York, and Marlissa had begged him to stay where he was. She had slipped easily into her native tongue on the phone, which also and unreasonably had irritated her. But most annoying of all was the fact that his voice excited her so greatly that she had to work hard to keep hers flat.

"Why are you here? Why are you coming to San Francisco?"

His familiar voice, a bit stiff after their long absence and formalized by his awareness of the cost of the call he was making, was as matter-of-fact as if they had talked only the night before. "To be with you, Marlissa. No, that is presumptuous of me. To see you, Marlissa. To find out for myself what has changed your mind toward me."

She had almost forgotten his direct nature. His statement left her floundering for a suitable answer. However direct he was with her, she could not possibly tell him her thoughts on the matter. She could not hurt him that way. In the end she was forced to restate what she had already said when she left Meiringen.

"I told you already. All our lives we have known nothing but each other. You are content to live the same way as your parents, and their parents before them. I want a different kind of life! Olivia DeSante gave me my passport to another world, Ernst. It is a world you would detest. But I am happy here, do you understand? Please don't come. It would only make matters difficult for both of us."

"Are you saying that you don't wish to see me, Marlissa?" He didn't give her a chance to respond. "We must see each other! This is absurd. Do you think perhaps that I would force a relationship you do not want? I, too, desire a change. There is nothing for me in Meiringen. I am tired of Europe. A good carpenter can find work anywhere in the world. I will live in your San Francisco, but I ask nothing more than to see and talk with you whenever it is convenient. You're a busy woman now, I understand. We are lifelong friends, Marlissa. Beyond that . . . we shall see."

She had met his plane the following month and had been unable to hide her pleasure at seeing him again. At the same time she found herself uncomfortably conscious of his poorly tailored, ill-fitting suit, the cheap luggage he carried, his thickly accented English. Ashamed, she concentrated instead on his intelligent blue eyes, his familiar and dear face and the welcome bits of trivia he related about their home. He had seen her family just before leaving Switzerland and had gifts and messages to deliver. Her parents had come for a visit less than three months before, but it had seemed like years.

Ernst had already made arrangements to move into an apartment with Hans Freyer, a second or third cousin he'd met many years before, not too far away from her house in St. Francis Wood. Marlissa was relieved to hear that he'd taken care of his living arrangements beforehand—for over a week she had scouted the city for a suitable but inexpensive rental, and all the time her massive house with its half-dozen unused bedrooms had rebuked her silently. She no longer knew how to classify Ernst. As he had pointed out on the phone, they were primarily friends. Had any other friends come from home to San Francisco, she would have insisted on their staying at her house for as long as they wished.

But this was Ernst, the first man—the only man—she had ever loved, and in spite of the time and distance between them, nothing seemed changed. Even her sensitivity about his clothing and the way he spoke had a proprietary flavor. She wouldn't have minded or even noticed in a friend, but Ernst and everything connected to him still seemed a reflection on her, and she had instinctively reacted like a wife nagged by her husband's frayed collar, seeing in it her own incompetency.

Perhaps he had understood that she would be unable to ask him to stay at her house yet miserable if she had deposited him in some second-rate hotel, and he had put off coming to the West Coast until he had made the arrangement with Hans. With relief Marlissa saw that the apartment in which he would be living was large and comfortable, well furnished, and spotlessly clean. Hans was still in New York with his family, and after depositing Ernst's luggage in the bedroom that would be his, Marlissa took him out for dinner and a tour of the city.

He loved San Francisco immediately. His open excitement and appreciation delighted Marlissa, forcing her to realize that she liked the unique experience of being the sophisticate for once, of showing off her wonderful new world as an insider. This had been her role, being awed and thrilled; and with Ernst, she found that for all the pleasures of being with sophisticated men, she had missed the simple joy of childlike wonder she shared with this unpretentious man.

They nibbled seafood from paper cups at the wharf and had espresso coffee in a North Beach bistro. She played tour guide with relish. He was fascinated with the spectacular bridges over the bay, but sheepishly admitted expecting the Golden Gate to be gold rather than rusty orange. He had to ride a cable car on Powell Street and wander through the tourist traps in Chinatown. He made her promise to take him to the zoo. The day melted into a velvety night, and she drove to the top of Twin Peaks for a dazzling view of The City, its lights a cluster of flashing diamonds below. Afterward they wandered around the deserted Palace of Fine Arts, and she pointed out Olivia's house above in Pacific Heights and Thea's glass-fronted home on the Marina on the left. Famished, they went to The Patio, an unpretentious little restaurant on Castro Street, for a homemade soup-and-quiche dinner. Ernst stared at the unusual grouping of single-sex couples at the various tables but made no comment.

The final treat was the MagnifiScent building. Marlissa sat quietly in the car while Ernst silently absorbed the contrast between the Deloffres' quaint little shop in Meiringen and this huge, spectacular monument with its silver and gold awnings. Even the new factory in Meiringen hadn't prepared him for this building, and though it was late, he insisted on an immediate tour of MagnifiScent.

He said nothing but was obviously acutely aware of the diffidence of the security guards as they greeted Marlissa. She showed him everything with tremendous pride, saving her office and laboratory for last. The salons and creative complex stunned him, and he muttered almost worriedly about the vast amount of money expended on each department. Showing it all to him excited her, as if she were again seeing it for the first time. They strolled through the huge packaging wing with its machines and clutter, the perfume-vatting chamber with its special safety locks and the bookkeeping floor with its glassed-in computer that cost millions. They rode the elevator smoothly from floor to floor, peeking into Olivia's penthouse office, the spectacular nighttime view from her bronzed windows no more impressive than her fantastic office itself.

Finally they went to Marlissa's office for a drink, and she showed him her wonderful personal laboratory, explaining the marvels of science that had cost a fortune to ensure that she wanted for nothing as she compounded her formulas and constantly enlarged the prestigious MagnifiScent line.

"You have been responsible for all this," he said breathlessly when they were back in her office for their nightcap.

She felt a twinge of unexpected sadness at his awe, although she had deliberately planned to force such a reaction from him. It had been the only way she could think of to show him pointedly and without the need for crushing words how really different their lives had become. Still ahead was a brief stop at her house, which would cap off the contrast she was trying to illustrate. His face was already telling her that he was beginning to understand that he had no place in her new universe, could never belong and feel at home. Subtleties eluded him—he knew that she looked wonderful in her classically simple dress of black wool crepe, but he didn't realize it carried a Pierre Cardin label and cost more than seven hundred dollars. He admired the cut of her hair but gave no thought of the price such artistry commanded. But the MagnifiScent building and her house had the power to force recognition of her new status, and she loathed herself for the necessity of making such superficial distances between them essential.

She made the tour of her house brief, hiding the depression she felt at the mingled expression of surprise and intimidation in his eyes. A part of her wanted to blurt out that this was only window dressing, that she was still the same girl he had loved. The lovely day was ruined by this show of success—how could he compete, what could he offer? Marlissa thought of Olivia with Mark, remembering how Mark had fled from Olivia's offer that he move into her world, had come back only to leave for good when he learned that she had had a hand in getting him recognition. She had understood Mark's reaction, and she was sensitive to Ernst's feelings now. But at the same time she sympathized with Olivia's frustration that Mark would allow tangible symbols of success to keep them apart. Couldn't Ernst see that this display of materialism was nothing more than bits of metal and fabric, trinkets and glitter? But her feelings made no sense—she herself had chosen this life over him when she left Meiringen. Why were her emotions insisting that the luxury and comfort after which she had lusted were meaningless?

She had gone too far and shown Ernst too well that he had no place in her life. She walked into his arms as he opened them as a gesture of the measure of her success. She hugged him tightly, growing excited when, in his hunger and pain, he hesitated only a moment before tightening his arms around her.

"I've missed you so terribly," she whispered into his thick neck, no longer giving a damn about the absurdity of her surrender.

"Marlissa . . . My darling."

He was not as skillful in bed as she had remembered, and with sadness she knew that men like Brad Cavell far outdistanced him in technique and experience. Why, then, did she feel at home against Ernst's broad naked chest? Why did the slow, hesitant way he moved inside her thrill her infinitely more than Brad's expertise ever had? There was no need for words once they had passed into her bedroom, and the hours disappeared as they held each other tightly and worked a magic that dissolved time.

When the first stains of pink and gold morning lightened the room, Marlissa cried in shame while Ernst slept at her side. It was not their night of passion that had aroused this grief but rather her weakness, her stupid and stubborn love for him. Nothing had changed. Still warm from his body, she could imagine her embarrassment and shame at introducing Ernst, the farm boy, Ernst, the carpenter, to her San Francisco friends. Introducing him as her lover, her mate . . . it was impossible. It negated everything she had worked to achieve, exposing her new chic as a thin coating of illusion over the naked peasantry of a social-climbing farm girl. She remembered the game children played in the streets . . . *take two steps forward . . . now a giant step back.*

She knew she was not prepared to take even one small step backward, and to reinvest her emotions in Ernst was to take the dreaded giant step in the wrong direction.

Sitting in her office almost a year and a half later, she felt sickened at the memory of the cold way she had deposited

Ernst at the doorstep of his new apartment after their night of love, how she had refused to see him again for almost a year, and then only because he had promised that he would never again overstep the boundaries of friendship, tactfully willing to accept full responsibility for that moment in which she had moved into his arms.

During that year she had met new men and dated eagerly, sleeping with some of them, laughing and playing the sophisticate with greater and greater ease. But she had also started to look forward to an occasional outing with Ernst, and the night before, over dinner, she had known that before long she would again find herself luring him to her bed. She couldn't help comparing him to the others, knew that she would be bored had she kept her date with Matt for sailing. It was a relief that Olivia had organized this Saturday meeting. She needed time to think.

She had agreed to see Ernst again that night.

The stainless-steel grandfather clock sounded the hour with electronic precision. She gathered her notes and left her office.

CHAPTER 35

The meeting, necessitated by a problem of reorganization due to the rapidly expanding scope of the business, went smoothly.

After Miles Holbrook gave his report on the salons, he set up the itinerary for Olivia's next trip, scheduled for the following month. It would include stops at the newly opened branches in Hawaii and Alaska, Canada and Baja California.

Consideration of Olivia's new name for the skin smoother also was on the agenda. Second Chance sounded good, was easy to remember, and might even sell the product with its contrived ambiguity. Second Chance. It suggested a stolen moment in which a woman might appear young again. It would also make her think of some long-lost opportunity and how it might be repeated and improved.

Following a brief discussion of the quarterly budgets, the group disbanded, Miles to fly immediately to Hawaii, Marlissa to check something in her lab, the accountant to return to his office, and the three lawyers to hurry jointly to the golf course.

Thea had stayed as long as she dared, allowing just enough time to get to the airport to meet Everett for their flight to Los Angeles. Olivia had kept her promise to call after the meeting with her father, but Thea wanted to hear the story all over again, this time in greater detail.

And Olivia had her own list of eager questions for Thea.

But finally Thea had hurried off, and Myoko Harper, who had been on hand to take notes, also finished up and departed. The building was as quiet as a tomb, although there were probably two dozen people still on the premises, counting the cleaning crews and security.

Relishing the quiet, Olivia moved from her desk to the couch. She felt a faint desire for a cigarette and vaguely resented the fact that the urge for tobacco had never completely faded. She stared out her tinted bronze window, but from her angle on the couch she could only see limitless expanses of patchy blue sky coddled by billowy white clouds.

Her father had been in this office less than sixteen hours ago, and the echo of his voice seemed to cling to the furniture and reverberate from the walls. Not that his had ever been a loud or distinctive voice—Olivia had been surprised to discover she remembered it so well.

She had barely recognized her father.

He was older, of course, and smaller, although he had never been of imposing stature. His hair had turned that special white common to the very old, forming a beautifully burnished halo that revealed snatches of the baby-pink scalp underneath. His walk had slowed, his shoulders were stooped and his faintly familiar face had been deeply etched by the years.

But it was his eyes that had changed the most.

She remembered them containing a soft, sweet luminescence, at least when they turned to her. Unlike some fathers and daughters, James and Olivia had never romped and played together. Even when she was a child, he had been too old and dignified for such frivolity. But his eyes had communicated love, had mattered even more than the presents he had given her, even the cherished gift of her beloved movie theater.

It had been the vivid memory of those loving eyes that had kept hope alive after Olivia had been installed in that miserable Hollywood apartment with Nick and her mother. So more than anything, it was her father's eyes that had let her down, betrayed her so long ago.

But when he marched into her office the day before, those eyes flashed and snapped with the indignity of being escorted by the guard like a child taken before the principal.

Olivia had very nearly laughed.

He looked much like an unchubby, uncheerful Santa Claus, red-cheeked, snowy-haired, cherry-nosed. He was dressed the way she remembered, immaculate, conservatively suited, except his ivory-tipped metal cane gave him a whimsical jauntiness, and his obvious annoyance with the guard made him resemble a volatile leprechaun on the edge of an explosion.

How absurd that she had once looked to this little man as if to a savior.

Instantly some of the bitterness Olivia had long harbored crumbled to dust. If he was not savior, neither was he devil. He was just another of the men in her life who had let her down. The realization eradicated much of her bitterness. Quickly Olivia gathered her defenses. She must not weaken now out of misplaced sentimentality.

She nodded coldly to her father indicating the chair facing her desk. He sat down hesitantly while she thanked and dismissed the security guard.

"You know, if you had called, it would have given me time to think about why you wanted to see me," she began immediately after the guard left. "I suppose you have softened with age and finally remembered me." Olivia was pleased that her voice was unruffled and her long fingers were steady as they tapped the desk.

"My memory hasn't been affected by age, one way or the other." Olivia's father peered myopically at her through thick-lensed glasses rimmed in gold. "Your photographs do you an injustice. You're even more beautiful than they show." He shrugged. "But then you were always beautiful."

She was annoyed at the sluggish rise of pleasure she felt and realized that a child's desire for the approval of a parent could not be killed even when that parent had long ceased to act like one. "Beauty is my business. Looking attractive is as necessary in my position as wearing safety glasses is for a welder." Olivia wondered at her need to reduce his compliment to its most functional level.

"It's been such a long time, Olivia. I never stopped thinking about you," he said softly, leaning his folded pink hands over the ivory tip of his cane, his loose-fleshed chin on top of the fingers. His eyes had lost their irritation.

Olivia's eyes were playing tricks on her, snipping away the erosion of time, allowing her to see remembered features. He still had the same hesitant smile, the same thin but well-shaped lips. And the eyes were beginning to conform to memory, resting on her face with the same lingering affection.

She felt a tightness in her throat, a burning in her eyes. She got up and walked quickly to her window, unable to look at her father until the tide of emotion ebbed. "How are you? How's Florida?" she asked, her back to him as if something out in the distant bay had caught her eye. "I heard you lost your wife. I'm sorry."

"I have my health. My second wife died painlessly in her sleep. I appreciate your concern." He paused. "Olivia?"

"Yes?" she replied, staring fixedly at the calm blue bay.

"Won't you come back to your seat? Am I that hard to look at? Age isn't kind to the eyes. Mine . . . or yours."

She turned and looked at him, her features working in an effort to conceal her agitation.

"You've done well for yourself. All this!" He lifted a hand from the security of his cane.

She didn't move. "Why have you come? Now, after so damn long! Why?" she demanded, the question bursting from her tensed throat.

He laboriously got to his feet and took a careful step in her direction.

Olivia saw that his eyes were unnaturally bright behind the glittering glasses. "Why, Father?"

He shook his head at her final word. "That's why, Olivia. To find out . . ." his voice rose shakily, ". . . if I *am* your father!"

At first his words made no sense to her. They sank into her mind awkwardly, penetrating slowly. Then she understood, and disgust redeemed her from immediate anger. After all this time he still debated her mother's diabolical lie! He had used up all those years contemplating birth dates and estimates about the longevity of Marta's affair with Nick! When he could have been thinking about the foolish waste of his only child's youth that he might have shared, he had instead fretted over biology and genetics.

Olivia saw her choices strewn before her like pebbles on the ground. She could tell him the truth, that she was his daughter and admit that Marta had said Olivia was Nick's child to expedite the divorce. Or she could challenge her father to determine what constituted paternity, a chance seed or assuming the role of father. The choices were many. She could refuse to answer and let him go to his grave wondering. He was old now, and alone. Because of his willingness to believe the worst, she had been young and just as alone. The temptation was overwhelming. The hurt she had felt and was feeling again—because of his need surfacing long after he had anything to give to her—made her hungry for revenge, for this chance to flex the whip of pain on the man who had abandoned her.

She turned lightly in his direction, keeping her voice bland and cool. "That is the question, isn't it?" She even managed an impersonal smile. "I don't mean to be rude, but if you'll excuse me. . . . I'm really extraordinarily busy today."

He said nothing for a moment, the weight of his frail body resting hard on the cane. Then he nodded slowly. "Yes. Of course. I . . . I'll be at the St. Francis until the end of September," he added hesitantly.

Gathering his strength, he slowly walked out of Olivia's office.

The clouds were no longer a pure white, and they threatened rather than coddled the dwindling blue sky. Olivia shivered as if feeling the cooling of the weather, as if the temperature in her building wasn't a comfortable 82 degrees any longer.

She had skimmed over the details of her father's visit when she'd related the story to Thea, voicing her indignation that he should still be concerned with her legitimacy in the twilight of his life. She had resolutely shelved the emotions he had churned and been eager to find out what Thea had meant about knowing Mark's location.

Thea had apologized, first on the phone and then after the meeting when they were alone in this office. "I didn't want to raise any hopes, Olivia, love. But Everett collects paintings, you know, and he has a large abstract in his San Francisco office that he bought recently in Paris. I would have sworn that it was one of Mark's paintings. But the work was signed by an unfamiliar name. Everett had a clipping of the artist from a Paris newspaper. It was a story about four artists who had had an important local show. The picture was blurred, but it looked like Mark. The name given was faintly familiar. I looked again at the painting's signature and put it together! Earl! Isn't that Mark's middle name?"

Olivia had nodded excitedly, her cheeks pink, her heart barely beating at all. "Yes!"

"Anyway, Everett said that the clipping is over a year old, and that this Earl has made it really big in Europe and will soon be showing in America. He's already won several important awards, darling, and Everett is investing in him like mad." She impulsively hugged Olivia. "Oh, dear, I don't know if this news is good or bad! I kept thinking about what Mark said to you, how he had always planned to come after you when he'd finally arrived. But after that ghastly scene when he left your house . . . I can't bear to think he won't come because, you know, too much bloody water has passed under the bridge or something. Artists are so temperamental! They seem to want to go on suffering for their beastly art. And making people who love them suffer even more. . . ."

Now the clouds were shot with gray and silvered at the edges. Olivia thought of her lawyers, undoubtedly cursing at the sky over their golf clubs. Too much water under the bridge? Perhaps. But even so, she had to meet Howard to tell him that she couldn't possibly become his wife. Then she would be alone again, possibly forever. How could she hope that Mark would be back, even though he'd finally carved his destiny, and without question of his merit.

But Thea was right. Even if Olivia drowned in her frigid isolation, even if it cost her the love of a fine man like Howard, she could not settle for second best.

It was still not enough.

CHAPTER 36

The great striped tent stretched across and above the famous rock mound in the center of the rock-edged swimming pool, encompassing the patio with its spread of wrought-iron tables and chairs. A rock-fronted bar was half-hidden behind a mob of guests, some in dripping bathing suits and others in splendid formal attire. Beyond was the tennis court, now transformed into a roller-skate disco for those with an overabundance of energy despite the late hour.

Thea nibbled at a canapé and watched a bikini-clad couple swim through a waterfall and into Hugh Hefner's much-publicized grotto in the rock mound. She and Everett had inspected the grotto earlier from its walk-in servants' entrance. It was spectacular; the pool narrowed to a stream inside a rock-covered opening to little ponds of steaming Jacuzzi spas, with convenient abovewater padded benches flanked by neat stacks of fluffy towels. The last and biggest spa was known as the passion pit. It was deeper than the others and studded with strategically positioned water jets.

Unlike her sedate and conservative parents, Thea was delighted with both the luxuriousness and the eroticism of this famed mansion in Holmby Hills. It served as the corporate headquarters of Playboy Enterprises and as Hugh Hefner's main residence.

She had chatted with her pajama-clad host earlier, and found him charming but restrained. She had told him that the only bunnies she had seen so far were the furry ones hopping freely over the lawn. He had smiled, tamped down his pipe and indicated several beautiful young women, bright lights in the already-glittering crowd of the famous or merely the very rich.

With a squeeze of her hand, Everett excused himself to

zigzag through the mob to reach a black-vested waiter with a tray of drinks. The ring she had given him a day early flashed on his finger, and she tried not to mind that he had immediately placed it on his right rather than his left hand as she had intended.

Thea wished she were free to enjoy this party more, that her mind were less chaotic and stormy. She had taken pains to make sure Everett wouldn't sense her distress, and had dressed in the brightest costume she owned, a smashing beaded silk chiffon long-sleeved top over a black velvet skirt. She had accented the costume with long gold earrings that appeared to drip tiny diamonds to the curve of her jawbone. She had had her nails done in metallic pale gold, and she wore the MagnifiScent gold-dust line of makeup, still immensely popular as evidenced by the distinctive golden sheen on the lips, eyes, and skin of many of Hugh Hefner's glamorous guests. She knew she looked exceptionally lovely tonight, that none of her inner turmoil showed. But she didn't feel lovely. She felt frightened.

Everett returned with a fresh drink, smiling because he had just bumped into the daughter of one of his mother's closest friends who was comically relieved to see someone else from her set at the Hefner party.

Thea watched Everett from the corner of her eyes. In spite of the fact that there were a large number of remarkably beautiful women present, he showed no excitement over any of them. He had scrupulously lived up to his standard of discretion and was solidly attentive to Thea when they were together, as if he had no interest in other women. If only she could be certain that Everett had not been sleeping with one of the guests at this very party, unbeknownst to her. She despised herself for this streak of jealousy that had grown ever since her marriage to Everett.

She wondered if jealousy was a part of the dynamics of love, an emotion that others simply worked hard at overcoming or concealing. To be happy in love meant to fear the loss of the beloved, didn't it? And to fear the loss equated to a sense of danger when there was the possibility that another person enjoyed an intimacy with your mate. Wasn't it natural to feel jealousy when there was a frank agreement about extramarital affairs? How often has the line What she doesn't know won't hurt her been heard in song and story? But Thea did know—Everett had made it plain that he intended to see other women when they planned their marriage. Of course, he had granted her the same freedom.

A tall and almost obscenely handsome actor Thea recognized but couldn't name looked her way, then did a double-take, smiling in frank approval of her loveliness. He finally turned back to his pretty but ruffled partner, and Thea glanced at Everett. He had caught the flash of interest in his wife, and although his lips still held a smile, she noticed that his eyes were fastened on the actor's handsome profile with a barely detectable expression of annoyance. Thea let her mind stumble through a maze of ideas. Knowing she was grasping at straws, that what she was contemplating was adolescent and beneath her dignity and that of Everett, she couldn't help playing with the thought of somehow deliberately incurring his latent jealousy.

What if she were to pretend she had a devoted, serious lover in San Francisco? Perhaps a casual exercise on a bed wouldn't disturb his sophisticated mind, but wouldn't a full-blown, passionate love affair stimulate a little possibly helpful jealousy?

If she could just make Everett lose that damned composure for a moment—if she could crack open his self-confident shell, then he might begin to treasure the knowledge that his home was inviolable. And to ensure this condition, he might even finally suggest that she spend less time at MagnifiScent and live full-time with him in Beverly Hills. She didn't really want to detach herself completely from the business, but there was no real need for her daily presence, either. Her name and social standing were her biggest benefits to MagnifiScent, other than her willing service as Olivia's confidante and sounding board. She could easily hold a position on the board of the company and be with Everett more. Even in his travels abroad, she could be helpful in the international affairs of the conglomerate. She would lose nothing and gain everything. Now, more than ever, she wanted to live normally with her husband. She longed for a conventional marriage. The kind of life she had once thought she would despise now loomed like paradise in her mind. She had wanted it before but now it was imperative, because the doctor had confirmed her uneasy suspicions.

She was pregnant.

CHAPTER 37

Marlissa came awake suddenly. She sat up, head cocked to hear what had disturbed her slumber.

The only sound in the room was the familiar ticking of the Bavarian clock on her dresser, as comforting and integrated into her sleeping pattern as the pounding of a mother's heart to an unborn child. Then came a deep snore and a few disjointed words in Swiss-German.

She smiled in the darkness and eased back down next to Ernst's naked body. He frequently mumbled in his sleep, always in his native tongue, as restless in slumber as he was placid and economical of movement in his waking hours.

Marlissa pulled the blankets over his bare shoulders. It was cold in the room but cozy under the feather comforter. Both she and Ernst liked breathing cool air while they slept. It was a habit learned in childhood. The ancient farmhouses in which both had lived were heated by fires that died early in the long, frigid Alpine nights. San Francisco air didn't smell the same, but the breeze carried the fragrance of flowers and freshly cut grass.

Impulsively she leaned over and kissed Ernst's cheek. She did not deserve to be happy, but she was, happier than she'd been for a long time. Shamefully happy, an unsettling blend of emotions that went against her grain. She knew all the reasons for her happiness. Ernst was kind. He was gentle. He was unwavering in his love. She reveled in the sweet weight of his body next to hers in bed. No perfume she'd ever created smelled as appealing as the scent of his hair against her cheek. With other lovers she slept uneasily, consciously laboring to match the tempo of their breathing, conform her body to their angles and curves. But with Ernst, she was comfortable without having to make an effort. They fit together perfectly, as if nature had molded them for each other.

Marlissa deliberately put aside her contentment. She had no right to it. She was a liar and a cheat, a fraud to the one man who had ever really mattered. He slept peacefully in her bed, believing himself safely back inside the snug circle of her love. He thought he was once again the only man in her life, that she was as proud of their togetherness as he.

She moved an inch or two away from his sleeping form, feeling loathsome and unworthy. For a moment she had allowed herself to take unlimited pleasure in their union.

For over a month they had been lovers again. How long could it continue? What sort of evil game was she playing, with herself as well as with him? How could she go on allowing him to love her without telling him the truth?

The truth was ugly. She did love Ernst, but how could she tell him that she was ashamed of him, embarrassed by the way he looked, dressed, and spoke. And that she didn't want to be identified with him publicly.

Ernst was a sensitive man and fiercely proud. He would want no part of a clandestine affair. And he was too naive to realize that that was all she was offering him.

For an instant Marlissa turned her anger on Ernst. How could he fail to see through her thin excuses when she had a date with another man, an acceptable man with whom she could afford to be seen in public? Hadn't he realized that she'd failed to introduce him to a single friend, or become suspicious over her refusal to have him pick her up at work? Was her feigned need to get away from The City every single weekend so easily accepted that he never once suspected the reason? She could only allow herself to be seen with him among strangers. How dare he allow her to get away with the insult of being ashamed of him? He who in all ways that mattered was a far better man than any she had known.

The anger was redirected on its rightful target. Herself.

Until she told him the lie would continue to fester and grow. It was a kind of foul gangrene, and when the amputation could no longer be avoided, it would be shocking and extensive. Better to wake him now, this minute, tell him and be done with it. Watch his face lose its kindness, its adoration, turn hard with bitterness and pain.

Marlissa knew that he expected them to be married eventually. He had not pushed her to set the date and would not until he had opened his own business. He had been working as a carpenter for a large company since he had come to San Francisco. He had saved every penny possible and was already looking for the right building in which to set up shop. Because he was European and proud, he would not think of taking a wife until he had the means to support a family, despite Marlissa's obvious ability to provide amply for herself. No matter how much a wife of his earned, Ernst would expect to shoulder the full burden of his family. Marlissa's money would never be touched, would instead be passed down to their children. That was the old way of their people, and Ernst was not about to change. He might agree to live in her house after their marriage, but he would work day and night to pay for its upkeep without accepting help from her.

It was impossible. She had to stop it. Right now.

Marlissa thought about waking him and knew she couldn't do it. His lips on hers were too desirable. And there was always the possibility that he would change.

Marlissa turned uneasily in the bed, cursing the weakness that had prompted her to let him back into her life. When she took him to bed a month ago, she had told herself that she was simply adding another special man to her small list of lovers. They would date, sleep together, and avoid any strangling emotional involvement.

Hadn't she known even then that Ernst was constitutionally unable to accept the half-loaf of love she was offering? Certainly she had done nothing to clarify her position, allowing him to incorrectly assume that in letting him back into her bed, she had taken him again to her heart. He thought her surrender was a vow of love, a commitment. He had been silently grateful to break through the wall she had erected that kept them apart. Ernst was the last man in the world to settle for a casual affair, particularly with a woman who had once looked eagerly to the day she would be his wife.

Marlissa remembered her own awkwardness when she had first come to America, her lack of style and sophistication. She had had to learn everything, and she had learned slowly, hesitantly, as wobbly and uncertain as a child taking her first few steps. Brad Cavell had educated her with a fair amount of patience and a great deal of tact, and she had greatly benefited. But she had had strong motivation to change and grow, being acutely conscious of her foreign, gauche ways. She had studied the well-dressed women who came to the MagnifiScent salon and had the images of Olivia and Thea to learn from and emulate. She had bought fashion magazines, placed herself often painfully in the company of her betters, and dared to experiment and question to smooth the rough places in the facade she presented to the world.

What motivation did Ernst have? He didn't even have the need to change in order to please Marlissa, because she never directly indicated her displeasure with him.

Still there had been some changes. She compared him today to the man he had been on first arriving from Meiringen. She had made subtle suggestions about clothing and taken advantage of every birthday and holiday to improve his wardrobe. He looked well in his new shirts and slacks, the jacket she had given him for Christmas that had cost three hundred dollars. He would have worn it uneasily had he suspected its price, but instead he wore it proudly because it had been a gift from Marlissa. He was beginning to lose his small-town awe of things and no longer gaped at luxurious comforts or evaluated them in dollars and cents rather than appreciating them for their artistic or functional merits. She had encouraged him to buy her Peugeot at bottom dollar when she had moved on to the sleek Mercedes, convincing him that the trade-in value would be still lower for her than what she had charged him. The Peugeot was undented and smart-looking, and she was spared the embarrassment of being seen in his old Dodge, his first San Francisco investment. She had taken him to good restaurants in the beginning, when he was merely a friend and could be explained harmlessly had they encountered a friend or business associate. Now he was able to handle himself when faced with a weighty menu, and could command the attention of a waiter without stumbling like a farm hand on his first outing to the city.

Yes, there had been changes, and perhaps there would be more. If she could be patient she might effect the miracle Brad had wrought in her.

Marlissa pulled the pillow more tightly under her head, knowing that she couldn't afford Brad's luxury of being able to be seen with anyone he chose. He was deeply embedded in smart society, so safely entrenched that the worst his choice of her as a mate could have done was draw a good-natured chuckle about his playing Henry Higgins to her Eliza. But Eliza playing that position with a young man from the streets would have been presumptuous or viewed as still another case of water seeking its own level.

She trembled, although her flesh was warm.

Ernst turned, touched her breast in his sleep. His fingers fluttered in reflex, then appeared to carry the message of her soft warmth to his slumbering brain.

He awakened instantly, quick to be aroused by her perfumed body under the cover. "Marlissa?" he whispered, sensing that she was also awake.

"I'm here." She felt him move closer, sensed the heat of his arms before they enfolded her. She remembered that she had considered awakening him and telling him of her deceptions. Now he was awake, and she had only to open her mouth to end this lie for all time. She had been kidding herself. He would always be the simple carpenter, happiest in work clothes or while dipping crusts of bread into the garlicky cheese fondues of their homeland, in a hut warmed by an open fire. *Tell him!*

Her lips parted, but only to accept his kiss.

CHAPTER 38

"Olivia." Howard reached across the low table and took her hand. He inclined his silvering head toward her and focused his pale blue eyes directly on hers. "You're making one of the biggest mistakes of your life."

His voice was gentle, his eyes softly pained, and the hand that held hers was cool-fingered and tense. Howard had waited until she had finished her well-rehearsed speech of farewell before talking.

"Perhaps," she acknowledged, squeezing, then escaping his touch. "It wouldn't be my first mistake." She shrugged and took a sip of her sherry. She had expected to feel a sense of relief at telling this wonderful man that she had decided to end their relationship rather than accept his offer of marriage, if only because the undesirable task had been postponed so long while Howard was away on business, and in his absence telling him had loomed foremost in her mind, becoming more and more unpalatable with every passing day. Had she gone to him at once, directly following her conversation with Thea about Mark, this severing would be long over. Howard had been abroad more than a month, and she had lacked the coldness to tell him just before he left. She had called her delay a kindness, but she knew it was also a coward's reprieve.

"But it might be your largest." He also took a sip of the good sherry. "Has Mark Lyman returned?"

She shook her head, knowing she shouldn't be surprised at his assumption that Mark had something to do with her decision. "Not yet." She had told Howard about Mark long ago, while the pain of his disappearance was at its brutal peak. "But he's become the artist of the hour in Europe. He did it, Howard. By himself. He started all over, with no help from me, and he's made it at last." She managed a little laugh. "Thanks to me, he had to start all over." She looked up, met Howard's unwavering stare. "He's coming to the States on a tour of one-man shows."

"Has he called? Or written?" Howard set his glass on the table and leaned forward, resting his broad fingers with their neatly manicured tips on either side of the glass.

"No." She kept her eyes on the backs of his fingers with their little tufts of light brown hair.

"Not once since he's been gone? Not even to tell you of his success?"

She merely shook her head. Howard's fingers were white under the buffed nails, the only indication of his agitation.

The fingers relaxed, moved back from the table to intertwine over his suited chest, pressing down on knuckles and joints that cracked protestingly. "And yet you're prepared to end our relationship . . . our good, rewarding relationship . . . in the hope that Mark, in his success, will come back to you."

Olivia winced at the deliberate mockery in his voice. It took her a moment to realize that he'd put no emphasis on his words, that the sarcasm she heard was from the echo of his statement in her mind. He had merely been stating his assumption. It was she who read in the mockery. "I know it sounds foolish . . ."

"Foolish! Damn it, woman! Do you intend to continue throwing away every decent relationship you form on the strength of an idle dream?"

Surprised, Olivia looked up to meet Howard's angry glare. She had never before heard him raise his voice to anyone, much less to her. "The idle dream to which you refer is my life, Howard." She felt her cheeks grow hot. "The decision I've made to terminate our relationship now has less to do with whether or not Mark returns than the more important point that I might marry you for the wrong reasons."

"Wrong?" His strong, attractive face hardened. "Wrong, because you would have married me knowing you can't love me the same way you've loved Mark Lyman? Wrong, even knowing our life would be comfortable and happy, mutually supportive and constructive? You call it wrong, because we merely want the best for each other, rather than demand the impossible from each other and ourselves? Olivia, you're lost in a dream about some perfect passion, as if there were but one right mate allotted to each individual, and that settling for less is a sin against nature! Don't you see that? Mark isn't the only man in the world for you. I understand your feelings, believe me, I truly do. When my wife died, I felt the same way, I thought that no other woman could take Shelly's place." His face softened. "And I was right—no one can. But I also learned that Shelly's place didn't need filling. I found that I needed a woman to complete the other areas of my being. When Jennifer was born, I thought I could never love another child as deeply. Then Kevin came along, and I wondered at the vastness of my own ability to cherish children, because I had the same amount of love for him as for my daughter, yet I'd have sworn that I'd already given all the paternal love in me to my firstborn. Love isn't like a pie, with just so many slices and no more. What you've already given to Mark hasn't left you empty. I know that what you feel for me is love, a good, sustaining love on which you can build your future. Don't cancel me out with glib, unimportant comparisons! Don't cheat us both that way."

Olivia got gracefully to her feet and walked slowly over to Mark's portrait of her. The Modigliani influence in some of Mark's earlier work had an excellent vehicle in her face and her naturally elongated neck. She studied the sweeping lines and the amber tones thoughtfully. It was not a flattering portrait in the conventional sense. It didn't dwell on the fineness of her features or the delicacy of her bones. Instead it revealed the subject through the eyes of the artist, looking deeper through the skin and tissues to reveal determination and an indefinable integrity. "To marry you, Howard, would cheat us both." She turned to face him.

"Why?" He got to his feet but made no move to come to her.

"Because it would be second best for me. Because you deserve more than my emotional leavings. And that's all I have for any other man. You're right, of course. There is no one man for every woman, no one woman for any man. It's all a matter of fulfilling needs and desires, and you're also right that we fulfill just enough of each other's to have had a damn good chance at a good marriage. But Howard, dear God, your Shelly *is* gone, and you've buried her and reached that place of peace and contentment at last. You can come to another woman fully, without ties and doubts. Knowing where Mark is, that there's the slightest chance he'll come back. . . . Howard, as your wife, I'd come to you like an item at a basement sale, marked down and shopworn, yours only because . . ." she quickly put a hand over her eyes to stem the sudden flow of tears, ". . . I didn't go where I belonged." She bit down on the soft inside of her top lip, lowering her hand to look at him only when she had regained control. "Howard, I have to be free to wait for Mark's decision. I ruined things for us last time. He might never come back to me. I wouldn't blame him if he didn't. But I must wait."

Howard brushed flat the front panels of his dark blue suit and mechanically closed the buttons. "And if he doesn't come back? Am I to wait in the wings for a second chance?" He shook his head, anger and disappointment etched into his face. "Olivia, I really do love you. Damned if I won't probably be waiting in those wings when your artist doesn't make the curtain call. But let me leave you with something more to think about." He walked slowly to her, stopping an arm's length away.

She looked up at him, wondering at the chemistry that wouldn't allow her to prefer this kind-faced, tall, graying man who radiated warmth, energy and success.

"You talk of being rejected and shopworn, but I want you to remember that it was you who discarded Mark, not he you. You wouldn't settle for what he had to give. Even the last time, when by your manipulations of his career you proved to him that he was unacceptable without meeting your standard of fame and fortune—"

"But I told him I wanted him just as he was!" she interrupted.

"Only because you had enough of both for the two of you! Had he asked you to walk out on all you had, would you have gone?"

She lowered her head. "He did ask, and no, I didn't go."

He nodded, waiting until she had looked back at him. "Don't misunderstand, Olivia. I'd think you a fool to walk out on all you'd created, and I doubt that your Mark would have really expected that of you. But the test was effective, because it let both of you know that in the end the decision was still yours. You're no one's victim, dear. You've always been on top, whatever life handed you. They call you the swan. It's fitting. You hold your neck high above the muddy water. The men in your life haven't failed you. They just weren't able to reach high enough. Now I leave you to wonder if you've asked for too much. I can't answer that one for you. No one can but you."

She saw him to the door, hugged him briefly but tightly. "I'm sorry, Howard."

His voice was husky. "You don't have to be sorry. But you may have to do a little homework in order to be happy."

After he had left, Olivia picked up her glass with its dregs of sherry and refilled it. Then she doused the lights and walked hesitantly to her bedroom. She left the light off and stared out the huge window at the view of the Palace of Fine Art, its tiny lights distinct and twinkling in the clear night sky. It was very early, not yet ten. Her early dinner with Howard had brought them to her house less than an hour before. Olivia marveled at the brevity of time it took to change the direction of an entire life. Had she instead accepted his proposal, she would be with him still, planning a future so different from the empty expanse of time now hanging before her.

She drank from her glass and felt the heaviness of being alone. She knew that she did not believe Mark would be back. Despite the hopefulness of her words, the excitement in her voice when she had discussed the possibility with Thea, she suspected that Howard was correct. She was chasing an idle dream, and it would leave her in a nightmare of unfulfillment.

Yet she could not have made any other decision but to send Howard away.

An image of a pond came to her mind. Olivia could see it

clearly, complete with lily pads and reeds and noisy with the squawking of downy-feathered ducks as they bathed together at the water's edge. And always there was a swan, out alone where the water was clearest and deepest, poised and graceful, with only its own lovely reflection for company.

She put down her glass and went to the window, unconsciously wanting to blend with the busy city below. Had Howard been right? Had she demanded too much from the men in her life? Mark had always been ambitious about having his work recognized, but if she'd been willing to share his simple pleasure in the slow growth of his name, would he have so blindly accepted the unnaturally sudden blossoming of his fame? Hadn't she forced him into wanting the same dream she had created for herself? She had established the level of his success by setting her own so high. Now he seemed to be climbing to the same lofty altitude, but had she spoiled the rarefied air by getting there first, insisting on his immediate elevation to her heights?

She had muddied the water in their pond so long ago, yet she had never ceased longing for him. Now, at last, it was her turn to wait without pressure, to swim alone in the pond. She could offer nothing other than room for him someday to join her.

Howard had insisted that she asked for more than could be expected. Mark's success proved that she had asked no more of him than what he was capable of. She had just asked for it too soon. But what of other men? She had certainly expected too much of Jean-Pierre. She had wanted him to change from who he was to Mark, keeping at the same time his wealth, success, heritage, and vast sophistication.

She thought of her father, the only other man of importance in her life. Certainly she hadn't asked too much of him. She had merely expected him to be the father he had been when she was a child. He had left her; she hadn't left him.

Far below a ship ducked behind the dome of the palace, reappearing a moment later on the other side. She watched it move out of sight, returning the window to a still-life painting.

Or had she asked more of her father than he was capable of giving? Her fury with him in her office had come from the unforgotten pain of his desertion. But he had not walked out on her mother and her. In fact, they had left him alone in the great house. True, leaving was not her idea. She had resisted it with every fiber of her being. Yet she had walked out that door on her own two feet, and she had neglected to take the initiative to tell her father that she wanted to stay.

Olivia sat down on the edge of her bed, remembering the way the old man had looked when he had come to her office after their parting twenty-two years before. He had infuriated her with his demand to be told that he was indeed her real father. She had felt that he should not have had to ask. If she, as a child, could have seen through her mother's pathetic story of a supposed genetic link to Nick, her mature and sensible father should have recognized at once Marta's sly scheme. He should have insisted on visits with his daughter.

She fought down the rising anger, slowly understanding what Howard had meant by unrealistic expectations. Her father had been deeply wounded by Marta's stinging words. He was extremely vulnerable to a lie that implied his inability to parent a child. And certainly when Olivia hadn't called him even once after she left, how could he not have assumed that she was happy where she was? Happy, especially, with Nick, with a much younger man who possibly had the time and energy to take a young daughter to the zoo and school football games, a handsome young father to whom she would be proud to introduce her friends. How else could it have appeared to him, already an old man who no doubt suffered guilt over his failure to romp with his only child like younger fathers. There had been no children with his first wife—why wouldn't he have believed himself infertile? Marta had been clever in her calculations and had known him as a woman knows a man, not as a child its father. She had known exactly where to aim her poison dart.

Olivia thought of the many times she had been tempted to call her father while parties raged in the small living room of the Hollywood apartment, keeping her from sleep. Her pride had stood in the way. She was a child. He was an adult. It was his place to call, not hers. And when she had wanted the money for a European education and her mother had told her the scope of her deception, even then she had let pride stand in the way of her needs and desires. She had called that pride integrity. She had been the swan even then, keeping her neck above the water.

But how much integrity had she had when she had confronted the man who, after twenty-two years, had had the courage to come to her office? Where was her prized integrity when she had turned her father's question back on him, sending him away in humiliation?

Loneliness was like a great weight on her chest, and she longed for the comfort of an arm over her shoulders. Now she had everything she'd always told herself she desired, and she was still in need.

She was tired of pride. She had wasted enough time expecting the impossible. She was done writing scripts that others couldn't read.

Olivia reached out for the phone, called information, and calmly got the number she needed. She cradled the receiver tightly in her hand while the connection was made and her party reached.

She heard the voice and felt a great rush of happiness. Wondering why tears stung her eyes, Olivia brushed them away with the back of her hand as she said the words that would welcome her father back into her life.

CHAPTER 39

"I simply can't get over it!" Olivia held her glass of champagne high in still another toast. "A baby!"

Thea laughed and clicked glasses with Olivia and Marlissa. They had met for lunch at Jack's, San Francisco's oldest and, Thea thought, best French restaurant, at her invitation. She wanted to share her news with her friends, because she hadn't yet shared the secret with anyone, even Everett.

"Will you tell him tonight?" Marlissa asked. "Isn't he coming in later?"

"Tomorrow. Yes, probably. Oh, damn, I don't know! I'm dying to tell him, but I don't think the time is right yet. And I can't possibly tell Mother and Dad until I tell Everett. They'll tell the world instantly and fly in all kinds of imported specialists."

"Well, then, when do you suppose is the right time to tell Everett? When you can no longer wear a belt? Or are you planning on the baby simply introducing himself?" Olivia surgically extracted a sliver of fat from her steak and pushed it to the edge of her plate.

Marlissa laughed. "Why 'himself'? Who needs more men in this world? I vote for a sweet chubby little girl. A new customer for MagnifiScent!"

"A little girl," Thea said dreamily, distracted from thoughts of Everett into a pleasant, fragrant world of baby powder and pink-blanketed bassinets.

"Tell him as soon as he comes," Olivia urged, "and let's have a lovely party!"

Snapping out of her dream, Thea shook her head. "Not yet. There's something I have to take care of first, darling. First I have to secure the happy home, and then full steam ahead, damn the stops."

"Something is wrong?" Marlissa inquired, putting down her fork and leaning closer to Thea across the table.

Thea looked from one friend to the other, studying Olivia's stunning face, then swinging her eyes to Marlissa, who seemed to be growing steadily more attractive. She put down her glass, glanced at the plate she'd barely touched, and nodded. "Well, my dears, not wrong. Just not perfect," she began, speaking swiftly and simply, realizing as she spoke that she automatically excused Everett for the game rules he had established for their marriage. She heard herself defending him, citing herself for the discontent she felt over their arrangement. It still startled her, the depth of her love for this man.

Olivia was the first to speak. "Are you trying to say that the baby might not be Everett's?"

Thea laughed, stopped when she realized the laugh was a shade too near hysteria. "Good God! I haven't made myself clear at all. Darlings, there's been no other man, don't you understand? Your insatiable friend has found perfect contentment with the man with the nice knees." She smiled affectionately at Olivia, remembering her approval of Everett in his tennis outfit so many years ago. The smile faded. "I don't want to share him, can you believe that? I think I'll die from an overdose of suspicion if I have to live like this forever, with me here, Everett down in Beverly Hills, playing footsie with a pack of unpregnant dollies!"

"Wow." Olivia sat back with her glass of wine, the steak forgotten.

Marlissa, who had said nothing, stared thoughtfully across the table.

"Wow, indeed," Thea said self-consciously, feeling defensive and ridiculous. "It's ironic, isn't it? The setup is absolutely perfect for my former tastes, isn't it? And I can't even enjoy the freedom. I don't want the freedom. I just want to be another ghastly, boring little hausfrau. With a nanny on hand, of course, and a few servants for the nasty business of cooking and cleaning."

Olivia smiled, but Marlissa retained her state of contemplation.

"So what is it you have decided to do?"

Thea looked at Marlissa in surprise, then remembered mentioning she intended taking care of matters before telling Everett of his impending fatherhood. She smiled a little uncertainly. "I haven't cornered the market on jealousy, have I? After all, if I'm uptight about Everett, doesn't it stand to reason that he'd be just a teeny bit shattered by finding out that I was in the throes of a passionate love affair of my own?"

"I thought you said . . . oh, God, Thea, you can't be serious!" Olivia reached over and stayed Thea's hand before she drank more of the wine.

"Oh, can't I?" She giggled, but didn't resist Olivia's hand, letting it instead fall away from the thin glass stem.

Olivia released her hold on Thea. "Then you aren't serious?"

"Never more." She sighed. "Really, I'm a little desperate, and I apologize for letting it show. How theatrical! But one good shock to his system and Everett will think twice about this open-marriage thing. He'll want me by his side night and day. . . ."

"And spend the rest of his life wondering who really fathered the infant you're carrying!" Marlissa shuddered delicately.

Thea turned to her in confusion. "He wouldn't! I'd simply tell him. . . ." She hesitated. "Oh, dear, I hadn't thought of that."

"You'd better start thinking of that," Olivia advised, upset. "Or would you like me to tell you from firsthand experience how it feels to be a child of such a deception?"

"Oh, Olivia, I didn't think! It never entered my mind! I was thinking of myself, as usual. I thought it would be so simple . . . I wrote a note, you see. A masterpiece, if I say so myself, the sort of thing every woman wants to receive and keep to warm her blood in old age. Filled with lovely passion and urgings to leave my husband and fly off into the sunset. . . ."

"Damn it, Thea! Even if there were no baby, haven't you learned anything by seeing what my scheming did to Mark and me? Mine was also a harmless lie . . . no, even less, a sin of omission, really, and it may have cost me Mark! Who the hell do you think you are, to manipulate Everett's emotions in such a way? It isn't as if you entered into this marriage without knowing the score. Jean-Pierre didn't do me the honor of spelling out the rules when he asked me to marry him. Everett hasn't betrayed you—he simply offered what he thought you'd want! God, you'd made it clear enough to him that you weren't about to settle for a dull, conventional marriage. You proved that by the way you lived!" Olivia's anger was evident in the two blotches of color on her smooth cheeks.

"That was before!" Thea defended, sobered by Olivia's agitation. The simple plan she'd devised was beginning to grow horns. "I didn't realize then how I'd feel now!"

Marlissa reached over and patted her hand. "Thea, you have not told Everett your feelings in this matter?"

She swung her head toward her other friend, soothed by the calm face and voice. "How could I tell him? How could I admit being jealous?"

Marlissa nodded understandingly. "You are frightened to reveal your insecurity, yes? Yes? It is a sin, then, to show weakness? Thea, how can Everett know that you are not content with his kind of marriage? It is a petty plan, unworthy of you, to plot his jealousy. It may not be necessary. Go to him, Thea. Tell him with dignity, no, with humility, that you require the stability of a unified home. Be direct with him. Give him a chance to know your feelings, and let him express his own. You are concerned with what he thinks of you, that he will be disappointed to find you less worldly than you pretend to be. It is odd—you are the last person in the world I would have suspected of harboring the least tinge of insecurity, but I don't feel you have cheapened yourself by revealing this truth." She smiled musingly. "If I may say so, I think I like you more for knowing that you, too, are human, can feel and be hurt. Would it be so very terrible if your husband discovered he has a wife of flesh and blood? I think not. You might be surprised at what you learn about him, as well."

Thea glanced over at Olivia, saw that the anger had dissipated. "Olivia? What do you think?"

"I think I want very much for one of us to be truly happy, Thea," she said tiredly. "You have the man you love, and you're going to have a baby. I say burn the damned letter to ashes, sit Everett down and tell him you have no intention of raising your child with a part-time father, and tell him that he's man enough for you. Ask him just what it is that any other woman could give him that you don't have in abundance." She grinned. "I think he'll be delighted. He's wanted you for himself since he was seventeen years old. He's not about to walk away now."

"Are you sure?" Thea played with a cigarette before lighting it. "The doctor said I'd better cut down on these," she said softly, putting the cigarette out after one brief puff. "For the duration. Olivia, are you sure he'll understand?"

Olivia shrugged, smoothing the collar of her pale suede and silk suit. "I've never known life to offer any guarantees about anything. But I do know the consequences of deception. These days I'd put my money on playing it straight, given the chance."

Marlissa nodded, but her face seemed contorted by a personal sorrow. "Yes, tell him." She seemed to be talking to herself.

Thea smiled. "Okay, but lunch first! There's something to this eating-for-two business." She attacked her lunch with vigor. "Then it's home for a little ceremonial letter-burning." She felt as if a great weight had been lifted from her shoulders. She wondered if all pregnant women were a little mad. Maybe along with their bodies, their minds underwent drastic changes. She had allowed her fears to get out of hand. The worst that could happen would be that Everett would not want to give up his extramarital affairs, but that seemed less and less likely the more she rationally thought about it. After all, he had been eager to marry her. If there were another woman, he would have been content without marriage to complicate matters. She really didn't know his feelings on the subject. She had assumed the worst, afraid to admit directly that she might be the only one dissatisfied with their current arrangement. Even if he chose to end the marriage rather than solidify it, she would be more content than she was now.

And she would never be alone again. She would have the baby. For the first time her pregnancy became something other than a temporary condition. She was going to have a child! She and the baby would form a real home, no matter what Everett's decision! She would never again need pills to put herself to sleep or alcohol to help her through the days. She would have someone of her own for whom to live.

Her friends were right. She couldn't start this new life with lies. It would be a new and clean beginning for all three of them.

Feeling starved, she ate quickly, discussing the relative merits of giving her child a solid family name or thinking up an exotic and dramatic one. "Not Everett Junior. That's out. Definitely." She put down her fork and patted her lips. "Maybe."

Thea drove home wondering how she could have been stupid enough to write the letter. She had put it on the dresser where Everett would be certain to discover it tomorrow, and now she was ashamed of the childishness of her ploy. Someday, years later, she would tell Everett about it and together they would laugh.

She found him already at her house on the Marina, a day early, the letter in his hand.

"What the hell is this?"

Thea set down the packages in her arms and covered her face with her hands. "Oh, dear!" She would have laughed if he hadn't looked so distraught. Now that she had talked the whole thing out with Marlissa and Olivia, she felt more like a child discovered with its hand in the cookie jar than a desperate woman taking desperate steps to safeguard her marriage. "How can I explain?"

"I think this is self-explanatory." He looked down at the note as if it were so much filth in his fingers.

His incriminating tone immediately angered Thea, snapping her out of her chagrin. "Look, Everett, don't sound so pompous. You were the one who wanted us to be 'free,' remember." She wriggled her fingers at the childish note. "Don't worry about that thing. I wrote it myself." She sat down wearily, rummaging in her purse for a cigarette. "It was a stupid thing to do, I'll admit, but after all, you—"

"You wrote this?" Everett shook the note at her, his voice raising. "You expect me to believe . . . to actually believe you wrote this . . . this piece of pornography?"

Thea stifled a giggle. "Come on, darling, it's a bit graphic, but pornography is putting it—"

"Damn it, Thea, what kind of a fool do you think I am? Okay, I admit I may be off base, getting so upset . . ." He appeared to wrestle with his emotions for a moment, but when he resumed speaking, he sounded furious. "But coming home to find something like *this* in our bedroom . . . a goddamned love letter from another man . . ."

"I told you. . . ." She got her cigarette lit on the third try and noticed that her hands were actually shaking. Much as she had wanted to spark some reaction from Everett, to see some indication of a jealousy to match her own, she had envisioned remorse on his part, not this infuriating show of indignation.

"You really do think I'm a fool, don't you? You always did. Do you really think I'm so stupid that I'd believe you wrote this . . . thing?"

"Everett, I wrote the damn note!"

"How many lovers have you been parading through this house, anyway? What the hell's been going on in my absence? Who is this jerk, if I may ask?" Everett crossed the room to tower menacingly over her. "He really knows how to write, doesn't he? Is he this hot all the time?"

"I told you, Everett, I wrote that damned letter. Please sit down and let me explain."

"Explain!" He tried a laugh but it came out all wrong. He finger-combed his sandy brown hair nervously. "Explain, shit!"

"Yes, explain, though you don't deserve it!" she retorted, her face chalk white. "You were the one who sat on that couch and suggested we go right on having our tawdry little affairs! That came from your lips, not mine, remember?" She smashed the cigarette into the ashtray. "I almost wish the idiot letter did come from a man. But I was fucking *sick* of living like this—not knowing where you are, what you're doing, whom you're with. I thought that I could perhaps stun you to your senses by making you a little jealous." She met his eyes defiantly. "It was infantile, granted. I'd already decided to rip the thing up and tell you how I feel without such high drama. I tell you, the letter is a sham! There are no other men! Really, darling, I hate to admit it. There you are, off in Beverly Hills doing God knows what with any number of little whores, and I've been here by myself, pregnant, dying of jealousy and writing childish letters! It's really too funny—"

"Pregnant?" Everett stared down at his wife.

"Yes, pregnant!"

He held out the letter accusingly. "Whose child is it, mine or his? Or don't you know?"

Her laugh bordered on hysteria. It was laugh or cry, but he couldn't know that.

He crumpled the note in his clenched fist. "Keep on laughing, Thea." He threw the crushed letter to the floor. "I trust you won't be laughing alone for long."

He was gone long before the tears started.

CHAPTER 40

"I'm sorry, Olivia," Peter Berger said. "But don't let it distress you. The suit is undoubtedly being instituted by some half-baked, eager kid fresh out of law school, or more likely by a cheap ambulance chaser out for every cent he can get."

"But how could—" Olivia began and stopped. She picked up a newspaper clipping from her desk. "Just let me read this once more."

HOUSEWIFE SUES MAGNIFISCENT FOR $1,000,000

Woman disfigured while preparing for husband's company dinner

LOS ANGELES, June 27—Mrs. Fred Bickers of the Wilshire District was critically burned last night when applying MagnifiScent's well-known beauty lotion Second Chance. According to her husband, Mrs. Bickers had purchased the lotion just two days before, having saved for months to buy the entire MagnifiScent collection.

Mr. Bickers said he was waiting for his wife to finish dressing when he heard her scream. He ran upstairs and found her in the bathroom, shouting that her face was on fire. "It was horrible," he said. "Her face was all red and blistering and she couldn't see. I called the ambulance and then I started dousing her face

> with cold water. But it didn't do any good. Patty fainted, thank God. The pain was too much."
>
> Mrs. Bickers was rushed to Cedars-Sinai Hospital, where she is in stable condition. According to Mrs. Bickers' attorney, John F. Brady, Jr., his client has suffered third-degree facial burns and will require extensive plastic surgery. Mrs. Bickers is bringing suit against MagnifiScent for $1,000,000. . . .

Olivia put down the clipping and glanced at the other one next to it on her desk. Mark's unsmiling face above the caption "American artist comes home in triumph" seemed to be watching her.

"I don't understand," she said to Peter Berger, who was seated opposite her. "How could Second Chance do that? It's been on the market for over two years, and it was thoroughly tested long before. . . ."

"It can't," Berger assured her calmly. "It's clearly not the fault of the product. Our staff has already requested a complete analysis of the lotion. I wouldn't even bring this to your attention, but there's sure to be a furor raised by the press, and I wanted to prepare you. If you're contacted by the media, it's imperative that you treat the allegation without excitement. Under no circumstances act as if you're in the slightest degree concerned. We'll try to head off the press, but this sort of claim is the meat of a good many publications. 'Los Angeles housewife disfigured and blinded by the MagnifiScent cosmetics she sacrificed to buy.' It sells papers, and you'll be pressed for a comment, Olivia. Headlines like that can ruin a business. It's a nuisance claim. The woman can't afford the corrective surgery she'll need, and some hotshot lawyer told her she'll make a bundle suing MagnifiScent. If we're not careful, by the time MagnifiScent is completely cleared of any liability, your products won't move in a discount house! Our only hope is to act as if the whole thing is a setup by some hungry little housewife out to make an easy buck."

"Easy! The poor woman!" She was horrified at the thought of the struggling young wife who had saved from her household budget to look glamorous for an important evening out with her husband, only to end up disfigured and in a hospital bed.

"Yes, an easy buck!" the lawyer thundered. "It happens all the time. I'm not implying that the woman intentionally burned her face, but who knows what she did to herself? I only know that Second Chance couldn't possibly be responsible. We'll be off the hook as soon as the analysis is completed, but until then you must be prepared to treat the matter as a deliberate hoax. The slightest expression of concern by the owner of MagnifiScent will do more damage than can be fixed by a thousand retractions in the newspaper! Let those women out there nurture the slightest doubt about the safety of your products, and you can close down your shops. Olivia, claims like these—and God knows they come to all companies sooner or later—can ruin a business. No woman in her right mind is going to put something on her face if she entertains the faintest suspicion that she might end up like this Patty Bickers woman. There are any number of nuisance claims that are easier to buy off than fight. But not one of this nature! You've worked too hard for too long to lose everything because one person injures herself and sees a way to turn it into a profit!"

Olivia listened to the lawyer repeat his instructions to coolly disclaim any responsibility for the accident, but her mind was flooded with sympathy for the poor woman.

When Peter Berger finally left her office, Olivia sat at her desk without moving, remembering the Oscar Wilde fairy tale of the Happy Prince she had read as a child. The Happy Prince had been sheltered all of his life, dwelling in a great castle surrounded by a wondrous garden. But after he'd died, his soul had gone into a large statue of himself erected in the town square. The statue was crusted with gold, with precious jewels for eyes and lips, and from his lofty perch he could see the suffering of others, from which he had been shielded while he'd lived. With the aid of a helpful swallow that paused in its flight south for the winter, the Happy Prince divested himself of his gold and jewels one by one, to lessen the suffering he viewed.

Olivia thought of herself as a realist, but she was also aware that her great wealth sheltered her from such realities as the Los Angeles housewife had experienced. She had no desire to end up as the Happy Prince, stripped bare of his gold, but she also could and did ache for the obviously terrified Patty Bickers, in need of surgery to reconstruct her face but without the means to buy a miracle. Peter Berger and her other attorneys were blinded by facts and legal precedents. They couldn't afford to let their hearts bleed with pity, and they owed a solid, uncompromising loyalty to those who retained their services. But Olivia, without such restraints, could see the inequality of enormous wealth for some and destitution for others. She was particularly geared for such realizations because, unlike Thea, she had personally known what it was to be in need. For a long time she had had the means of buying anything she needed or desired. A bauble for her finger cost far more than the expense of the housewife's entire operation. One single painting in her house or office could procure the services of the best surgeon. Not that Olivia would have to part with a bauble or a painting to rescue the woman. She had long since given up any attempt to calculate the extent of her fortunes, content to let experts attend to such matters while she put her energy toward swelling her wealth even more.

Olivia felt helpless to console this woman she'd never met, had not known existed until her lawyer told her about the case.

MagnifiScent was important to Olivia. It was her life, her dream. But she had always known it from the top, had looked upon the endless outpouring of bottles and jars with the proud and fretting eye of a mother watching over her babies. To Patty Bickers, MagnifiScent meant something entirely different. It meant hope, an element of glamour in an undistinguished life, and those tiny bottles and jars had represented a sacrifice of daily necessities.

Olivia didn't cloud her mind with the question of what had hurt the Bickers woman. She was secure in the lawyer's opinion that Patty's injury was caused by a completely different substance. Marlissa had unwaveringly demanded boundless proof that her creations were flawlessly pure, harmless to even the most sensitive skin. Second Chance was a special moisturizing lotion with a dense oil that attracted and held makeup and actually medicated aging flesh, restoring the softness and tone of youth. The product would swiftly be exonerated, but Patty would remain disfigured forever unless someone cared enough to come to her aid.

Knowing the pitfalls of her intended action, Olivia sternly reminded herself of her promise to stop playing God. The housewife's problems had nothing to do with her. When she had meddled in Mark's career, she had also called her manipulations kind involvement. To help this poor, mutilated woman was to invite trouble. The offer to take care of Patty's medical bills would be misinterpreted as a confession of responsibility. Peter Berger had made it abundantly clear that she couldn't afford to become involved. She had a responsibility to the hundreds of people who directly depended on MagnifiScent for their jobs and the thousands who were involved less immediately, and even to the faithful customers who had the right to use her products in complete confidence.

But she was living, Olivia thought wryly, in a world that increasingly feared involvement, among physicians who feared aiding accident victims in the street out of concern for resulting lawsuits, the witnesses of crimes who refused to step forward, the teachers who looked the other way when they saw signs of child abuse, the passersby who ignored a call for help. She was cradled in luxury, removed from ugliness on her high perch of absolute comfort; but with the scribble of her signature, she could at least save Patty Bickers from a blighted future.

She made three calls, first to Thea, then to Marlissa, and, after a moment of deliberation, a final call to a travel agent. Thea had only grasped a fraction of Olivia's impassioned message but with a sigh had said she supposed that there was no stopping Olivia's irrepressible do-gooder streak. Marlissa had listened quietly, afterward murmuring support and encouragement, sure that the vindication of Second Chance would soothe the public in time.

Then she realized she had to call and prepare Peter for what she was about to do. But first she asked Maureen to pack the small traveling case she carried on even the briefest trip, smiling faintly because she knew it would contain the inevitable jar of Second Chance, which she used daily.

Steeling herself for Peter's reaction, Olivia lifted the phone to make the necessary call, grateful that it would be a short one. Her flight to Los Angeles was only an hour away.

CHAPTER 41

Thea put down the phone and watched George, her houseman, clear the dining-room table of the dinner she had barely touched.

Olivia never ceased to amaze her. Not that the tale of the mutilated housewife wasn't horrible; yet there was a certain hint of Pollyanna about the unquestionably sophisticated Olivia that perplexed and often made Thea a touch uncomfortable. Marlissa, understandably, had her endless causes and was sensitive to the minor triumphs of those under her. It had been typical of Marlissa to rush out to buy an elaborate wedding gift for Rita Bannerman when, after her divorce from the formula-stealing realtor, she had suddenly remarried. That was different, of course. In some strange way Marlissa had seemed to identify with Rita and had been very anxious about her decision to keep Stephen Vanalden's crime from Rita. Yet Marlissa's discretion had seemed well placed—Rita had ended the marriage shortly afterward for reasons of her own, apparently, and Marlissa had been as excited over the news of Rita's plans to take a second husband as if Rita's fate were her own. For months Marlissa had rhapsodized over Rita's happiness with Milton Bannerman and talked constantly to Olivia and Thea about that and Rita's triumph over her weight problem. When Rita Bannerman became pregnant, Marlissa had mothered the older woman shamelessly. Marlissa loved happy endings.

But for Olivia to defy her own attorney to become involved with some woman she didn't even know, a woman who had the audacity to threaten MagnifiScent's excellent reputation, seemed to be pushing a passion for charity too far. Yet MagnifiScent was Olivia's business, to do with as she wished, and Thea had been flattered that her friend had sought her approval before flying away on her mission of mercy.

"Will there be anything else, Mrs. Hamlinton?"

Thea looked up, then waved the houseman away. "No, thank you, George. You may leave early tonight if you'd like."

Thanking her, he slipped noiselessly from the room.

Thea watched the lights play over the water of the bay, tempted to call George back to fix her a stiff drink. She wanted him more for the company than because she was incapable of doing for herself. Then she considered calling Olivia back and offering her company on the flight to Los Angeles. While Olivia played fairy godmother to Patty Bickers, Thea could drop in on Everett. Perhaps he would feel forced to see her if she dropped in unexpectedly.

She turned on the couch so that her face was half-concealed in the satin pillows. One hand rubbed firmly over her still-flat belly, as if to find the life that was taking form there. Since Everett had left two nights before, she had found it increasingly difficult to believe that she was really pregnant, and yet she was surprised at her mounting pleasure at the thought of having a child. Until she had returned from her lunch with Olivia and Marlissa to find Everett with that inane letter she had written, all thoughts of the baby were tied tightly to her relationship with Everett. Other than a vague pleasure that a child would keep her from loneliness, the pregnancy represented tangible proof of her love for her husband, her hold on him that took precedence over his affairs with other women.

But now Everett was gone, and she hadn't heard from him once during his absence. Everything had gone wrong. She had meant to tell him about the baby after they had a long, open discussion about their relationship, hopefully after hearing him admit that he, too, was ready to settle down to a full-time marriage. Instead she had blurted out her secret and had heard him turn it into an ugly, dirty joke.

Thea got up, went to the bar, and fixed herself a drink. The bay beyond the window seemed to roll with her movements, and she pushed the gin and tonic away, a wave of nausea negating her desire for a drink. She closed her eyes and felt the threatened spasm pass. The realization that she was indeed pregnant made her feel giddy. It was so strange to think of sharing her body with a tiny creature she couldn't see, couldn't even yet feel. She had never even thought about having children or needing them in the way that Olivia occasionally talked about. Of the three of them, Marlissa seemed the most likely to want to bear children. She was motherly and gentle, earthy. Yet it was happening to her, not Marlissa. In less than seven short months she would have a baby. Soon her trim, athletic body would change, her flat stomach would swell, her small, firm breasts would fill out. With a proud Everett by her side, she would have welcomed this eventuality. But now she was alone.

Thea brought the tips of her fingers to her abdomen. She smiled faintly. No, not alone.

Leaving the drink where it was, she went to her room and put on a white satin nightgown, covering it with the exquisite silver-edged black robe Everett had brought back from his last trip to New York. She would have that drink, and then she would try to sleep. Her body was already taking over, demanding sleep, giving her a taste for bacon-and-egg breakfasts, diminishing the acute need for tobacco she'd had since she was sixteen. With or without Everett, she'd be healthy and plump through this pregnancy, and afterward, well, afterward there would be the baby to make the house less lonely. She left her bedroom, ready now for her drink.

Everett was standing at the bar. "I've made you a fresh one. Your ice cubes are melting."

"You'll notice there's only one drink there," she said faintly, indicating her gin and tonic.

He smiled gently, looking older and pale, as if he'd huddled sleeplessly in his house since leaving San Francisco. "I know, Thea." He put his arm around her, guided her to the starkly modern couch, then handed her one of the glasses he had filled. "Sit down, please."

He sat down and put his untouched glass on a low table. "I want to apologize for the scene I made the other day. I don't know what happened. When I found that letter . . . I suppose I was suddenly that rejected boy again, chasing after you, never able to catch up."

He shook his head. "Look, when you agreed to marry me, I thought . . . I don't know, I suppose I thought it was just another of your whims. I thought you'd be bored by marriage. I was scared. All you ever seemed to care about was your own freedom. I thought that if I could give you freedom within our marriage, you wouldn't run from me someday. I wanted to make it seem that I was a man of the world. I wouldn't intrude in your life so heavily that you'd ever want to eject me from it completely. I don't even need the house in

Beverly Hills anymore. For more than a year the San Francisco office has been our main West Coast branch of the business."

"Then why . . . ?"

He shook his head. "I didn't know what the hell you had going up here! Half the nights I've called you, I was at the Mark Hopkins a few miles from here. When I found that damned letter . . . it was like realizing all at once that I still didn't have you; I was still that kid waiting in the wings for the girl he loved to come home. I couldn't believe you would feel the same. I suppose in a sick way I didn't want to believe that there really isn't anyone else. I was too used to my old role. At last I had a vehicle for my pent-up anger, and I suppose I didn't want to give it up until I'd gotten it all out."

She didn't understand. "What are you saying, Everett?"

"Thea, darling, there have never been any other lovers for me, either. I wanted you to think there were. You wrote a letter to make me jealous. I lived a life to attempt to make you jealous! I thought that perhaps someday you'd want to settle down and be with just one man. I wanted to be around when that time finally came. You've always seemed like a chimera to me, an impossible illusion that would vanish again if I dared come too close and stay too long."

She put her glass down and took his hand, pressing it flat against her belly. "Chimeras don't have babies. And we are going to have a baby." She looked at him worriedly. "You do believe me about the letter? Because if you don't—"

"I believe you. But even if it had been true, I'd have no one to blame but myself." He probed her stomach delicately. "Are you sure there's something in there?"

She laughed against his shoulder. "Only time," she said, as his arms came around her, "will tell."

CHAPTER 42

Marlissa pushed back from the table, her plate still nearly full. "It is a shame to waste so much food." She doubted that she'd ever lose her European disapproval over the casual way most Americans regarded waste. She wasn't sure she wanted to acclimate that completely.

"It's only a dinner," Matt teased, knowing it was always easy to draw her into a spirited conversation when he pretended total indifference to the sufferings of a good part of the world. He was aware that Marlissa contributed heavily to charities dedicated to the feeding of the poor in this and other countries, and she had already bullied him into supporting almost as many needy children in India and Africa as she.

"Only a dinner!" she said with indignation, looking down at the expensive steak he had insisted on ordering although she had claimed little appetite. Then she realized that he was merely trying to draw her out of her thoughtful shell. "Ah, Matt . . . I told you I would be no good tonight. You should have let me go home and ponder black thoughts in a dark room."

"Do you want to talk about it? My ex-wife—the last one, that is—said the one redeeming feature about my rather oversize ears is that they listen quite nicely now and then."

She smiled at him. "You're a nice man, Matthew Douglas. And a good friend."

"Not a bad lover, either, huh? So if you'd like to do your talking in bed . . ."

She shook her head gravely, apologetically. Although she had dated him regularly since resuming her affair with Ernst, it had been quite a while since she had allowed Matt into her bed. "I'm sorry, Matt, I—"

"Uh-uh." He held a hand up, palm toward her, to stop her

explanation. "My honor prohibits excuses for being sexually rejected. To say nothing of my ego. I'd rather think you suffer from a common feminine complaint than hear you tell me about the other guy."

She looked at him, visibly upset by his teasing words. "What do you mean?"

He laughed, his handsome, tanned face revealing a large expanse of very white, even teeth. "Hit home, did I? Well, don't tell me about it. I'll listen to any complaints you want to list about the hard time the gorgeous Olivia is giving you at work. Or you can cry over a formula that isn't working. I'll even listen sympathetically if you want to bitch about what my man Reagan is doing in the White House. But I got an *F* in tact when it comes to listening to my women sob about their other lovers."

She smiled faintly. "It's no wonder your wives left you. You have an uncanny and disconcerting way of . . . how do you say, hitting the nail on the head. I had no idea my gloom stemmed from thoughts of a man until you mentioned it. But perhaps all black thoughts involve men. Yours is a wicked sex," she intoned, teasing him back. But her heart wasn't in it, because it wasn't Ernst who was wicked but she.

Marlissa went unprotestingly to see a performance by the Canadian ballet company at the opera house, grateful that there would be no chance to continue their conversation.

Since her lunch with Olivia and Thea, she had been uncomfortably conscious of a strange incongruity of thoughts and feelings. Reviewing her words to Thea, words that counseled honesty and humility, Marlissa had wondered at her nerve. That she of all people should speak out for the putting aside of unnecessary ego in the interests of a wholesome and candid relationship was ironic. At this very minute Ernst believed she was at Olivia's house, ironing out some problems with a new product. Her own lies far outdistanced Thea's attempt at deception. Who had she been to offer advice?

Yet she had not been able to hold her tongue. She had keenly felt Thea's pain. She thought wryly of the simplicity of the problems of others, the overwhelming complexity of one's own.

At work following the extended lunch, Marlissa had resolved firmly to tell Ernst the truth about her feelings toward him. She would not put off the inevitable another day. Then she remembered promising to meet Matt for dinner and the ballet, and breathed easier knowing she could not act upon her decision until the following night. Then she would tell Ernst, and she would have time enough to plan her words carefully.

As the afternoon progressed, she realized there was no need to be cruel. She could simply tell Ernst that she was not yet ready to settle down, that she felt it necessary to date others and for him to do the same. He would be upset, certainly, but he might even see the logic in seeking other partners if he felt a need to marry and begin a family. She would hurt him more by stringing him along indefinitely, and more still if she told him that she was ashamed of how he looked, spoke, and earned his living.

By the time she met Matt at the Iron Horse, her mood had swung to the other extreme and she was actively brooding over a future without Ernst.

Graceful dancers glided across the stage, and Marlissa found her thoughts going back to Thea and Everett. She was still excited by the news of Thea's pregnancy, and jealous, too. All of her friends in Meiringen had babies by now. Frequently she found herself in the nursery department of shops, buying presents to send home to girls who had once been school chums and were now mothers, most of them with toddlers as well as newborns to care for. She had a niece she had yet to see and two nephews she adored. She felt a strong maternal urge to reproduce, to nurse a tiny infant at her breast. And Ernst would be a wonderful father; gentle, instructive, and playful.

A lovely dancer in a white tutu came onstage, and the lights dimmed, one white beam following her elfin prance to center stage. Marlissa followed her movements without being conscious of her excellent performance.

He would be a fine husband as well, Ernst. He would never ask a wife to share him with others. There was no doubt that she loved him, either. Or he her. And yet she was about to send him away, possibly forever. Because he embarrassed her.

Marlissa glanced over at her date. She liked Matt but couldn't imagine him as her husband. Basically they were too different, and despite his charm and friendship, his values were flighty and insubstantial. Ernst was like a rock, steady and dedicated, deeply aware of what was sincerely important in the world and what was mere frosting. They thought alike. They shared the same points of reference. Why, then, did she care what others thought?

Who, in fact, were the others whose opinion she feared? It was the first time Marlissa had ever asked herself the question directly. Who really mattered in her life? Her friends? The people she had come to know since coming to San Francisco were by and large simple acquaintances. What they thought about her—if, indeed, they peered beyond the shell of their own lives—mattered very little. Olivia? Marlissa tried to imagine Olivia's reaction to the idea of Marlissa marrying Ernst. But Olivia, dealing with her own unhappy loss of the man she loved, would only wish her well. Olivia was far too confident and secure to worry about what others thought. Mark was an artist, and she wanted him even as an unknown. Others, unaware of Olivia and Mark's long history as lovers, might have thought Olivia was marrying beneath her had Mark stayed with her. It had never occurred to Marlissa to think that. But if Olivia were influenced by the petty suspicions of outsiders, she might have sent Mark away herself. Olivia was famous, world-known. As such, she was the vulnerable target for speculation, much of it inspired by jealousy. The press might have had a field day with the story of Mark and Olivia, especially when he was an unknown artist with few worldly goods to his name. Yet Olivia had not once worried about what others would think.

Thea, then? Was she worried about Thea? Olivia teased Thea about being a snob, and Thea had obligingly lived up to the title. But Thea had her own problems, and for the first time Thea had allowed Marlissa to see beneath her surface, to witness Thea's own vulnerability. Certainly Marlissa couldn't imagine Thea marrying an Ernst. But Thea wouldn't be comfortable with a Mark, either. Of the three of them, Thea most needed the safe nest of impeccable society to keep her from catching glimpses of a world not coddled in silks and priceless furs. Thea might well wonder why Marlissa would choose to settle down with a simple carpenter from her hometown when she had sampled men Thea would label more acceptable. But Thea's friendship certainly ran deeper than that or she would have been put out by Olivia's choice of a love rather than sharing Olivia's pain of loss.

While the full company of dancers finished the second act, Marlissa contemplated the future. What was it she was trading for social acceptability? Whom would she find to replace Ernst? Matt? He had a place in her life, but never could he fill her needs in that special way. Other men like Matt? She would be alone and lonely. She would have traded style for substance. Who would hold her hand during the empty years ahead? Oh, yes, she'd be envied by some. She would have her beautiful house and her prestigious position at MagnifiScent. She'd never be an object of pity, nor would her simple beginnings be glimpsed behind her smooth facade of sophistication. Without Ernst, she'd eventually be a polished jewel, if not as flawless as Olivia, at least almost as shining and enviable. And over the years she'd come to regret her choice more and more.

Slowly Marlissa began to feel as weightless and free as the feathery dancers who leaped and turned, seeming never to touch the ground. She had chided Thea for a lack of gut-level confidence. But Marlissa had always been proud of her personal strength. It had carried her through difficult times. She felt something long lost reenter her being.

What was she doing here with Matt, watching some dancers float through the air? Ernst was waiting for her. Ernst.

They had a wedding to plan.

CHAPTER 43

Ernst had been especially quiet during dinner at a small, unpretentious restaurant at the wharf. Marlissa had wanted to celebrate and had suggested an elaborate West Indian place she had often gone to with Brad Cavell. But Ernst had suggested the restaurant on the wharf, pointing out that he couldn't afford the other, not if he hoped to open his own business in the near future.

As they ate, she reminded herself that she must take care to remember his pride and that she faced a lifetime of living within Ernst's means if they married. With that thought she really didn't give a damn where they ate, as long as they were together. She felt wonderful, as if the weight of the world had been lifted from her shoulders. She was in love and proud of it. She wondered at her new peace—Ernst was still the humble carpenter, and his hands were just as rough, his accent no lighter.

"Ernst," she said shyly, reaching across the coffee cups to take his callused hand, "do we really have to wait until you open your shop to be married?" It was the first time the word had been brought into the open since they'd begun seeing each other again. Her heart seemed to fill her chest.

His eyes touched her with a tender sorrow. "Come, we are finished here. Let us take a drive, yes? We will talk."

He was a cautious driver, peering intently over the wheel as he piloted the Peugeot through the one-way streets and out of the city. They drove across the bay to Berkeley, where the hills over East Bay inevitably reminded them of Meiringen. They parked at Grizzly Peak and rolled down the windows to let in the night air, fragrant with the scent of eucalyptus, oak, and pine trees.

"It's been a long time since we've been here," Marlissa commented, looking contentedly out at the greenery.

"Perhaps because it is a little too close to home for you." Ernst turned to look at her.

Marlissa experienced a twinge of discomfort. "What do you mean?"

Ernst seemed to be picking his words carefully. "When we go out at all lately, it is to drive far away from The City." He reached for her hand, held, then kissed it softly. "Marlissa, tonight is the first time you have mentioned marriage in a very long time. It was once heavily on our minds. Now . . . I don't know if it is such a good thought."

She looked down at their entwined fingers. "Don't you want to marry me anymore, Ernst?" She started to withdraw the hand he held.

He shook his head slowly. "It is not I who have changed but you, Marlissa. And that is perhaps the trouble. My life is the same here as it was in Switzerland. I did not understand what a difference they make—money and position. If I had I would not have come to San Francisco. I would not have allowed our love to fill you with shame. Tonight you mention marriage." He smiled without humor. "Tonight I was going to tell you of my decision to end our relationship."

Marlissa grasped his hand tightly, as if refusing to let him go. "No! But why?"

His free hand went to her face, tracing the bones to her pointed, proud chin. "Because you love me but are ashamed of that love. Because I deserve more than such a love. Because once I am out of your life forever, you will again be free to find the kind of a man who shares your dreams. Ah, what do I know of such a glamorous existence? What to wear, where to go, how to talk. I make no apology for who and what I am, Marlissa. Yet in your arms I feel shame. You deserve a man you can introduce to your friends with pride, not one you must hide away in your fine house. A man who causes you to tremble at the ring of your bell."

"Never! I would never . . ." Marlissa then remembered the Sunday morning when Danuta, the wife of the doctor next door, neat and pretty in her immaculate little tennis dress, had come by to see if her neighbor had noticed a stray dog. Then Ernst *had* seen the irrepressible flinch at the ringing of the doorbell, *had* noticed the way she'd glanced uneasily at him in his old work pants and shirt.

Her shoulders sagged, but she turned squarely to face him. "No, you are right. I was ashamed. But not half so much as I am right now. Ernst, there is much I have learned since coming to this city. But none of it is as important as what I have learned about myself in one short day."

Strangely the tension was completely gone now. Subconsciously Marlissa had dreaded this moment above all, when she'd either have to tell him or he'd find out on his own that she'd been treating their affair like a shameful secret, tucking it away from the rest of her world. Yet now she was free to see that her embarrassment was nothing more than a barometer of her own insecurity and not an accusation against Ernst.

"Oh, Ernst, my darling," she said, "I wasn't ashamed of you. It was shame for myself! I have been a vain and foolish woman, belittling my own humble beginnings. How I envied Thea and Olivia. I wanted to be like them. You . . . you only reminded me of who I am. And that filled me with shame! Imagine!" She smiled at him gently.

"But yesterday . . ." she continued hesitantly, ". . . yesterday I saw the truth. Yesterday I realized that we are the same. Three women with joys and troubles. The same and yet different. I have not changed inside. My feelings for you have not altered. It was my feelings about myself that were confused, uncertain. I don't want you to leave me. I want you to forgive me. I would be proud to be your wife. I will try to make you proud of me."

"I will still be just a simple carpenter, Marlissa," he said warningly. "I will still be the same."

She brought his hand to her lips, kissed the callused fingers. "You will still be a carpenter, Ernst, but you will not remain the same. Nor shall I. Life will change us. Life changes all of us. Not always in the way we have hoped to change. But however we change, we will change together."

"But you will have your important job, and I will still be working with my hands. How will you feel, introducing your husband the carpenter to your fine friends?"

Marlissa thought of Olivia, so beautiful, so alone. "I will feel sad," she answered truthfully, "introducing you to them. I will worry that they will never be as happy as I am." Then she remembered Olivia's mission south. She was fiercely proud of Olivia's decision to help the injured Los Angeles housewife but was fully aware that what she was doing could well destroy MagnifiScent. Marlissa had been tempted to offer alternatives, to suggest that the woman's hospital bill be paid quietly, anonymously. But Marlissa had sensed that Olivia had reached a point in her life when it was necessary to take a firm stand for humanity, to risk her own security and be done with the polished manipulations that had failed her so greatly in her personal life. "My fine job might not last forever. I may have to come to you for a job before long," she added, smiling.

Ernst didn't try to understand. He stared at her instead, weighing and measuring the future. Then he started the engine. "Come, we must phone your mother."

"In Meiringen? Now?"

He nodded, the flash of his broad grin the only part of his face that was discernible as they drove through the shadows of the huge trees. "My future mother-in-law is a nervous woman. If she is to plan a wedding, she must be told at once."

Marlissa laughed and fought down a mad urge to hug him as he maneuvered the Peugeot through the trees. But he was already in his standard driving position, alertly hunched over the wheel.

CHAPTER 44

"I can't see him! Send him away!"

The nurse hesitated uncertainly before the bed. "But Mrs. Bickers, your husband has been out there since yesterday. He's terribly eager to see you."

"Send him away!" Patty shrieked hysterically, painfully twisting her bandaged neck away from the gentle, concerned voice. Only a shifting of grays indicated that she was facing the window now, but in the few days of her imprisonment in the gauze cage, she had already become an expert at reading the shades of light that came through the waffle-threaded bandages, which now told her that the low afternoon sun was fast sinking into the ocean beyond the hospital. "See!" she said bitterly. "I can't see him . . . I can't see anything! Don't you understand, I won't let him see me like this!"

"But Mrs. Bickers," the nurse reminded, her voice firm but backed with compassion, "he's already seen you. He sat by your side all night long after you were treated and bandaged."

"I don't care," she sobbed miserably. "Tell him to go home to the kids." She knew that her mother-in-law was with Nicki and Brian, but that they would be frightened at finding their mother gone so long despite the cookies and endless stories their grandmother was feeding them. But the pain she felt about her children was swallowed in the greater reality of what had happened to her. "I don't ever want to see him again. I'm ugly . . . ugly. . . ." She fisted her unbandaged hand and struck the bed.

"There, there. . . ." The nurse took her hand, patted it, then tucked it under the covers. "Don't be upsetting yourself like this, Mrs. Bickers. It will be all right, you'll see. Why, it's amazing what medical science can do! We had a little boy in here who was so badly burned by acid he scarcely had a face at all. And he turned out just fine in time."

Time, Patty thought, as the nurse, believing Patty had cried herself to sleep, quietly tiptoed out of the room. Again she was face to face with the two enemies of time and money. The physicians had already told her about time and money. She would need a series of operations if she ever hoped to have her face restored, and they would cost far more than the pittance covered by Fred's insurance.

Only hours before, the senior partner of the law firm she had engaged to sue MagnifiScent had told Patty that the company could not be held responsible for what its product had done to her. Mr. Neilson had come personally, apologetic about his firm's newest lawyer's unsubstantiated claim that the cosmetics company could be held for damages.

"He should have waited until the bottle of Second Chance was analyzed, Mrs. Bickers," the man had explained. "Our private analysis has established now that most of the actual cosmetic was removed and replaced with sulfuric acid. Nothing in the formula of the manufactured product could have contributed to your injury." He had cleared his throat.

"There is, however, the possibility of suing the shop from which you purchased the lotion, the jobbers who distributed the line, the owners or owner and employees who sold the item and what we refer to as John and Jane Does, the as-yet unestablished person or persons who may have tampered with the cosmetic that resulted in your grave injury. The suit would be leveled at the manufacturer and the Does, one through twenty-one, to cover all possible responsible parties. But first we must buy several bottles of Second Chance from this shop and others serviced by the jobber and conduct other relevant investigations. The police will be involved at such time that we establish criminal intent rather than negligence." He sighed.

"At this point we don't know if the acid was introduced to that bottle deliberately or out of negligence," Mr. Neilson had continued. "This determines if we're dealing with a crime or merely a tort. Had the product or one of its standard ingredients been at fault, there would be no question of speedy compensation either by court action or, more likely, by settlement directly with the company. If we weren't dealing with a personal product like cosmetics, the company might be induced to settle even if its responsibility were minimal or unlikely, simply to remove the threat of damaging publicity. But in this case MagnifiScent couldn't risk any suggestion that it might be responsible for your injury. It would be foolish of them to imply responsibility by paying you off as if yours were a nuisance claim. The public would avoid their products, out of concern for their safety. No, I don't believe there's any point to proceeding with a direct claim against the company."

Patty had listened to the lawyer's words despondently. "But my face!" she cried, when he had stopped talking.

The lawyer had tried to soothe her. "I didn't say we wouldn't try to get medical compensation, Mrs. Bickers. We'll continue our investigation, then file for a court hearing. But it will take time."

After he had gone, Patty had cried tearlessly. Her physician had examined her at length that morning, had attempted to cheer her with the news that the damage to her right eye was not critical. She would keep her sight after the delicate tissues had healed. She would be able to see the look of horror in the eyes of everyone who saw the rest of her face.

The one ray of hope to which she'd been clinging since regaining consciousness in the hospital was that MagnifiScent would be made to pay for the extensive operations she would need. With unlimited money she could have had the services of the best surgeons. She had kept that one thought above all else, ignoring the discomfort and pain, fighting back the panic that pushed at the edges of her mind. All she'd ever had was a pretty face. Other women were clever, had bright careers or husbands who adored them however they looked. But she couldn't be sure Fred would stay with a wife who had a hideous, scarred face. For the last two months Fred had been "working late," and Patty was terrified he was seeing another woman.

Fred was young, handsome. He wanted to get somewhere in this world. Having a wife with a mutilated face would make him a freak, too. And her children . . . they were babies now, but soon they'd be going to school. The other children would be cruel, gaping at her, avoiding Brian and Nicki. It would be better if she were dead if she couldn't have the necessary operations.

Patty could imagine the months of legal entanglements ahead while things like cause and responsibility were bantered back and forth. Mr. Neilson hadn't discussed the legal fees that would be consumed by lengthy court battles, but she was alert enough to read through his words and understand that unless liability could quickly be established, these would have to be considered as well. It might take years before she could begin the skin grafts and plastic surgery she needed, and she would be a blight on her family and herself for all that time.

She had been silently praying for death when the nurse returned to tell her again that her husband was still waiting to see her, and again she turned her face to the wall. She knew he was hurt, that her unwillingness to be seen was directed toward him alone. He would know she had seen the lawyer and a reporter from the *Times,* to whom she'd revealed her earlier intention to sue MagnifiScent. But she couldn't see Fred. She had sent him a message begging him to go home and leave her in peace. If there were to be no operations, she would never see him again. He could take her sweet-faced children and leave her to make some sort of life for herself. Never, never would she suffer the agony of seeing the faces of the ones she loved when they looked at her.

She was sobbing quietly, facing away from the light of the overhead lamp, as the door opened again. She stiffened, praying that it was anyone but Fred who had slipped into her room.

"Mrs. Bickers? Are you awake?"

Patty turned at the unfamiliar, clear voice. "Who is it?" She made an effort to contain her crying. "Please . . . I don't want to talk to anyone."

"I understand how you must be feeling, Mrs. Bickers. I only want to talk to you for a minute. My name is Olivia DeSante. I own MagnifiScent."

Patty half-turned on the bed, staring with her good eye through the gauze that covered it to keep out an excessive amount of light until the natural secretions had cleansed it completely. She was stunned out of her sorrow by the identity of her visitor. She couldn't see the woman now, but she had seen her before, on the pages of countless magazines and newspapers and on television talk shows. It was like having a movie star come to see her, and for a moment she was shocked out of her pain and misery. "Olivia DeSante!" Her exclamation was muffled by the gauze, reminding Patty of how she looked. Instinctively her hand flew to cover her almost completely bandaged head. The foolishness of her gesture penetrated, and she let the hand fall weakly to its bandaged mate, lost in the blankets.

"I heard about your injury only this morning, from my legal staff."

Patty turned her head away from the soft voice. "Tell them they don't have to worry," she interrupted in a hoarse whisper. "Something was mixed into the Second Chance. Sul . . . sulfuric acid!" Her shoulders trembled with an effort to keep the tears from running out of her good eye. She felt a comforting hand rest lightly on her arm.

"My God!" There was a pause. "Mrs. Bickers, I didn't come because I thought our product could be responsible for what happened to you. I only wanted you to know that I've made arrangements to underwrite the expenses for the surgery you'll require. I understand that your face can be restored with the right treatment."

Patty turned sharply toward the voice. "But you aren't liable! My lawyer made that clear just a few hours ago!"

The hand patted her arm gently. "So my attorneys tell me. But you'll still need the surgery, won't you? I'd like to know that it's taken care of properly. We at MagnifiScent like to keep our new customers."

Patty could almost see the smile on the beautiful face over her. "I . . . I don't know what to say."

The hand patted briefly and there was a catch to Olivia's voice. "Just get better. I'll be in touch."

"Thank you," Patty answered faintly, her head turned toward the softly retreating steps. At the click of the door, Patty gingerly allowed her head to fall back against the pillows. For the first time since before she had unknowingly put the sulfuric acid on her face, she tried to twist her blistered mouth into a smile.

She thought of Mr. Neilson's words about the inadvisability of MagnifiScent assuming any responsibility for her injury. From what Olivia DeSante had said, the woman was also aware of the likely repercussions resulting from her generous offer of badly needed help. The press would believe that Olivia had picked up her medical tab because the Second Chance in some way had ruined Patty's face. Unless Patty did something, Olivia DeSante's kindness would cost the famous woman dearly.

Yet the woman's generosity would save, at the very least, years of anguish for Patty. She would have lost everything she cherished, her husband, her children . . . She would have dreaded being seen, would have grown old and bitter even if she had eventually found some target for a lawsuit. Now she would have her operations, and one day she would again be free to face the world, be a mother to her children. All because this woman, who could only be hurt by her action, had cared.

Patty tried to remember the name of the reporter who had come to see her. Then she rang for the nurse.

CHAPTER 45

Lights flashed in her face as she closed the door behind her, and before she could get her footing to make her way through the path of photographers and newsmen pressing in on her, Olivia felt a strong arm fall over her shoulder.

"Now, now, boys, back off and leave Mrs. DeSante alone. Give her air!"

Olivia smiled hesitantly at the grim-faced lawyer she had argued with only hours before.

Peter Berger firmly steered her toward the elevator. "Mrs. DeSante has no comment at this time." He paused as a cameraman, bent under the weight of his shouldered minicam with the bold CBS logo, stepped in front of them, blocking their escape. The attorney forced his face into a pleasant smile, sighed before speaking into the thrusting mike. "Out of the goodness of her heart—and against my counsel, I might add," he said carefully, "Mrs. DeSante has personally offered to underwrite the entire cost of Mrs. Bickers's medical bill."

Olivia knew that Peter was also taking note of the smug expressions on the newsmen's faces. She kept her own face immobile.

"We have already secured proof that our product was in no way responsible for Mrs. Bickers's unfortunate injury. It was caused by deliberate, outside tampering with the product. Mrs. Bickers was the victim of some unknown person who removed the contents of the product and then filled the bottle . . ." he paused for dramatic effect, "with sulfuric acid." He looked at Olivia with pride and warmth. "When Mrs. DeSante heard that Mrs. Bickers was unable to afford the necessary treatment for her injury, she generously decided to come to her aid. Even though MagnifiScent is in no way responsible for what has happened to Patty Bickers!"

Olivia felt the pressure behind her shoulders intensify and she stepped forward, eyes straight ahead, seeing but not acknowledging the disbelieving smirks on the faces of the newsmen. Peter's words would be heard and printed, but the readers would largely share the opinion so evident on the faces she passed—that she wouldn't have made her offer unless she believed MagnifiScent to be responsible.

". . . buy her silence?"

". . . settle out of court for an undisclosed sum . . ."

Peter groaned as he pushed Olivia into the elevator and slapped his palm over the button that closed the sliding doors in the middle of the comments and questions.

"Jesus, this is going to be a bitch!" He touched the street button, hesitated, then pressed the button for the floor below. "Come on, Olivia, this place is crawling with press. We'll wait them out over coffee."

The elevator stopped and they got out. Down the hall was a little alcove with hot- and cold-drink machines. He fumbled in his pocket, inserted some coins, waited nervously for the paper cup to fill with the black brew, handed the hot cup to Olivia, and repeated the process.

They carried the cups cautiously through the hall, passing nurses, doctors, other visitors, and open-doored rooms with their stiffly blanketed beds, and others with patients in their cotton hospital gowns. No one paid them any attention, and they quietly slipped into an empty waiting room.

Olivia sank gratefully into a brown vinyl lounge chair and tasted her coffee. It was strong and flavored by the cardboard, but she drank it. "Thank you for coming, Peter."

"Damn, Olivia, if you had to do this, there were better ways to accomplish the same end." The lawyer let his anger show.

"Is it really so terrible to let people know we care?"

He looked at her disbelievingly, then grudgingly smiled. "Yes, Olivia, I'm afraid it is. Nobody cares anymore, unless he has something to hide." He rubbed a graying sideburn tiredly. "I talked to Fredricks in packaging. We're going to ask for a recall of the entire inventory and ring the bottles with sealing wax, if you approve. That will guarantee that there will never be a repeat of what's happened with one of our products again. The recall will cost us a fortune, but it might save the company. Other than that, I think we should put our own investigators on the case. The police won't do much to find out who put the acid in that bottle unless we can prove that it wasn't a simple case of negligence. If we're able to prove that her husband or some enemy was trying to kill her, that will get the company off the hook."

"God." Olivia shuddered, imagining how the poor woman must have felt, the acid eating into her flesh.

Peter looked at her with undisguised curiosity. "Why did you do it, Olivia? It won't make life easier for you. They say the road to hell is paved with good intentions. The road to ruin, too."

She smiled and thought of Mark. "I don't know, exactly. I suppose because I wanted to do one thing in my life that wasn't exclusively for my own comfort."

He looked at her as if doubting her sanity. "Remember that the next time I want to up my retainer. Believe me, it'll cost you a good deal less."

Because Peter wanted to stay on in Los Angeles to arrange for a thorough investigation of the Bickers matter, Olivia flew home alone. Grateful for the solitude, she opened her traveling case and took out the newspaper clippings she had been reading when Peter Berger had interrupted her.

She could see that Mark had aged during his absence. His face was thinner, and new lines under his eyes testified to hard work and little sleep. But he had done it, had proved his ability without any help other than that of his own talent.

She let the clippings rest in her lap as she stared out the narrow window at the night. The jet seemed to be treading water through the darkness. Olivia had no sense of movement. She thought about stars but could see none. If Mark was now a star in its ascendancy, she was perhaps a meteor, plunging in fiery demise. Even if MagnifiScent rallied from this threat against it, she felt as if she and Mark were again traveling in different directions.

She thought of his claimed intention to come to her when he'd proved himself, but had she ever been worthy of him? She had left him for a more glamorous life, had found gold and tried to use some of it to buy him back. She had scoffed at his pride, and yet she had valued her own above all else. He had asked only one thing of her: to be given the time to make it on his own.

I'll do anything for you, except get off your back....

Well, she was off his back now. She smoothed the clippings in her lap. They said that Mark would be in San Francisco in three months, once more showing his work at Neftale's Gallery.

She closed her eyes to the night, vowing that she would find the strength to keep from calling him, begging him to return. She would wait, as he asked. And if he didn't call, she would go on waiting.

CHAPTER 46

The nurse brought Fred into Patty's room, but instead of tactfully making her exit, she lingered on to do the things nurses can't resist doing. She straightened the blanket and sheet over Patty, pushed the glass with its accordion-pleated straw closer to the bed, straightened a chair. With a last look to assure herself that there was nothing further to take care of, she smiled brightly and left.

Patty was glad she had waited until the bandage over her good eye was removed before seeing Fred. The eye felt weak and sensitive to the light, but she could see well enough to make out the way stress had tightened his face. She realized with a rush of feeling that her ordeal had been almost as terrible for him as it had been for her. But before she could blurt out the speech she had prepared to explain why she'd refused to see him, Fred started talking.

"I want you to know that I understand why you wouldn't see me, Patty." He looked at her face wrapped in its gauze mask, his eyes unnaturally bright. "God, you must hate me, baby. And I don't blame you."

"Hate you?" Her lips were less swollen now. Her voice sounded more familiar in her own ears.

He sat down by the side of her bed. "Any decent husband would be able to take care of his wife!" He buried his face in his hands, rubbed angrily at his eyes, looked at her again. "How many times I meant to get a decent insurance policy for us. But no, I had to get a new car instead. And a color TV! Now look at you, and there isn't a fucking thing I can do about it!"

"But, Fred, honey, the doctors say—"

"They say it will take two, maybe three operations to fix you up! Operations I can't afford." He stood up, put a hand lightly on her leg, then pulled it away, sitting down again. "I talked to the lawyer after he came to see you yesterday. He told me they don't even know who to sue yet. What if they never collect from anyone?" He reached over and grasped her good hand. "I don't give a damn for myself, baby. You know that, don't you?" His mouth tried a weak smile. "You'll always be beautiful to me, however you look. And to the kids, too. They miss you so much. They drew pictures for me to bring you." He patted the pockets of his suit jacket. "I'll find them later. Patty, do you think you can ever forgive me? I'll do anything to make it up to you, anything. I swear! I'll work nights . . ." He looked down at her hand, swallowed up in his larger one. "I've already got a second job. Did you know? Those nights I was supposed to be working for Homwell."

She twisted her neck stiffly to see him better. The bandages gave her tunnel vision, forcing her to turn her whole head in the direction of what she wanted to see. "A second job? Fred, I don't know what you're talking about. Didn't anyone tell you—"

"It was supposed to be a surprise. I've been installing car stereos at Cal Sound. You know, where we got the stereo for the car. I've been saving for your birthday. For a down payment on a new Pinto station wagon. The one you wanted."

She found she could smile. "Fred, darling! I thought . . . it doesn't matter what I thought. Oh, Fred, I don't care about a new car! I just want you home nights." She squeezed his hand. All this time she had been so sure that he had been with someone else, and he'd been working to surprise her with a new car to take the place of her broken-down station wagon.

Then she remembered the rest of what he'd said. Was it possible that he didn't know about Olivia DeSante's offer? "Fred, weren't you here late yesterday afternoon?"

"Not after you said you wouldn't see me for the third time. I went home, saw Mom and the kids, then I drove around for most of the night. I couldn't sleep. I haven't been able to think about anything except you and those operations. I did some checking around this morning before coming over here. Listen, baby, there are ways to do this. I'm going to hit Homwell up for a raise. I can get another two nights a week at Cal Sound. Mom hasn't much, but she's going to help. I'm going to talk to the doctors, see if I can't work out something—"

"Fred," she interrupted quietly, realizing he didn't know that her hospital and doctor bills were going to be taken care of by Olivia DeSante. But before telling him, she had to know something. "What if . . . what if the operations don't work? What if I end up ugly?" All her life Patty had put a great deal of stock in her face. But even without the acid, her face wouldn't have been pretty forever. Time would take its toll even on the most beautiful face.

"What do you mean?" He looked at her.

She saw the fear in his eyes. Her heart felt tight against her chest. "What if I'm not pretty ever again? Will you . . . will you still love me?" How many times had she wanted to ask him this? Why was it so easy now? "Will you go on loving me even if I'm not pretty?"

His eyes filled with tears. "How can you ask me that, baby? How can you even ask?" The tears spilled over, but he paid them no attention. "I thought you were going to die the other night! And if you had . . . Patty, I don't think I could have gone on living without you. I'd have had to, for the kids. God, I was so scared! I didn't realize how much I love you, honey. I mean, I knew, you know, but almost losing you. . . . I don't give a damn what you *look* like! Look, when we first met, when all I wanted to do was get it on with you, then, sure, it mattered. It always matters then, because that's all there is in the beginning. And yeah, I like the other guys seeing that my wife is great-looking. It's a kind of shot in the ego, I guess. And I wanted Homwell to be impressed with what he saw. But all that stuff doesn't matter, honey. It's you I love, not the way you look on the outside. I want you to be pretty again for *you*. What else do you have? A husband who can't take care of his family right, kids who take all of your time and energy—"

"Oh, Fred," she interrupted, rubbing his arm, what she could reach of it. "It's going to be all right! And it doesn't even matter so much now. The woman who owns Magnifi-Scent, Olivia DeSante—you know who she is, don't you?"

She waited for his nod. "She was here yesterday. To see me. She's taken care of all my medical bills! All of them! I'm going to have the operations just as soon as I'm ready for them. The doctor swears my face will be fine."

He shook his head. "Olivia DeSante? Here? But your lawyer told me—"

"I know! She's doing it anyway. I don't know why. From what I've heard, it makes it look like Second Chance was responsible, but it wasn't. She's fantastic, Fred. She said it was to keep me as a customer, can you believe that? She's doing it because she felt bad about what happened to me, because it happened with one of her products, I guess. I called the reporter who came to see me. I told him what Olivia had done, and that I'd already dropped the suit against her, that we were still looking for the person who had put the stuff in the jar. I wanted him to write about how fantastic she is, how she's taking care of me when she doesn't have to, when it only makes her look guilty." She sighed. "But I think he thought I was trying to do my end of some deal I'd made with her. Maybe I shouldn't have accepted, Fred. But she has so much . . . Was I wrong?"

"Of course not, baby," he said, getting up. "Patty, if I'm very careful, can I hold you, do you think?"

"You'd better!"

He held her so gently that she couldn't repress a giggle. She reached out and rubbed him boldly.

"Hey!" He jumped back, startled but grinning.

"I didn't think I'd ever . . . you know, feel that way again, but I do. I didn't think I'd ever feel like a woman again. But just knowing you love me, and that my face is going to be normal again. . . ." She held out her good arm to him.

The nurse came in then, her eyes excited. "I don't know if you want to see this . . ." She held out the latest newspaper and pointed.

Fred twisted around to read along with Patty.

GRIEF-CRAZED WIDOW LEAVES SUICIDE NOTE ABSOLVING MAGNIFISCENT

Ex-Employee of The Vanity put sulfuric acid in Second Chance Bottle

LOS ANGELES, June 30—Charlotte Burquin, a recent widow and ex-employee of The Vanity, a cosmetics shop on the Miracle

Mile, was found dead early this morning in her apartment, apparently from an overdose of sleeping pills. Mrs. Burquin left a suicide note on her kitchen table stating that she had previously worked for the current owner of The Vanity, Erika Halstead, but that Mrs. Halstead had dismissed her when she found money missing from The Vanity's bank account. At the time Mrs. Burquin admitted that she had taken the money to help pay for treatment for her husband, who died of cancer six weeks ago.

Mrs. Burquin's note admitted that she had sought revenge against Mrs. Halstead by substituting sulfuric acid for some of the lotion in a bottle of Second Chance. The note further stated: "My only thought at the time was to punish Mrs. Halstead for making me lose my job after so recently losing my husband. I wanted her to lose her shop. In my anger and grief I forgot that anyone other than Mrs. Halstead could get hurt. When I heard a radio news report about what had happened to Patty Bickers, I felt I could not go on. My life is over, but I pray that Mrs. Bickers can find it in her heart to forgive me for the pain I have caused."

Patty finished reading and sighed. "That poor woman. She lost her husband, her job, everything."

The nurse nodded. "The poor soul. I'm sorry, Mrs. Bickers, I know I shouldn't have sympathy for her after what she did to you. But I think the poor thing was half-crazy with grief." She shook her head.

Patty reached for Fred's hand. He got up and put his arms around her and hugged her gently.

The phone rang. Patty picked it up, twisting around to use her good hand. She brought the receiver to her bandaged ear carefully. "Hello?" She listened, then covered the mouthpiece with her hand. "It's the reporter from the *Times!*"

"Yes?" she said into the phone. "Yes, I know. I just read—A statement? Yes, I'm sorry for the woman. I believe that she wasn't thinking of who would get the lotion. Yes, I certainly do intend to use MagnifiScent products when my face is better!" She smiled at Fred, forgetting that he couldn't see her expression. "In fact, that's what I want my husband to get me for my birthday. Yes, Second Chance, too! And you can print that!"

She hung up the phone.

"No new car?" Fred asked, smiling.

"No, just the old husband home where he belongs."

The nurse slipped out of the room.

CHAPTER 47

The first nip of fall was in the air, but San Francisco seemed to welcome it eagerly. Indian summer came and lingered, followed by days of dampness and fog. Then the sun returned but kept a respectful distance, allowing the air to be cool and crisp and clear. Out beyond the dead walls of Alcatraz on its rock island, the fog continued to play hide-and-seek with the sun as ships fought the tide like toy boats in a choppy tub. Students poured into The City again in Volkswagen bugs and buses to party in town, merge with the mobs at Cal State, or journey back across the Bay Bridge to Berkeley, the primary campus of the University of California.

All of San Francisco seemed caught up in an undefined excitement, like a great engine starting up again after a comparative rest. Summer tourists had filtered out of The City, leaving the business of living to the seasoned natives. New shops opened with gay colored banners and closed as quickly, squashed by escalating rentals and fierce competition. On either side of the main branch of MagnifiScent, offices changed names and firmly established corporations drew greater and greater crowds.

MagnifiScent brought out its long-debated line of men's cosmetics and scents, but Thea paid less attention to the ever-booming business and more to the exclusive little boutiques that specialized in fabulous clothing for expectant mothers.

Everett had moved his offices to San Francisco, but they had decided to keep the house in Beverly Hills, if only to pacify the eagerly waiting grandparents in Southern California. It had been a busy and productive few months. The house on the Marina had been geared for Thea's needs and had catered to her tastes and life-style. Now it had been redone, and the starkly modern tone had been subdued to incorporate Everett's penchant for heavy leather furniture and casual comfort. The merging had been more successful than the decorator had envisioned, and the nursery was an absolute dream. They had put a door to the next room in the far wall, which had been turned into a bedroom and sitting room for the English nanny Everett had found on his last trip to London.

"Now let's have that party!" she suggested as Everett prowled through his new den. "To celebrate my glowing and growing condition. And for Marlissa and Ernst! They'll be back from Switzerland in two weeks. Shall we?"

Everett kissed her lightly on her shoulder, tickling his nose on her hair, which she'd decided to grow long again. "A party? Sure, why not?" He crossed the room to inspect the desk he'd had shipped from Los Angeles.

She watched him, warmed by his presence in the house she had once thought of as her private domain. Everything was perfect now, she and Everett, Marlissa and her carpenter, who seemed like a nice enough young man. Thea, Everett, and Olivia had flown to Meiringen for the old-fashioned wedding in the impossibly sweet church nestled against the Alps. Meiringen was even lovelier than Thea had remembered it from her visits to see Olivia, and Marlissa had been beautiful in the white lace gown her mother and grandmother had worn as brides.

Afterward she and Everett had gone to Paris and then to Florence, where she'd stuffed herself on the delectable pastries and bought masses of lovely Florentine leather gloves and purses. Her body seemed to adore being pregnant. She'd never looked healthier or prettier, and already she was wondering if it wasn't a good idea to think about a brother for her baby girl or a sister for the boy she would have in less than five short months.

Olivia, however, had refused to join them on their European holiday. She had had enough of Europe when she had lived in Switzerland all those years, she insisted, but Thea suspected that mingled thoughts of Jean-Pierre and Mark had hastened her return to San Francisco.

Thea felt a pang of sadness for Olivia. Olivia the beautiful, Olivia the famous, the envied one. By the time they had flown to Switzerland for Marlissa's wedding, Mark was already in New York, the first stop on his tour of the major cities.

As Mark went from city to city, his fame was spreading in

advance of every show. His paintings were being bought for the best museums and snatched up by the most knowledgeable collectors. In Paris he had moved more heavily into sculpture, working chiefly in marble, and Everett, who already owned several of Mark's paintings, had placed a bid on a large white Italian marble piece he had seen in Europe. There was a strength and a purity to his work in both media, and he was displaying an amazing versatility, which caused the critics to make comparisons between Mark and Picasso, a frightening, awesome comparison that left Thea stunned and even more fearful for Olivia.

Her own knowledge of art and artists was unexceptional, but she trusted Everett's judgment implicitly. He had already written the forewords for two art books, and his private collection had more than tripled in value due to his sage buying. And Everett's opinions about Mark's work were completely formed. He considered Mark to be well on the road to expanding a talent that would make him one of the most important artists of his time.

Thea had met and liked Mark years before, and when she had seen him again for the short time he and Olivia were together, she appreciated what her friend had seen in the handsome artist. He had a boyish enthusiasm that was contagious and exhilarating. She had no doubt that he loved Olivia. It seemed pure tragedy that now that they were both at the top, they were further apart than ever.

Olivia hadn't mentioned Mark once since Thea had told her where he was. But Thea knew Olivia, like her, was following his slow and glittering migration west. Olivia would know the exact date of Mark's opening in San Francisco, and she would wait silently to see if he would call. It would be a lonely vigil for her, and her pride would see to it that no one witnessed her suffering.

"So when are you going to have this party?"

"Party?" Her thoughts lingered on Mark and Olivia. If only Olivia could know the kind of peace and happiness Thea had found.

"The party. For Marlissa and Ernst. For the baby." Smiling, Everett snapped his fingers as if to awaken her from a vaguely disorienting dream.

"Oh, yes!" If only, she mused, Mark and Olivia could be meeting now for the first time. She also began to smile. "The party! Of course. Wait a minute." She left the room and was gone long enough to give Everett the time to mix them drinks.

She came back slowly, a newspaper clipping in her hand. She was reading the small print. "Let's make it on the first."

He held out his hand for the clipping, knowing his wife well enough by now to understand that she had something more important than a party on her mind.

He looked up from the clipping, smiling broadly. "The first it is." He handed over the scrap of paper. "I certainly hope you know what you're doing."

She exhaled slowly and picked up her drink. "So do I."

CHAPTER 48

Meiringen was exactly as Marlissa had left it. Nothing had aged or been replaced. The same shops occupied the same little stone and mortar buildings, and the same faces joyously greeted her from behind their counters. Any replacements were caused by the one inevitable change, death. Even then the sons and daughters of the shopkeepers took over, wearing the same aprons and selling the same wares.

Here and there little concessions to progress had been hesitantly incorporated into the picture. The largest market in town had taken on some of the flavor of a modern supermarket, with wider lanes between the stocked shelves, a greater variety of imported goods, and shining shopping carts to urge the customers to buy more than they could carry. But the candy counter still contained the same excellent Swiss chocolates, and the spirits department still dazzled the eye with its selection of fine brandies and local wines, including the spectacular pear brandy bottle holding a massive whole pear that had been grown in the bottle that was then filled with brandy. And the townspeople still shopped with their net bags, magically stretching to encompass the largest order.

The whole town is frozen in time! Marlissa was delighted with the realization. The setting of her happy childhood was as unmarked by time and progress as a cherished crèche laid under the tree at Christmas, then wrapped in batting and tucked safely away for the rest of the year.

Only the huge, modern MagnifiScent factory was new, and even that was half-hidden in the shadow of the Alps, surrounded by ferns and long, sweet grass. Everything else was as she had left it. The only thing that was different was her, and, she discovered in great surprise, Ernst.

She knew she had changed, then changed again, and she was glad. Her parents had already seen the obvious changes on their trips to San Francisco, but she enjoyed the look of awe on the faces of the rest of her family and in the eyes of the friends she had left behind. They touched the superb clothes she wore so matter-of-factly now, exclaimed over the cut of her hair, the strikingly attractive cast of her face with its artfully applied makeup.

But the more meaningful changes could not be seen, not even by those who had loved Marlissa the most. She had returned home with a calmness she'd never had before. They didn't know, because she'd kept her previous dissatisfaction to herself and, in many ways, *from* herself. To these loving friends and relatives, she had merely returned for an event they'd all anticipated, to become the wife of her childhood sweetheart.

After the wedding they spent the first night of their honeymoon in the quaint old inn by a little waterfall tucked against the Alps, making love on a feather mattress under a handmade quilt while a fire in the hearth provided just enough flickering light to enable them to see the pleasure they gave and took.

There were so many places to revisit, such a multitude of people to see. Her entire family and all its branches called Meiringen or nearby Innertkirchen, Iseltwald, and Bönigen on the Brienzer See home, coming together in knots of laughing, crying excitement. Marlissa hadn't known how terribly homesick she had been for these people and places until she saw it all again.

Ernst's family welcomed her warmly. They, too, had always been family, his old grandmother, his brothers and sisters, his parents. He also had cousins and aunts and uncles and their children, all of whom would have been hurt if they were not visited.

Marlissa couldn't help noticing that Ernst also stood apart from the others, not quite blending into the easy conversation, comfortable but somehow removed. She began to watch him carefully, listening with a questioning ear to the words he said, the idioms he used, the things that amused him and the subjects that raised a small light of impatience in his eyes.

It was more than the way he now conducted himself in a restaurant or dressed for a dinner party. It went beyond the fact that he could now draw from so many more points of reference. He had seen something of the world, adjusted to a strikingly different environment, tasted the delights and failures of starting a new life. He had left a small town where he was unthinkingly loved and cared for, to throw himself into the demanding bustle and impersonality of a big city. He had become used to small comforts unknown in Meiringen.

He had changed without Marlissa even being aware of the subtlety of the changing. He was still the good, sincere, hard-working man she had known, but the sandpaper of experience had rubbed against the vague, unformed edges of his being. She had wanted nothing more than to make this country boy a sophisticate. Now she saw that it had happened without her. It made Marlissa happy and sad, because she knew that he was perfect as he was, but that time would steadily define and polish the rough diamond he had always been.

Marlissa no longer wanted to be Olivia or Thea, however secure they were in their confrontations with the world. She wanted always to remember that the important ingredients in life were not determined by price or reflected in the eyes of others. She needed the discipline and satisfaction of work and the deep and secure love of one good man. The work may have brought her recognition, a fine house and a swelling bank account, but all that was icing on the cake, not its substance. She had looked only for the icing when she had dated other men, impressed by glib manners and worldly ease, and she had starved on glamour.

"Don't ever change," she had begged Ernst while picnicking on cold chicken and wine during an outing along the Brunig Pass.

He had laughed at her seriousness. "Of course I shall change. Change is the only constant factor in life. We will both change, and we will both stay the same. I will bend to you, and you to me." He had pointed to two trees, swaying in unison in the breeze. "'Fate, Time, Occasion, Chance, and Change? To these all things are subject but eternal Love.'"

She smiled, remembering when they had both discovered and fallen in love with Shelley.

"That is what really troubles you, my Marlissa. That in my changing I will cease to love you. In your change you momentarily left me behind, and you fear that I will falter in the same way. Yes?"

She had nodded, frightened by the fragile bonds that held them together, an emotion that she had found could be shrugged aside by glitter and false pride.

"I did falter. When I saw the shame in your eyes when we were together in San Francisco. For a moment I, too, forgot. But we are both builders, Marlissa. When you create a new essence, is it not sometimes necessary to start over with the same chemicals, blending them in a new and better fashion? When I erect a new structure, I must sometimes take down what I have begun. The wood is right, but the pieces need planing or sanding to make them fit as they should. Or the foundation must be shored more firmly. So it is with lovers. The timber is sound, but the real work is in the building, the fitting together of pieces. I will make concessions to your needs, and you to mine." He had taken her into his strong arms. "Would you like to hear more of Shelley?" He kissed her gently. "'Life may change, but it may fly not; Hope may vanish, but can die not; Truth be veiled, but still it burneth; Love repulsed—but it returneth!'"

Marlissa sighed, as comforted by his arms and lips as the remembered and beloved words of Shelley. She said, "Thou may look for the tinsel, but must not forget the tree."

He looked at her dubiously, a little smile on the edges of his lips. "Shelley?"

She laughed and pushed him back on the blanket they had brought. "No. Marlissa. A much wiser Marlissa."

CHAPTER 49

Olivia stood in her dressing room, her eyes fixed on the white and gold phone on its glass stand by the door. "Ring! Please." It remained silent.

She sat down on the chair in the middle of the mirrored, cagelike room. Under the bright lights she looked surprisingly fresh. There was no evidence of the last two restless nights, during which she had awakened again and again at the imagined ringing of the telephone.

The newspaper clippings had mounted in the drawer of her bedside table, neatly scissored, most showing Mark's face and all containing samples of his amazing works. She had resisted the urge to order some of them. Thea's husband had become an ardent collector, but she dared not contribute to Mark's success in any way. Determined never again to interfere in Mark's life or career without his implicit invitation, Olivia had resisted the intense desire to call him when he arrived in San Francisco two days earlier. She had followed every step he had taken since his arrival in New York. It was increasingly easier to know where he was, what he was doing. The papers were filled with word of his actions. James Lacy, in San Francisco for the opening of his special project, the Impressionist museum to which Olivia had contributed, had talked with Mark both in New York and Chicago. And Mark had become an important new name, showing up with regularity in society columns in papers throughout the country. Olivia had several clippings with mention of his appearance at a benefit or ball, or dining out at fashionable restaurants. Often well-known women were shown at his side, and Olivia had followed the articles with a trace of panic, terrified that his engagement or marriage to one of these beauties might be announced.

Slowly she smoothed Second Chance over her face, distracted for a moment by thoughts of Patty Bickers. She had been unable to use the product since without thinking of the woman, who, after her first operation, was almost completely normal again. When Olivia's jar of the facial setting lotion was gone, she'd open the newly packaged Cling! the same excellent product under a new name and in a differently shaped bottle, also with the wax seal around its neck that was now a standard feature of all MagnifiScent products. Olivia had known that it would be a long time before any woman would feel comfortable using Second Chance, and that thought brought her back to Mark again, to the painful realization that he had not called and probably never would. *Other women had suffered greater tragedies than losing a lover,* she told herself, waiting for the lotion to dry. The woman who had mixed sulfuric acid into Second Chance had lost her husband and her job, and then her life. *Once Mark has had his show here and goes back to Europe or New York, I'll put him out of my mind!*

She closed her eyes and tightly compressed her lips, hating the need to lie to herself. Never would she forget Mark! Never would she stop hoping he'd return!

The setting lotion had dried to a barely perceptible sheen. Olivia applied a light coat of foundation, then blusher, touching the soft brush to the point of her chin and the center of her forehead as well as the curve of her cheekbone. She used cotton to blend the color into the skin cream, then dusted her face with a film of Feathertouch # 3 powder.

She opened the exquisitely crafted glass case of the newest of the MagnifiScent eye shadows, The Elements, a lovely blend of earth, sea, and sky colors to be worn on the upper lid like a subdued rainbow of browns, greens, and blues. She concentrated intently on what she was doing, steeling herself against thoughts of why she was going through this elaborate process of beautification. *First the chocolate, then the dust, next the two shades of green . . .* She worked a little brush through the well of aquamarine eye shadow, applied it over the narrow band of jade, brought a fresh brush to the turquoise, swept it above the aquamarine all the way to the edge of her well-shaped eyebrow. She leisurely repeated her actions on the second lid, ignoring the little voice in her mind that warned her that she would be late for Thea's party.

She outlined her eyes in smoky gray and brought out her eyelashes with a darker mascara. She studied her work in the mirror, daring herself to cry now that her eyes were done. Satisfied with the exotic and yet subtle artistry, Olivia applied Golden Oranges to her mouth, wiped off the excess, brought her lips to dazzling life with gloss. She poured a few drops of Premier Enfant on her fingertips, lightly touched the backs of her ears, the hollow of her throat.

Standing up, she removed the white protective cloth from her neck and looked at herself, keeping eye contact with her reflection while she brought her most famous piece of jewelry to her neck. It was five strands of rare golden pearls, perfectly matched and roped together, caught at the throat by a diamond band on yellow gold, in which was set a five-carat flawless emerald. It seemed to carry all the light to her neck, emphasizing its slender length, illuminating her beautiful face with its exquisite features and exotically painted eyes. Her hair, longer and fuller now, seemed a platinum tiara.

Olivia stepped back, allowing herself to be captured in the mirrors. She knew she had never looked more beautiful. The floor-length, St. Laurent satin gown had been made especially to be worn with this necklace. It was tight and sleek at the throat and sleeves, snugly hugging her body, its color exactly matching the hammered gold of the unusual pearls, a shade so unique that Olivia seemed bathed in shimmering light rather than fabric and jewels. Only the emerald cast a definite color, picking up the blue of her eyes and upper lids. Her skin, her hair, even her lips echoed the pale beaten gold of the pearls.

Wondering how she could look as she did and feel so unspeakably desolate, Olivia turned away from the mirrors and left the room.

Welcoming the traffic as a distraction, she drove herself to the Marina in the black Rolls-Royce. More than once she had suspected that Thea had chosen this particular night for her party because it was also the opening of Mark's exhibit at Neftale's Gallery. Although Thea hadn't said a word about Mark in a month or more, Olivia knew that her friend was acutely aware that she was counting the days until his San Francisco opening. It would be like Thea to arrange her party to coincide with the opening so that Olivia would find it impossible to be alone on this night in the eventuality of Mark's not calling.

Olivia stopped for a light, staring straight ahead and trying not to notice the car full of people on her right who were gaping at the big Rolls and its driver, wrapped tightly in white mink. An old blue Dodge edged dangerously forward to see her face, the people in it recognizing her now and wanting a better look at the famous owner of MagnifiScent.

Relieved when the light changed to green, Olivia moved ahead of the Dodge, her thoughts returning to Thea. She realized that Thea's sensitivity to her pain was actually a recently acquired dimension of her friend's personality. The Thea she had known as a girl and young woman had lacked subtle compassion. Being married to Everett had changed Thea, instilled a softness, broken through the brittle shell that had made others think her shallow and self-serving.

Taking a right on Market Street, Olivia understood that time had altered Thea, Marlissa, and her. Both of her friends were married and settled now, and Thea would soon be a mother. The Thea who had taken her to Europe so long ago would have been appalled at the thought of having a child. And now she could talk of little else, rhapsodic about the nursery she'd had done, looking forward to the changes in the body she'd pampered so carefully in the past. And Marlissa had been a lovely bride, her eyes leaving no doubt about the happiness she'd found with Ernst. It struck Olivia suddenly that both Thea and Marlissa had run from these men, only to find their greatest peace ultimately in the very arms they'd avoided. Thea and Marlissa had gone in a circle, and only she was drifting eternally out into space. Acutely lonely, wretchedly weary, Olivia gripped the wheel tightly to avoid turning around and going back to her empty house. Much as she appreciated Thea's kind concern, she wanted nothing more than to be by herself tonight, a wounded animal seeking darkness to nurse her pain.

The house on the Marina was brilliantly lit. It seemed as if Thea knew everyone in San Francisco, and Olivia thought they might all be at her party tonight. Sighing, she found a space behind Marlissa's Mercedes and parked. As she got out, she prepared herself for the night ahead. She was not going to dampen Thea's party, no matter how she felt. She had dressed her best, and she was determined to act as if she weren't devastated by Mark's failure to call. But every step she took toward Thea's door seemed harder than the one before.

Thea answered the door herself, falling on her in near-panic. "My God, darling, I thought you weren't coming! Here, George, take this beautiful thing before I steal it!"

Radiant in a bright red Chinese silk gown, Thea tossed

Olivia's white mink to her houseman, then grasped her friend by the hand. "Everyone's here! Dozens of people I don't even know, but lovely, all of them!"

Olivia, smiling faintly, thought Thea might be right. The spacious rooms were packed with beautifully dressed, bejeweled women and handsomely tailored men. She saw Marlissa and Ernst at the far end of the room. Marlissa smiled and waved but couldn't leave her corner without a small army to force a path through the bodies.

Thea looked her up and down and grinned mischievously. "Perfect. My God, I must be insane to associate with anyone who looks like you. But it's wonderful, because I have someone special you really must meet. But first we'll get you something to drink. . . ." She pulled Olivia into the room, losing her for a few moments while Olivia exchanged greetings with people she knew.

Everett slipped away from a knot of guests and gave her a quick kiss. Then he shrugged as if in apology. "Sorry, none of this is my doing," he whispered, disappearing again.

Wondering if he were apologizing for the hordes of people or for forcing her out of her quiet home on this particular night, Olivia accepted a glass of champagne and found herself again being tugged further into the crowd by Thea.

The party had been going full blast for quite a while, and the noise was deafening. Thea was trying to tell her something, but Olivia couldn't hear what she was saying. She saw Marlissa working her way toward her, and escaped Thea's urging hand long enough to welcome Marlissa back home with a warm hug. Marlissa was looking at Thea and laughing, her eyes shifting to the far side of the room, where a ring of people were circling a tall, dark-haired man. For an instant the man looked exactly like Mark, and Olivia felt her heart pound.

Then she stopped despite Thea's insistent tug on her hand. Surely Thea would not have planned a meeting with Mark for her in the middle of this horrible crush of people? Or would she? Thea could think of it as an easy way to break the ice.

Thea tugged again on her hand. "Come on, darling, it's only a bit further."

"Thea . . ." Olivia started to protest. But they were almost at the far end of the room now, and the dark-haired man was laughing at something a lovely red-headed woman was saying. It was Mark.

He was looking at her. His eyes held no surprise, only a

subdued excitement. Olivia couldn't speak, couldn't breathe. She was overwhelmed, thrilled, frightened, and she had to make a superhuman effort to hold back tears. Before she could formulate her thoughts or speak his name, Thea put a supportive arm around her waist. She was beginning to feel numb as she watched Mark excuse himself and come over to them.

Olivia stared at him and then turned to Thea in utter confusion. "Thea, have you gone mad? I don't understand." She turned back to Mark and stared at him helplessly. "Mark," she said, her whispered greeting lost in the din.

"Olivia, darling, I want to present Mark Lyman, the artist Everett is so excited about. Mark, this is my dearest friend, Olivia DeSante." Thea laughed delightedly.

Mark took her hand, drew her closer. "Don't look so astonished, Olivia. I asked for the introduction." Seeing that she didn't understand, he laughed. Then he kissed her.

"My fans call. I know you two will excuse me." Thea kissed Olivia's cheek. "Don't faint, darling. Just, for once in your life, be happy." She was immediately swallowed up in the crowd, a flash of red.

Mark led her to a relatively quiet corner. He looked deeply into her ice blue eyes and touched her lips again with his own, his mouth working into the familiar small smile just before they kissed.

"We are, you know,"—he smiled again—"meeting as if for the first time."

She watched him glance reluctantly at his watch.

"Damn, we've got to fight our way out of here in about five minutes. My show opens at Neftale's Gallery in less than an hour, and I don't want us to be late." He looked at her with concern. "You will come with me, won't you? I had this planned down to the word ever since Thea called, but I see you haven't changed—you're still late."

She couldn't help laughing, although she could hardly see him through the film of uncontrollable tears. "Yes, of course I'll come." She blinked rapidly until his soft smile was clearly in focus. "But I still don't understand—what do you mean, meeting as if for the first time?"

"But we are, Olivia. Now, for the very first time, we're finally meeting as equals. Don't you see?" He touched the regal length of her beautiful white neck above its exquisite rope of golden pearls.

"Two swans, Olivia. Two swans," he said into her ear.

"Swans who have always belonged together, and at last will have their chance."

"Mark. . . ." But he was looking beyond her now, nervously surveying the crowds that stood between them and the door.

"We'll have time to talk later. All the time in the world. A lifetime of days and nights. To talk . . . to catch up." He grinned the old grin, and once again melted away the years. "But now we'd better make a run for it."

Once more a hand was firmly urging her into the packed, glittering room. Bodies moved between them, but they were inseparably linked, their fingers tightly entwined.

"Who, then," she called out loudly, knowing that her words were lost in the laughter and noise, "are the geese? Mark? Who are the geese?"

He looked back at her as he smiled an apology to guests on either side of the lane he was creating. His eyes were shining with excitement. "What?"

Olivia shook her lovely head, returning his smile, and silently answered her own question. She realized that she had always known the answer.

The geese were simply swans who had settled for less than the best.

M